Anthony Hope

The King's Mirror

Anthony Hope

The King's Mirror

ISBN/EAN: 9783743398047

Manufactured in Europe, USA, Canada, Australia, Japa

Cover: Foto ©Andreas Hilbeck / pixelio.de

Manufactured and distributed by brebook publishing software (www.brebook.com)

Anthony Hope

The King's Mirror

THE KING'S MIRROR

"I'm not a king for my own pleasure."

(See page 14.)

THE KING'S MIRROR

A NOVEL

BY ANTHONY HOPE

Author of The Chronicles of Count
Antonio • The Prisoner of Zenda •
The God in the Car • Phroso •
Rupert of Hentzau, etc. • • • •

NEW YORK
D. APPLETON AND COMPANY
1899

CONTENTS.

LIST OF ILLUSTRATIONS

THE KING'S MIRROR.

CHAPTER I.

A PIOUS HYPERBOLE.

BEFORE my coronation there was no event in childhood that impressed itself on my memory with marked or singular distinction. My father's death, the result of a chill contracted during a hunting excursion, meant no more to me than a week of rooms gloomy and games forbidden; the decease of King Augustin, my uncle, appeared at the first instant of even less importance. I recollect the news coming. The King, having been always in frail health, had never married; seeing clearly but not far, he was a sad man: the fate that struck down his brother increased his natural melancholy; he became almost a recluse, withdrew himself from the capital to a retired residence, and henceforward was little more than a name in which Prince von Hammerfeldt conducted the business of the country. Now and then my mother visited him; once she brought back to me a letter from him, little of which I understood then, although I have since read often the touching words of his message. When he died, there was the same gloom as when my father left us; but it seemed to me that I was treated a little differently; the servants stared at me, my mother would look long at me with a half-admiring, half-amused expression, and Victoria let me have all her toys. In Baroness von Krakenstein (or Krak, as we called her) alone, there was no difference; yet the explanation came from her, for when that evening I reached out my little hand and snatched a bit of cake from the dish, Krak caught my wrist, saying gravely,

"Kings must not snatch, Augustin."

"Victoria, what do you get when you are a king?" I asked my sister that night. I was hardly eight, she nearing ten, and her worldly wisdom seemed great.

"Oh, you have just what you want, and do what you like, and kill people that you don't like," said she. "Don't you remember the Arabian Nights?"

"Could I kill Krak?" I asked, choosing a concrete and tempting illustration of despotic power.

Victoria was puzzled.

"She'd have to do something first, I suppose," she answered vaguely. "I should have been queen if you hadn't been born, Augustin." Her tone now became rather plaintive.

"But nobody has a queen if they can get a king," said I serenely.

It is the coronation day that stands out in memory; the months that elapsed between my accession and that event are merged in a vague dimness. I think little difference was made in our household while we mourned the dead King. Krak was still sharp, imperious, and exacting. She had been my mother's governess, and came with her from Styria. I suppose she had learned the necessity of sternness from her previous experience with Princess Gertrude, for that lady, my mother, a fair, small, slim woman, who preserved her girlishness of appearance till the approach of middle age, was of a strong and masterful temper. Only Krak and Hammerfeldt had any power over her; Krak's seemed the result of ancient domination, the Prince's was won by a suave and coaxing deference that changed once a year or thereabouts to stern and uncompromising opposition. But with my early upbringing, and with Victoria's, Hammerfeldt had nothing to do; my mother presided, and Krak executed. The spirit of Styria reigned in the nursery, rather than the softer code of our more Western country; I doubt whether discipline were stricter in any house in Forstadt than in the royal palace.

They roused me at eight on my coronation day. My mother herself came to my bedside, and knelt down for a few minutes by it. Krak stood in the background, grim and gloomy. I was a little frightened, and asked what was afoot.

"You're to be crowned to-day, Augustin," said my mother. "You must be a good boy."

"Am I to be crowned king, mother?"

"Yes, dear, in the cathedral. Will you be a good king?"

"I'll be a great king, mother," said I. The Arabian Nights were still in my head.

She laughed and rose to her feet.

"Have him ready by ten o'clock, Baroness," she said. "I must go and have my coffee and then dress. And I must see that Victoria is properly dressed too."

"Are you going to be crowned, mother?" I asked.

"No," she said. "I shall be only Princess Heinrich still."

I looked at her with curiosity. A king is greater than a princess; should I be greater than my mother? And my mother was greater than Krak! Why, then—but Krak ended my musings by whisking me out of bed.

It was fine fun to ride in the carriage by my mother's side, with Victoria and old Hammerfeldt opposite. Hammerfeldt was President of the Council of Regency; but I, knowing nothing of that, supposed my mother had asked him into our carriage because he amused us and gave us chocolates. My mother was very prettily dressed, and so was Victoria. I was very glad that Krak was in another vehicle. There were crowds of people in the street, cheering us more than they ever had before; I was taking off my hat all the time. Once or twice I held up my sword for them to see, but everybody laughed, and I would not do it any more. It was the first time that I had worn a sword, but I did not see why they should laugh. Victoria laughed most of all; indeed, at last my mother scolded her, saying that swords were proper for men, and that I should be a man soon.

We reached the cathedral, and with my hand in my mother's I was led up the nave, till we came to the front of the High Altar. There was a very long service; I did not care about or heed much of it, until the archbishop came down on to the lowest step, and my mother took my hand again and led me to him, and he put the crown on my head. I liked that, and turned round to see if the people were looking, and was just going to laugh at Victoria, when I saw Krak frowning at me; so I turned back and listened to the archbishop. He was a nice old man, but I did not understand very much of what he said. He talked about my uncle, my father, and the country, and what a king ought to do; at last he leaned down toward me, and told me in a low but very distinct voice that henceforward God was the only Power above me, and I had no lord except the King of kings. He was a very old man with white hair, and when he had said this he seemed not to be able to go on for a minute. Perhaps he was tired, or did not know what to say next. Then he laid his hand on my head—they had taken the crown off because it was so heavy for me—and said in a whisper, " Poor child! " but then he raised his voice, so that it rang all through the cathedral, and blessed me. Then my mother made me get up and turn and face the people; she put the crown on my head again; then she knelt and kissed my hand. I was very much surprised, and I saw Victoria trying hard not to laugh—because Krak was just by her. But I didn't want to laugh; I was too much surprised.

So far memory carries me; the rest is blurred, until I found myself back in our own home divested of my military costume, but allowed, as a special treat, to have my sword beside me when we sat down to tea. We had many good things for tea, and even Krak was thawed into amiability; she told me that I had behaved very well in the cathedral, and that I should see the fireworks from the window presently. It was winter and soon dark. The fireworks began at seven; I remember them very well. Above all, I recollect the fine excitement of seeing my own name in great long golden letters, with a word after them that Krak told me I ought to know meant "king," and was of the third declension. "*Rex, Regis*," said Krak, and told poor Victoria to go on. Victoria was far too excited, and Krak said we must both learn it to-morrow; but we were clapping our hands, and didn't pay much heed. Then Hammerfeldt came in and held me up at the window for a few minutes, telling me to kiss my hand to the people. I did as he told me; then the crowd began to go away, and Krak said it was bedtime.

Now here I might conclude the story of my coronation day; but an episode remains trivial and ludicrous enough, yet most firmly embedded in my memory. Indeed, it has always for me a significance quite independent of its obvious import; it seems to symbolize the truth which the experience of all my life has taught me. Perhaps I throw dignity to the winds in recording it; I intend to do the like all through what I write; for, to my thinking, when dignity comes in at the door sincerity flies out of the window. I was not tired after the day, or I was too excited to feel tired. My small brain was agog; my little head was turned. Amidst all that I did not understand I understood enough to conceive that I had become a great man. I saw Victoria led off to bed, and going meekly. But I was not as Victoria; she was not a king as I was; mother had not knelt before her; the archbishop had not told Victoria that she had no lord except the King of kings. Perhaps I was hardly to blame when I took his words as excluding the domination of women, of Krak, even of the mother who had knelt and kissed my hand. At any rate, I was in a wilful mood. Old Anna, the nurse, had put Victoria to bed, and now came through the door that divided our rooms and proposed to assist me in my undressing. I was wilful and defiant; I refused most flatly to go to bed. Anna was perplexed; unquestionably a new and reverential air was perceptible in Anna; the detection of it was fuel to my fires of rebellion. Anna sent for Krak; in the interval before the governess's arrival I grew uneasy. I half wished I had gone to bed quietly, but now I was in for the battle. Had there been any meaning in what the archbishop said, or had there not? Was it true, or had he misled me? I had believed him, and was minded to try the issue; I sat in my chair attempting to whistle as my groom had taught me. Krak came; I whistled on; there was a whispered consultation between Anna and Krak; then Krak told me that I was to go to bed, and bade me begin the process by taking off my shoes. I looked her full and fair in the face.

"I won't till I choose," said I. "I'm king now"; and then I quoted to Krak what the archbishop had said. She lifted her hands in amazement and wrath.

"I shall have to fetch your mother," she said.

"I'm above my mother; she knelt to me," I retorted triumphantly.

Krak advanced toward me.

"Augustin, take off your shoes," said she.

I had no love for Krak. Dearest of all gifts of sovereignty would be the power of defying Krak.

"Do you really want me to take them off?" I asked.

"This instant," commanded Krak.

I do not justify my action; yet, perhaps, the archbishop should have been more careful of what he said. My answer to Krak was, "Take them, then." And I snatched off one of them and threw it at Krak. It missed most narrowly the end of her long nose, and lodged, harmlessly enough, on Anna's broad bosom. I sat there exultant, fearful, and defiant.

Krak spoke to Anna in a low whisper; then they both went out, leaving me alone in the big room. I grew afraid, partly because I was alone, partly for what I had done. I could undress myself, although I was not, as a rule, allowed to. I tumbled quickly out of my clothes, and had just slipped on my nightshirt, when the door opened, and my mother entered, followed by Krak. My mother looked very young and pretty, but she also looked severe.

"Is this true, Augustin?" she asked, sitting down by the fire.

"Yes, mother," said I, arrested in my flight toward bed.

"You refused to obey the Baroness?"

"Yes. I'm king now."

"And threw your shoe at her?"

"The archbishop said——" I began.

"Be quiet," said my mother, and she turned her head and listened to Krak, who began to whisper in her ear. A moment later she turned to me.

"You must do as you are told," she said; "and you must apologize to the Baroness."

"I'd have taken them off if she had asked me," I said, "but she ordered me."

"She has a right to order you."

"Is she God?" I asked, pointing scornfully at Krak. Really the archbishop must bear some of the responsibility.

Krak whispered again; again my mother turned to me.

"Will you apologize, Augustin?" she said.

"No," said I stubbornly.

Krak whispered again. I heard my mother say,

with a little laugh, " But to-day, Baroness!" Then she sighed and looked round at me.

" Do apologize, Augustin," said she.

" I'll apologize to you, not to her," I said.

She looked at the Baroness, then at me, then back to the Baroness; then she smiled and sighed.

" I suppose so. He must learn it. But not much to-night, Baroness. Just enough to—to show him."

Krak came toward me; a moment later I occupied a position which, to my lively discomfort, I had filled once or twice before in my short life, but which I had not supposed that I should fill again after what the archbishop had said. I set my teeth to endure; I was full of bewilderment, surprise, and anger. The archbishop had played me terribly false; the Arabian Nights were no less delusive. Krak was as unmoved and business-like as usual. I was determined not to cry—not to-night. I was not very hard tried; almost directly my mother said, " That will do." There was a pause; no doubt Krak's face expressed a surprised protest. " Yes, that's enough to-day," said my mother, and she added, " Get into bed, Augustin. You must learn to be an obedient boy before you can be a good king."

The moment I was released I ran and leaped into bed, hiding my face under the clothes. I heard my mother come and say, " Won't you kiss me? " but I was very angry; I did not understand why they made me a king, and then beat me, because I behaved like all the kings I had been told or read about. Moreover, I had begun to cry now, and I would have been killed sooner than let Krak see that. So presently my mother went away, and Krak too. Then Anna came and tried to turn down the clothes, but I would not let her. I hung on to them hard, for

I was still crying. I heard Anna sigh, " Poor dearie ! " then she went away ; but directly after Victoria's voice came, saying, " Anna says I may come in with you. May I, please, Augustin ? " I let her move the bedclothes and get in with me ; and I put my arms round her neck. Victoria comforted me as best she could.

" You'll be a real king when you grow up," she said.

A thought struck me—a rapturous thought, born of the Arabian Nights. (In the archbishop lay no comfort at all.)

" Yes," I cried, " and then I'll bastinado Krak ! " With this comforting thought I fell asleep.

A strange day, this of my coronation, odd to pass through, to the highest degree illuminating in retrospect. I did not live to bastinado Krak ; nor would I now had I the power. What they did was perhaps a little cruel, a little Styrian, as Victoria and I used covertly to say of such harsh measures ; but how valuable a lesson on the state and fortune of kings ! The King is one, the man another. The King is crowned, the man is lashed ; they give us greatness in words : in fact, we are our servants' servants. Little as I liked the thing at the time, I can not now regret that I was chastised on my coronation day. I was thus put into an attitude eminently conducive to the perception of truth, and to a realization of the facts of my position. I forgive thee the blows, Krak —Lo, I forgive thee !

CHAPTER II.

A MAN'S *puerilia* are to himself not altogether
puerile; they are parcel of the complex explanation
of his existent self. He starts, I suppose, as something, a very malleable something, ready to be ham-
mered into the shape that the socket requires. The
two greatest forces at work on the yielding substance
are parents and position, with the gardener's boy
beneath my window crusts and cuffs, with me at the
window kingship and Styrian discipline. In the
latter there was to me nothing strange; I had grown
into it from birth. But now it became suddenly
noticeable, as a thing demanding justification, by reason of its patent incongruity with my kingship. I
have shown how swiftly and sharply the contrast
was impressed on me; if I have not made that point,
then my story of a nursery tragedy ·is unexcused.
I was left wondering what manner of king he was
who must obey on pain of blows. I was very young,
and the sense of outrage did not last, but the puzzle
persisted, and Victoria's riper philosophy was taxed
to allay it. Waiting seemed the only thing, waiting
till I could fling my shoes at whom I would, and sit
on my throne to behold the bastinadoing of Krak.
My mother told me that I must be an obedient boy
first. Well and good; but then why make me a king

now? In truth I was introduced over-early to the fictions of high policy. A king without power seems to a child like a bird without wings; but a bird without wings is a favourite device of statesmanship.

The matter did not stand even here. My kingship not only lacked the positive advantages with which youthful imagination (aided by the archbishop's pious hyperbole) had endowed it; it became in my eyes the great and fertile source of all my discomfort, the parent of every distasteful obligation, the ground on which all chosen pleasures were refused. It was ever " Kings can not do this," or " Kings must do that," and the " this " was always sweet, the " that " repellent; in Krak's hands monarchy became a cross between a treadmill and a strait-waistcoat. " What's the use of being a king?" I dared once to cry to her.

" God did not make you a king for your own pleasure," returned Krak solemnly. I recollect thinking that her remark must certainly be true, yet wondering whether God quite realized how tiresome the position was.

It may be supposed that I had many advantages to counterbalance these evils that pressed so hardly on me. I do not recollect being conscious of them. Even my occasional parades in public, although they tickled my vanity, were spoiled for me by the feeling that nobody would look at me with admiration, envy, or even interest, if he knew the real state of the case. I may observe that this reflection has not vanished with infancy, but still is apt to assail me. Of course I was well fed, well housed, and well, though firmly, treated. Alas, what we have not is more to us than all we possess. I was thankful under protest; prohibitions outweighed privileges. I have not the experience necessary for any generalization, but my own childhood was not very happy.

A day comes into my mind almost as clear and distinct in memory as my coronation day. I was nine years old, and went with my mother to pay a visit to a nobleman of high rank. He had just married and brought to his house a young American lady. We were welcomed, of course, with infinite courtesy and deference. Princess Heinrich received such tributes well, with a quiet, restrained dignity and a lofty graciousness. I was smart in my best clothes, a miniature uniform of the Corps of Guards, and my hand flew up to my little helmet when the Countess curtseyed very low and looked at me with merry, sparkling blue eyes. Her husband was a tall, good-looking fellow, stiff in back and manner, as are most of our folk, but honest and good-hearted, as are most of them also. But I paid little heed to him; the laughing Countess engrossed me, and I found myself smiling at her. Her eyes seemed to enter into confidence with me, and I knew she was rather sorry for me. The day was damp and chill, and, although my mother would not refuse to go round the Count's gardens, of which he was proud, she declared that the walk was not safe for me, and asked the Countess to take care of me. So she and I were left alone. I stood rather shyly by the table, fingering the helmet that my mother had told me to take off; presently looking up, I saw her merry eyes on me.

"Sire," said the Countess, "if you sat down I would."

I bowed and sought a chair; there was a high wooden arm-chair, and I clambered into it; my legs dangled in mid-air. Another little laugh came from

the Countess as she brought me a high footstool. I
tried to jump down in time to stop her, but she would
not let me. Then she knelt herself on the stool, her
knees by my feet.

"What beautiful military boots!" she said.

I looked down listlessly at my shining toes. She
clasped her hands, crying:

"You're a beautiful little king! Oh, isn't it lovely to be a king!"

I looked at her doubtfully; her pretty face was
quite close to mine. Somehow I wanted very much
to put my arms round her neck, but I felt sure that
kings did not hug countesses. Imagine Krak's verdict on such a notion!

"I'm not a king for my own pleasure," said I,
regarding my hostess gravely. "I am a king for
the good of my people."

She drew a long breath and whispered in English
(I did not understand then, but the sound of the
words stayed with me), "Poor little mite!" Then
she said:

"But don't you have a lovely time?"

I felt that I was becoming rather red, and I knew
that the tears were not far from my eyes.

"No," said I, "not very."

"Why not?"

"They—they don't let me do any of the things
I want to."

"You shall do anything you want to here," she
whispered. I was very much surprised to see that
her bright eyes had grown a little clouded.

"We've no kings in my country," she said, taking my hand in hers.

"Oh, I wish I'd been born there," said I; then
we looked at one another for a minute, and I put

out my arms and took hold of her, and drew her face near mine. With a little gulp in her throat she sprang up, caught me in her arms, kissed me a dozen times, and threw herself into the big chair with me on her knees. Now I was crying, and yet half laughing; so I believe was she. We did not say very much more to one another. Soon I stopped crying; she looked at me, and we both laughed.

"What babies we are, your Majesty!" said she.

"They might let me do a little more, mightn't they? It's all Krak, you know. Mother wouldn't be half so bad without Krak."

"Oh, my dear, and is Krak so horrid?"

"Horrid," said I, with grave emphasis.

The Countess kissed me again.

"You'll grow up soon," she said. Somehow the assurance comforted me more from her lips than from Victoria's. "Will you be nice to me when you grow up?"

"I shall always be very, very fond of you," said I.

She laughed a funny little laugh, and then sighed.

"If God sends me a little son, I hope he'll be like you," she whispered, with her cheek against mine.

"He won't be a king," said I with a sigh of envy.

"You poor dear!" cooed she.

Then came my mother's clear, high-bred voice, just outside the door, descanting on the beauty of the Count's parterres and orangery. A swift warning glance flew from me to my hostess. I scampered off my perch, and she stood up in respectful readiness for the entrance of Princess Heinrich.

"Don't tell mother," I whispered urgently.

"Not a word!"

" Whatever they do to you? "

" No, whatever they do to me! "

My mother was in the room, the Count holding the door for her and closing it as she passed through. I felt her glance rest on me for a moment; then she turned to the Countess and expressed all proper admiration of the gardens, the house, and the whole demesne.

" And I hope Augustin has been a good boy? " she ended.

" The King has been very good, madame," returned the Countess. Then she looked in an inquiring way at her husband, as though she did not quite know whether she were right or not, and with a bright blush added, " If you would let him come again some day, madame! "

My mother smiled quite graciously.

" You mustn't leave me out of the invitation," she said. " We will both come, won't we, Augustin? "

" Yes, please, mother," said I, relapsed into shyness and in great fear lest our doings should be discovered.

" Say good-bye now," commanded the Princess.

I should have liked to kiss the Countess again, but such an act would have risked a betrayal. Our adieu was made in proper form, the Countess accompanying us to the door. There we left her curtseying, while the Count handed my mother into the carriage. I looked round, and the Countess blew me a surreptitious kiss.

When we had driven a little way, my mother said :

" Do you like the Countess von Sempach? "

" Yes, very much."

" She was kind to you? "

" Very, mother."

" Then why have you been crying, Augustin? "

" I haven't been crying," said I. The lie was
needful to my compact with the Countess; my honour was rooted in dishonour.

" Yes, you have," said she, but not quite in
the accusing tones that generally marked the detection of falsehood. She seemed to look at me
more in curiosity than in anger. Then she bent
down toward me. " What did you talk about? " she
asked.

" Nothing very particular, mother. She asked
me if I liked being king."

" And what did you say? "

" I said I liked it pretty well."

My mother made no answer. I stole a look at
her handsome clean-cut features; she was frowning
a little.

" I didn't tell her much," said I, aiming at pro-
pitiation.

" Much of what? " came sharply, but not unkindly. Yet the question posed me.

" Oh, I don't know! " I murmured forlornly; and
I was surprised when she turned and kissed me,
saying:

" We all love you, Augustin; but you have to be
king, and you must learn how."

" Yes," I assented. The thing was quite inevitable; I knew that.

Silence followed for a little while. Then my
mother said:

" When you're ten you shall have a tutor, and
your own servants, Augustin."

Hastily I counted the months. There were nine;

but what did the proposal mean? Was I to be a free man then?

"And we women will leave you alone," my mother went on. She kissed me again, adding, "You don't like us, do you?"

"I like you, mother," I said gravely, "at least generally—not when you let Kr—the Baroness——"

"Never mind the Baroness," she interrupted. Then she put her arm round my neck and asked me in a very low voice, "You didn't like the Countess better than me, did you, Augustin?"

"N—no, mother," said I, but I was an unaccomplished hypocrite, and my mother turned away. My thoughts were not on her, but on the prospect her words had opened to me.

"Do you mean that the Baroness won't be my governess any more?"

"Yes. You'll have a governor, a tutor."

"And shall I——?"

"I'll tell you all about it soon, dear."

The rest of our drive was in silence. My mind was full to overflowing of impressions, hopes, and wonders; my mother's gaze was fixed on the windows of the carriage.

We reached home, and together went up to the schoolroom. It was not tea-time yet, and lesson-books were on the table. Krak sat beside it, grave, grim, and gray. Victoria was opposite to her. Victoria was crying. Past experience enlightened me; I knew exactly what had happened; Victoria had a delightfully unimpressionable soul; no rebuke from Krak brought her to tears; Krak had been rapping her knuckles, and her tears were an honest tribute to pain, with no nonsense of merely wounded sensibility about them. My mother went up and whispered to Krak. Krak had, of course, risen, and stood now listening with a heavy frown. My mother drew herself up proudly; she seemed to brace herself for an effort; I heard nothing except " I think you should consult me," but our quick children's eyes apprehended the meaning of the scene. Krak was being bearded. There was no doubt of it; for presently Krak bowed her head in a jerky unwilling nod and walked out of the room. My mother stood still for a moment with a vivid red colour in her cheeks. Then she walked across to Victoria, lifted one of her hands from the table, and kissed it.

" You're going to have tea with me to-day, children," said she, " and we'll play games afterward. Augustin shall play at not being a king."

I remember well the tea we had and the games that followed, wherein we all played at being what we were not, and for an evening cheated fate of its dues. My mother was merriest, for over Victoria and myself there hung a veil of unreality, a consciousness that indeed we played and set aside for an hour only the obstinate claims of the actual. But we were all merry; and when we parted—for my mother had a dinner-party—we both kissed her heartily; me she kissed often. I thought that she wanted to ask me again whether I liked the Countess better than her, but was afraid to risk the question. What I wanted to say was that I liked none better if she would be always what she was this evening; but I found no skill adequate to a declaration of affection so conditional. It would be to make a market of my kisses, and I had not yet come to the age for such bargains.

Then we were left alone, Victoria and I, to sit together for a while in the dusk; and, sitting there, we totted up that day's gains. They were uncertain, yet seemed great. All that had passed I told Victoria, save what in loyalty to my countess I might not; Victoria imparted to me the story of the knuckle-rapping. For her an added joy lay in the fact that on this occasion, if ever, she had deserved the affliction; she had been gloriously naughty, and gloried in it now; did not her sinfulness enhance the significance of this revolution? So carried away were we by our triumph that now again, after a long interval, we allowed our imagination to paint royalty in glowing colours, and our Arabian Nights and fairy tales seemed at last not altogether cunningly wrought deceptions. When we had gone to bed, again we met, I creeping into her room, and rousing her to ask whether in truth a new age had come and the yoke of Krak been broken from off our backs. Victoria sat up in bed and discussed the problem gravely. For me she was sanguine, for herself less so; for, said she, they go on worrying the girls for ever so long. "She won't rap your knuckles any more," I suggested, fastening on a certain and tangible advantage. Victoria agreed that in all likelihood her knuckles would henceforth be inviolate; and she did not deny such gain as lay there. Thus in the end I won her to cheerfulness, and we parted merrily, declaring to one another that we were free; and I knew that in some way the pretty American countess had lent a hand to knocking off our chains.

Free! A wonderful word that, whether you use it of a child, a man, a state, a world, an universe! That evening we seemed free. In after-days I received from old Hammerfeldt (a great statesman, as history will one day allow) some lectures on the little pregnant, powerful, empty word. He had some right to speak of freedom; he had seen it fought for by

Napoleon, praised by Talleyrand, bought by Castle-reagh, interpreted by Metternich.   Should he not then know what it was, its value, its potency, and its sweetness, why men died for it, and delicate women who loved them cheered them on?   Once also in later years a beautiful woman cried to me, with white arms outstretched, that to be free was life, was all in all, the heart's one satisfaction.   Her I pressed, seeking to know wherein lay the attraction and allurement that fired her to such extravagance.   And' I told her what the Prince had said to me half-way through his pinch of snuff.

"'Sire,' said he, 'to become free—what is it? It is to change your master.'"

The lady let her arms fall to her side, reflected a moment, smiled, and said:

"The Prince was no fool, sire."

As the result of this day that I have described, I had become free.   I had changed my master.

We did not, however, pay any more visits to the Countess.

CHAPTER III.

SOME SECRET OPINIONS.

EVEN such results as might be looked for on Prince von Hammerfeldt's theory of the meaning of freedom were in my case arrested and postponed by a very serious illness which atacked me on the threshold of my eleventh year. We had gone to Schloss Artenberg, according to our custom in the summer; it was holiday-time; Krak was away, the talked-of tutor had not arrived. The immediate fruit of this temporary emancipation was that I got my feet very wet with dabbling about the river, and, being under no sterner control than Victoria's, lingered long in this condition. Next day I was kept in bed, and Victoria was in sore disgrace. To be brief, the mischief attacked my lungs. Soon I was seriously ill; a number of grave, black-coated gentlemen came and went about the bed on which I lay for several weeks. Of this time I have many curious impressions; most of them centre round my mother. She slept in my room, and I believe hardly ever left me. I used to wake from uneasy sleep and look across to her bed; always in a few moments she also awoke, came and gave me what I needed or asked for, and then would throw a dressing-gown round her and walk softly to and fro on bare feet, with her long fair hair hanging about her shoulders.

Her face looked different in those days; yet it was not soft as I have seen mothers' faces when their sons lay sick or dead, but rather excited, urgent, defiant; the lips were set close, and the eyes gleamed. She did not supplicate God, she fought fate, or, if God and fate be one, then it was God whom she fought; and her battle was untiring. I knew from her face that I might die, but, so far as I can recall my mood, I was more curious about the effect of such an event on her and on Victoria than concerning its import to myself. I asked her once what would happen if I died; would Victoria be queen? She forbade me to ask the question, but I pressed it, and she answered hastily, "Yes, yes, but you won't die, Augustin; you shan't die." I was not allowed to see very much of Victoria, but a day or two afterward she sat with me alone for a little while, and I told her she would be queen if I died.

"No. Mother would kill me," she said with absolute conviction, in no resentment or fear, but in a simple certitude.

"Why? Because you didn't bring me in when I got wet?"

"Yes—if you died of it," nodded Victoria.

"I don't believe it," I said boldly. "Why shouldn't she like you to be queen?"

"She'd hate it," said Victoria.

"She doesn't hate me being king."

"You're a boy."

I wondered dimly then, and I have wondered since (hardly with more knowledge), what truth or whether any lay behind my sister's words; she believed that, apart from any unjust blame for my misfortune, her mother would not willingly see her queen. Yet why not? I have a son, and would be glad to lay down my burden and kiss his hand as he sat on the throne. Are all fathers such as I? Nay, and are all mothers such as mine? I know not; and if there be any position that opens a man's mind to the Socratic wisdom of knowing his own ignorance it is that in which my life has been spent. But it can hardly be that the curious veiled opposition which from about this time began to exist between my mother and my sister was altogether singular. It was a feeling not inconsistent with duty, with punctilious observance, not even with love; but there was in it a sort of jealousy, of assertion and counter-assertion. It seemed to me, as I became older, to have roots deeper than any accidental occurrence or environment, and, so far, I came near to the difficult analysis, to spring from the relation of one woman who was slowly but surely being forced to lay down what she had prized most in her womanhood and another who, slowly but surely, also became aware that hers was the prize in her turn, and thrust forward a tentative hand to grasp it. If I am at all right in this notion, then it is plain that feelings slight and faint, although not non-existent in ordinary homes, might be intensified in such a family as ours, and that a new and great impulse would have been imparted to them by such an artificial accentuation of the inevitable as must have resulted had I died, and my sister been called to the first place. Among men the cause for such an antagonism is far less powerful; advancing years take less from us and often bring what, to older eyes, is a good recompense for lost youth, and seems to youth itself more precious than any of its own possessions. Our empire, never so brilliant as a woman's in its prime, is of stuff more durable and less shaken by the wind of Time's fluttering garment as he passes by.

My confessor came to see me sometimes. He was an eminent divine, nominated to his post by Hammerfeldt in reward, I believe, for some political usefulness. I do not think he saw far into a child's heart, or perhaps I was not like most children. He was always comforting me, telling me not to be afraid, that God was merciful, Christ full of love, and the saints praying for me. Now I was not in the least afraid; I was very curious about death— I had never seen it—but I was, as I have said, more curious about the world I should leave behind. I wanted to know what would be done when I was dead, and where I was to be buried. Would they fire the guns and parade the troops? I did not rise to the conception of myself, not knowing anything of what they did. I thought I should be there somehow, looking on from heaven; and I think that I rather enjoyed the prospect. A child is very self-centred; I had no doubt that I should be the object of much attention in heaven on that day at least. I hinted something of what was passing in my mind to the confessor. He did not appear to follow the drift of my thoughts. He told me again that I had been a good boy, and that now, if I prayed and was sorry for my faults, I should be happy and should please God. This did not touch the point that engaged my attention. I tried whether my mother could help me, and I was surprised when the tears started into her eyes, and she bade me, almost roughly, to be quiet. However, when Victoria came we talked it all over. Victoria cried a little, but she was quite clear as to her own position in the procession, and we had rather an animated dispute about it. She said also that some one in heaven would hold me, and we differed again as to the celestial personage in whose lap I was to sit. I am afraid that here our imaginations were assisted by the picture of the Holy Family in the chapel of the Schloss.

Not the least tiresome incident of this time was that Krak felt it her duty to display affection. I do not mean to assert that Krak was not and had not been all along fond of me, but in ordinary seasons to feel affection was with Krak no reason at all for displaying it. I do more justice to Krak now; then I did not appreciate the change in her demeanour. On questioning Victoria, I found that Krak's softness did not extend beyond the limits of my sick-room; she had indeed ceased the knuckle-rapping, but in its place she curtailed Victoria's liberty and kept her nose to the grindstone pitilessly. Why should caresses be confined to the sick, and kindness be bought only at the price of threatened death? I was inclined to refuse to kiss Krak, but my mother made such a point of compliance that I yielded reluctantly. In days of health Krak had exacted, morning and evening, a formal and perfunctory peck; if I gave her no more now she looked aggrieved, and my mother distressed. Had Krak been possessed by a real penitence, I would have opened my arms to her, but I was fully aware that her mood was not this; she merely wanted to know that I bore no malice for just discipline, and it went to my heart even apparently·to concede this position. There seemed to me something a little unfair in her proceedings; they were attempts to obtain from me admissions that I should have repudiated scornfully in hours of health. I knew that concessions now would prejudice my future liberty. In days to come (supposing I recovered) my hostility to Krak would be met by " Remember how kind she was to you when you were ill," or " Oh, Augustin, you didn't say that of the Baroness when she brought you grapes in your illness." I had plenty of grapes. There are few things which human nature resents more than a theft of its grievances. I was polite to Krak, but I lodged a protest with my mother and confided a passionate repudiation of any treaty to Victoria's sympathetic ear. Victoria was all for me; my mother was stern for a moment, and then, smiling faintly, told me to try to sleep.

After several months I took a decided and rapid turn toward recovery. This, I think, was the moment in which I realized most keenly the fictitious importance which my position imparted to me. The fashion of everybody's face was changed; mother, doctors, nurses, servants, all wore an air of victory. When I was carried out on to the terrace at Artenberg, rows of smiling people clapped their hands. I felt that I had done something very meritorious in getting better, and I hoped secretly that they would give me just as fine a procession as though I had died. Victoria got hold of a newspaper and, before she was detected and silenced, read me a sentence:

" By the favourable news of the King's health a great weight is lifted from the heart of the country. There is not a house that will not be glad to-day." I was pleased at this, although rather surprised. Taking thought with myself, I concluded that, although kingship had hitherto failed to answer my private expectations and desires, yet it must be a more important thing even in these days than I had come to suppose. I put a question to my mother, pointing at one of the gardeners.

"If Josef's son was ill and I was ill," said I, "which would Josef wish most to get better?"

"The King should be before a thousand sons to him," she answered quickly, and in a proud, agitated voice. But a moment later she bade me not ask foolish questions. I remember that I studied her face for some moments. It was a little difficult to make out how she really felt about me and my kingship.

Convalescence was a pleasant season. Styrian discipline was relaxed, and I was allowed to do very nearly all that my strength enabled me. Victoria shared in the indulgence of this time; I remember we agreed that there would be something to be said for never getting quite well. Had getting quite well meant going back to Krak, I should have felt this point of view most strongly, but I was not to go back to Krak. There was a talk of a governor, of tutors, and masters. Hammerfeldt came down and had a long conversation with my mother. She came out from the interview with flushed cheeks, seeming vexed and perturbed, but she was composed again when the Prince took his leave, and said to him pleasantly:

"You mustn't take him away from me altogether, Prince."

"We rely on your influence above everything, madame," was Hammerfeldt's courtly answer, but my mother watched his retreating figure with a rather bitter smile. Then she turned to me and asked:

"Shall you be glad to have tutors?"

Krak was in the distance with Victoria; my

mother perceived my eyes travelling in that direction.

"Poor old Baroness! You never liked her, did you, Augustin?"

"No," said I, emboldened by this new and confidential tone.

"Try to think more kindly of her," she advised; but I saw that she was not in the least aggrieved at my want of appreciation. "You don't like women, do you?"

"Only you, and Victoria, and——" I hesitated.

"And Anna?"

"Oh, of course, old Anna."

"Well, and who else?"

"The Countess von Sempach," said I, a little timidly.

"Haven't you forgotten her?" asked my mother, and her smile became less bright.

"No, I've—I've not forgotten her," I murmured. "Does she ever come to see you, mother—here at Artenberg, I mean?"

"No, darling," said my mother.

I did not pursue the subject. I had eyes good enough to see that my dislike for Krak was pleasanter to my mother than my liking for the Countess. Women seem to me to have the instinct of monopoly, and not to care for a share of affection. Such, at least, was my mother's temperament, intensified no doubt by the circumstance that in future days my favour and liking might be matters of importance. She feared from another woman just what she feared from Hammerfeldt, his governor, and his tutors; probably her knowledge of the world made her dread another woman more than any number of men. She feared even Victoria, her own daughter and my sister; but a woman, very pretty and sympathetic, who would be only twenty-eight when I was eighteen, must have seemed to her mind the greatest peril of all. It is one of the drawbacks of conspicuous place that a man's likings and fancies, his merest whims, are invested by others with an importance that throws its reflection back on to his own mind; he is able to recollect only with an effort that even in his case there are a good many things of no importance. I did not make these observations as a small boy at Artenberg, but even as a small boy I knew very well that the Countess von Sempach would not be invited to the Schloss. Nor was she. My mother guarded the gate, a jealous angel.

Thus a pleasant summer passed at Artenberg, and in the autumn we returned to Forstadt. Then I had my procession, though it seemed scarcely as brilliant or interesting as that wherein Victoria had held first place while I looked down, a highly satisfied spectator, from heaven. I was eleven years old now, and perhaps just the first bloom was wearing off the wonder of the world. For recompense, but not in full requital, I was more awake to the meaning of things around me, and I fear much more awake to the importance of myself, Augustin. Now I appropriated the cheers at which before I had marvelled, and approved the enthusiasm that had before amused me. My mother greeted these signs in me; since I was to leave the women she would now have me a man as soon as might be; besides, she had a woman's natural impatience for my full growth. They love us most as babies, when they are Providence to us; least as boys, when we make light of them; more again when as men we return to rule and be ruled, bartering slavery in one matter for

dominion in another, and working out the equilibrium of power.

But after my procession in the cathedral, when I
was giving thanks for rescue from a death that had
never been terrible and now seemed remote and impossible, I saw my countess. She was nearly opposite to me; her husband was not with her: he was
on guard in the nave with his regiment. I wanted
to make some sign to her, but I had been told that
everybody would be looking at me. When I was
crowned, "everybody" had meant Krak, and I had
feared no other eye. I was more self-conscious now.
I was particularly alert that my mother should observe nothing. But the Countess and I exchanged
a glance; she nodded cautiously; almost immediately afterward I saw her wipe her eyes. I should
have liked to talk to her, tell her that I liked being
a king rather better, and give her the glad tidings
that the dominion of Krak had ended; but I got no
chance of doing anything of the sort, being carried
away without coming nearer to her.

Victoria was in very low spirits that evening.
It had suddenly come upon her that she was to be
left to endure Krak all alone. Victoria and I were
not somehow as closely knit together as we had been;
she was now thirteen, growing a tall girl, and I was
but a little boy. Yet our relations were not, I imagine, quite what they would have been between
brother and sister of such relative ages in an ordinary case. The authority which elder sisters may
be seen so readily to ape and assume was never
claimed by Victoria; my mother would not have endured such presumption for a moment. I think Victoria regarded me as a singularly ignorant person,
who yet, by fortune's freak, was invested with a

strange importance and the prospect at least of great and indefinite power. She therefore took a good deal of pains to make me understand her point of view, and to convert me to her opinions. Her present argument was that she also ought to be relieved from Krak.

" Krak was mother's governess till mother was eighteen," I reminded her.

" Awful ! " groaned poor Victoria.

" In fact, mother's never got rid of Krak at all."

" Oh, that's different. I shouldn't in the least mind keeping Krak as my daughter's governess," said Victoria. " That would be rather fun."

" It would be very cruel, considering what Krak does," I objected.

Dim hintings of the grown-up state were in Victoria ; she looked a little doubtful.

" It wouldn't matter when she was quite young," she concluded. " But I'm nearly fourteen. Augustin, will you ask mother to send Krak away when I'm fifteen ? "

" No," said I. I had a wholesome dread of straining the prerogative.

" Then when I'm sixteen ? "

" I don't see what I've got to do with it," said I restlessly.

Victoria became huffy.

" You're king, and you could do it if you liked," she said. " If I was king, I should like to do things for people, for my sister anyhow." She pouted in much vexation.

" Well, perhaps I'll try some day," said I reluctantly.

" Oh, you dear boy ! " cried Victoria, and she immediately gave me three kisses.

I was certainly on my way to learn the secret of popularity. In my experience Victoria's conception of the kingly office is a very common one, and Victoria's conduct in view of a refusal to forward her views, and of consent, extremely typical. For Victoria took no account of my labours, or of the probable trouble I should undergo, or of the snub I should incur. She called me a dear boy, gave me three kisses, and went off to bed in much better spirits. And all the while my own secret opinion was that Krak was rather good for Victoria. It has generally been my secret opinion that people had no business to receive the things which they have asked me to give to or procure for them. When the merits are good the King's help is unnecessary.

CHAPTER IV.

PHYSICALLY my parents' child, with my father's
tall stature and my mother's clean-cut features, in-
tellectually I was more son to Hammerfeldt than
to any one else. From the day when my brain
began to develop, his was the preponderating influence. I had a governor, a good soldier, General
von Vohrenlorf; I had masters; I had one tutor, of
whom more presently (he for a time bade fair to dispute the Prince's supremacy); but above them all,
moulding me and controlling them, was this remarkable old man. At this time he was seventy years
old; he had been a soldier till thirty, since then a
diplomatist and politician. I do not think in all
things as Hammerfeldt thought; time moves, and
each man's mind has its own cast; but I will make
no claim to originality at the cost of depreciating
what I learned from him. He was a solitary man;
once he had taken a wife; she left him after two
years; he used to talk about her as though she had
died at the date when she ran away, without bitterness, with an indulgent kindness, with a full recognition of her many merits. Those who did not know
the story little supposed that the lady lived still in
Paris. His conduct in this matter was highly characteristic. He regarded passions and emotions as

things altogether outside and independent of the rational man. Their power could not be denied in their own sphere and season; he admitted that they must be felt—raw feeling was their province; he denied that they should affect thought or dominate action. In others they were his opportunity, in himself a luxury that had never been dangerous, or an ailment that was troublesome but never fatal. He was hard on a blunder; as a necessary presupposition to effective negotiation or business he recognised a binding code of honour; he has frequently told me he did not understand the theological conception of sin. He had eaten of our salt and was our servant; thus he would readily have died for us; but he prayed pardon if we asked him to believe in us. "Conduct," he said once, "is the outcome of selfishness limited by self-conceit." It was his way so to put things as to strip them of friendly, decent covering; had he said self-interest limited by self-respect, the axiom would have been more accepted and less quoted. A superficial person used to exclaim to me, "And yet he is so kind!" A man without ideals finds kindness the easiest thing in the world. In truth he was kind, and in a confidential sort of way that seemed to chuckle and wink, saying, "We're rogues together; then I must lend you a hand." But he could be ruthless also, displaying a curious aloofness from his fellow-men and an unconsciousness of any suffering he might inflict that left mere cruelty far behind. If I were making an automaton king, I would model my machine on the lines of Hammerfeldt. He had no belief in a future life, but would sometimes trifle whimsically with the theory of a transmigration of souls; he traced all beliefs in immortality to the longing of those who were unfortunate here (and who did not think himself so?) for a recompense (a revenge he called it) hereafter, and declared transmigration to be at once the most ingenious and the most picturesque embodiment of this yearning. He played billiards extremely well, and excused his skill on the ground that he was compelled to pass the time while foreign diplomatists and his own colleagues were making up their mind. I do not think that he ever hesitated as to what he had best do. He was of an extremely placid and happy temper. As may be anticipated from what I have said, he regarded no man as utterly lost unless he were completely under the influence of a woman.

Yet it was by Hammerfeldt's will that Geoffrey Owen became my daily companion and familiar friend. Vohrenlorf visited me once or twice a week, and exercised a perfunctory superintendence. I had, of course, many masters who came and went at appointed hours. Owen lived with me both at Forstadt and at Artenberg. At this time he was twenty-five; he excelled my own adult stature, and walked with the free grace of a well-bred English gentleman. His dark hair grew thick, rising from his forehead in a wave; his face was long and thin, and a slight mustache veiled a humorous tender mouth. There was about the man a pervading sympathy; the desire to be friends was the first characteristic of his manner; he was talkative, eager, enthusiastic. If a man were good it seemed to Owen but natural; if he were a rogue my tutor would set it down to anything in the world save his own fault. Everybody could be mended if everybody else would try. Thus he brought with him into our conservative military court and society the latest breath of generous hope and human aspiration that had blown over Oxford.

Surely this was a strange choice of Hammerfeldt's! Was it made in ignorance of the man, or with some idea that my mind should be opened to every variety of thought, or in a careless confidence that his own influence was beyond shaking, and that Owen's spirit would beat hopelessly against the cage and never reach mine in its prison of tradition?

A boy that would not have worshipped such a man as Geoffrey Owen must have wanted heart and fire. I watched him first to see if he could ride; he rode well. When he came he could not fence; in six months he was a good hand with the foils; physical fatigue seemed as unknown to him as mental inertia. There was no strain and no cant about him; he smoked hard, drank well after exertion, with pleasure always. He delighted to talk to my mother, chaffing her Styrian ideas with a graceful deference that made her smile. Victoria adored him openly, and Krak did not understand why he was not odious. Thus he conquered the Court, and I was the first of his slaves. It would be tedious to anybody except myself to trace the gradual progress of our four years' intimacy and friendship, of my four years' training and enlightenment. Shall I summarize it and say that Owen taught me that there were folks outside palaces, and that the greatness of a station, even as of a man, stood not in the multitude of the things that it possessed? The summary is cold and colourless; it smacks of duty, of obligations unwillingly remembered, of selfish pleasures reluctantly foregone. As I became old enough to do more than listen entranced to his stories, it seemed to me that to be such a man as he was, and not knowing that he himself was admired, could be no duty, but only a happy dream. There has been in my family, here

and there, a vein of fancy, or of mysticism turning
sometimes to religious fervour, again sometimes to
soldierly enthusiasm and a knight-errantry in arms,
the ruin and despair of cool statesmanship. On this
element Owen's teaching laid hold and bent it to a
more modern shape. I would not be a monk or a
Bayard, but would serve humanity, holding my
throne a naked trust, whence all but I might reap
benefit, whereon I must sit burdened with the sorrows of all; and thus to be burdened was my joy.
With some boys no example could have made such
ideas acceptable, or won anything but scornful wonder for them; in me they struck answering chords,
and as I rambled in the woods at Artenberg already
in my mind I was the perfect king.

Where would such a mood have led? Where
would it have ended? What at the last would have
been my state and fame?

On my fifteenth birthday Prince von Hammerfeldt, now in his seventy-fifth year, came from Forstadt to Artenberg to offer me congratulations.
Though a boy may have such thoughts as I have
tried to describe, for the most part he would be
flogged to death sooner than utter them; to the
Prince above all men an instinct bade me be silent.
But Owen rose steadily to the old man's skilful fly;
he did not lecture the minister nor preach to him,
but answered his questions simply and from the heart,
without show and without disguise. Old Hammerfeldt's face grew into a network of amused and tol-
erant wrinkles.

"My dear Mr. Owen," said he, "I heard all this
forty—fifty—years ago. Is it not that Jean Jacques
has crossed the Channel, turning more sickly on the
way?"

Owen smiled. Mine was the face that grew red in resentment, mine the tongue that burned to answer him.

"I know what you mean, sir," laughed Owen. "Still doesn't the world go forward?"

"I see no signs of it," replied Hammerfeldt with a pinch of snuff, "unless it be progress to teach rogues who aren't worth a snap to prate of their worth. Well, it is pretty enough in you to think as you think. What says the King to it?" He turned to me with a courteous smile, but with an unceremoniously intent gaze in his eyes.

I had no answer ready; I was still excited.

"I have tried to interest the King in these lines of thought," said Owen.

"Ah, yes, very proper," assented Hammerfeldt, his eyes still set on my face. "We must have more talk about the matter. Princess Heinrich awaits me now."

Owen and I were left together. He was smiling, but rather sadly; yet he laughed outright when I, carried beyond boyish shame by my indignation, broke into a tirade and threw back at him something of what he had taught me. Suddenly he interrupted me.

"Let's go for a row on the river and have one pleasant afternoon," he said, laying his hand on my shoulder. "The Prince does not want us any more to-day."

The afternoon dwells in my memory. In my belief Owen's quick mind had read something of the Prince's purpose; for he was more demonstrative of affection than was his wont. He seemed to eye me with a pitiful love that puzzled me; and he began to talk (this also was rare with him) of my special position, how I must be apart from other men, and to speculate in seeming idleness on what a place such as mine would be to him and make of him. All this came between our spurts of rowing or among our talk of sport or of flowers as we lay at rest under the bank.

"If there were two kings here, as there were in Sparta!" I cried longingly.

"There were ephors, too," he reminded me, and we laughed. Hammerfeldt was our ephor.

There was a banquet that night. I sat at the head of the table, with my mother opposite and Hammerfeldt at her right hand. The Prince gave my health after dinner, and passed on to a warm and eloquent eulogy on those who had trained me. In the course of it he dwelt pointedly on the obligation under which Geoffrey Owen had laid me, and of the debt all the nation owed to one who had inspired its king with a liberal culture and a zeal for humanity. I could have clapped my hands in delight. I looked at Owen, who sat far down the table. His gaze was on Hammerfeldt, and his lips were parted in a smile. I did not understand his smile, but it persisted all through the Prince's graceful testimony to his services. It was not like him to smile with that touch of satire when he was praised. But I saw him only for an instant before I went to bed, and others were with us, so that I could ask no explanation.

The next morning I rose early, and in glee, for I was to go hunting. Owen did not accompany me; he was, I understood, to confer with Hammerfeldt. My jovial governor Vohrenlorf had charge of me. A merry day we had, and good sport; it was late when we came home, and my anxious mother

awaited me in the hall with dry slippers. She had a
meal spread for me, and herself came to share it.
Never had I seen her so tender or so gentle. I had
a splendid hunger, and fell to, babbling of my skill
with the gun between hearty mouthfuls.

"I wish Owen had been there," I said.

My mother nodded, but made no answer.

"Is the Prince gone?" I asked.

"No, he is here still. He stayed in case you
should want to see him, Augustin."

"I don't want him," said I with a laugh, as I
pushed my chair back. "But I was glad he talked
like that about Owen last night. I think I'll go and
see if Owen's in his room." I rose and started toward the door.

"Augustin, Mr. Owen is not in his room," said
my mother in a strangely timid voice.

I turned with a start, for I was sensitive to every
change of tone in her voice.

"Do you know where he is?" I asked.

"He is gone," said she.

I did not ask where, nor whether he would return. I sat down and looked at her; she came,
smoothed my hair back from my forehead, and
kissed me.

"I have not sent him away," she said. "I
couldn't help it. The Prince was resolved, and he
has power."

"But why?" burst from my lips.

"It is the Prince's doing, not mine," she reminded me. "The Prince is here, Augustin."

Why, yes, at least old Hammerfeldt would not
run away.

My lips were quivering. I was nearer tears than
pride had let me be for three years past, grief and

4

anger uniting to make me sore and desolate. There seemed a great gap made in my life; my dearest companion was gone, the source of all that most held my fancy and filled my mind dried up. But before I could speak again a tall, lean figure stood in the doorway, helmet in hand. Hammerfeldt was there; he was asking if the King would receive him. My mother turned an inquiring glance on me. I bowed my head and choked down a sob that was in my throat. The old man came near to me and stood before me; there was a little smile on his lips, but his old eyes were soft.

"Sire," said he, addressing me with ceremonial deference and formality, "her royal highness has told you what I have done in your Majesty's service. I should be happy in your Majesty's approval."

I made him no answer.

"A king, sire," he went on, "should sip at all cups and drain none, know all theories and embrace none, learn from all men and be bound to none. He may be a pupil, but not a disciple; a hearer, but always a critic; a friend, never a devotee."

I felt my mother's hand resting on my shoulder; I sat still, looking in the Prince's eyes.

"Mr. Owen has done his work well," he went on, "but his work is done. Do you ask, sire, why he is gone? I will give you an answer. I, Prince von Hammerfeldt, would have Augustin and not Geoffrey for my master and my country's."

"Enough for to-night, Prince. Leave him now," my mother urged in a whisper.

The Prince bent his head slightly, but remained where he stood for a moment longer. Then he bowed very low to me, and drew back a step, still

Hammerfeldt came to me and kissed my hand.

facing me. My mother prompted me with what I suppose was the proper formula.

" You are convinced of the Prince's wisdom and devotion in everything, aren't you, Augustin? " she said.

" Yes," said I. " Will Mr. Owen write to me? "

" When your Majesty is older, your Majesty will, of course, use your own pleasure as to your correspondence," returned Hammerfeldt.

He waited for a moment longer, and then drew back further to the door.

" Speak to the Prince, Augustin," said my mother.

" I am very grateful to the Prince for his care of me," said I.

Hammerfeldt came quickly up to me and kissed my hand. " I would make you a true king, sire," said he, and with that he left us.

So they took my friend from me, and not all the kindness with which I was loaded in the time following his loss lightened the grief of it. Presently I came to understand better the meaning of these things, and to see that the King might have no friend; for his friend must be an enemy to others, perhaps even to the King himself. Shall I now blame Hammerfeldt? I do not know. I was coming to the age when impressions sink deep into the mind; and Geoffrey Owen was a man whose mark struck very deep. Besides, he had those theories! It was not strange in Hammerfeldt to fear those theories. Perhaps he was right; with his statecraft it may well be that he could have done no other than what he did. But to my fifteen-years-old thoughts these reflections were not present. They had taken my friend from me. In my bed that night I wept for him, and my

days seemed empty for the want of him. It was to
me as though he had died, and worse than that; there
are things as final as death, yet lacking death's gentleness. Such is it to be cut off, living friend from
living friend, and living heart from heart, not grown
cold in the grave. I have told this story of my tutor
and myself first, for the influence Owen had on me
more than for the effect wrought in me by the manner in which I lost him. There must be none very
near me; it seemed as though that stern verdict had
been passed. There must be a vacant space about
the throne. Such was Hammerfeldt's gospel. He
knew that he himself soon must leave me; he would
have no successor in power, and none to take a place
in love that he had neither filled nor suffered to be
filled. As I wandered, alone now, about the woods
at Artenberg I mused on these things, and came to
a conclusion rather bitter for one of my years. I
would tie no more bonds, to have them cut with the
sword; if love must be slain, love should be born
no more; to begin was but to prepare a sad ending.
I would not be drawn on to confidence or friendship.
I chose not to have rather than to lose, not to taste
rather than leave undrained the cup of sweet intimacy. Thus I armed my boyhood at once against
grief and love. In all that I did in after days this
determination was always with me, often overborne
for the time by emotions and passions, but always
ready to reassert itself in the first calm hour, and
relentlessly to fetter me in a prison of my own making. My God, how I have longed for friends sometimes!

Geoffrey Owen I saw but once again. I had
written twice to him, and received respectful, friendly,
brief answers. But the sword had passed through

his heart also; he did not respond to my invitation, nor show a desire to renew our intimacy. Perhaps he was afraid to run the risk; in truth, even while I urged him, I was half afraid myself. Had he come again, it would not have been as it had been between us. Very likely we both in our hearts preferred to rest in memories, not to spoil our thoughts by disappointment, to be always to one another just what we had been as we rowed together that last afternoon at Artenberg, when the dim shadow of parting did no more than deepen our affection and touch it to a profounder tenderness.

And that time when I saw him again? I was driving through the gates of an English palace, encircled by a brilliant troop of soldiers, cheered by an interested, good-humoured throng. Far back in their ranks, but standing out above all heads, I saw his face, paler and thinner, more gentle even and kindly. He wore a soft hat crushed over his forehead; as I passed he lifted and waved it, smiling his old smile at me. I waved my hand, leaning forward eagerly; but I could not stop the procession. As soon as I was within I sent an equerry to seek him, armed with a description that he could not mistake. But Geoffrey Owen was nowhere to be found, he had not awaited my messenger. Having signalled a friend's greeting across the gulf between us, he was gone. I could have found him, for I knew that he dwelt in London, working, writing, awakening hope in many, fear in some, thought in all. But I would not seek him out, nor compel him to come to me, since he would not of his own accord. So he went his way, I mine, and I have seen him no more. Yet ever on my birthday I drain a cup to him, and none knows to whom the King drinks a full glass silently. It is my libation on a friendship's grave. Perhaps it would support an interpretation more subtle. For when I stood between Owen and Hammerfeldt, torn this way and that, uncertain whom I should follow through life, was not I the humble transitory theatre of a great and secular struggle? It seems to me that then the Ideal and the Actual joined in battle over me; Hector and Achilles, and I the body of Patroclus! Alas, poor body! Greatly the combatants desire it, little they reck of the roughness it suffers in their struggle! The Spirit and the World—am I over-fanciful if I seem to see them incarnated in Geoffrey Owen and old Hammerfeldt? And victory was with the world. Yet the conquered also have before now left their mark on lands which they could not hold.

CHAPTER V.

SOMETHING ABOUT VICTORIA.

I FEEL that I give involuntarily a darker colour to my life than the truth warrants. When we sit down and reflect we are apt to become the prey of a curious delusion; pain seems to us the only reality, pleasure a phantasm or a dream. Yet such reality as pain has pleasure shares, and we are in no closer touch with eternal truth when we have headaches (or heartaches) than when we are free from these afflictions. I wonder sometimes whether a false idea of dignity does not mislead us. Would we all pose as martyrs? It is nonsense; for most of us life is a tolerable enough business—if we would not think too much about it. We need not pride ourselves on our griefs; it seems as though joy were the higher state because it is the less self-conscious and rests in fuller harmony with the great order that encircles us.

As I grew older I gained a new and abiding source of pleasure in the contemplation and study of my sister Victoria. I have anticipated matters a little in telling of my tutor's departure; I must hark back and pick up the thread of Victoria's history from the time when I was hard on thirteen and she near fifteen—the time when she had implored me to rid her of Krak. I had hated Krak with that healthy full-blooded antipathy whose faculty one seems to lose in later years. It is a tiresome thing to be driven by experience to the discovery of some good in everybody; your fine black fades to neutral gray; often I regret the delightfully partial views of earlier days. And so many people succeed in preserving them to a green and untutored old age! They are Popes always to their heretics. Such was and is Victoria; she never changed in her views of other people. In contrast she was, as regards herself, of a temperament so elastic that impressions endured hardly a moment beyond the blow, and pleasures passed without depositing any residuum which might form a store against evil days. If Krak had cut her arm off, its perpetual absence might have made Victoria remember the fault which was paid for by amputation; the moral effect of rapid knuckles disappeared with the comfort that came from sucking them. Perhaps her disposition was a happy chance for her; since the Styrian discipline (although not, of course, in this blankly physical form later on) persisted for her long after it had been softened for me. I touch again perhaps on a point which has caught my attention before; undoubtedly my mother kept the status of childhood imposed on Victoria fully as long as nature countenanced the measures. Krak did not go; a laugh greeted my hint. Krak stayed till Victoria was sixteen. For my part, since it was inevitable that Krak should discipline somebody, I think heaven was mild in setting her on Victoria. Had I stayed under her sway I should have run mad. Victoria laughed, cried, joked, dared, submitted, offended, defied, suffered, wept, and laughed again all in a winter's afternoon. She was by way of putting on the dignity of an elder with me and shutting off from my gaze her trials and reverses.

But there was no one else to tell the joke to, and I had it all each night before I slept.

But now Victoria was sixteen; and Krak, elderly, pensioned, but unbroken, was gone. She went back to Styria to chasten and ultimately to enrich (I would not for the world have been privy to their prayers) some nephews and nieces. It seemed strange, but Krak was homesick for Styria. She went; Victoria gave her the tribute of a tear, surprised out of her before she remembered her causes for exultation. Then came their memory, and she was outrageously triumphant. A new era began; the buffer was gone; my mother and Victoria were face and face. And in a year as Victoria said, in two or three as my mother allowed, Victoria would be grown up.

I was myself, most unwillingly, a cause of annoyance to Victoria, and a pretext for her repression. Importance flowed in on me unasked, unearned. To speak in homely fashion, she was always "a bad second," and none save herself attributed to her the normal status of privileges of an elder sister. Her wrath was not visited on me, but on those who exalted me so unduly; even while she resented my position she was not, as I have shown, above using it for her own ends; this adaptability was not due to guile; she forgot one mood when another came, and compromised her pretensions in the effort to compass her desires. Princess Heinrich seized on the inconsistency, and pointed it out to her daughter with an exasperating lucidity.

" You are ready enough to remember that Augustin is king when you want anything from him," she would observe. " You forget it only when you are asked to give way to him."

Victoria would make no reply—the Krak traditions endured to prevent an answer to rebukes—but when we were alone she used to remark, " I should think an iceberg's rather like a mother. Only one needn't live with icebergs."

Quite suddenly, as it seemed, it occurred to Victoria that she was pretty. She lost no time in advertising the discovery through the medium of a thousand new tricks and graces; a determined assault on the affections of all the men about us, from the lords-in-waiting down to the stablemen—an assault that ignored existing domestic ties or pre-arranged affections—was the next move in her campaign. When she was extremely angry with her mother she would say, " How odious it must be not to be young any more ! " I thought that there was sometimes a wistful look in my mother's eyes; was she thinking of Krak, Krak in far-off Styria? Perhaps for once, when Victoria was hitting covertly at Krak, my mother remarked in a very cold voice:

" You remember your punishments, you don't remember your offences, Victoria."

I could linger long on these small matters, for I find more interest and incitement to analysis in the attitude of women toward women than in their more obvious relations with men; but I must pass over a year of veiled conflict, and come to that incident which is the salient point in Victoria's girlish history. It coincided almost exactly in time with the dismissal of Geoffrey Owen, and my pre-occupation with that event diverted my attention from the earlier stages of Victoria's affair. She was just seventeen, grown up in her own esteem (and she adduced many precedents to fortify her contention), but in my mother's eyes still wanting a year of quiet home life before she should be launched into society. Victoria acquiesced perforce, but turned the flank of the decree by ensuring that the home life should be by no means quiet. She set to work to prepare for us a play; comedy or tragedy I knew not then, and am not now quite clear. Our nearest neighbour at Artenberg dwelt across the river in the picturesque old castle of Waldenweiter; he was a young man of twenty-two at this time, handsome, pleasant, and ready for amusement. His father being dead, Frederick was his own master—that is to say, he had no master. Victoria fell in love with him. The Baron, it seemed, was not disinclined for a romance with a pretty princess; perhaps he thought that nothing serious would come of it, and that it was a pleasant way enough of passing a summer; or, perhaps, being but twenty-two, he did not think at all, unless to muse on the depth of the blue in Victoria's eyes, and the comely lines of her figure as she rowed on the river. To say truth, Victoria gave him small time for reflection.

As I am convinced, before he had well considered the situation he had fallen into the habit of attending a *rendezvous* in a backwater of the stream about a mile above Artenberg. Victoria never went out unaccompanied, and never came back unaccompanied; it was discovered afterward that the trusted old boatman could be bought off with the price of beer, and used to disembark and seek an ale house so soon as the backwater was reached. The meeting over, Victoria would return in high spirits and displaying an unusual affection toward my mother, either as a blind, or through remorse, or (as I incline to think) through an amiability born of triumph; there was at times even a touch of commiseration in her manner, and more than once she spoke to me, in a tone of philosophical speculation, on the uselessness of endeavouring to repress natural feelings and the futility of treating as children persons who were already grown up. This mood lasted some time, so long, I suppose, as the stolen delight of doing the thing was more prominent than the delight in the thing itself. A month passed and brought a change. Now she was silent, absent, pensive, very kind to me, more genuinely submissive and dutiful to her mother. The first force of my blow had left me, for Owen had been gone now some months; I began to observe my sister carefully. To my amazement she, formerly the most heedless of creatures, knew in an instant that she was watched. She drew off from me, setting a distance between us; my answer was to withdraw my companionship, since only thus could I convince her that I had no desire to spy. I had not guessed the truth, and my mother had no inkling of it. Princess Heinrich's ignorance may seem strange, but I have often observed that persons of a masterful temper are rather easy to delude; they have such difficulty in conceiving that they can be disobeyed as to become ready subjects for hoodwinking; I recollect old Hammerfeldt saying to me, " In public affairs, sire, always expect disobedience, but be chary of rewarding obedience." My mother adopted the second half of the maxim but disregarded the first. She always expected obedience; Victoria knew it and built on her knowledge a confident hope of impunity in deceit.

Now on what harsh word have I stumbled? For deceit savours of meanness. Let me amend and seek the charity, the neutral tolerance, of some such word as concealment. For things good and things bad may be concealed, things that people should know and things that concern them not, great secrets of State and the flutterings of hearts. Victoria practised concealment.

I found her crying once, crying alone in a corner of the terrace under a ludicrous old statue of Mercury. I was amazed; I had not seen her cry so heartily since Krak had last ill-treated her. I put it to her that some such affliction must be responsible for her despair.

"I wish it was only that," she answered. "Do go away, Augustin."

"I don't want to stay," said I. "Only if you want anything——"

"I wonder if you could!" she said with a sudden flush. "No, it's no use," she went on. "And it's nothing. Augustin, if you tell mother you found me crying, I'll never——"

"You know quite well that I never tell anybody anything," said I, rather offended.

"Then go away, dear," urged Victoria.

I went away. I had been feeling very lonely myself, and had sought out Victoria for company's sake. However, I went and walked alone down to the edge of the river. It was clear that Victoria did not want me, and apparently I could do nothing for her. I have never found myself able to do very much for people, except those who did not deserve to have anything done for them. Perhaps poor Victoria didn't, but I was not aware of her demerits then. I repeated to the river my old reflection: "I don't see that it's much use being king, you know," said I as I flung a pebble and looked across at the towers of Waldenweiter. "That fellow's better off than I am," said I; and I wished again that Victoria had not sent me away. There is a period of life during which one is always being sent away, and it is not quite over for me yet in spite of my dignity.

At last came the crash. A little carelessness born of habit and impunity, the treachery of the old boatman under the temptation of a gold piece, the girl's lack of *savoir faire* when charged with the offence— here was enough, and more than enough. I recollect being summoned to my mother's room late one evening, just about my bedtime. I went and found her alone with Victoria. The Princess sat in her great arm-chair; Victoria was leaning against the wall when I entered; her handkerchief was crushed in one hand, the other hand clenched by her side.

"Augustin," said the Princess, "Victoria and I go to Biarritz to-morrow."

Victoria's quick breathing was her only comment. My mother told me in brief, curt, offensive phrases that Victoria had been carrying on a flirtation with our opposite neighbour. I have no doubt that I looked surprised.

"You may well wonder!" cried my mother. "If she could not remember what she was herself, she might have remembered that the King was her brother."

"I've done nothing——" Victoria began.

"Hold your tongue," said my mother. "If you were in Styria, instead of here, you'd be locked up in your own room for a month on bread and water; yes, you may think yourself lucky that I only take you to Biarritz."

"Styria!" said Victoria with a very bitter smile. "If I were in Styria I should be beheaded, I daresay, or—or knouted, or something. Oh, I know what Styria means! Krak taught me that."

"I wish the Baroness was here," observed the Princess.

"You'd tell her to beat me, I suppose?" flashed out my sister.

"If you were three years younger——" began my mother with perfect outward composure. Victoria interrupted her passionately.

"Oh, never mind my age. I'm a child still. Come and beat me!" she cried, assuming the air of an Iphigenia.

To this day I am of opinion that she ran a risk in giving this invitation; it was well on the cards that the Princess might have accepted it. Indeed had it been Styria—but it was not Styria. My mother turned to me with a cold smile.

"You perceive," said she, "the spirit in which your sister meets me because I object to her compromising herself with this wretched baron. She accuses me of persecution, and talks as though I were an executioner."

I had been looking very curiously at Victoria. She was in a dressing-gown, having been called, apparently, from her bedroom; her hair was over her shoulders. She looked most prettily woe-begone—like Juliet before her angry father, or, as I say, Iphigenia before the knife. In a moment she broke out again.

"Nobody feels for me," she complained. "What can Augustin know of it?"

"I know," observed my mother. "But although I know——"

"Oh, you've forgotten," cried Victoria scornfully.

For a moment my mother flushed. I was glad on all accounts that Victoria did not repeat her previous invitation now. On the contrary, when she had looked at Princess Heinrich, she gave a sudden frightened sob, rushed across the room, and flung herself on her knees at my feet.

"You're the king!" she cried. "Protect me, protect me!"

Throughout all this very painful interview I seemed to hear as it were echoes of the romances which I had read on Victoria's recommendation; the reminiscence was particularly strong in this last exclamation. However, it is not safe to conclude that feelings are not sincere because they are expressed in conventional phrases. These formulas are moulds into which our words run easily; though the moulds be hollow, the stuff that fills them may be solid enough.

"Why, you don't want to marry him?" I exclaimed, much embarrassed at being prematurely forced into functions of a *père de famille.*

"I'll never marry anybody else," moaned Victoria. My mother's face was the picture of disgust and scorn.

"That's another thing," said she. "At least the King would not hear of such a marriage as this."

. "Do you want to marry him?" I asked Victoria, chiefly, I confess, in curiosity. I had risen—or fallen—in some degree to my position, and it seemed strange to me that my sister should wish to marry this Baron Fritz.

"I—I love him, Augustin," groaned Victoria.

"She knows it's impossible, as well as you do," said my mother. "She doesn't really want to do it."

Victoria cried quietly, but made no reply or protest. I was bewildered; I did not understand then how we may passionately desire a thing which we would not do, and may snatch at the opposition of others as an excuse alike for refusal and for tears. Looking back, I do not think had we set Victoria free in the boat, and put the sculls in her hands, that she would have rowed over to Waldenweiter. But did she, then, deserve no pity? Perhaps she deserved more; for not two weak creatures like the Princess (I crave her pardon) and myself stood between her and her wishes, but she herself—the being that she had been fashioned into, her whole life, her nature, and her heart, as our state had made them. If our soul be our prison, and ourself the jailer, in vain shall we plan escape or offer bribes for freedom; wheresoever we go we carry the walls with us, and if death, then death alone can unlock the gates.

The scene grew quieter. Victoria rose, and threw herself into a chair in a weary, puzzled desolation; my mother sat quite still, with eyes intent on the floor, and lips close shut. A sense of awkwardness grew strong on me; I wanted to get out of the room. They would not fight any more now; they would be very distant to one another; and, moreover, it seemed clear that Victoria did not propose to marry Baron Fritz. But what about poor Baron Fritz? I approached my mother, and whispered a question. She answered me aloud.

"I have written to Prince von Hammerfeldt. A letter from him will, I have no doubt, be enough to insure us against further impertinence."

Victoria dabbed her eyes, but no protest came from her.

"We shall start mid-day to-morrow," the Princess pursued, "unless, of course, Victoria refuses to accompany me." Her voice took a tinge of irony.

5

" Possibly your wishes may persuade her, Augustin,
if mine can not."

Victoria raised her head suddenly, and said very
distinctly :

" I will do what Augustin tells me."   The emphatic word in that sentence was " Augustin."

My mother smiled bitterly; she understood well
enough the implicit declaration of war, the appeal
from her to me, the shifting of allegiance.   I daresay
that she saw the absurdity of putting a boy not yet
sixteen into such a position; but I know that I felt
it much more strongly.

" Oh, you'd better go, hadn't you?" I asked
uncomfortably. " You wouldn't be very jolly here,
you know."

" I'll do as you tell me, Augustin."

" Yes, we are both at your orders," said my
mother.

It crossed my mind that their journey would not
be a very pleasant one, but I did not feel able to
enter into that side of the question.   I resented this
reference to me, and desired to be rid of the affair.

" I should like you to do as mother suggests,"
said I.

" Very well, Augustin," said Victoria, and she
rose to her feet. She was a tall, graceful girl, and
looked very stately as she walked by her mother.
The Princess made no movement or sign; the grim
smile persisted on her lips. After a moment or two
of wavering I followed my sister from the room. She
was just ahead of me in the passage, moving toward
her bedroom with a slow, listless tread. An impulse
of sympathy came upon me; I ran after her, caught
her by the arm, and kissed her.

" Cheer up," I said.

"Oh, it's all right, Augustin," said she. "I've only been a fool."

There seemed nothing else to do, so I kissed her again.

"Fancy, Biarritz with mother!" she moaned. Then she turned on me suddenly, almost fiercely. "But what's the good of asking anything of you? You're afraid of mother still."

I drew back as though she had struck me. A moment later her arms were round my neck.

"Oh, never mind, my dear," she sobbed. "Don't you see I'm miserable? Of course, I must go with her."

I had never supposed that any other course was practicable. The introduction of myself into the business had been but a move in the game. Nevertheless it marked the beginning of a new position for me, as rich in discomfort as, according to my experience, are most extensions of power.

CHAPTER VI.

A STUDENT OF LOVE AFFAIRS.

THE departure to Biarritz was carried through
without further overt hostilities. It chanced to be
holidays with me, all my tutors were on their vaca-
tion, my governor, Vohrenlorf, on a visit at Berlin.
Hearing of my solitude, he insisted on making arrangements to return speedily; but for a few days
I was left quite alone, saving for the presence of my
French body-servant Baptiste. I liked Baptiste; he
was by conviction an anarchist, by prejudice a free-
thinker; one shrug of his shoulders disposed of the
institutions of this world, another relegated the next
to the limbo of delusions. He was always respectful,
but possessed an unconquerably intimate manner; he
could not forget that man spoke to man, although
one might be putting on the other's boots for him.
He regarded me with mingled affection and pity. I
had overheard him speaking of *le pauvre petit roi;*
the point of view was so much my own that from the
instant my heart went out to Baptiste. Since he attributed to me no sacro-sanctity, he was not officious
or persistent in his attendance while he was on duty;
in fact he left me very much to my own devices.
To my mother he was polite but cold; he adored
Victoria, declaring that she was worthy of being
French; his great hatred was for Hammerfeldt,

whom he accused of embodying the devil of Teutonism. Hammerfeldt was aware of his feelings and played with them, while he trusted Baptiste more than anybody about me. He did not know how attached I was to the Frenchman, and I did not intend that he should learn. I had received a sharp lesson with regard to parading my preferences.

It was through Baptiste that I heard of Baron Fritz's side of the case, for Baptiste was friendly with Fritz's servants. The Baron, it appeared, was in despair. "They watch him when he walks by the river," declared Baptiste with a gesture in which dismay and satisfaction were curiously blended.   ·

"Poor fellow!" said I, leaning back in the stern of the boat. To be in such a state on Victoria's account was odd and deplorable.

Baptiste laid down the sculls and leaned forward smiling.

"It is nothing, sire," said he. "It must happen now and again to all of us. M. le Baron will soon be well. Meanwhile he is—oh, miserable!"

"Is he all alone there?" I asked.

"Absolutely, sire. He will see nobody."

I looked up at Waldenweiter.

"He has not even his mother with him," said Baptiste; the remark, as Baptiste delivered it, was impertinent, and yet so intangibly impertinent as to afford no handle for reproof. He meant that the Baron was free from an aggravation; he said that he lacked a consolation.

"Shall I go and see him?" I asked. In truth I was rather curious about him; it was a pleasure to me to break out of my own surroundings.

"What would the Prince say?" said Baptiste.

"He need not know. Row ashore there."

" You must not go, sire. It would be known, and they would say——" Baptiste's shrug was eloquent.

" Do they always talk about everything one does ? "

" Certainly, sire, it is your privilege," smiled my servant. " But I think he might come to you. That could be managed; not in the Schloss, but in the wood, quite privately. I can contrive it."

Baptiste did contrive it, and Baron Fritz came. I was now just too old to scorn love, just too young to sympathize fully with it. There is that age in a boy's life, but since he holds his tongue about it, it is.apt to escape notice, and people jest on the sudden change in his attitude toward women. Nothing in nature is sudden; no more, then, is this transition. I looked curiously at Fritz; he was timid with me. I perceived that he was not an ordinary young nobleman, devoted only to sport and wine; he had something of Owen's romance, but in him it was self-centred, not open wide to embrace the universe of things beautiful and ugly. He thanked me for receiving him in a rather elaborate and artificial fashion. I wondered at once that he had caught Victoria's fancy; her temperament seemed too robust for him. He began to speak of her in some very poetical phrases; he quoted a line of poetry about Diana and Endymion. I had been made to turn it into Latin verses, and its sentiment fell cold on my soul. He spoke of his passion with desperation, and I thought with pride. He said that, happen what might, his whole life was the Princess's; but he did not mention Victoria's name, he said " her " with an air of mystery, as though spies lurked in the woods. There was nobody save Baptiste, standing sentry to guard this secret meeting. I gave the

Baron a cigarette, and lit one myself; I had begun the habit, though still surreptitiously.

"You must have known there'd be a row?" I suggested.

"Tell me of her!" he cried. "Is she in great grief?"

I did not want to tell him about Victoria; I wanted him to tell me about himself. As soon as he understood this, I am bound to say that he gratified me at once. I sat looking at him while he described his feelings; all at once he turned and discovered my gaze on him. ,

"Go on," said I.

The Baron appeared uncomfortable. His eyes fell to the ground, and he tried to puff at his cigarette which he had allowed to go out. I daresay he thought me a strange boy; but he could not very well say so.

"You don't understand it?" he asked.

"Partly," I answered.

"We never had any hope," said he, almost luxuriously.

"But you enjoyed it very much?" I suggested; I was quite grave about it in my mind, as well as in my face.

"Ah!" sighed he softly.

"And now it's all over!"

"I see her no more. I think of her. She thinks of me."

"Perhaps," said I meditatively. I was wondering whether they did not think more about themselves. "Didn't you think you might manage it?"

"Alas, no. Sorrow was always in our joy."

"What are you going to do now?"

"What is there for me to do?" he asked despairingly. "Sometimes I think that I can not endure to live."

"Baptiste told me that they watched you when you walked by the river."

He turned to me with a very interested expression of face.

"Do they really?" he asked.

"So Baptiste said."

"I promised her that, whatever happened, I would do nothing rash," said he. "What would her feelings be?"

"We should all be very much distressed," said I, in my best court manner.

"Ah, the world, the world!" sighed Baron Fritz. Then with an air of great courage he went on. "Yet, how am I so different from her?"

"I think you are very much alike," said I.

"But she is—a Princess!"

I felt that he was laying a sort of responsibility on me. I could not help Victoria being a Princess. He laughed bitterly; I seemed to be put on my defence.

"I think it just as absurd as you do," I hastened to say.

"Absurd!" he echoed. "I didn't say that I thought it absurd. Would not your Majesty rather say tragic? There must be kings, princes, princesses —our hearts pay the price."

I was growing rather weary of this Baron, and wondering more and more what Victoria had discovered in him. But my lack of knowledge led me into an error; I attributed what wearied me in no degree to the Baron himself, but altogether to his condition. "This, then, is what it is to be in love," I was saying to myself; I summoned up the relics

of my scorn once so abundant and vigorous. The
Baron perhaps detected the beginnings of *ennui;* he
rose to his feet.

"Forgive me, if I say that your Majesty will
understand my feelings better in two or three years,"
he observed.

"I suppose I shall," I answered, rather uneasily.

"Meanwhile I must live it down; I must master it."

"It's the only thing to do."

"And she——"

"Oh, she'll get over it," I assured him, nodding
my head.

I am inclined sometimes to count it among my
misfortunes, that the first love affair with which I
was brought into intimate connection and con-
fronted at an age still so impressionable, should have
been of the shallow and somewhat artificial character betrayed by the romance of my sister and Baron
Fritz. She was a headstrong girl; longing to exercise power over men, surprised when a temporary
gust of feeling carried her into an emotion unex-
pectedly strong; he was a self-conscious fellow, hugging his woes and delighting in the picturesqueness
of his misfortune. The notion left on my mind was
that there was a great deal of nonsense about the
matter. Baptiste strengthened my opinion.

"I ask your pardon, sire," he said with a shrug,
"but we know the sentimentality of the Germans.
What is it? Sighs and then beer, more sighs and
more beer, a deluge of sighs and a deluge of beer.
A Frenchman is not like that in his little affairs."

"What does a Frenchman do, Baptiste?" I had
the curiosity to ask.

"Ah," laughed Baptiste, "if I told your Majesty

now, you would not care to visit Paris; and I long
to go to Paris with your Majesty."

I did not pursue the subject. I was conscious of
a disenchantment, begun by Victoria, continued by the
Baron. The reaction made in favour of my mother.
I acknowledged the wisdom of her firmness and
an excuse for her anger. I realized her causes for
annoyance and shame, and saw the hollowness of the
lovers' pleas. I had thought the Princess very hard;
I was now inclined to think that she had shown as
much self-control as could be expected from her.
Rather to my own surprise I found myself extend-
ing this more favourable judgment of her to other
matters, entering with a new sympathy into her disposition, and even forgiving some harsh thing which
I had never pardoned. The idea suggested itself to
my mind, that even the rigours of the Styrian discipline had a rational relation to the position which
the victims of it were destined to fill. She might
be right in supposing that we could not be allowed
the indulgence accorded to the common run of children. We were destined for a special purpose, and,
if we were not made of a special clay, yet we must
be fashioned into a special shape. It is hard to dis-
entangle the influence of one event from that ex-
erted by another. Perhaps the loss of Owen, and
the consequently increased influence of Hammerfeldt over my life and thoughts, had as much to do
with my new feelings as Victoria's love affair; but
in any case I date from this time a fresh development
of myself. I was growing into my kingship, beginning to realize the conception of it, and to fill up
that conception in my own mind. This moment was
of importance to me; for it marked the beginning
of a period during which this idea of my position

was very dominant and coloured all I did or thought.
I did not change my opinion as to the discomfort
of the post; but its importance, its sacredness, and
its paramount claims grew larger and larger in my
eyes. It seems curious, but had Baron Fritz been
a different sort of lover, I think that I should have
been in some respects a different sort of a king. It
needs a constant intellectual effort to believe that
there is anything except accident in the course of
the world.

Hammerfeldt's persistent pressure drove the love-
lorn Baron, still undrowned (had the watchers been
too vigilant?), on a long foreign tour, and in three
months the Princess and Victoria returned. I saw
at once that the new relations were permanently established between them; my mother displayed an
almost ostentatious abdication of authority; her
whole air declared that since Victoria chose to walk
alone, alone in good truth she should walk. It was
the attitude of a proud and domineering nature that
answers any objection to its sway by a wholesale
disclaimer at once of power and responsibility. Victoria accepted her mother's resolution, but rather
with resentment than gratitude. They had managed
the affair badly; my mother had lost influence without gaining affection; my sister had forfeited guidance but not achieved a true liberty. She was hardly
more her own mistress than before; Hammerfeldt,
screened behind me, now trammelled her, and she
had a statesman to deal with instead of a mother.
Only once she spoke to me concerning the Baron
and his affair; the three months had wrought some
change here also.

"I was very silly," she said impatiently. "I know
that well enough."

" Then why don't you make it up with mother? "
I ventured to suggest.

" Mother behaved odiously," she declared.   " I
can never forgive her the way she treated me."

The grievance then had shifted its ground; not
what the Princess had done, but the manner in which
she had done it was now the head and front of her
offence. It needed little acquaintance with the world
to recognise that matters were not improved by this
change; one may come to recognise that common
sense was with the enemy; vanity at once takes refuge
in the conviction that his awkwardness, rudeness, or
cruelty in advancing his case was responsible for all
the trouble.

" If she had been kind, I should have seen it
all directly," said Victoria.   And in this it may
very well be that Victoria was not altogether
wrong.

The position was, however, inconsistent with even
moderate comfort. There was a way of ending it,
obvious, I suppose, to everybody save myself, but
seeming rather startling to my youthful mind.   In
six months now Victoria would be eighteen, and
eighteen is a marriageable age. Victoria must be
married; my mother and Hammerfeldt went hus-
band-hunting. As soon as I heard of the scheme
I was ready with brotherly sympathy, and even cherished the idea of interposing a hitherto untried royal
veto on such premature haste and cruel forcing of
a girl's inclination. Victoria received my advances
with visible surprise. Did I suppose, she asked,
that she was so happy at home as to shrink from
marriage? Would not such a step be rather an
emancipation than a banishment? (I paraphrase and
condense her observation.) Did I not perceive that

she must hail the prospect with relief? I was to know that her mother and herself were at one on this matter; she was obliged for my kindness, but thought that I need not concern myself in the matter. Considerably relieved, not less puzzled, with a picture of Victoria sobbing and the Baron walking (well watched) by the river's brink, I withdrew from my sister's presence. It occurred to me that to take a husband in order to escape from a mother was a peculiar step; I have since seen reason to suppose that it is more common than I imagined.

The history of my private life is (to speak broadly) the record of the reaction of my public capacity on my personal position; the effect of this reaction has been almost uniformly unfortunate. The case of Victoria's marriage affords a good instance. It might have been that here at least I should be suffered to play a fraternal and grateful part. My fate and Hammerfeldt ruled otherwise. There were two persons who suggested themselves as suitable mates for my sister; one was the reigning king of a country which I need not name, the other was Prince William Adolphus of Alt-Gronenstahl, a prince of considerable wealth and unexceptionable descent but not in the direct succession to a throne, not likely to occupy a prominent position in Europe. Victoria had never quite forgiven fortune (or perhaps me either) for not making her a queen in the first instance; she was eager to repair the error. She came to me and begged me to exert my influence in behalf of the king, who was understood through his advisers to favour the suggestion. I was most happy to second her wishes, although entirely sceptical as to the value of my assistance. I recollect very well the interview that followed between Hammerfeldt and myself;

throughout the Prince treated me *en roi*, speaking with absolute candour, disclosing to me the whole question, and assuming in me an elevation of spirit superior to merely personal feelings.

"After your Majesty," said he, "the Princess is heir to the throne. We have received representations that the union of the two countries in one hand could not be contemplated by the Powers. Now you, sire, are young; you are and must be for some years unmarried; life is uncertain and" (here he looked at me steadily) "your physicians are of opinion that certain seeds of weakness, sown by your severe illness, have not yet been eradicated from your constitution. It is necessary for me to offer these observations to your Majesty."

The old man's eyes were very kind.

"It's all right, sir," said I. "Go on."

"We all trust that you may live through a long reign, and that your son may reign after you. It is, indeed, the only strong wish that I have left in a world which I have well-nigh done with. But the other possibility has been set before us and we can not ignore it."

From that moment I myself never ignored it.

"It was suggested that Princess Victoria should renounce her rights of succession. I need not remind your Majesty that the result would be to make your cousin Prince Ferdinand heir-presumptive. I desire to speak with all respect of the Prince, but his succession would be an unmixed calamity." The Prince took a pinch of snuff.

Ferdinand was very liberal in his theories; and equally so, in a rather different sense, in his mode of life.

I thought for a moment.

"I shouldn't like the succession to go out of our branch," said I.

"I was sure of it, sire," he said, bowing. "It would break your mother's heart and mine."

I was greatly troubled. What of my ready inconsiderate promise to Victoria? And apart from the promise I would most eagerly have helped her to her way. I had felt severely the lack of confidence and affection that had recently come about between us; I was hungry for her love, and hoped to buy it of her gratitude. I believe old Hammerfeldt's keen eyes saw all that passed in my thoughts. The Styrian teaching had left its mark on my mind, as had the Styrian discipline on my soul. "God did not make you king for your own pleasure," Krak used to say with that instinctive knowledge of the Deity which marks those who train the young. No, nor for my sister's, nor even that I might conciliate my sister's love. Nay, again, nor even that I might make my sister happy. For none of these ends did I sit where I sat. But I felt very forlorn and sad as I looked at the old Prince.

"Victoria will be very angry," said I. "I wanted to please her so much."

"The Princess has her duties, and will recognise yours," he answered.

"Of course, if I die it'll be all right. But if I live she'll say I did it just out of ill-nature."

The old man rose from his chair, laying his snuff-box on the table by him. He came up to me and held out both his hands; I put mine into them, and looked up into his face. It was moved by a most rare emotion. I had never seen him like this before.

"Sire," said he in a low tone, "do not think that nobody loves you; for from that mood it may

come that a man will love nobody. There is an old
man that loves you, as he loved your father and your
grandfather; and your people shall love you." He
bent down and kissed me on either cheek. Then he
released my hands and stood before me. There was
a long silence. Then he said:

"Have I your Majesty's authority and support in
acting for the good of the kingdom?"

"Yes," said I.

But, alas! for Victoria's hopes, ambitions, and
vanity for her crown, and her crowned husband.
Alas, poor sister! And, alas, poor brother, hungry
to be friends again!

CHAPTER VII.

THINGS NOT TO BE NOTICED.

I HAVE not the heart to set down what passed between my sister and myself when I broke to her the news that I must be against her. Impulsive in all her moods, and ungoverned in her emotions, she displayed much bitterness and an anger that her disappointment may excuse. I have little doubt that I, on my part, was formal, priggish, perhaps absurd; all these faults she charged me with. You can not put great ideas in a boy's head without puffing him up; I was doing at cost to myself what I was convinced was my duty; it is only too likely that I gave myself some airs during the performance. Might I not be pardoned if I talked a little big about my position? The price I was paying for it was big enough. It touched me most nearly when she accused me of jealousy, but I set it down only to her present rage. I was tempted to soften her by dwelling on my own precarious health, but I am glad that an instinct for fair play made me leave that weapon unused. She grew calm at last, and rose to her feet with a pale face.

"I have tried to do right," said I.

"I shall not forget what you have done," she retorted as she walked out of the room.

I have been much alone in my life—alone in spirit, I mean, for that is the only loneliness that has power to hurt a man—but never so much as during the year that elapsed before Victoria's marriage was celebrated. Save for Hammerfeldt, whose engagements did not allow him to be much in my company, and to whom it was possible to open one's heart only rarely, I had nobody with whom I was in sympathy. For my mother, although she yielded more readily to the inevitable, was yet in secret on Victoria's side on the matter of marriage. Victoria had been for meeting the foreign representatives by renouncing her succession; my mother would not hear of that, but was for defying the protests. Nothing, she had declared, could really come of them. Hammerfeldt overbore her with his knowledge and experience, leaving her defeated, but only half convinced, sullen, and disappointed. She was careful not to take sides against me overtly, but neither did she seek to comfort or to aid me. She withdrew into a neutrality that favoured Victoria silently, although it refused openly to espouse her cause. The two ladies thus came closer together again, leaving me more to myself. The near prospect of independence reconciled Victoria to a temporary control; my mother was more gentle from her share in her daughter's disappointment. For my part I took refuge more and more in books and my sport.

Amusement is the one great consolation that life offers, and even in this dreary time it was not lacking. The love-lorn Baron had returned to Waldenweiter; he wrote to Hammerfeldt for permission; the Prince refused it; the Baron rejoined that he was about to be married; I can imagine the grim smile with which the old man withdrew his objection. The Baron came home with his wife. This event nearly broke the new alliance between my mother and my sister; it was so very difficult for my mother not to triumph, and Victoria detected a taunt even in silence. However, there was no rupture, the Baron was never mentioned; but I, seeking distraction, made it my business to pursue him as often as he ventured into his boat. I overtook him once and insisted on going up to Waldenweiter and being introduced to the pretty young Baroness. She knew nothing about the affair, and was rather hurt at not being invited to Artenberg. The Baron was on thorns during the whole interview—but not so much because he must be looking a fool in my eyes, as because he did not desire to seem light of love in his wife's. Unhappily, however, about this time a pamphlet was secretly printed and circulated, giving a tolerably accurate account of the whole affair. The wrath in " exalted quarters " may be imagined. I managed to procure (through Baptiste) a copy of this publication and read it with much entertainment. Victoria, in spite of her anger, borrowed it from me. It is within my knowledge that the Baroness received a copy from an unknown friend, and that the Baron, being thus driven into a corner, admitted that the Princess had at one time distinguished him by some attentions—and could he be rude? Now, curiously enough, the report that got about on our bank of the river was, that there was no foundation at all for the assertions of the pamphlet, except in a foolish and ill-mannered persecution to which the Princess had, during a short period, been subjected. After this there could be no question of any invitation passing from Artenberg to Waldenweiter. The subject dropped; the printer made some little scandal and a pocket full of money, and persons who, like myself, knew the facts and could appreciate the behaviour of the lovers gained considerable amusement.

My second source of diversion was found in my future brother-in-law, William Adolphus, of Alt-Gronenstahl. He was, in himself, a thoroughly heavy fellow, although admirably good-natured and, I believe, a practical and competent soldier. He was tall, dark, and even at this time inclining to stoutness; he became afterward exceedingly corpulent. He did not at first promise amusement, but a rather malicious humour found much in him, owing to the circumstance that the poor fellow was acquainted with the negotiations touching the marriage first suggested for Victoria, and was fully aware that he himself was in his lady's eyes only a *pis-aller*. His dignity might have refused such a situation; but in the first instance he had been hardly more of a free agent than Victoria herself, and later on, as though he were determined to deprive himself of all defence, he proceeded to fall genuinely in love with my capricious but very attractive sister. I was sorry for him, but I am not aware that sympathy with people excludes amusement at them. I hope not, for wide sympathies are a very desirable thing. William Adolphus, looking round for a friend, honoured me with his confidence, and during his visits to Artenberg used to consult me almost daily as to how he might best propitiate his deity and wean her thoughts from that other alliance which had so eclipsed his in its prospective brilliance.

" Girls are rather difficult to manage," he used to say to me ruefully. " You'll know more about them in a few years, Augustin."

I knew much more about them than he did already. I am not boasting; but people who learn only from experience do not allow for intuition.

"But I think she's beginning to get fonder of me," he would end, with an uphill cheerfulness.

She was not beginning to get the least fonder of him; she was beginning to be interested and excited in the stir of the marriage. There were so many things to do and talk about, and so much desirable prominence and publicity attaching to the affair, that she had less time for nursing her dislike. The shock of him was passing over; he was falling into focus with the rest of it; but she was not becoming in the least fonder of him. I knew all this without the few words; with them he knew none of it. It seems to be a mere accident who chances to be previous to truth, who impervious.

In loneliness for me, in perturbation for poor William Adolphus, in I know not what for Victoria the time passed on. There is but one incident that stands out, flaming against the gray of that monotony. The full meaning of it I did not understand then, but now I know it better.

I was sitting alone in my dressing-room. I had sent Baptiste to bed, and was reading a book with interest. Suddenly the door was opened violently. Before I could even rise to my feet, Victoria—the door slammed behind her—had thrown herself on her knees before me. She was in her nightdress, barefooted, her hair loose and tumbled on her shoulders; it seemed as though she had sprung up from her bed and run to me. She caught my arms in her hands, and laid her face on my knees; she said nothing, but sobbed violently with a terrible gasping rapidity.

"My God, what's the matter?" said I.

For a moment there was no answer; then her voice came, interrupted and half-choked by constant sobs.

"I can't do it, I can't do it. For God's sake, don't make me do it.

"Do what?" I asked.

Her sobs alone answered me, and their answer was enough. I sat there helpless and still, the nervous tight clutching of her hands pinning my arms to my side.

"You're the king, you're the king," she moaned.

Yes, I was the king; even then I smiled.

"You don't know," she went on, and now she raised her face streaming with tears. "You don't know—how can you know what it is? Help me, help me, Augustin."

The thing had come on me with utter suddenness, the tranquillity of my quiet room had been rudely rent by the invasion. I was, in an instant, face to face with a strange dim tragedy, the like of which I had never known, the stress of which I could never fully know. But all the tenderness that I had for her, my love for her beauty, and the yearning for comradeship that she herself had choked rose in me; I bent my head till my lips rested on her hair, crying, "Don't, darling, don't."

She sprang up, throwing her arm about my neck, and looking round the room as though there were something that she feared; then she sat on my knee and nestled close to me. She had ceased to sob now, but it was worse to me to see her face strained in silent agony and her eyes wept dry of tears.

"Let me stay here, do let me stay here a little,"

she said as I passed my arm round her and her head fell on my shoulder. "Don't send me away yet, Augustin," she whispered, "I don't want to be alone."

"Stay here, dearest, nobody shall hurt you," said I, as I kissed her. My heart broke for her trouble, but it was sweet to me to think that she had fled from it to my arms. After all, the old bond held between us; the tug of trouble revealed it. She lay a while quite still with closed eyes; then she opened her eyes and looked up at me.

"Must I?" she asked.

"No," I answered. "If you will not, you shall not."

Her arm coiled closer round my neck and she closed her eyes again, sighing and moving restlessly. Presently she lay very quiet, her exhaustion seeming like sleep. How long had she tormented herself before she came to me?

My brain was busy, but my heart outran it. Now, now if ever, I would assert myself, my power, my position. She should not call to me in vain. What I would do, I did not know; but the thing she dreaded should not be. But although I was in this fever, I did not stir; she was resting in peace; let her rest as long as she would. For more than an hour she lay there in my arms; I grew stiff and very weary, but I did not move. At last I believe that in very truth she slept.

The clock in the tower struck midnight, and the quarter, and the half-hour. I had rehearsed what I should say to my mother and what to Hammerfeldt. I had dreamed how this night should knit her and me so closely that we could never again drift apart, that now we knew one another and for each of us what was superficial in the other existed no more, but was swept away by the flood of full sympathy. She and I against the world if need be!

A shiver ran through her; she opened her eyes wide and wider, looking round the room no longer in fear, but in a sort of wonder. Her gaze rested an instant on my face, she drew her arm from round my neck and rose to her feet, pushing away my arm. There she stood for a moment with a strange, fretful, ashamed look on her face. She tossed her head, flinging her hair back behind her shoulders. I had taken her hand and still held it; now she drew it also away.

"What must you think of me?" she said. "Good gracious, I'm in my nightgown."

She walked across to the looking-glass and stood opposite to it.

"What a fright I look!" she said. "How long have I been here?"

"I don't know; more than an hour."

"It was horrid in bed to-night," she said in a half-embarrassed yet half-absent way. "I got thinking about—about all sorts of things, and I was frightened."

The change in her mood sealed my lips.

"I hope mother hasn't noticed that my room's empty. No, of course not; she must be in bed long ago. Will you take me back to my room, Augustin?"

"Yes," said I.

She came up to me, looked at me for a moment, then bent down to me as I sat in my chair and kissed my forehead.

"You're a dear boy," she said. "Was I quite mad?"

" I meant what I said," I declared, as I stood up. " I mean it still."

" Ah," said she, flinging her hands out, " poor Augustin, you mean it still! Take me along the corridor, dear, I'm afraid to go alone."

Sometimes I blame myself that I submitted to the second mood as completely as I had responded to the first; but I was staggered by the change, and the old sense of distance scattered for an hour was enveloping me again.

One protest I made.

" Are we to do nothing, then? " I asked in a low whisper.

" We're to go to our beds like good children," said she with a mournful little smile. " Come, take me to mine."

" I must see you in the morning."

" In the morning? Well, we'll see. Come, come."

Now she was urgent, and I did as she bade me. But first she made me bring her a pair of my slippers; her feet were very cold, she said, and they felt like ice against my hand as I touched them in putting on the slippers for her. She passed her hand through my arm and we went together. The door of her room stood wide open; we went in; I saw the bed in confusion.

" Fancy if any one had come by and seen! " she whispered. " Now, good-night, dear."

I opened my lips to speak to her again.

" No, no; go, please go. Good-night, dear." I left her standing in the middle of her room. Outside the door I waited many minutes; I heard her moving about and getting into bed; then all was quiet; I returned to my own room.

I was up early the next morning, for I had been able to sleep but little. I wanted above all things to see Victoria again. But even while I was dressing Baptiste brought me a note. I opened it hurriedly, for it was from her. I read:

"Forget all about last night; I was tired and ill. I rely on your honour to say nothing to anybody. I am all right this morning."

She was entitled to ask the pledge of my honour, if she chose. I tore the note in fragments and burned them.

It was about eleven o'clock in the morning when I went out into the garden. There was a group on the terrace—my mother, Victoria, and William Adolphus. They were laughing and talking and seemed very merry. As a rule I should have waved a " good morning " and passed on for my solitary walk. To-day I went up to them. My mother appeared to be in an excellent temper, the Prince looked quite easy and happy. Victoria was a little pale but very vivacious. She darted a quick look at me, and cried out the moment I had kissed my mother:

" We're settling the bridesmaids! You're just in time to help, Augustin."

We " settled " the bridesmaids. I hardly knew whether to laugh or to cry during this important operation. Victoria was very kind to her *fiancé*, receiving his suggestions with positive graciousness: he became radiant under this treatment. When our task was done, Victoria passed her arm through his, declaring that she wanted a stroll in the woods; as they went by me she laid her hand lightly and affectionately on my arm, looking me full in the face the while. I understood; for good or evil my lips were sealed.

My mother looked after the betrothed couple as they walked away; I looked at my mother's fine high-bred resolute face.

"I'm so glad," said she at last, "to see Victoria so happy. I was afraid at one time that she'd never take to it. Of course we had other hopes."

The last words were a hit at me. I ignored them; that battle had been fought, the victory won, and paid for by me in handsome fashion.

"Has she taken to it?" I asked as carelessly as I could. But my mother's eyes turned keenly on me.

"Have you any reason for thinking she hasn't?" came in quick question.

"No," I answered.

The sun was shining and Princess Heinrich opened her parasol very leisurely. She rose to her feet and stood there for a moment. Then in a smooth, even, and what I may call reasonable voice, she remarked:

"My dear Augustin, from time to time all girls have fancies. We mothers know that it doesn't do to pay any attention to them. They soon go if they're let alone. We shall meet at lunch, I hope?"

I bowed respectfully, but perhaps I looked a little doubtful.

"It really doesn't do to take any notice of them," said my mother over her shoulder.

So we took no notice of them; my sister's midnight flight to my room and to my arms was between her and me, and for all the world as though it has never been, save that it left behind it a little legacy of renewed kindliness and trust. For that much I was thankful; but I could not forget the rest.

A month later she was married to William Adolphus at Forstadt.

CHAPTER VIII.

DESTINY IN A PINAFORE.

THE foreign tour I undertook in my eighteenth year has been sufficiently, or even more than sufficiently, described by the accomplished and courtly pen of Vohrenlorf's secretary. I travelled as the Count of Artenberg under my Governor's guidance, and saw in some ways more, in some respects less, than most young men on their travels are likely to see. Old Hammerfeldt recommended for my reading the English letters of Lord Chesterfield to his son, and I studied them with some profit, much amusement, and an occasional burst of impatience; I believe that in the Prince's opinion I, like Mr. Stanhope, had hitherto attached too little importance to, and not attained enough proficiency in, " the graces "; concealment was the life's breath of his statescraft, and " the graces " help a man to hide everything—ideals, emotions, passions, his very soul. It must have been an immense satisfaction to the Prince, on leaving the world at a ripe age, to feel that nobody had ever been sure that they understood him; except, of course, the fools who think that they understood everybody.

As far as my private life is concerned, one incident only on this expedition is of moment. We paid a visit to my father's cousins, the Bartensteins, who

possessed a singularly charming place in Tirol. The
Duke was moderately rich, very able, and very indolent. He was a connoisseur in music and the arts.
His wife, my Cousin Elizabeth, was a very good-
natured woman of seven or eight and thirty, noted for
her dairy and fond of out-of-door pursuits; her devotion to these last had resulted in her complexion
being rather reddened and weather-beaten. We were
to stay a week, an unusually long halt; and even before we arrived I detected a simple slyness in my
good Vohrenlorf's demeanour. When a secret was
afoot, Vohrenlorf's first apparent effort was to draw
everybody's attention to the fact of its existence.
Out of perversity I asked no questions, and left him
to seethe in his over-boiling mystery. I knew that
I should be enlightened soon enough. I was quite
right; before I had been a day with my relatives it
became obvious that Elsa was the mystery. I suppose that it is not altogether a common thing for a
youth of eighteen, feeling himself a man, trying to
think himself one, just become fully conscious of
the power and attraction of the women he meets, to
be shown a child of twelve, and given to understand
that in six years' time she will be ready to become
his wife. The position, even if not as uncommon as
I suppose, is curious enough to justify a few words
of description.

I saw Elsa first as she was rolling down a hill,
with a scandalized governess in full chase. Elsa
rolled quickly, marking her progress by triumphant
cries. She " brought up " at the foot of the slope
in an excessively crumpled state; her short skirts
were being smoothed down when her mother and I
arrived. She was a pretty, fair, blue-eyed child, with
a natural merriment about her attractive enough.

She was well made, having escaped the square solidity of figure that characterized Cousin Elizabeth. Her features were still in an undeveloped condition, and her hair, brushed smooth and plastered down on her forehead, was tormented into ringlets behind. She looked at my lanky form with some apprehension.

"Was it a good roll, Elsa?" I asked.

"Splendid!" she answered.

"You didn't know Cousin Augustin was looking on, did you?" asked her mother.

"No, I didn't." But it was plain that she did not care either.

I felt that Cousin Elizabeth's honest eyes were searching my face.

"Give me a kiss, won't you, Elsa?" I asked.

Elsa turned her chubby cheek up to me in a perfection of indifference. In fact, both Elsa and I were performing family duties. Thus we kissed for the first time.

"Now go and let nurse put on a clean frock for you," said Cousin Elizabeth. "You're to come downstairs to-day, and you're not fit to be seen. Don't roll any more when you've changed your frock."

Elsa smiled, shook her head, and ran off. I gathered the impression that even in the clean frock she would roll again if she chanced to be disposed to that exercise. The air of Bartenstein was not the air of Artenberg. A milder climate reigned. There was no Styrian discipline for Elsa. I believe that in all her life she did at her parents' instance only one thing that she seriously disliked. Cousin Elizabeth and I walked on.

"She's a baby still," said Cousin Elizabeth presently, "but I assure you that she has begun to develop."

"There's no hurry, is there?"

"No. You know, I think you're too old for your age, Augustin. I suppose it was inevitable."

I felt much younger in many ways than I had at fifteen; the gates of the world were opening, and showing me prospects unknown to the lonely boy at Artenberg.

"And she has the sweetest disposition. So loving!" said Cousin Elizabeth.

I did not find anything appropriate to answer. The next day found me fully, although delicately, apprised of the situation. It seemed to me a strange one. The Duke was guarded in his hints, and profuse of declarations that it was too soon to think of anything. Good Cousin Elizabeth strove to conceal her eagerness and repress the haste born of it by similar but more clumsy speeches. I spoke openly on the subject to Vohrenlorf.

"Ah, well, even if it should be so, you have six years," he reminded me in good-natured consolation. "And she will grow up."

"She won't roll down hills always, of course," I answered rather peevishly.

In truth the thing would not assume an appearance of reality for me; it was too utterly opposed to the current of my thoughts and dreams. A boy of my age will readily contemplate marriage with a woman ten years his senior; in regard to a child six years younger than himself the idea seems absurd. Yet I did not put it from me; I had been well tutored in the strength of family arrangements, and the force of destiny had been brought home to me on several occasions. I had no doubt at all that my visit to

Bartenstein was part of a deliberate plan. The person who contrived my meeting with Elsa had a shrewd knowledge of my character; he knew that ideas long present in my mind became as it were domiciled there, and were hard to expel. I discovered afterward without surprise that the stay with my relatives was added to my tour at Prince von Hammerfeldt's suggestion.

Many men, or youths bordering on manhood, have seen their future brides in short frocks and unmitigated childhood, but they have not been aware of what was before them. I was at once amused and distressed; my humour was touched, but life's avenue seemed shortened. Even if it were not Elsa it would be some other little girl, now playing with her toys and rolling down banks. Imagination was not elastic enough to leap over the years and behold the child transformed. I stuck in the present, and was whimsically apprehensive of a child seen through a magnifying glass, larger, but unchanged in form, air, and raiment. Was this my fate? And for it I must wait till the perfected beauties who had smiled on me passed on to other men, and with them grew old—aye, as it seemed, quite old. I felt myself ludicrously reduced to Elsa's status; a long boy, who had outgrown his clothes, and yet was no nearer to a man.

My trouble was, perhaps unreasonably, aggravated by the fact that Elsa did not take to me. I did my best to be pleasant; I made her several gifts. She accepted my offerings, but was not bought by them; myself she considered dull. I had not the flow of animal spirits that appeals so strongly to children. I played with her, but her young keenness detected the cloven hoof of duty. She told me I need not play unless I liked. Cousin Elizabeth apologized for me; Elsa was gentle, but did not change her opinion. The passage of years, I reflected, would increase in me all that the child found least to her taste. I was, as I have said, unable to picture her with tastes changed. But a failure of imagination may occasionally issue in paradoxical rightness, for the imagination relies on the common run of events which the peculiar case may chance to contradict. As a fact, I do not think that Elsa ever did change greatly. I began to be sorry for her as well as for myself. Considered as an outlook in life, as the governing factor in a human being's existence, I did not seem to myself brilliant or even satisfactory. I had at this time remarkable forecasts of feelings that were in later years to be my almost daily companions.

"And what shall your husband be like, Elsa?" asked the Duke, as his little daughter sat on his knee and he played with her ringlets.

I was sitting by, and the Duke's eyes twinkled discreetly. The child looked across to me and studied my appearance for some few moments. Then she gave us a simple but completely lucid description of a gentleman differing from myself in all outward characteristics, and in all such inward traits as Elsa's experience and vocabulary enabled her to touch upon. I learned later that she took hints from a tall grenadier who sometimes stood sentry at the castle. At the moment it seemed as though her ideal were well enough delineated by the picture of my opposite. The Duke laughed, and I laughed also; Elsa was very grave and business-like in defining her requirements. Her inclinations have never been obscure to her. Even then she knew perfectly well what she wanted, and I was not that.

7

By the indiscretion of somebody (the Duke said his wife, his wife said the governess, the governess said the nurse) on the day before I went, Elsa got a hint of her suggested future. Indeed it was more than a hint; it was enough to entangle her in excitement, interest, and, I must add, dismay. Children play with the words "wife" and "husband" in a happy ignorance; their fairy tales give and restrict their knowledge. Cousin Elizabeth came to me in something of a stir; she was afraid that I should be annoyed, should suspect, perhaps, a forcing of my hand, or some such manœuvre. But I was not annoyed; I was interested to learn what effect the prospect had upon my little cousin. I was so different from the Grenadier, so irreconcilable with Elsa's fancy portrait.

"I'm very terribly vexed!" cried Cousin Elizabeth. "When it's all so—all no more than an idea!"

"She's so young she'll forget all about it," said I soothingly.

"You're not angry?"

"Oh, no. I was only afflicted with a sense of absurdity."

Chance threw me in Elsa's way that afternoon. She was with her nurse in the gardens. She ran up to me at once, but stopped about a yard from the seat on which I was sitting. I became the victim of a grave, searching, and long inspection. There was a roundness of surprise in her baby blue eyes. Embarrassed and amused (I am inclined sometimes to think that more than half my life has been a mixture of these not implacable enemies), I took the bull by the horns.

"I'm thin, and sallow, and hook-nosed, and I can't sing, and I don't laugh in a jolly way, and I can't fly kites," said I, having the description of her ideal in my mind. " You wouldn't like me to be your husband, would you?"

Elsa, unlike myself, was neither embarrassed nor amused. The mild and interested gravity of her face persisted unchanged.

" I don't know," she said meditatively.

With most of the faults that can beset one of my station, I do not plead guilty to any excessive degree of vainglory. I was flattered that the child hesitated.

" Then you like me rather?" I asked.

" Yes—rather." She paused, and then added: " If I married you I should be queen, shouldn't I, Cousin Augustin?"

" Yes," I assured her.

" I should think that's rather nice, isn't it?"

" It isn't any particular fun being king," said I in a burst of confidence.

" Isn't it?" she asked, her eyes growing rounder. " Still, I think I should like it." Her tone was quite confident; even at that age, as I have observed, she knew very well what she liked. For my part I remembered so vividly my own early dreams and later awakenings that I would not cut short her guileless visions; moreover, to generalize from one's self is the most fatal foolishness, even while it is the most inevitable.

During the remaining hours of my visit Elsa treated me, I must not say with more affection, but certainly with more attention. She was interested in me; I had become to her a source of possibilities, dim to vision but gorgeous to imagination. I knew so well the images that floated before a childish mind, able to gape at them, only half able to grasp them.

I had been through this stage. It is odd to reflect that I was in an unlike but almost equally great delusion myself. I had ceased to expect immoderate enjoyment from my position, but I had conceived an exaggerated idea of its power and influence on the world and mankind. Of this mistake I was then unconscious; I smiled to think that Elsa could play at being a queen, the doll, the bolster, the dog, or whatever else might chance to come handy acting the regal *rôle* in my place. I do not now altogether quarrel with my substitutes.

The hour of departure came. I have a vivid recollection of Cousin Elizabeth's overwhelming tact; she was so anxious that I should not exaggerate the meaning or importance of the suggestion which had been made, that she succeeded in filling my mind with it, to the exclusion of everything else. The Duke, having tried in vain to stop her, fell into silence, cigarettes, and drolly resigned glances. But he caught me alone for a few moments, and gave me his word of advice.

"Think no more about this nonsense for six years," said he. "The women will match-make, you know."

I promised, with a laugh, not to anticipate troubles. He smiled at my phrase, but did not dispute its justice. I think he shared the sort of regret which I felt, that such things should be so much as talked about in connection with Elsa. A man keeps that feeling about his daughter long after her mother has marked a husband and chosen a priest.

My visit to my cousins was the last stage of my journey. From their house Vohrenlorf and I travelled through to Forstadt. I was received at the railway station by a large and distinguished company.

My mother was at Artenberg, where I was to join her that evening, but Hammerfeldt awaited me. and some of the gentlemen attached to the Court. I was too much given to introspection and self-appraisement not to be aware that my experiences had given me a lift toward manhood; my shyness was smothered, though not killed, by a kind of mechanical ease born of practice. After greeting Hammerfeldt I received the welcome of the company with a composed courtesy of which the Prince's approval was very manifest. Ceremonial occasions such as these are worthy of record and meditation only when they surround, and, as it were, frame some incident really material. Such an incident occurred now. My inner mind was still full of my sojourn with the Bartensteins, of the pathetic, whimsical, hypothetical connection between little Elsa and myself, and of the chains that seemed to bind my life in bonds not of my making. These reflections went on in an undercurrent while I was bowing, saluting, grasping hands, listening and responding to appropriate observations. Suddenly I found the Count von Sempach before me. His name brought back my mind in an instant from its wanderings. The Countess was recalled very vividly to my recollection; I asked after her; Sempach, much gratified, pointed to a row of ladies who (the occasion being official) stood somewhat in the background. There she was, now in the maturity of her remarkable beauty, seeming to me the embodiment of perfect accomplishment. I saluted her with marked graciousness; fifty heads turned instantly from me toward her. She blushed very slightly and curtseyed very low. Sempach murmured gratification; Hammerfeldt smiled. I was vaguely conscious of a subdued sensation running all through the com-

pany, but my mind was occupied with the contrast
between this finished woman and the little girl I had
left behind. From feeling old, too old, sad, and
knowing for poor little Elsa, I was suddenly trans-
ported into an oppressive consciousness of youth and
rawness. Involuntarily I drew myself up to my full
height and assumed the best air of dignity that was
at my command. So posed, I crossed the station to
my carriage between Hammerfeldt and Vohrenlorf.

"Your time has not been wasted," old Hammerfeldt whispered to me. "You are ready now
to take up what I am more than ready to lay
down."

I started slightly; I had for the moment forgotten that the Council of Regency was now discharged
of its office, and that I was to assume the full burden
of my responsibilities. I had looked forward to this
time with eagerness and ambition. But a man's emotions at a given moment are very seldom what he
has expected them to be. Some foreign thought in-
trudes and predominates; something accidental sup-
plants what has seemed so appropriate and certain.
While I travelled down to Artenberg that evening,
with Vohrenlorf opposite to me (Vohrenlorf who himself was about to lay down his functions), the assumption of full power was not what occupied my
mind. I was engrossed with thoughts of Elsa, with
fancies about my Countess, with strange dim speculations that touched me—the young man, not the
king about whom all the coil was. Had I been called
upon to condense those vague meditations and emotions into a sentence, I would have borrowed what
Vohrenlorf had said to me when we were with the
Bartensteins. He did not often hit the nail exactly

on the head, but just now I could give no better summary of all I felt than his soberly optimistic reminder: " Ah, well, even if it should be so, you have six years ! "

The thought that I treasured on the way to Artenberg that evening was the thought of my six years.

CHAPTER IX.

Soon after my return my mother and I went into
residence at Forstadt. My time was divided between mastering my public duties under Hammerfeldt's tuition, and playing a prominent part in the
gaieties of the capital. Just now I was on cordial,
if not exactly intimate, terms with the Princess. She
appeared to have resigned herself to Hammerfeldt's
preponderating influence in political affairs, and to
accept in compensation the office of mentor and guide
in all social matters. I was happy in the establish-
ment of a *modus vivendi* which left me tolerably free
from the harassing trifles of ceremonial and etiquette.
To Hammerfeldt's instructions I listened with avidity
and showed a deference which did not forbid secret
criticism. He worked me hard; the truth is (and
it was not then hidden either from him or from me)
that his strength was failing; age had not bent, but
it threatened to break him; the time was short in
which he could hope to be by my side, binding his
principles and rivetting his methods on me. He was
too shrewd not to detect in me a curiosity of intellect that only the strongest and deepest preposses-
sions could restrain; these it was his untiring effort
to create in my mind and to buttress till they were
impregnable. To some extent he attained his ob-

ject, but his success was limited; and his teaching affected by what I can only call a modernness of temperament in me, which no force of tradition wholly destroyed or stifled. That many things must be treated as beyond question was the fruit of his maxims; it is a position which I have never been able to adopt; with me the acid of doubt bit into every axiom. I took pleasure in the society and arguments of the liberal politicians and journalists who began to frequent the court as soon as a rumour of my inclinations spread. I became the centre and object of a contention between the Right and the Left, between Conservative and Liberal forces—or, if I apply to each party the nickname accorded to it by the enemy, between the Reaction and the Revolution.

Doubtless all this will find an accomplished, and possibly an impartial, historian. Its significance for these personal memoirs is due chiefly to the accidental fact that, whereas my mother was the social centre of the orthodox party and in that capacity gave solid aid to Hammerfeldt, the unorthodox gathered round the Countess von Sempach. Her husband was considered no more than a good soldier, a man of high rank, and a devoted husband; by her own talents and charm this remarkable woman, although a foreigner, had achieved for herself a position of great influence. She renewed the glories of the political *salon* in Forstadt; but she never talked politics. Eminent men discussed deep secrets with one another in her rooms. She was content to please their taste without straining their intellects or seeking to rival them in argument. By the abdication of a doubtful claim she reigned absolute in her own dominion. It was from studying her that I first learned both how far-reaching is the inspiration of a woman's personality, and how it gathers and conserves strength by remaining within its own boundaries and refusing alien conquests. The men of the Princess's party, from Hammerfeldt downward, were sometimes impatient of her suggestions and attempted control; the Countess's friends were never aware that they received suggestions, and imagined themselves to exercise control. I think that the old Prince was almost alone in penetrating the secret of the real power his charming enemy exercised and the extent of it. They were very cordial to one another.

" Madame," he said to her once, " you might convince me of anything if I were not too old."

" Why, Prince," she cried, " you are not going to pretend that your mind has grown old?"

" No, Countess, my feelings," he replied with a smile. Her answer was a blush.

This was told to me by Wetter, a young and very brilliant journalist who had once given me lessons in philosophy, and with whom I maintained a friendship in spite of his ultra-radical politics. He reminded me now and then of Geoffrey Owen, but his enthusiasm was of a dryer sort; not humanity, but the abstract idea of progress inspired him; not the abolition of individual suffering, but the perfecting of his logical conceptions in the sphere of politics was his stimulating hope. And there was in him a strong alloy of personal ambition and a stronger of personal passion. Rather to my surprise Hammerfeldt showed no uneasiness at my friendship with him; I joked once on the subject and he answered:

" Wetter only appeals to your intellect, sire. There I am not afraid now."

His answer, denying one apprehension, hinted

another. It will cause no surprise that I had renewed an old acquaintance with the Countess, and had been present at a dinner in her house. More than this, I fell into the habit of attending her receptions on Wednesdays; on this night all parties were welcome, and the gathering was by way of being strictly non-political. Strictly non-political also were the calls that I made in the dusk of the evening, when she would recall our earlier meetings, our glances exchanged, our thoughts of one another, and lead me to talk of my boyhood. These things did not appeal only to the intellect of a youth of eighteen or nineteen when they proceeded from the lips of a beautiful and brilliant woman of twenty-eight.

I approach a very common occurrence; but in my case its progress and result were specially modified and conditioned. There was the political aspect, looming large to the alarmed Right; there was the struggle for more intimate influence over me, in which my mother fought with a grim intensity; in my own mind there was always the curious dim presence of an inexorable fate that wore the incongruous mask of Elsa's baby face. All these were present to me in their full force during the earlier period of my friendship with the Countess, when I was still concealing from myself as well as from her and all the world that I could ever desire to have more than friendship. The first stages past, there came a time when the secret was still kept from all save myself, but when I knew it with an exultation not to be conquered, with a dread and a shame that tormented while they could not prevail. But I went more and more to her house. I had no evil intent; nay, I had no intent at all in my going; I could not keep away. She alone had come to satisfy me; with her alone, all of me—thoughts, feelings, eyes, and ears—seemed to find some cause for exercise and a worthy employment of their life. The other presences in my mind grew fainter and intermittent in their visits; I gave myself up to the stream and floated down the current. Yet I was never altogether forgetful nor blind to what I did; I knew the transformation that had come over my friendship; to myself now I could not but call it love; I knew that others in the palace, in the chancellery, in drawing-rooms, in newspaper offices, ay, perhaps even in the very street, called it now, not the king's friendship nor the king's love, but the king's infatuation. Not even then could I lose altogether the external view of myself.

We were sitting by the fire one evening in the twilight; she was playing with a hand-screen, but suffering the flames to paint her face and throw into relief the sensitive merry lips and the eyes so full of varied meanings. She had told me to go, and I had not gone; she leaned back and, after one glance of reproof, fixed her regard on the polished tip of her shoe that rested on the fender. She meant that she would talk no more to me; that in her estimation, since I had no business to say, I was already gone. An impulse seized me. I do not know what I hoped nor why that moment broke the silence which I had imposed on myself. But I told her about the little, fair, chubby child at the Castle of Bartenstein. I watched her closely, but her eyes never strayed from her shoe-tip. Well, she had never said a word that showed any concern in such a matter; even I had done little more than look and hint and come.

"It's as if they meant me to marry Toté," I ended. Toté was the pet name by which we called her own eight-year-old daughter.

The Countess broke her wilful silence, but did not change the direction of her eyes.

"If Toté were of the proper station," she said ironically, "she'd be just right for you by the time you're both grown up."

"And you'd be mother-in-law?" ₁

"I should be too old to plague you. I should just sit in my corner in the sun."

"The sun is always in your corner."

"Don't be so complimentary," she said with a sudden twitching of her lips. "I shall have to stand up and curtsey, and I don't want to. Besides, you oughtn't to know how to say things like that, ought you, Cæsar?"

Cæsar was my—shall I say pet-name?—used when we were alone or with Count Max, only in a playful satire.

A silence followed for some time. At last she glanced toward me.

"Not gone yet?" said she, raising her brows. "What will the Princess say?"

"I go when I please," said I, resenting the question as I was meant to resent it.

"Yes. Certainly not when I please."

Our eyes met now; suddenly she blushed, and then interposed the screen between herself and me. A glorious thrill of youthful triumph ran through me; she had paid her first tribute to my manhood in that blush; the offering was small, but, for its significance, frankincense and myrrh to me.

"I thought you came to talk about Wetter's Bill," she suggested presently in a voice lower than her usual tones.

"The deuce take Wetter's Bill," said I.

" I am very interested in it."

" Just now? "

" Even just now, Cæsar." I heard a little laugh behind the screen.

" Hammerfeldt hates it," said I.

" Oh, then that settles it. You'll be against us, of course! "

" Why of course? "

" You always do as the Prince tells you, don't you? "

" Unless somebody more powerful forbids me."

" Who is more powerful—except Cæsar himself? "

I made no answer, but I rose and, crossing the rug, stood by her. I remember the look and the feel of the room very well; she lay back in a low chair upholstered in blue; the firelight, forbidden her face, played on the hand that held the screen, flushing its white to red. I could see her hair gleaming in the fantastically varying light that the flames gave as they left and fell. I was in a tumult of excitement and timidity.

" More powerful than Cæsar? " I asked, and my voice shook.

" Don't call yourself Cæsar."

" Why not? "

There was a momentary hesitation before the answer came low:

" Because you mustn't laugh at yourself. I may laugh at you, but you mustn't yourself."

I wondered at the words, the tone, the strange diffidence that infected even a speech so full of her gay bravery. A moment later she added a reason for her command.

" You're so absurd that you mustn't laugh at

The firelight played on the hand that held the screen.

yourself. And, Cæsar, if you stay any longer, or—come again soon—other people will laugh at you."

To this day I do not know whether she meant to give a genuine warning, or to strike a chord that should sound back defiance.

"If ten thousand of them laugh, what is it to me? They dare laugh only behind my back," I said.

She laughed before my face; the screen fell, and she laughed, saying softly, "Cæsar, Cæsar!"

I was wonderfully happy in my perturbation. The great charm she had for me was to-day alloyed less than ever before by the sense of rawness which she, above all others, could compel me to feel. To-day she herself was not wholly calm, not mistress of herself without a struggle, without her moments of faintness. Yet now she appeared composed again, and there was nothing but merriment in her eyes. She seemed to have forgotten that I was supposed to be gone. I daresay that not to her, any more than to myself, could I seem quite like an ordinary boy; perhaps the more I forgot what was peculiar about me the more she remembered it, my oblivion serving to point her triumph.

"And the Princess?" she asked, laughing still, but now again a little nervously.

My exultation, finding vent in mischief and impelled by curiosity, drove me to a venture.

"I shall tell the Princess that I kissed you," said I.

The Countess suddenly sat upright.

"And that you kissed me—several times," I continued.

"How dare you?" she cried in a whisper; and

her cheeks flamed in blushes and in firelight. My little device was a triumph. I began to laugh.

"Oh, of course, if she asks me when," I added, "I shall confess that it was ten years ago."

Many emotions mingled in my companion's glance as she sank back in her chair; she was indignant at the trap, amused at having been caught in it, not fully relieved from embarrassment, not wholly convinced that the explanation of my daring speech covered all the intent with which it had been uttered, perhaps not desirous of being convinced too thoroughly. A long pause followed. Timidity held me back from further advance. For that evening enough seemed to have passed; I had made a start —to go further might be to risk all. I was about to take my leave when she looked up again, saying:

"And about Wetter's Bill, Cæsar?"

"You know I can do nothing."

"Can Cæsar do nothing? If you were known to favour it fifty votes would be changed." Her face was eager and animated. I looked down at her and smiled. She flushed again, and cried hastily:

"No, no, never mind; at least, not to-night."

I suppose that my smile persisted, and was not a mirthful one. It stirred anger and resentment in her.

"I know why you're smiling," she exclaimed. "I suppose that when I was kind to you as a baby, I wanted something from you too, did I?"

She had detected the thought that had come so inevitably into my mind, that she should resent it so passionately almost persuaded me of its injustice. I turned from it to the pleasant memory of her earlier impulsive kindness. I put out my hands and grasped hers. She let me hold them for an instant and then drew them away. She gave rather a forced laugh.

"You're too young to be bothered about Bills," she said, "and too young for—for all sorts of other things, too. Run away; never mind me with my Bills and my wrinkles."

"Your wrinkles!"

"Oh, if not now, in a year or two; by the time you're ready to marry Elsa."

As she spoke she rose and stood facing me. A new sense of her beauty came over me; her beauty's tragedy, already before her eyes, was to me remote and impossible. Because it was not yet very near she exaggerated its nearness; because it was inevitable I turned away from it. Indeed, who could remember, seeing her then? Who save herself, as she looked on my youth?

"You'll soon be old and ugly?" I asked, laughing.

"Yes, soon; it will seem very soon to you."

"What's the moral?" said I.

She laughed uneasily, twisting the screen in her hands. For an instant she raised her eyes to mine, and as they dropped again she whispered:

"A short life and a merry one?"

My hand flew out to her again; she took it, and, after a laughing glance, curtseyed low over it, as though in formal farewell. I had not meant that, and laughed in my turn.

"I shan't be old—well, by to-morrow," she murmured, and glanced ostentatiously at the clock.

"May I come to-morrow?"

"I never invite you."

"Shall you be here?"

"It's not one of my receiving days."

8

"I like a good chance better than a poor certainty. At least there will be nobody else here."

"Max, perhaps."

"I don't think so."

"You don't think so? What do you mean by that, Cæsar? No, I don't want to know. I believe it was impertinent. Are you going?"

"Yes," said I, "when I have kissed your hand."

She said nothing, but held it out to me. She smiled, but there seemed to me to be pain in her eyes. I pressed her hand to my lips and went out without speaking again. As I closed the door I heard her fling herself back into her chair with a curious little sound, half-cry, half-sigh.

I left the house quickly and silently; no servant was summoned to escort me. I walked a few yards along the street to where Wetter lived. My carriage was ordered to come for me at Wetter's; it had not yet arrived. To be known to visit Wetter was to accept the blame of a smaller indiscretion as the price of hiding a greater. The deputy was at home, writing in his study; he received me with an admirable unconsciousness of where I had come from. I was still in a state of excitement, and was glad to sit smoking quietly while his animated, fluent talk ran on. He was full of this Bill of his, and explained its provisions to me with the air of desiring that I should understand its spirit and aim, and of being willing then to leave it to my candid consideration. He did not attempt to blink the difficulties.

"Of course we have the Prince and all the party of Reaction against us," he said. "But your Majesty is not a member of any party."

"Not even of yours yet," said I with a laugh.

He laughed in his turn, openly and merrily.

"I'm a poor schemer," he said. "But I don't know why it should be wrong for you to hear my views any more than Hammerfeldt's."

The servant entered and announced the arrival of my carriage. Wetter escorted me to it.

"I'll promise not to mention the Bill, if you'll honour me by coming again, sire," he said as he held the brougham door.

"I shall be delighted to come again; I like to hear about it," I answered. His bow and smile conveyed absolutely nothing but a respectful gratification and a friendly pleasure. Yet he knew that the situation of his house was more responsible for my visit than the interest of his projects.

In part I saw clear enough even at this time. It was the design and hope of Wetter and his friends to break down Hammerfeldt's power and obtain a political influence over me. Hammerfeldt's political dominance seemed to them to be based on a personal ascendency; this they must contrive to match. Their instrument was not far to seek. The Countess was ready to their hand, a beautiful woman, sharpest weapon of all in such a strife. They put her forward against the Prince in the fight whereof I was the prize. All this I saw, against it all I was forewarned, and forearmed. Knowledge gave security. But there was more, and here with the failure of insight safety was compromised. What was her mind? What was her part, not as it seemed to these busy politicians, but as her own heart taught it her? Here came to me the excitement of uncertainty, the impulse of youth, the prick of vanity, the longing for that intimate love of which my life had given me so little. Was I to her also only something to be used in the game of politics, a tool that she, a defter tool, must shape

and point before it could be of use? I tried to say
this to myself and to make a barrier of the knowledge. But was it all the truth? Remembering her
eyes and tones, her words and hesitations, I could
not accept it for the whole truth. There was more,
what more I knew not. Even if there had been no
more I was falling so deep into the gulf of passion
that it crossed my mind to take while I gave; and,
if I were to be used, to exact my hire. In a tumult
of these thoughts, embracing now what in the next
moment I rejected, revolting in a sudden fear from
the plan which just before seemed so attractive, I
passed the evening and the night. For I had taken
up that mixed heritage of good and evil, of pain and
power, that goes by the name of manhood; and
when a new heir enters on his inheritance there is a
time before he can order it.

CHAPTER X.

A FEW days later my mother informed me that Victoria and her husband had proposed to pay us a long visit. I could make no objection. Princess Heinrich observed that I should be glad to see Victoria again, and should enjoy the companionship of William Adolphus. In my mind I translated her speech into a declaration that Victoria might have some influence over me although my mother had none, and that William Adolphus would be more wholesome company than my countesses and Wetters and such riff-raff. I was unable to regard William Adolphus as an intellectual resource, and did not associate Victoria with the exercise of influence. The weakness of the Princess's new move revealed the straits to which she felt herself reduced. The result of the position which I have described was almost open strife between her and me; Hammerfeldt's powerful bridle alone held her back from declared rupture. His method of facing the danger was very different. He sought to exercise no veto, but he kept watch; he knew where I went, but made no objection to my going; any liberal notions which I betrayed in conversation with him he received with courteous attention, and affected to consider the result of my own meditations. Had my feelings been less deeply involved I think his method would have succeeded; even as it was he checked and retarded what he could not stop. The cordiality of our personal relations remained unbroken and so warm that he felt himself able to speak to me in a half-serious, half-jesting way about the Countess von Sempach.

"A most charming woman indeed," said he. "In fact, too charming a woman."

I understood him, and began to defend myself.

"I'm not in love with the Countess," I said; "but I give her my confidence, Prince."

He shook his head, smiled, and took a pinch of snuff, glancing at me humorously.

"Reverse it," he suggested. "Be in love with her, but don't give her your confidence. You'll find it safer and also more pleasant that way."

My confidence might affect high matters, my love he regarded as a passing fever. He did not belong to an age of strict morality in private life, and his bent of mind was utterly opposed to considering an intrigue with a woman of the Countess's attractions as a serious crime in a young man of my position. "Hate her," was my mother's impossible exhortation. "Love her, but don't trust her," was the Prince's subtle counsel. He passed at once from the subject, content with the seed that he had sown. There was much in him and in his teaching which one would defend to-day at some cost of reputation; but I never left him without a heightened and enhanced sense of my position and my obligations. If you will, he lowered the man to exalt the king; this was of a piece with all his wily compromises.

Victoria arrived, and her husband. William Adolphus's attitude was less apologetic than it had been before marriage; he had made Victoria mother

to a fine baby, and claimed the just credit. He was
jovial, familiar, and, if I may so express myself,
brotherly to the last degree. Happily, however, he
interpreted his more assured position as enabling him
to choose his own friends and his own pursuits; these
were not mine, and in consequence I was little troubled with his company. As an ally to my mother
he was a passive failure; his wife was worse than
inactive. Victoria's conduct displayed the height of
unwisdom. She denounced the Countess to my face,
and besought my mother to omit the Sempachs from
her list of acquaintances. Fortunately the Princess
had been dissuaded from forcing on an open scandal; my sister had to be content with matching her
mother's coldness by her rudeness when the Countess came to Court. Need I say that my attentions
grew the more marked, and gossip even more rife?

Wetter's Bill came up for discussion, and was
hurled in vain against Hammerfeldt's solid phalanx
of country gentlemen and wealthy *bourgeoisie.* I had
kept a seal on my lips, and in common opinion was
still the Prince's docile disciple. Wetter accepted
my attitude with easy friendliness, but he ventured
to observe that if any case arose which enabled me
to show that my hostility to his party was not in-
veterate, the proof would be a pleasure to him and
his friends, and possibly of no disadvantage to me.
Not the barest reference to the Countess pointed
his remark. I had not seen her or heard from her
for nearly a week; on the afternoon of the day after
the Bill was thrown out I decided to pay her a visit.
Wetter was to take luncheon at her house, and I
allowed him to drop a hint of my coming. I felt
that I had done my duty as regards the Bill; I was
very apprehensive of my reception by the Countess.

The opposition that encircled me inflamed my passion for her; the few days' separation had served to convince me that I could not live without her.

I found her alone; her face was a little flushed and her eyes bright. The moment the door was shut she turned on me almost fiercely.

"Why did you send to say you were coming?"

"I didn't send; I told Wetter. Besides, I always send before I go anywhere."

"Not always before you come to me," she retorted. "You're not to hide behind your throne, Cæsar. I was going out if you hadn't prevented me."

"The hindrance need not last a moment," said I, bowing.

She looked at me for an instant, then broke into a reluctant smile.

"You haven't sent to say you were coming for a week," she said.

"No; nor come either."

"Yes, of course, that's it. Sit down; so will I. No, in your old place, over there. Max has been giving me a beautiful bracelet."

"That's very kind of Max."

She glanced at me with challenging witchery.

"And I've promised to wear it every day—never to be without it. Doesn't it look well?" She held up her arm where the gold and jewels sparkled on the white skin as the sleeve of her gown fell back.

I paid to Max's bracelet and the arm which wore it the meed of looks, not of words.

"I've been afraid to come," I said.

"Is there anything to be afraid of here?" she asked with a smile and a wave of her hands.

"Because of Wetter's Bill."

"Oh, the Bill! You were very cowardly, Cæsar."

"I could do nothing."

"You never can, it seems to me." She fixed on me eyes that she had made quite grave and invested with a critically discriminating regard. "But I'm very pleased to see you. Oh, and I forgot—of course I'm very much honoured too. I'm always forgetting what you are."

On an impulse of chagrin at the style of her reception, or of curiosity, or of bitterness, I spoke the thought of my mind.

"You never forget it for a moment," I said. "I forget it, not you."

She covered a start of surprise by a hasty and pretty little yawn, but her eyes were inquisitive, almost apprehensive. After a moment she picked up her old weapon, the firescreen, and hid her face from the eyes downward. But the eyes were set on me, and now, it seemed, in reproach.

"If you think that, I wonder you come at all," she murmured.

"I don't want you to forget it. But I'm something besides."

"Yes, a poor boy with a cruel mother—and a rude sister—and——" She sprang suddenly to her feet. "And," she went on, "a charming old adviser. Cæsar, I met Prince von Hammerfeldt. Shall I tell you what he said to me?"

"Yes."

"He bowed over my hand and kissed it and smiled, and twinkled with his old eyes, and then he said, 'Madame, I am growing vain of my influence over his Majesty.'"

"The Prince was complimenting you," I remarked, although I was not so dull as to miss either Hammerfeldt's mockery or her understanding of it.

"Complimenting me? Yes, I suppose he was—on not having done you any harm. Why? Because I couldn't!"

"You wouldn't wish to, Countess?"

"No; but I might wish to be able to, Cæsar."

She stood there the embodiment of a power the greater because it feigned distrust of its own might.

"No, I don't mean that," she continued a moment later. "But I should——" She drew near to me and, catching up a little chair, sat down on it, close to my elbow. "Ah, how I should like the Prince to think I had a little power!" Then in a low coaxing whisper she added, "You need only to pretend—pretend a little just to please me, Cæsar."

"And what will you do just to please me, Countess?" My whisper was low also, but full where hers had been delicate; rough, not gentle, urging rather than imploring. I was no match for her in the science of which she was mistress, but I did not despair. She seemed nervous, as though she distrusted even her keen thrusts and ready parries. I was but a boy still, but sometimes nature betrays the secrets of experience. Suddenly she broke out in a new attack, or a new line of the general attack.

"Wouldn't you like to show a little independence?" she asked. "The Prince would like you all the better for it." She looked in my face. "And people would think more of you. They say that Hammerfeldt is the real king now—or he and Princess Heinrich between them."

"I thought they said that you——"

"I! Do they? Perhaps! They know so little. If they knew anything they couldn't say that."

To be told they gossiped of her influence seemed to have no terror for her; her regret was that the talk should be all untrue and she in fact impotent. She stirred me to declare that power was hers and I her servant. It seemed to me that to accept her leading was to secure perennial inspiration and a boundless reward. Was Hammerfeldt my schoolmaster? I was not blind to the share that vanity had in her mood nor to ambition's part in it, but I saw also and exulted in her tenderness. All these impulses in her I was now ready to use, for I also had my vanity—a boy's vanity in a tribute wrung from a woman. And, beyond this, passion was strong in me.

She went on in real or affected petulance:

"Can they point to anything I have done? Are any appointments made to please me? Are my friends ever favoured? They are all out in the cold, and likely to stay there, aren't they, Cæsar? Oh, you're very wise. You take what I give you; nobody need know of that. But you give nothing, because that would make talk and gossip. The Prince has taught you well. Yes, you're very prudent." She paused, and stood looking at me with a contemptuous smile on her lips; then she broke into a pitying little laugh. "Poor boy!" said she. "It's a shame to scold you. You can't help it."

It is easy enough now to say that all this was cunningly thought of and cunningly phrased. Yet it was not all cunning; or rather it was the primitive, unmeditated cunning that nature gives to us, the instinctive weapon to which the woman flew in her need, a cunning of heart, not of brain. However inspired, however shaped, it did its work.

"What do you ask?" said I. In my agitation I was brief and blunt.

"Ask? Must I ask? Well, I ask that you should show somehow, how you will, that you trust us, that we are not outcasts, riff-raff, as Princess Heinrich calls us, lepers. Do it how you like, choose anybody you like from among us—I don't ask for any special person. Show that some one of us has your confidence. Why shouldn't you? The King should be above prejudice, and we're honest, some of us."

I tried to speak lightly, and smiled at her.

"You are all I love in the world, some of you," I said.

She sat down again in the little chair, and turned her face upward toward me.

"Then do it, Cæsar," she said very softly.

It had been announced a few days before that our ambassador at Paris had asked to be relieved of his post; there was already talk about his successor. Remembering this, I said, more in jest than seriousness:

"The Paris Embassy? Would that satisfy you?"

Her face became suddenly radiant, merry, and triumphant; she clapped her hands, and then held them clasped toward me.

"You suggested it yourself!" she cried.

"In joke!"

"Joke? I won't be joked with. I choose that you should be serious. You said the Paris Embassy! Are you afraid it'll make Hammerfeldt too angry? Fancy the Princess and your sister! How I shall love to see them!" She dropped her voice as she added, "Do it for me, Cæsar."

"Who should have it?"

"I don't care. Anybody, so long as he's one

of us. Choose somebody good, and then you can defy them all."

She saw the seriousness that had now fallen on me; what I had idly suggested, and she caught up with so fervent a welcome, was no small thing. If I did it, it would be at the cost of Hammerfeldt's confidence, perhaps of his services; he might refuse to endure such an open rebuff. And I knew in my heart that the specious justifications were unsound; I should not act because of them, they were the merest pretext. I should give what she asked to her. Should I not be giving her my honour also, that public honour which I had learned to hold so high?

"I can't promise to-day; you must let me think," I pleaded.

I was prepared for another outburst of petulance, for accusations of timidity, of indifference, again of willingness to take and unwillingness to give. But she sat still, looking at me intently, and presently laid her hand in mine.

"Yes, think," she said with a sigh.

I bent down and kissed the hand that lay in mine. Then she raised it, and held her arm up before him.

"Max's bracelet!" she said, sighing again and smiling. Then she rose to her feet, and walking to the hearth, stood looking down into the fire. I did not join her, but sat in my chair. For a long while neither of us spoke. At last I rose slowly. She heard the movement and turned her head.

"I will come again to-morrow," I said.

She stood still for a moment, regarding me intently. Then she walked quickly across to me, holding out her hands. As I took them she laughed nervously. I did not speak, but I looked into her eyes, and then, as I pressed her hands, I kissed her cheek. The nervous laugh came again, but she said nothing. I left her standing there and went out.

I walked home alone through the lighted streets. It has always been, and is still, my custom to walk about freely and unattended. This evening the friendly greetings of those who chanced to recognise me in the glare of the lamps were pleasant to me. I remember thinking that all these good folk would be grieved if they knew what was going on in the young King's mind, how he was torn hither and thither, his only joy a crime, and the guarding of his honour become a sacrifice that seemed too great for his strength. There was one kind-faced fellow in particular, whom I noticed drinking a glass at a *café*. He took off his hat to me with a cheery " God bless your Majesty! " I should have liked to sit down by him and tell him all about it. He had been young, and he looked shrewd and friendly. I had nobody whom I could tell about it. I don't remember ever seeing this man again, but I think of him still as one who might have been a friend. By his dress he appeared to be a clerk or shop-keeper.

I had an appointment for that evening with Hammerfeldt, but found a note in which he excused himself from coming. He had taken a chill, and was confined to his bed. The business could wait, he said, but went on to remark that no time should be lost in considering the question of the Paris Embassy. He added three or four names as possible selections; all those mentioned were well-known and decided adherents of his own. I was reading his letter when my mother and Victoria came in. They had heard of the Prince's indisposition, but on making inquiries were informed that it was not serious. I sent at once to inquire after him, and handed his note to the Princess.

"Any of those would do very well," she said when she finished it. "They have all been trained under the Prince and are thoroughly acquainted with his views."

"And with mine?" I asked, smiling.

A look of surprise appeared on my mother's face; she looked at me doubtfully.

"The Prince's views are yours, I suppose?" she said.

"I'm not sure I like any of his selections," I observed.

I do not think that my mother would have said anything more at the time; her judgment having been convinced, she would not allow temper to lead her into hostilities. Here, as so often, the unwise course was left to my dear Victoria, who embraced it with her usual readiness.

"Doesn't Wetter like any of them?" she asked ironically.

I remained silent. She came nearer and looked into my face, laughing maliciously.

"Or is it the Countess? Haven't they made enough love to the Countess, or too much, or what?"

"My dear Victoria," I said, "you must make allowances. The Countess is the prettiest woman in Forstadt."

My sister curtseyed with an ironical smile.

"I mean, of course," I added, "since William Adolphus carried you off to Gronenstahl."

My mother interrupted this little quarrel.

"I'm sure you'll be guided by the Prince's judgment," she observed.

Victoria was not to be quenched.

"And not by the beauty of the prettiest woman in Forstadt." And she added, "The creature's as plebeian as she can be."

As a rule I was ready enough to spar with my sister; to-night I had not the spirit. To-night, moreover, she, whom as a rule I could treat with good-humoured indifference, had power to wound. The least weighty of people speaking the truth can not be wholly disregarded. I prepared to go to my room, remarking:

"Of course, I shall discuss the matter with the Prince."

Again Victoria rushed to the fray.

"You mean that it's not our business?" she asked with a toss of her head.

I was goaded beyond endurance, and it was not their business. Princess Heinrich might find some excuse in her familiarity with public affairs, Victoria at least could urge no such plea.

"I am always glad of my mother's advice, Victoria," said I, and with a bow I left them. As I went out I heard Victoria cry, "It's all that hateful woman!"

Naturally the thing appeared to me then in a different light from that in which I can see it now. I can not now think that my mother and sister were wrong to be anxious, disturbed, alarmed, even angry with the lady who occasioned them such discomfort. A young man under the influence of an older woman is no doubt a legitimate occasion for the fears and efforts of his female relatives. I have recorded what they said not in protest against their feelings, but to show the singularly unfortunate manner in which they made what they felt manifest; my object is not to blame what was probably inevitable in them, but to show how they overreached themselves and became not a drag on my infatuation, as they hoped, but rather a spur that incited my passion to a quicker course.

That spur I did not need. She seemed to stand before me still as I had left her, with my kiss fresh on her cheeks, and on her lips that strange, nervous, helpless laugh, the laugh that admitted a folly she could not conquer, expressed a shame that burned her even while she braved it, and owned a love so compact of this folly and this shame that its joy seemed all one with their bitterness. But to my younger heart and hotter man's blood the folly and shame were now beaten down by the joy; it freed itself from them and soared up into my heart on a liberated and triumphant wing. I had achieved this thing—I, the boy they laughed at and tried to rule. She herself had laughed at me. She laughed thus no more. When I kissed her she had not called me Cæsar; she had found no utterance save in that laugh, and the message of that laugh was surrender.

9

CHAPTER XI.

AN ACT OF ABDICATION.

THE night brought me little rest and no wisdom.
As though its own strength were not enough, my
passion sought and found an ally in a defiant obstinacy, which now made me desirous of doing what
the Countess asked for its own sake as well as for
hers. Being diffident, I sought a mask in violence.
I wanted to assert myself, to show the women that
I was not to be driven, and Hammerfeldt that I was
not to be led. Neither their brusque insistence nor
his suave and dexterous suggestions should control
me or prevent me from exercising my own will. A
distorted view of my position caused me to find its
essence in the power of doing as I liked, and its dignity in disregarding wholesome advice because I
objected to the manner in which it was tendered.
This mood, ready and natural enough in youth, was
an instrument of which my passion made effective
use; I pictured the consternation of my advisers with
hardly less pleasure than the delight of her whom
I sought to serve. My sense of responsibility was
dulled and deadened; I had rather do wrong than
do nothing, cause harm than be the cause of nothing, that men should blame me rather than not can-
vass my actions or fail to attribute to me any initi-
ative. I felt somehow that the blame would lie with

my counsellors; they had undertaken to guide and control me. If they failed they, more than I, must answer for the failure. Sophistry of this kind passes well enough with one who wants excuses, and may even array itself in a cloak of plausibility; it was strong in my mind by virtue of the strong resentment from which it sprang, and the strong ally to which its forces were joined. Passion and self-assertion were at one; my conquest would be two-fold. While the Countess was brought to acknowledge my sway, those who had hitherto ruled my life would be reduced to a renunciation of their authority. The day seemed to me to promise at once emancipation and conquest; to mark the point at which I was to gain both liberty and empire, when I should become indeed a king, both in my own palace and in her heart a king.

In the morning I was occupied in routine business with one of the Ministers. This gentleman gave me a tolerably good account of Hammerfeldt, although it appeared that the Prince was suffering from a difficulty in breathing. There seemed, however, no cause for alarm, and when I had sent to make inquiries I did not deem it necessary to remain at home and await the return of my messenger. I paid my usual formal visit to my mother's apartments. The Princess did not refer to our previous conversation, but her manner toward me was even unusually stiff and distant. I think that she had expected repentance. When I in my turn ignored the matter she became curt and disagreeable. I left her, more than ever determined on my course. I was glad to escape an interview with Victoria, and was now free to keep my appointment with Wetter. I had proposed to lunch with him, saying that I had

one or two matters to discuss. Even in my obstinacy
and excitement I remained shrewd enough to see
the advantage of being furnished with well-sound-
ing reasons for the step that I was about to take.
Wetter's forensic sharpness, ready wit, and per-
suasive eloquence would dress my case in better
colours than I could contrive for myself. It mattered little to me how well he knew that arguments
were needed, not to convince myself, but to flourish
in the faces of those who opposed and criticised
me. It was also my intention to obtain from him
the name of two or three of his friends who, apart
from their views, were decently qualified to fulfil
the duties of the post in the event of their nomi-
nation.

It was no shock, but rather a piquant titillation
of my bitter humour, when I disentangled from Wetter's confident and eloquent description of the Ideal
Ambassador a tolerably accurate, if somewhat partial, portrait of himself. I was rather surprised at
his desire for the position. Subsequently I learned
that pecuniary embarrassments made him willing to
abandon, for a time at least, the greater but more
uncertain chances of active political warfare. However, given that he desired the Embassy, it caused
me no surprise that he should ask for it. To ap-
point him would be open war indeed; he was the
Prince's *bête noire*, my mother's pet aversion; that
he was totally untrained in diplomacy was a minor,
but possibly serious, objection; that he was extreme
in his views seemed to me then no disqualification.
I allowed him to perceive that I read his parable,
but, remembering the case of the Greek generals
and Themistocles, ventured to ask him to give me
another name.

"The only name that I could give your Majesty with perfect confidence would be that of my good friend Max von Sempach," said he, with an admirable air of honesty, but, as I thought, a covert gleam of amusement in his deep-set eyes. I very nearly laughed. The only man fit for the Embassy, except himself, was Count Max! And if Count Max went, of course the Countess would go with him; equally of course the King must stay in Forstadt. I saw Wetter looking at me keenly out of the corner of his eye; it did not suit me that he should read my thoughts this time. I appeared to have no suspicion of the good faith of his suggestion, and said, with an air of surprise:

"Max von Sempach! Why, how is he suitable?"

With great gravity he gave me many reasons, proving not that Max was very suitable, but that everybody else was profoundly unsuitable, except the unmentioned candidate whose name was so well understood between us.

"These," I observed, "would seem to be reasons for looking elsewhere—I mean to the other side—for a suitable man."

He did not trouble to argue that with me. He knew that his was not the voice to which I should listen.

"If your Majesty comes to that conclusion, my friends and I will be disappointed," he said, "but we must accept your decision."

There was much to like in Wetter. Men are not insincere merely because they are ambitious, dishonest merely because they are given to intrigue, selfish merely because they ask places for themselves. There is a grossness of moral fibre not in itself a good thing, but very different from rottenness. Wetter was a keen and convinced partisan, and an ardent believer in himself. His cause ought to win, and, if his hand could take the helm, would win; this was his attitude, and it excused some want of scruple both in promoting the cause and in insuring to it his own effective support. But he was a big man, of a well-developed nature, hearty, sympathetic, and free from cant, full of force, of wit, of unblunted emotion. He would not, however, have made at all a good ambassador; and he would not have wanted to be one had he not run into debt.

Max von Sempach, on the other hand, would fill the place respectably, although not brilliantly. Wetter knew this, and the fact gave to the mention of the Count's name a decent appearance without depriving it of its harmlessness. He named a suitable but an impossible person—a person to me impossible.

Soon after the meal I left him, telling him that I should come in again later, and had ordered my carriage to call for me at his house at five o'clock. Turning down the quiet lane that led to the Countess's, I soon reached my destination. I was now in less agitation than on the day before. My mind was made up; I came to give what she asked. Wetter should have his Embassy. More than this, I came no longer in trepidation, no longer fearing her ridicule even while I sought her love, no more oppressed with the sense that in truth she might be laughing while she seemed to encourage. There was the dawning of triumph in my heart, an assurance of victory, and the fierce delight in a determination come to at great cost and to be held, it may be, at greater still. In all these feelings, mighty always, there were for me the freshness, the rush of youth, and the venturous joy of new experience.

On her also a crisis of feeling had come; she was not her old self, nor I to her what I had been. There was a strained, almost frightened look in her eyes; a low-voiced "Augustin" replacing her bantering "Cæsar." Save for my name she did not speak as I led her to a couch and sat down by her side. She looked slight, girlish, and pathetic in a simple gown of black; timidity renewed her youth. Well might I forget that she was not a maiden of meet age for me, and she herself for an instant cheat time's reckoning. She made of me a man, of herself a girl, and prayed love's advocacy to prove the delusion true.

"I have been with Wetter," said I. "He wants the Embassy."

I fancy that she knew his desire; her hand pressed mine, but she did not speak.

"But he recommended Max," I went on.

"Max!" For a moment her face was full of terror as she turned to me; then she broke into a smile. Wetter's advice was plain to her also.

"You see how much he wants it for himself," said I. "He knows I would sooner send a gutter-boy than Max. And you know it?"

"Do I?" she murmured.

I rose and stood before her.

"It is yours to give, not mine," said I. "Do you give it to Wetter?"

As she looked up at me her eyes filled with tears, while her lips curved in a timid smile.

"What—what trouble you'll get into!" she said.

"It's not a thousandth part of what I would do for you. Wetter shall have it then—or Max?"

"Not Max," she said; her eyes told me why it should not be Max.

"Then Wetter," and I fell on one knee by her, whispering, "The King gives it to his Queen."

"They'll blame you so; they'll say all sorts of things."

"I shan't hear them; I hear only you."

"They'll be unkind to you."

"They can't hurt me if you're kind to me."

"Perhaps they'll say I—I got it from you."

"I am not ashamed. What is it to me what they say?"

"You don't care?"

"For nothing in the world but you and to be with you."

She sat looking up at me for an instant; then she threw her arm over the end of the sofa and laid her face on the cushion; I heard her sob softly. Her other hand lay in her lap; I took it and raised it to my lips. I did not know the meaning of her tears. I was triumphant. She sobbed, not loudly or violently, but with a pitiful gentleness.

"Why do you cry so, darling?" I whispered.

She turned her face to me; the tears were running down her cheeks. "Why do I cry?" she moaned softly. "Because I'm wicked—I suppose I'm wicked—and so foolish. And—and you are good, and noble, and—and you'll be great. And "—the sobs choked her voice, and she turned her face half away—"and I'm old, Augustin."

I could not enter into her mood; joy pervaded me; but neither did I scorn her nor grow impatient. I perceived dimly that she struggled with a conflict of emotions beyond my understanding. Words were unsafe, likely to be wrong, to make worse what they sought to cure. I caressed her, but trusted my tongue no further than to murmur endearments. She grew calmer, sat up, and dried her eyes.

"But it's so absurd," she protested. "Augustin, lots of boys are just as absurd as you; but was any woman ever as absurd as I am?"

"Why do you call it absurd?"

"Oh, because, because"—she moved near me suddenly—"because, although I've tried so hard, I can't feel it the least absurd. I do love you."

Here was her prepossession all the while—that the thing would seem absurd, not that there was sin in it. I can see now why her mind fixed on this point; she was, in truth, speaking not to me who was there by her, me as I was, but to the man who should be; she pleaded not only with herself, but with my future self, praying the mature man to think of her with tenderness and not with a laugh, interceding with what should one day be my memory of her. Ah, my dear, that prayer of yours is answered! I do not laugh as I write. At you I could never have laughed; and if I set out to force a laugh even at myself I fall to thinking of what you were, and again I do not laugh. Then what is it that the world outside must have laughed with a very self-conscious wisdom? Its laughter was nothing to us then, and to-day is to me as nothing. Is it not always ready to weep at a farce and laugh at a tragedy?

"But you've nobody else," she went on softly. "I shouldn't have dared if you'd had anybody else. Long ago—do you remember?—you had nobody, and you liked me to kiss you. I believe I began to love you then; I mean I began to think how much some woman would love you some day. But

I didn't think I should be the woman. Oh, don't look at me so hard, or—or you'll see——"

"How much you love me?"

"No, no. You'll see my wrinkles. See, if I do this you can't look at my face." And putting her arms round my neck she hid her face.

I was strangely tongue-tied, or, perhaps, not strangely; for there comes a time when the eyes say all that there is desire or need to say. Her pleadings were in answer to my eyes.

"Oh, I know you think so now!" she murmured. "But you won't go on thinking so—and I shall." She raised her head and looked at me; now a smile of triumph came on her face. "Oh, but you do think so now!" she whispered in a voice still lower, but full of delight. "You do think so now," and again she hid her face from me. But I knew that the triumph had entered into her soul also, and that the shadows could no longer altogether dim its sunshine for her.

The afternoon became full, and waned to dusk as we sat together. We said little; there were no arrangements made; we seemed in a way cut off from the world outside, and from the consideration of it. The life which we must each lead, lives in the main apart from one another, had receded into distance, and went unnoticed; we had nothing to do save to be together; when we were together there was little that we cared to say, no protestations that we had need to make. There was between us so absolute a sympathy, so full an agreement in all that we gave, all that we accepted, all that we abandoned. Doubts and struggles were as though they had never been. There is a temptation to think sometimes that things so perfectly justify themselves that conscience is not discrowned by violence, but signs a willing abdication, herself convinced. For passion can simulate right, even as in some natures the love of right becomes a turbulent passion in the end, like most of such, destructive of itself.

"Then I am yours, and you are mine? And the Embassy is Wetter's?"

"The Embassy is whose you like," she cried, "if the rest is true."

"It is Wetter's. Do you know why? That everybody may know how I am yours."

She did not refuse even the perilous fame I offered.

"I should be proud of it," she said, with head erect.

"No, no; nobody shall breathe a letter of your name," I exclaimed in a sudden turn of feeling. "I will swear that you had nothing to do with it, that you hate him, that you never mentioned it."

"Say what you like," she whispered.

"If I did that, I should say to all Forstadt that there's no woman in the world like you."

"You needn't say it to all Forstadt. You haven't even said it to me yet."

We had been sitting together. Again I fell on one knee, prepared to offer her formal homage in a sweet extravagance. On a sudden she raised her hand; her face grew alarmed.

"Hark!" she said. "Hark!"

"To your voice, yours only!"

"No. There is a noise. Somebody is coming. Who can it be?"

"I don't care who it is."

"Why, dearest! But you must care. Get up, get up, get up!"

I rose slowly to my feet. I was indeed in a mood when I did not care. The steps were close outside. Before they could come nearer, I kissed her again.

"Who can it be? I am denied to everybody," she said, bewildered.

There was a knock at the door.

"It is not Max," she said, with a swift glance at me. I stood where I was. "Come in," she cried.

The door opened, and to my amazement Wetter stood there. He was panting, as though he had run fast, and his air displayed agitation. The Countess ran to him instantly. His coming seemed to revive the fears which her love had laid to rest.

"What is it?" she cried. "What's the matter?"

Wetter took absolutely no notice of her. Walking on as though she were not there, he came straight up to me. He spoke in tones of intense emotion, and with the bluntness that excitement brings.

"You must come with me at once," he said in an imperious way. "They've sent for you to my house; we can get in together by the back door."

"But what's the matter, man?" I cried, divided between puzzle and anger.

"You're wanted; you must go to Hammer-feldt's."

"To Hammerfeldt's?"

"Yes. He's dying. Come along."

"Dying! My God!"

"The message is urgent. There's no time to lose. If you want to see him alive, come. I said you were lying down in my study. If you don't come quickly, it will be known where you are."

"I don't care for that."

"He's sent for you himself."

The Countess had moved to my side.

"You must go," she said now, laying her hand on my arm.

I turned to look at her. Her eyes were full of a vague alarm. I was like a man suddenly roused half-way through a vivid entrancing dream, unable still to believe that the real is true and the phantasm not the only substance.

"Come, come," repeated Wetter urgently and irritably. "You can't let him die without going to him."

"Go, Augustin," she whispered.

"Yes, I'll go. I'm going; I'm going at once," I stammered. "I'm ready, Wetter. Take me with you. Is he really dying?"

"So they say."

"Hammerfeldt dying! Yes, I'll come with you."

I turned to the Countess; Wetter was already half-way to the door. He looked back over his shoulder, and his face was impatient. My eyes met hers, I read the fear that was in hers. I was strangely fearful myself, appalled at such a breaking of our dream.

"Good-bye," I said. "I'll come again soon; to-morrow, some time to-morrow."

"Yes, yes," said she, but hardly as though she believed me.

"Good-bye." I took her hand and kissed it; Wetter looked on, saying nothing. The thought of concealment did not occur to me. I kissed her hand two or three times.

"Shall you find him alive?" she murmured, in speculation more than in question.

"I don't know. Good-bye."

She herself led me to where Wetter was standing.

" It's his breathing," said Wetter. " He can't get his breath; can't speak at all. Come along."

" I'm ready; I'll follow you."

As I reached the door I turned. She was not looking at me; she had sat down in a chair by the fire and was gazing fixedly at the flames. I have had that picture of her often in my mind.

Wetter led me downstairs and out into the street at a rapid pace. I followed him, trying to gather myself together and think coherently. Too sudden a change paralyzes; the mind must have time for readjustment. Hammerfeldt was and had always been so large a figure and a presence so important in my life; I could only whisper to myself, " He's dying; it's his breathing; he can't get his breath."

We went in by the back door as we had arranged, and gained the study.

" Quick!" whispered Wetter. " Remember you were in here. Don't make any excuses about delay. Or put it on me; say I hesitated to rouse you."

I listened little to all that he said, and paid small heed to the precautions that his wariness suggested.

" I hope he won't be dead when you get there," he added as we started for the hall. " Here's your hat."

I caught at the word " dead."

" If he's dead——" I repeated aimlessly. " If he's dead, Wetter——"

Then for an instant he turned to me, his face full of expression, his eyes keen and eager. He shrugged his shoulders.

" He's an old man," said he. " We must all die. And if he's dead——"

" Well, Wetter, well ? "

" Well, then you're king at last."

With this he opened the door of my carriage and stood holding it. I looked him full in the face before I stepped in. He did not flinch; he nodded his head and smiled.

" You're king at last," he seemed to say again.

CHAPTER XII.

KING AT A PRICE.

THE death of Prince von Hammerfeldt furnished the subject of a picture exhibited at Forstadt with great success a few years ago. The old man's simple room, its plain furniture, the large window facing the garden, were faithfully given; the bed was his bed and no other bed; the nurses were portraits, the doctors were portraits, the Prince's features were exactly mapped; I myself was represented sitting in an armchair by his side, with a strong light on my face as I leaned forward to catch his faint words. The artist's performance was, in fact, a singularly competent reproduction of every external object, human or other, in the room; and with the necessary alteration of features and title the picture would have served to commemorate the death-bed of any aged statesman who had a young prince for his pupil. Hammerfeldt is evidently giving a brief summary of his principles, providing me with a *vade mecum* of kingship, a manual on the management of men. I listen with an expression of deep attention and respectful grief. By a touch which no doubt is dramatic, the other figures are gazing intently at me, on whom the future depends, not at the dying man whose course is run. Looking at the work as a whole, I am not in the least surprised that I was recommended to bestow the Cross of St. Paul on the painter. I consented without demur. In mere matters of taste I have always considered myself bound to reflect public opinion.

Now for reality. An old man struggling hard for breath; gasps now quicker, now slower; a few words half-formed, choked, unintelligible; eyes that were full of an impotent desire to speak; these came first. Then the doctors gathered round, looked, whispered, went away. I rose and walked twice across the room; coming back, I stood and looked at him. Still he knew me. Suddenly his hand moved toward me. I bent my head till my ear was within three inches of his lips; I could hear nothing. I saw a doctor standing by, watch in hand; he was timing the breath that grew slower and slower. "Will he speak?" I asked in a whisper; a shake of the head answered me. I looked again into his eyes; now he seemed to speak to me. My face grew hot and red; but I did not speak to him. Yet I stroked his hand, and there was a gleam of understanding in his eyes. A moment later his eyes closed; the gasps became slower and slower. I raised my head and looked across at the doctor. His watch had a gold front protecting the glass; he shut the front on the face with a click.

Very likely there were no proper materials for a picture here; the sentiment, the historical interest, the situation would all have been defective. Men die in so very much the same way, and in so very much the same way men watch them dying. Death is the triumph of the physical. I must not complain that the painter imported some sentiment.

In twenty minutes I was back again in my carriage, being driven home rapidly. My dinner was ready and Baptiste in attendance. "Ah, he is dead?" said Baptiste, as he fashioned my napkin into a more perfect shape.

"Yes, Baptiste, he's dead," said I. "Bring me some slippers."

"Your Majesty will not dress?"

"A smoking jacket," said I.

While I ate my dinner Baptiste chattered about the Prince. There was a kindly humanity in the man that gave a whimsical tenderness to what he said.

"Ah, now, M. le Prince knew the world well. And where is he gone? Well, at least he will not be disappointed! To die at eighty! It is only to go to bed when one is tired. What use would there be in sitting up with heavy eyes? That is to bore yourself and the company."

"Has the Princess expressed a wish to see me?" I asked.

"Certainly, sire, at your leisure. I said, 'But his Majesty must dine.' The Princess is much upset it seems. She was greatly attached to the Prince." He looked at me shrewdly. "She valued the Prince very highly," he added, as though in correction of his previous statement.

"I'll go directly I've done dinner. Send and say so."

I was not surprised that consternation reigned in the heart of my mother and extended its sway to Victoria. Victoria was crying, Princess Heinrich's eyes were dry, but her lips set in a despairing closeness. Both invited me to kiss them.

"What will you do without him?" asked Victoria, dabbing her eyes.

"You have lost your best, your only guide," said my mother.

I told them what I had to tell about Hammerfeldt's death. Victoria broke into compassionate comments, my mother listened in silence.

"Poor old Hammerfeldt!" I ended reflectively.

"Where were you when you got the news?" asked Victoria.

I looked at her. Then I answered quietly:

"I was calling on the Countess von Sempach. I lunched with Wetter and went on there."

There was a pause. I believe that my candour was a surprise; perhaps it seemed a defiance.

"Did you tell the Prince that?" my mother asked.

"The Prince," I answered, "was not in a state to listen to anything that I might have said, not even to anything of importance."

"Fancy if he'd known! On his death-bed!" was Victoria's very audible whisper.

My mother looked at me with a despairing expression. I am unwilling to do either her or my sister an injustice, but I wondered then how much thought they were giving to the old friend we had lost. It seemed to me that they thought little of the man we knew, the man himself; not grief, but fear was dominant in them. Wetter's saying, "You're king at last," came into my mind. Perhaps their mood was intelligible enough and did not want excuse. They had seen in Hammerfeldt my schoolmaster; his hand was gone, and could no longer guide or restrain me. To one a son, to the other a younger brother, by both I was counted incapable of standing alone or choosing my own path. Hammerfeldt was gone; Wetter remained; the Countess von Sempach remained. There was the new position. The Prince's death then might well be to them so great a calamity as to lose its rank among sorrows, regrets for the past be ousted by terror for the future, and the loss of an ally obliterate grief for a friend.

"But you know his wishes and his views," said my mother. "I hope that they will have an increased sacredness for you now."

"He may be looking down on you from heaven," added Victoria, folding her handkerchief so as to get a dry part uppermost.

I could not resist this provocation: I smiled.

"If it is so, Victoria," I remarked, "nobody will be more surprised than the Prince himself."

Victoria was very much offended. She conceived herself to have added an effective touch: I ridiculed her.

"You might at least pretend to have a little decent feeling," she cried.

"Come, come, my dear, don't let's squabble over him before he's cold," said I, rising. "Have you anything else to say to me, mother?"

At this instant my brother-in-law entered. He smelt very strongly of tobacco, but wore an expression of premeditated misery. He came up to me, holding out his hand.

"Good evening," said I.

"Poor Hammerfeldt!" he murmured. "Poor Hammerfeldt! What a blow! How lost you must feel!"

He had been talking over the matter with Victoria. That was beyond doubt.

"I happen to have been thinking," I rejoined, "more of him than of myself."

"Of course, of course," muttered William Adolphus in some confusion, and (as I thought) with a reproachful glance at his wife.

"We have lost the Prince," said my mother, "but we can still be guided by his example and his principles. To follow his counsels will be the best monument you can raise to his memory, Augustin."

I kissed her hand and then she gave me her cheek. Going to Victoria, I saluted her with brotherly heartiness. I never allowed myself to forget that Victoria was very fond of me, and I never lost my affection for her.

"Now don't be foolish, Augustin," she implored.

"What is being foolish?" I asked perversely.

"Oh, you know! You know very well what people say, and so do I."

"And poor old Hammerfeldt in heaven—does he know too?"

She turned away with a shocked expression. William Adolphus hid a sheepish smile with a large hand. In the lower ranges of humour William Adolphus sometimes understood one. I declined his offer of company over a cigar, but bade him good-night with a mild gratitude; he desired to be pleasant to us all, and the realization of his ambition presented difficulties.

I was very tired and fell into a deep sleep almost the moment I was in bed. At four o'clock in the morning I awoke. My fatigue seemed gone; I did not think of sleeping again. The events of the day before came back to me with an extraordinary vividness of impression, the outcome of nerves strained to an unhealthy sensitiveness. It would have needed but a little self-delusion, a little yielding to the current of my thoughts, to make me see Hammerfeldt by my bed. The Countess and Wetter were in mental image no less plain. I rose and pulled up the blinds; the night had begun to pass from black to gray; for a moment I pictured the Prince, not looking down from heaven, but wandering somewhere in such a dim cold twilight. The message that his eyes had given me became very clear to me. It had turned my cheek red; it sent an excitement through me now. It would not go easily into words, but, as I sought to frame it, that other speech came back to me—the speech of the Prince's enemy. Wetter had said, " You're king at last." What else had Hammerfeldt meant to say? Nothing else. That was his message also. From both it came, the same reminder, the same exhortation. The living man and the dead joined their voices in this brief appeal. It did not need my mother's despair or Victoria's petulance to lend it point. I was amazed to find how it came home to me. Now I perceived how, up to this time, my life had been centred in Hammerfeldt. I was obeying him or disobeying, accepting his views or questioning them, docile or rebellious; when I rebelled, I rebelled for the pleasure of it, for the excitement it gave, the spice of daring, the air of independence, for curiosity, to see how he would take it, what saying he would utter, what resource of persuasion or argument he would invoke. It was strange to think that now if I obeyed I should not gratify, if I disobeyed I could make him uneasy no more. If I went right, there was none to reap credit; if I went wrong, none who should have controlled me better; none to say, " You are wise, sire "; none to smile as he said, " We must all learn wisdom, sire." It was very strange to be without old Hammerfeldt.

" You're king at last." By Wetter's verdict and by the Prince's own, his death made me in very truth king. So they said; what did they think? Wetter's thought was, " Here is a king, a king to be shaped and used." I read Wetter's thought well enough. But the old man's? His was a plea, a hope, a prayer. " Be king." A sudden flash of feeling came upon me—too late! For I had gone to his bedside fresh from signing my abdication. It mattered nothing at whose bidding or with what eager obedience I had taken off the crown. My sovereignty was my possession and my trust. I had laid it down. In those dim hours of the night, when men die (so they say), passion is cold, the blood chill, and we fall prey to the cruelties of truth, then I knew to what I had put my hand, why Wetter exulted, why Hammerfeldt's eyes spoke one unspoken prayer. It was not that Wetter went Ambassador, but that he went not of my will, by my act, or out of my mind; he went by another's will, that other on whose head I had put my crown.

Strange thoughts for a man not yet grown? I am not altogether of that mind. For then my trust seemed very great, almost holy, armed with majesty; I had not learned the little real power that lay in it. To-day, if I threw away my crown, I should not exaggerate the value of my sacrifice. Then it seemed that I gave a great thing, and great was my betrayal. Therefore I could not rest for the thought of what I had put my hand to, chafed at Wetter's words that sounded now like a taunt, and seemed again to see old Hammerfeldt dying and to flush red in shame before the utterance of his eyes. The Prince had served his masters, his country, and the cause that he held right. Wetter, if he served himself, served his principles also. What and whom did I serve in this thing that I was about to do? I could answer only that I served her whose image rose now before me. But when I turned to her for comfort she accused, and did not delight.

I am aware that my feelings will probably appear exaggerated to those not brought up in the habit of thought nor subjected to the influences which had ruled my mind. I give them for what they are worth. At this moment the effect of the contrast between my position and my desires was a struggle of peculiar severity—one of the battles of my life.

Irony was not to be wanting, comedy claimed her accustomed share. The interview which I have already set down might seem enough to have satisfied my sister. It was not; after I had breakfasted Victoria sent William Adolphus to me. I am inclined now and then to think that there is, after all, something mystic in the status of husbandhood, some supernatural endowment that in the wife's eyes attaches to her own man, however little she values him, at however low a rate she sets his natural qualities. How otherwise could Victoria (whose defect was more in temper than in perception) send William Adolphus to talk to me?

He came; the *rôle* of the man of the world was his choice. "I'm a bit older than you, you know," he began; then he laughed, and said that women were all very well in their places. I must not suppose that he was a Puritan. Heavens, I supposed nothing about him! I knew he was a fool, and rested in that sufficient knowledge. The Countess, he said, was a damned pretty woman. "We shan't quarrel about that, anyhow," he added, with the sort of laugh that I had so often seen poor old Hammerfeldt wince at. But come now, did I mean to——? Well, I knew what he meant, didn't I?

"My dear William Adolphus," said I, "I am so infinitely obliged to you. You have made me see the matter in quite a new light. It's surprising what a talk with a man of the world does for one. I am very young, of course."

"Oh, you'll learn. You're no fool," said William Adolphus.

"I suppose Victoria doesn't know you've come?"

He turned rather red, and, like a fool, lied where he need not, out of pride, not policy.

"No; I came off my own bat," he answered.

"You have done me a great service."

"My dear fellow!" beamed he with the broadest of smiles. "Now Hammerfeldt's gone, I thought a friendly word or two would not come amiss."

Hammerfeldt was dead; now came William Adolphus. *Il n'y a pas d'homme nécessaire.*

"Of course you can do nothing abrupt," he continued. "But I should think you might gradually——"

"I understand you absolutely," said I, rising to my feet.

"What I mean is——"

"My dear fellow, not another word is needed."

"You don't mind if I mention to Victoria that I have——?"

"Put it in the evening papers, if you like," said I.

"Ha, ha!" he laughed. "That wouldn't be a bad joke, would it?"

What a man! With his little bit of stock wisdom, "You can do nothing abruptly"! Nothing abruptly! I must not check myself abruptly on the edge of the precipice, but go quietly down half-way to the gulf, and then come up again! If I were ever to do anything, it must be done abruptly—now, to-day; while the strength was on me, while there was still a force, fresh and vigorous, to match the other great force that drew me on. And across this consiousness came a queer little remorse for not having rescued Victoria from this husband whom she sent to teach me. When Baptiste brought me lunch I was laughing.

That afternoon the thought of Geoffrey Owen was much with me. Perhaps I summoned it first in a sort of appeal against Hammerfeldt. But I knew in my heart that the two could not be antagonists here. Geoffrey would wish me to show favour, or at least impartiality, toward Liberal opinions; for the sake of such a manifestation he might overlook certain objections and acquiesce in my giving the Embassy to Wetter. But with what face would he hear an honest statement of the case—that Wetter was to have the Embassy because the King desired to please Countess von Sempach? I smiled drearily as I imagined his incredulous indignation. No; everybody was against me, saints and sages, Geoffrey and Hammerfeldt, women and men; even the fools gave no countenance to my folly. William Adolphus thought that I might gradually——!

At five o'clock I sent for Wetter. He came with remarkable promptness. He was visibly excited, and could hardly force himself to spend a moment on the formal and proper expressions of regret for the Prince's death. He seemed to be watching me closely and eagerly. I made him sit down, and gave him a cigar. I had meant to approach the matter with a diplomatic deviousness. I had overrated my skill and self-control. Wetter made me feel young and awkward. I was like a schoolboy forced to confess the neglect of his task, and speaking in fear of the cane. Ignoring the reserve that had marked our former conversation, I blurted out:

" I can't send you to Paris."

The man's face went white, but he controlled himself.

" Your Majesty knows that I did not ask for it," he said with considerable dignity.

" I know; but you wanted it."

He looked straight at me; he was very pale.

" Truly, yes," he said. " I wanted it; since your Majesty is plain, I'll be plain too."

" Why did you want it? Why are you pale, Wetter? "

He put his cigar in his mouth and smoked fiercely, but did not answer.

" You must have wanted it," I said, " or you wouldn't have tried to get it in that way."

" My God, I did want it."

" Why? "

" If I can't have it, what matter? " He rose to his feet and bowed. " Good-bye, sire," said he. Then he gave a curious laugh. " *Moriturus te saluto*," he added, laughing still.

" What's the matter, man? " I cried, springing up and catching him by the arm.

" I haven't a shilling in the world; my creditors are in full chase; I'm posted for a card debt at the club. If I had this I could borrow. Good God, you promised it to her! "

" Yes, I promised it to her."

" Have you seen her again?"

" No. I must."

" To whom will you give it?"

" I don't know. Not to you."

" Why not?"

" You're not fit for it."

He took out his handkerchief and wiped his forehead.

" I was no more fit for it yesterday," he said.

" I won't argue it."

" As you please, sire," said he with a shrug, and he seemed to pull himself together. He rose and stood before me with a smile on his lips.

I sat down, took a piece of paper, wrote a draft, leaving the amount unstated, and pushed it across to him. He looked down at it in wonder. Then his face lit up with eagerness.

" You mean—you mean——? " he stammered.

" My ransom," said I.

" Mine! " he cried.

" No, it is mine, the price of my freedom."

He lifted the piece of paper in a hand that trembled.

" It's a lot of money," he said. " Eighty or ninety thousand marks."

" My name is good for that."

He looked me in the face, opening his lips but not speaking. Then he thrust out his hand to me. I took it; I was as much moved as he.

" Don't tempt me again," I said.

He gripped my hand hard and fiercely; when he released it I waved it toward the door. I could trust myself no more. He turned to go; but I called to him again:

"My ransom," said I. "The price of my freedom."

" Don't say anything to her. I must see her."

He faced me with an agitated look.

" What for? " he asked.

I made him no answer, but lay back in my chair. He came toward me slowly and with hesitation. I looked up in his face.

" I'll pay you back," he said.

" I don't want the money."

" And I don't mean the money. In fact, I'm bad at paying money back. Why have you done it? "

" I have done it for myself, not for you. You owe me nothing. My honour was pawned, and I have redeemed it. I was bound; I am free."

His eyes were fixed intently on me with a sort of wonder, but I motioned him again to the door. He obeyed me without another word; after a bow he turned and went out. I rose, and having walked to the window, looked down into the street. I saw him crossing the roadway with a slow step and bent head. He was going toward his club, not to his house. I stood watching him till he turned round a corner and disappeared. Then I drew a long breath and returned to my chair. I had hardly seated myself when Baptiste came in with a note. It was from the Countess. " Aren't you coming to-day? " That was all.

" There is no answer," I said, and Baptiste left me.

For I must carry the answer myself; and the answer must be, " Yes, to-day, but not to-morrow."

There was doubtless some extravagance in my conception of the situation, and I have not sought to conceal or modify it. It seemed to me that I could play my part only at the cost of what was dearest to me in the world. Money had served with Wetter; it would not serve here. My heart must pay, my heart and hers. I remember that I sat in my chair murmuring again and again, " To-day, but not to-morrow."

CHAPTER XIII.

I PROMISE NOT TO LAUGH.

I TAKE it that generally when middle age looks
back on the emotions of youth and its temptations,
it is to smile at the wildness of the first and to marvel
at the victories of the second. That is not my mood
when I recall the relation between the Countess and
myself. For sometimes, while passion becomes less
fierce, aspiration grows less exalted. The man who
calls most, if not all, things vanity, will yield to desires which some high-strung ideal in the boy would
rout. At forty the feelings are not so strong as at
twenty, but neither are the ambitions, the dreams,
the conception of self. It is easier to resist, but it
may not seem so well worth while. Thus it is with
me. I wonder not at the beginning or progress of
my first love, but at the manner of its end, asking
myself incredulously what motive or what notion
had power to hold back the flood of youth, seeking
almost in vain to re-discover the spring that moved
me then. Yet, though I can not feel it again, I know
dimly what it was, that high, strange, noble, ludicrous ideal of my office which so laid hold on me
as to scatter passion's forces and wrest me from the
arms of her I loved. I can not now so think of my
kingship, so magnify its claim, or conceive that it
matters so greatly to the world how I hold it or

what manner of man I show myself. I come to the conclusion (though it may seem to border on paradox) that in a like case I could not, or should not, do now what I did then. I suppose that it is some such process as this, a weakening of emotion parallel with a lowering of ideal, that makes us, as we grow older, think ourselves so much wiser and know ourselves to be so little better.

I had charged Wetter to say nothing to the Countess, but he disobeyed me. He had been to her and told her all that passed between us. I knew this the moment I entered her room. Her agitated nervous air showed me that she had been informed of the withdrawal of my gift, was aware that the Embassy was no longer hers to give to Wetter or another, and was wondering helplessly what the meaning of the change might be. To her, as to Wetter, the death of Hammerfeldt must have seemed the removal of an impediment; only through the curious processes of my own mind did it raise an obstacle insurmountable. She had liked the Prince, but feared him; she imagined my feelings to have been the same, and perhaps in his lifetime they were. Then should not I, who had been brought to defy him living, more readily disregard him dead?

But against her knowledge of me and her quick wit no preconception could hold out long. She was by me in a moment, asking:

"What has happened? What's wrong, Augustin?"

I had pictured myself describing to her what I felt, making her understand, sympathize, and, even while she grieved, approve. The notion was so strong in me that I did not doubt of finding words for it—words eloquent of its force and dignity. But before her simple impulsive question I was dumb. A wave of shyness swept over me; not even to her could I divulge my thoughts, not even from her risk the smile of ridicule or the blankness of non-apprehension. I became wretchedly certain that I should be only absurd and priggish, that she would not believe me, would see only excuse and hypocrisy in what I said. It was so difficult also not to seem to accuse her, to charge her with grasping at what I had freely offered, with having, as the phrase runs, designs on me, with wishing to take power where she had been impelled to bestow love. She pressed me with more questions, but still I found no answer.

"I can't do it," I was reduced to stammering. "I can't do it. He's not the man. I must find another."

"Of the Prince's party?" she asked quickly.

"I don't know. I must find somebody; I must find somebody for myself."

I had sat down, and she was standing opposite to me.

"Find somebody for yourself?" she repeated slowly. "For yourself? What do you mean by that, Augustin?"

"I must choose a man for myself."

"You mean—you mean without my help?"

I returned no answer, but sat looking at her with a dreary appealing gaze. She was silent for a few moments; then she said suddenly:

"You haven't offered to kiss me."

I rose and kissed her on the lips; she stood still and did not kiss me.

"Thank you," she said. "I asked you to kiss

11

me, and you've kissed me. Thank you." She paused and added, " Have I grown so much older in a day? "

" It is not that. It's——"

" It is that," she said. She turned away and seated herself on the sofa, where she sat with her eyes fixed on the ground. Then she gave a short laugh. " I knew it would come," she said, " but this is—is rather sudden."

I ran to her and threw myself on my knees by her. I lifted my arm and put it round her neck and drew her face down to mine.

" No, no, no," I whispered passionately. " It's not that."

She let me kiss her now many times, and presently returned my kisses. Her breath caught in gasps, and she clutched my hand imploringly.

" You do love me? " she murmured.

" Yes, yes."

" Then why—why? Why do you do this? " She drew back, looking in my face in a bewildered way. Then a sudden brightness came into her eyes. " Is it for me? Are you thinking of me? "

" No," said I in stubborn honesty, " I was not thinking of you."

" Don't! " she cried, for she did not believe me. " What do I care? I cared once; I don't care now."

" It wasn't because of you," I repeated obstinately.

" Then tell me, tell me! Because I believe you still love me."

I made shift to tell her, but my stumbling words belittled the great conception: I could not find the phrases that alone might convey the truth to her;

but I held on, trying to say something of what I meant.

"I never tried to interfere," she broke in once.

"I made you interfere, I myself," was my lame answer; and the rest I said was as lame.

"I don't understand," she murmured forlornly and petulantly. "Oh, I suppose I see what you mean in a way; but I don't believe it. I don't see why you should feel like that about it. Do men feel like that? Women don't."

"I can't help it," I pleaded, pressing her hand. She drew it away gently.

"And what will it mean?" she asked. "Am I never to see you?"

"Often, often, I hope, but——"

"I'm not to talk to you about—about important things, things we both care about?"

I felt the absurdity of such a position. The abstract made concrete is so often made absurd.

"Then you won't come often; you won't care about coming." Something in her thoughts made her flush suddenly. She met my eyes and took courage. "You asked a good deal of me," she said.

I made no answer; she understood my silence. She rose, leaving me on my knees. I threw myself on the sofa and she went to the hearthrug. She knew that what I had asked of her I asked no more. There was a long silence between us. At last she spoke in a very low voice.

"It's only a little sooner than it must have been," she said. "And I—I suppose I must be glad that it's come home to me now instead of—later. I daresay you'll be glad of that too, Augustin."

"How are we to live, how are we to meet, what are we to be to one another?" she broke out the next moment. "We can't go on as if nothing had happened."

"I don't know."

"You don't know! Yet you're hard as iron about it. Oh, I daresay you're right; you must be. It's only a little sooner."

She turned her back to me, and stood looking down into the fire. I was trying to answer her question, to realize how it would be between us, how, having lived in the real, we must now dwell in the unreal with one another. I was wondering how I could meet her and not show that I loved her, how I could love her and yet be true to my idol, the conception that governed me. Suddenly she spoke, without turning or lifting her head.

"Whom shall you send to Paris?"

"I don't know. I haven't settled."

"Wetter mentioned somebody else—besides himself?"

"Only Max," said I, with a dreary laugh.

"Hadn't you better send Max? That is, if you think him fit for it."

I thought that she was relieving her petulance by a bitter jest; but a moment later she said again, still without turning round:

"Send Max."

I rose and walked slowly to where she stood. Hearing my movement, she faced me.

"Send Max," she said again, holding out her hands toward me, clasped together. "I—I can't stay here like—in the way you say. And you? How could you do it?"

"You would go with him?" I exclaimed.

"Of course."

"For five years?"

"When I come back," she said, "you will be twenty-five. You will be married to Elsa. I shall be thirty-four. There will be no difficulty about how we are to treat one another when I come back, Augustin."

"My God!" I murmured, looking in her eyes. As I looked they filled with tears.

"My dear, my dear," she said, raising her arms and setting her hands on my shoulders, "I have never forgotten that I was a fool. Yes, once, for a few moments yesterday. I shall remember at Paris what a fool I was, and I shan't forget it when I come back. Only I wish it didn't break one's heart to be a fool."

"I won't let you go; I won't send him. I can't."

"Will it be better to have it happen here gradually before my eyes every day? I should kill myself. I couldn't bear it. I should see you finding out, changing, forgetting, laughing. Oh, what a miserable woman I am!" She turned away suddenly and flung herself into an armchair.

"Why did you do it?" she cried. "Why did you?"

"I loved you."

"Yes, yes, yes. That's the absurdity, the horrible absurdity. And I loved you, and I love you. Isn't it funny?" She laughed hysterically. "How funny we shall think it soon! When I come back from Paris! No, before then! We shall laugh about it!" She broke into sobs, hiding her face in her hands.

"I shall never laugh about it," I said.

"Shan't you?" she asked, looking up and gazing intently at me. Then she rose and came toward me. " No, I don't think you will. Don't, dear. But I don't think you will. You won't laugh about it, will you? You won't laugh, Cæsar?"

I bent low and kissed her hand. I should have broken down had I tried to speak. As I raised my head from her hand, she kissed my brow. Then she wiped her eyes, saying:

" You'll send Max to Paris? You promised me this Embassy. You shall be good and great and independent, and all you say you mean to be and must be afterward. But you promised me this Embassy. Well, I ask your promise of you. I ask it for Max."

" You would go away from me?"

" Yes. I want to grow old away from you. I ask the Embassy for Max."

I stood silent, wretched, undecided. She came near to me again.

" Don't refuse me, dear," she said in a low unsteady voice. " I don't ask much of you; just to let me go, and not to laugh. I shall never ask anything again of you. I have given you so much, and I would have given you anything you asked. Don't refuse me."

" It breaks my heart."

" Poor heart, poor heart!" she whispered softly, with a sad mocking smile. " It will mend, Cæsar."

" You—you mean it?"

" With all my heart and soul."

" Then so be it."

She came to me and held out her arms. I clasped her in mine, and we kissed one another. Then both of us sat down again, and there was silence. Only once she spoke.

"How soon shall we go?" she asked.

"In about three weeks or a month, I suppose," I answered.

We were sitting silent when we heard a step on the stairs. "Hark!" she said. "It's Max's step." She rose quickly and turned the lamp lower, then seated herself in shadow. "May I tell him about it now?" she asked.

"Yes—if it must be so."

"Yes, it must." She kissed her hand to me, saying, "Good-bye." The door opened, and Max von Sempach came in. Before he could greet me she began:

"Max, what do you think brings the King here to-day?"

Max professed himself at a loss.

"He's come about you," she said. "We've been talking about you."

"Have you? What about me?" he asked, going up to her. She rose and laid her hand on his arm.

"The King is going to give our side a turn," she said with a marvellous composure and even an appearance of gaiety.

"What?" cried Max. "Are you going to send Wetter to Paris, sire?"

"No," said I. "Not Wetter. He doesn't want it now, and anyhow he's not fit for it."

"He doesn't want it! Oh, but he does!"

"Max, you mustn't contradict the King. But one of our people is to have it. Guess who it is!"

He shrugged his shoulders.

"I don't know who it is if it's not Wetter."

"It's you," she said. "Isn't it, sire?"

"If he likes it," said I. "Do you like it?"

"Like it!" he exclaimed. "Oh, but- I can't believe it! Something of the sort has been the dream of my life."

"It is yours if you will have it," said I.

"And the dream of your life will come true," she said. "Fancy that! I didn't know it ever happened." And she glanced at me.

"Yes, the dream of his life shall come true," said I. "You're very fit for it, and I'm very glad to give it to one of your side."

"The King belongs to no party," said she. She paused and added, "And to no person. He stands apart and alone."

I hardly heeded Max's profuse thanks and honest open exultation.

"It's too good to be true," said he.

This has always seemed to me a strange little scene between us three. The accepted conventions of emotion required that it should raise in me and in her a feeling of remorse; for Max was so honest, so simple, so exclusively given over to gratitude. So far as I recollect, however, I had no such feeling, and I do not think that the Countess differed from me in this respect. I was envious of him, not because he took her with him (for he did not take her love), but simply because he had got something he liked, was very pleased, and in a good temper with the world and himself. The dream of his life, as he declared impetuously, was fulfilled. The dream of ours was shattered. How were we to reproach ourselves on his account? It would have been the Quixotry of conscience.

"I daresay you won't like it so much as you think," said I, with a childish desire to make him a little less comfortable.

"Oh, yes, I shall! And you'll like it, won't you?" He turned to his wife affectionately.

"As if I should let you take it if I didn't like it," she answered, smiling. "Think how I shall show off before all my good countrywomen in Paris!"

"I don't know how to thank your Majesty," said Max.

"I don't want any thanks. I haven't done it for thanks. I thought you the best man."

"No, no," he murmured. "I like to think it's partly friendship for my wife and me. Everybody will say so."

I looked up with a little start.

"I suppose they will," said I.

"Yes, you'll be handsomely abused."

"That'll be rather funny," I remarked almost unconsciously, as I looked across to the Countess, smiling.

"I mean—you don't mind my saying?" asked Max; and when I nodded, he went on, "They'll point out that you're turning to our side the moment that the Prince is dead. Yes, it will make a good deal of talk; they'll call it the beginning of a new era."

"Perhaps they'll be right," said she in a low voice.

I rose to my feet. I recognised the truth in what Max said, and it seemed to add a touch of irony that the situation had lacked. Hammerfeldt himself, if he looked down from heaven (as Victoria picturesquely suggested), would be amused at the interpretation put on my action; it would suit his humour well to see the great sacrifice that I had made at the shrine of his teaching twisted into a repudiation of his views and a prompt defiance of the authority which he in life had exercised. His partisans would be furious with me, they would say I flouted his memory. That would be strange to hear when the figure of the Countess was still fresh before my eyes, and the sound of her sobs rang yet in my ears. I shrugged my shoulders.

"There are harder things to bear than a little abuse and a little gossip. I can't help it if they don't understand the grounds of my action."

"It's so soon after the Prince's death," said Max.

"The thing could not be delayed; it had to be done at once," said I.

I moved toward her to take my leave. She was standing close by her husband's side; her face was still in shadow.

"We shall have so much to do before we go," she said, "that we can hope to see very little more of your Majesty."

"Yes," broke in Max, "we must go down and arrange everything on the estate; we're going to be away for so long."

"Oh, but I shall hope to see you again. You must come and say good-bye to me. Now I must leave you."

"Good-bye, and again thank you," she said.

She came with me to the door, and down the stairs. Max walked in front, and went on to open the door and see that my carriage was in readiness. For an instant I clasped her hand.

"I shan't see you again," she whispered. "Good-bye."

I left her standing on the lowest step, her head proudly erect and a smile on her lips. It was as she said, I did not see her again; for they went to the country the next day, and when Max came to take a formal leave of me she excused herself on the score of indisposition.

To complete the picture I ought to describe the wrath of those who had formed Hammerfeldt's *entourage*, the gleeful satisfaction of the opposing party, the articles in the journals, the speculations, guesses, and assertions as to my reasons, temper, intention, and expressions. I should paint also my mother's mingled annoyance and relief, vexation that I favoured the Liberals, and joy that the Countess von Sempach went to Paris; Victoria's absolute bewilderment and ineffectual divings and fishings for anything that might throw light on so mysterious a matter; William Adolphus' intense self-complacency in my following of his advice, accompanied by a patronizing rebuke for my having thought it necessary to " do it so abruptly." All these good people, as they acted their little parts and filled their corners of the stage, had their own ideas of the meaning of the play and their own estimate of the importance of the characters. They all fitted into their places in my conception of it, so that not one was superfluous; all were needed, and all worked in unconsciousness to heighten the irony, to point the comedy, and to frame the tragedy in its most effective, most incongruous setting. For in this real life the stage-manager takes no pains to have all things in harmony nor to lead us through gradual and well-attempered emotions to the climax of exalted feeling, nor to banish from our sight all that jars and clashes with the pathos of the piece. Rather he works by contrasts, by strange juxtapositions, by surprises, careless how many of the audience follow his mind, not heeding dissatisfaction or pleasure, recking nothing whether we applaud or damn his play.

Well, here was I, Augustin, twenty years of age, and determined to reign alone. And my Countess was gone to Paris. Did you look down from heaven, old Hammerfeldt? Victoria thought you did. Well, then, was not the boy's work absurdly, extravagantly, bravely done?

CHAPTER XIV.

PLEASURE TAKES LEAVE TO PROTEST.

DURING the months that followed the departure
of the Sempachs I engaged myself busily in public
affairs, in the endeavour to gain better acquaintance
with the difficult trade which was mine. I do not
throw off impressions lightly, and I was disinclined
for gaiety, or for more society than the obligations
of my position demanded. My mother approved of
my zeal; a convinced partisan, she enjoyed that happy
confidence in her own views which makes people
certain that everybody can study their opinions only
to embrace them. Attention is the sole preliminary
to conversion. I will not speak further of this matter here than to say that I was doomed to disappoint
Princess Heinrich in this respect. I am glad of it.
The world moves, and although it is very difficult for
persons so artificially situated as I have been to move
with it, yet we can and must move after it, lumbering
along in its wake more or less slowly and awkwardly.
We hold on this tenure; if we do not perform it—
well, we end in country-houses in England.

It was, I suppose, owing to these occupations that
I failed to notice the relations between Victoria and
her husband until they had reached a rather acute
crisis. Either from a desire to re-enforce the number
of my guardian angels, or merely because they found

themselves very comfortable, the pair had taken up a practically permanent residence with me. I was very glad to have them, and assigned them a handsome set of apartments quite at the other end of the house. Here they lived in considerable splendour, seeing a great deal of company and assuming the position of social leaders. Victoria at least was admirably suited to play such a part, and I certainly did not grudge it to her; for my mother I can not speak so confidently. William Adolphus, having abandoned his military pursuits, led an idle lounging life. In consequence he grew indolent; his stoutness increased. I mention this personal detail merely because I believe that it had a considerable influence on Victoria's feelings toward him. Her varied nature included a vivid streak of the romantic, and with every expansion in his belt and every multiplication of the folds of his chin William Adolphus came to satisfy this instinct in her less and less. She sought other interests; she contrived to combine very dexterously the *femme incomprise* with the leader of fashion; she posed as a patron of letters and the arts, indulging in intellectual flirtations with professors and other learned folk. There was no harm in this, and William Adolphus would not have been in the smallest degree disturbed by it. He had all the self-confidence given by a complete want of imagination. Unhappily, however, she began to treat him with something very like contempt, allowed him to perceive that his company did not satisfy her spiritual and mental requirements, and showed herself more than willing that he should choose his own associates and dispose of his own time. He was not resentful; he confessed that his wife's friends bored him, and availed himself amply and good-naturedly of

the liberty which her expressed preferences afforded
him. He devoted himself to his sport, his dogs, and
his horses; this was all very well. He also became
a noted patron of the lighter forms of the drama;
this, for reasons that I shall indicate directly, was
not quite so well. Out of this last taste of William
Adolphus came the strained relations between his
wife and himself to which I have referred.

Among those who have crossed my path few have
stamped themselves more clearly on my memory
than Coralie Mansoni. She was by no means so
great a force in my life as was the Countess von
Sempach, but she remains a singularly vivid image
before my eyes. Born heaven knew where, and of
parents whom I doubt whether she herself could
name, seeming to hail from the borderland of Italy
and France, a daughter of the Riviera, she had
strayed and tumbled through a youth of which she
would speak in moments of expansion. I, however,
need say nothing of it. When I saw her first she
was playing a small part in a light opera at Forstadt.
A few weeks later she had assumed leading *rôles*,
and was the idol of the young men. She was then
about twenty-three, tall, dark, of full figure, doomed
to a brevity of beauty, but at the moment magnifi-
cence itself. Every intellectual gift she appeared to
lack, except a strangely persistent resolution of purpose and an admirably lucid conception of her own
interest. She was not in the least brilliant or even
amusing in general conversation. She worshipped
her own beauty; she owed to it all she was, and paid
the debt with a defiant assertion of its supremacy.
None could contradict her. She was very lazy as
regards physical exertion, extremely fond of eating and drinking, a careful manager of her money.

All this sounds, and was, very unattractive. On the other side of the account may be put a certain simplicity, an indolent kindness, a desire to make folks comfortable, and (what I liked most) a mental honesty which caused her to assess both herself and other people with a nearness to her and their real value that was at times absolutely startling. It seemed as though a person, otherwise neither clever nor of signally high character, had been gifted with a *clairvoyance* which allowed her to read hearts, and a relentless fine sincerity that forced her to declare what she read to all who cared to listen to her. Whatever she did or did not in that queer life of hers, she never flattered man or woman, and fashioned no false image of herself.

William Adolphus made her the rage, so strangely things fall out. He went five nights running to see her. Next week came a new piece, with Coralie in the chief part. My brother-in-law had sent for her to his box. He was a Prince, a great man, exalted, of what seemed boundless wealth. Coralie was languidly polite. William Adolphus' broad face must have worn a luxurious smile. He did Coralie the honour of calling on her at her pretty villa, where she lived with her aunt-in-law (oddly selected relationship!), Madame Briande. He was received with acquiescence; enthusiasm was not among Coralie's accomplishments. However, she lazily drawled out the opinion that *Monseigneur* was *bon enfant*. William Adolphus mounted into the seventh heaven. He came home and did not tell his wife where he had been. This silence was significant. As a rule, if he but visited the tailor or had his hair cut, he told everybody all about it. He had really no idea that some things were uninteresting. I do not

mean to say that this trait constitutes exactly a peculiarity.

My brother-in-law and I were very good friends. He proposed that I should accompany him to the theatre, and afterward be his guest, for he was to entertain Coralie at supper.

"But where?" I asked with a smile.

"There is an excellent restaurant where I have a private room," he confessed.

"And they don't know you?"

"Of course they know me."

"I mean, where they would be willing to know neither you nor me."

"Oh, I see what you mean. That's all right."

So I went with William Adolphus. Several men whom I knew were present, among them Wetter and M. le Vicomte de Varvilliers, second secretary of the French Embassy and a mirror of fashion. We were quite informal. Varvilliers sat on my left and employed himself in giving me an account of my right-hand neighbour Coralie. I listened absently, for the sight of Wetter had stirred other thoughts in my mind. I had not yet spoken to Coralie; my brother-in-law monopolized her.

"I ought to speak to her, I suppose?" I said to Varvilliers at last.

"A thousand pardons for engrossing your Majesty!" he cried. "Yes, I think you should."

William Adolphus' voice flowed on in the account of a match between one of his horses and one of somebody else's. I turned to follow Varvilliers' advice; rather to my surprise, I found Coralie's eyes fixed on me with an appearance of faint amusement. She began to address me without waiting for me to say anything.

12

"Why do you listen to what Varvilliers says about me instead of finding out about me yourself?" she asked.

"How do you know he talked of you, mademoiselle?"

She shrugged her shoulders and returned to her salad. William Adolphus asked her a question; she nodded without looking up from the salad. I began to eat my salad.

"It's a good salad," I observed, after a few mouthfuls.

"Very," said Coralie; she turned her great eyes on me. "And, *mon Dieu*, what a rare thing!" she added with a sigh.

Probably she would expect a touch of gallantry.

"The perfection of everything is rare," said I, looking pointedly in her face. She put up her hand, lightly fingered the curls on her forehead, smiled at me, and turned again to her salad. I laughed. She looked up again quickly.

"You laugh at me?" she asked, not resentfully, but with an air of frank inquiry.

"No, at the human race, mademoiselle. It is we, not you, who excite laughter."

She regarded me with apparent curiosity, and gradually began to smile. "Why?" she asked, just showing her level white teeth.

"You haven't learned yet?"

William Adolphus began to speak to her. You would have sworn she had a deaf ear that side. She had finished her salad and sat turned toward me. If a very white shoulder could at all console my brother-in-law, he had an admirable view of one. Apparently he was not content; he pushed his chair back with a noise and called to me:

"Shall we smoke? I have eaten enough."

"With all my heart," I answered.

"In fact he has eaten too much," observed Coralie, by no means in an "aside." "He and I—we both eat too much. He is fat already. I shall be."

"You are talkative to-night, mademoiselle," said Varvilliers, who was offering her a cigarette.

"I believe there is to-night some one worth talking to," she retorted.

"Alas, and not last night?" he cried in affected despair.

I, however, thinking that it would ill become me to eat my brother-in-law's supper and then spoil his sport, bowed to the lady and crossed over to where Wetter was standing. Near him was a group of young men laughing and talking with Madame Briande; he seemed to pay little heed to their chatter. Varvilliers followed me, and William Adolphus sat down by Coralie. But I had not been talking to Wetter more than two minutes when the lady rose, left my brother-in-law, and came to join our group. She took her stand close by me. Half attracted and half repelled by her, young enough still to be shy, I was much embarrassed: the other men were smiling—I must except William Adolphus—and Varvilliers whispered to me:

"*Les beaux yeux de votre couronne, sire.*"

Coralie overheard his warning; she was not in the least put out.

"Don't disturb yourself," she said to Varvilliers. "The King is not a fool; he doesn't suppose that people forget what he is."

"You've judged him on short acquaintance," said Varvilliers, rather vexed.

"It's my way; and why shouldn't I give my opinion?"

Wetter laughed, and said to the Frenchman:

"You had better not ask for your character, I think, Vicomte."

"Heavens, no!" cried he. "Come, I see Monseigneur all alone!"

"You are right," said Coralie. "Go and talk to him. The King and I will talk."

They went off, Wetter laughing, Varvilliers still a little ruffled by his encounter. Coralie passed her arm through mine and led me to a sofa. I had recovered my composure, was interested, and amused.

"Briande," she said suddenly, "is always deploring my stupidity. 'How will you get on,' she says, 'without wit? Men are ruled by wit though they are won by faces.' So she says. Well, I don't know. Wit is not in my line." She looked at me half questioningly, half defiantly.

"I perceive no deficiency in the quality, mademoiselle," said I.

"Then you have not known witty women," she retorted tranquilly. "But I am not altogether dull. I am not like Monseigneur there."

"My brother-in-law?"

"So I am told."

As she said this she looked again at me and began to laugh. I laughed also. But I could not very well discuss William Adolphus with her.

"What man do you desire to rule with this wit?" I asked.

"One can't tell when it might be useful," said she, with a barely perceptible smile.

"Surely beauty is more powerful?"

"With Monseigneur?"

" Oh, never mind Monseigneur."

" But not with men of another kind."

" Some men are not to be ruled by any means."

" You think so? "

" Take Wetter now? "

" I would give him a week's resistance."

" Varvilliers? "

" A day."

I did not put the third question, but I looked at her with a smile. She saw my meaning, of course, but she did not tell me how long a resistance she would predict for me. I thought that I had talked enough to her, and, since she would not let me alone, I determined to take my leave. I wished her good-night. She received my adieu with marked indifference.

" I am very glad to have made your acquaintance," said I.

" Why, yes," she answered. " You are thinking that I am a strange creature, a new experience," and with this she turned away, although I was about to speak again.

Varvilliers' way lay in the same direction as mine, and I took him with me. He chatted gaily as we went. What I liked in the Vicomte was his confident denial of life's alleged seriousness. He seemed much amused at the situation which he proceeded to unfold to me. According to him, Wetter was passionately, my brother-in-law inanely, enamoured of Coralie. Wetter was ready to ruin himself in purse and prospects for her, and would gladly marry her. William Adolphus would be capable of defying his wife, his mother-in-law, and public opinion. But Coralie, he explained, cared little for either. Wetter could give her nothing, from William Adolphus she had already gained the advancement which it was in his power to secure for her.

"She wanted something new, so she made him bring your Majesty," he ended, laughing.

"Was my brother-in-law unwilling?"

"Oh, no. He didn't understand," laughed Varvilliers. "He was proud to bring you."

"It's rather awkward for me. I suppose I oughtn't to have come?"

"Ah, sire, when we have enjoyed ourselves, let us not be ungrateful. She amused you?"

"She certainly interested me."

He shrugged his shoulders. "What more do you want?" he seemed to ask. But I was wondering whether I should be justified in lending countenance to these distractions of William Adolphus. The Frenchman's quick wit overtook my thoughts.

"If you wish to rescue the Prince from danger, sire," he said, laughing, "you can't do better than come often."

"It seems to me that I'm in danger of quarrelling either with my sister or with my brother-in-law."

"If I were you, I should feel myself in a danger more delightful."

"But why not yourself equally, Vicomte? Aren't you in love with her?"

"Not I," he answered, with a laugh and a shake of his head.

"But why not?" I asked, laughing also.

"Can you ask? There is but one possible reason for a man's not being in love with Coralie Mansoni."

"Tell me it, Vicomte."

"Because he has been, sire."

"A good safeguard, but of no use to me."

"Why, no, not at present," answered Varvilliers.

The carriage drew up at his lodgings. I was not inclined for sleep, and readily acceded to his request that I should pay him a visit. Having dismissed the carriage (I was but a little way from my own house), I mounted the stairs and found myself in a very snug room. He put me in an armchair and gave me a cigar. We talked long and intimately as the hours of the night rolled on. He spoke, half in reminiscence, half in merry rhapsody, of the joys of living, the delight of throwing the reins on the neck of youth. As I looked at his trim figure, his handsome face, merry eyes, and dashing air, all that he said seemed very reasonable and very right; there was a good defence for it at the bar of nature's tribunal. It was honest too, free from cant, affectation, and pretence; it was a recognition of facts, and enlisted truth on its side. It needed no arguing, and he gave it none; the spirit that inspired also vindicated it. I could not help recalling the agonies and struggles which my passion for the Countess von Sempach had occasioned me. At first I thought that I would tell him about this affair, but I found myself ashamed. And I was ashamed because I had resisted the passion; it would have been very easy to tell him had I yielded. But the merry eyes would twinkle in amusement at my high-strung folly, as I had seen them twinkle at my brother-in-law's stolidity. He said something incidentally which led me to fancy that he had heard about the Countess and had received a mistaken impression of the facts; I did not correct what appeared to be his idea. I neither confirmed nor contradicted it. I said to myself that it was nothing to me what notion he had of my conduct; in reality I did not desire him to know the truth. I clung to the conviction that I could justify what had seemed my hard-won victory, but I did not feel as though I could justify it to him. He would laugh, be a little puzzled, and dismiss the matter as inexplicable. His own creed was not swathed in clouds, nor dim, nor hard clearly to see and picture; it was all very straightforward. Properly it was no creed; it was a course of action based on a mode of feeling which neither demanded nor was patient of defence or explanation. The circumstances of my life were such that never before had I been brought into contact with a similar temperament or a similar practice. When they were thus suddenly presented to me they seemed endowed with a most attractive simplicity, with a naturalness, with what I must call a wholesomeness; the objections I felt to be overstrained, unreal, morbid. Varvilliers' feet were on firm ground; on what shaking uncertain bog of mingled impulses, emotions, fancies, and delusions might not those who blamed him be found themselves to stand?

I am confident that he spoke without premeditation, with no desire to win a proselyte, merely as man to man, in unaffected intimacy. I think that he was rather sorry for me, having detected a gloominess in my view of life and a tendency to moody and fretful introspection. Once or twice he referred, in passing jest, to the difference of national characteristics, the German tendency to make love by crying (so he put it) as contrasted with the laughing philosophy of his own country. At the end he apologized for talking so much, and pointed out to me a photograph of Coralie that stood on the mantelpiece more than half-hidden by letters and papers, saying, " I suppose she set me off; somehow she seems to me a sort of embodiment of the thing."

It was three o'clock when I left him; even then I went reluctantly, traversing again in my mind the field that his tongue had easily and lightly covered, and reverting to the girl who, as he said, was a sort of embodiment of the thing. The phrase was definite enough for its purpose, and struck home with an undeniable truth. He and she were the sort of people to live in that sort of world, and to stand as its representatives. A feeling came over me that it was a fair fine world, where life need not be a struggle, where a man need not live alone, where he would not be striving always after what he could never achieve, waging always a war in which he should never conquer, staking all his joys against most uncertain shadowy prizes, which to win would bring no satisfaction. I cried out suddenly, as I walked by myself through the night, " There's no pleasure in my life." That protest summed up my wrongs. There was no pleasure in my life. There was everything else, but not that, not pure, unmixed, simple pleasure. Had I no right to some? I was very tired of trying to fill my place, of subordinating myself to my position, of being always Augustin the King. I was weary of my own ideal. I felt that I ought to be allowed to escape from it sometimes, to be, as it were, *incognito* in soul as well as in body, so that what I thought and did should not be reckoned as the work of the King's mind or the act of the King's hand. I envied intensely the lot and the temper of my friend Varvilliers. When I reached the palace and entered it, it seemed to me as though I were returning to a prison. Its walls shut me off from that free existence whose sweetness I had tasted, and forbade me to roam in the fields whither youth beckoned and curiosity lured me. That joy could never be mine.

My burden was ever with me; the woman I had loved was gone; the girl I must be made husband to was soon to come. I was not and could not be as other young men.

That all this, the conversation with Varvilliers, its effect on me, my restless discontent and angry protests against my fate, should follow on meeting Coralie Mansoni at supper will not seem strange to anybody who remembers her.

CHAPTER XV.

THE HAIR-DRESSER WAITS.

WHEN my years and my mood are considered, it may appear that I had enough to do in keeping my own life in the channel of wisdom and discretion. So it seemed to myself, and I was rather amused at being called upon to exert a good influence or even a wholesome authority over William Adolphus; it was so short a time since he had been summoned to perform a like office toward me. Yet after breakfast the next day Victoria came to me, dressed in a subdued style and speaking in low tones; she has always possessed a dramatic instinct. She had been, it seemed, unable to remain unconscious of the gossip afoot; of her own feelings she preferred to say nothing (she repeated this observation several times); what she thought about was the credit of the family; and of the family, she took leave to remind me, I was (I think she said, by God's will) the head. I could not resist remarking how times had changed; less than a year ago she had sent William Adolphus, sober, staid, panoplied in the armour of contented marriage, to wrestle with my errant desires. Victoria flushed and became just a little less meek.

"What's the good of going back to that?" she asked.

"None; it is merely amusing," said I.

The flush deepened.

"Will you allow me to be insulted?" she cried.

"Let us be cool. You've yourself to thank for this, Victoria. Why aren't you pleasanter to him?"

"Oh, he's—I'm all I ought to be to him."

"I don't know what you are to him, you're very little with him."

I suppose that these altercations assume much the same character in all families. They are necessarily vulgar, and the details of them need not be recalled. For myself I must confess that my sister found me in a perverse mood; she, on her side, was in the unreasonable temper of a woman who expects fidelity but does not show appreciation. I suggested this point for her consideration.

"Well, if I don't appreciate him, whose fault was it I married him?" she cried.

"I don't know. Whose fault is it that I'm going to marry Elsa Bartenstein? Whose fault is anything? Whose fault is it that Coralie Mansoni is a pretty woman?"

"I've never seen her."

"Ah, you wouldn't think her pretty if you had."

Victoria looked at me for a few seconds; then she suddenly drew up a low chair and sat down at my feet. She turned her face up toward mine and took my hand. Well, we never really disliked one another, Victoria and I.

"Mother's so horrid about it," she said.

It was an appeal to an old time-honoured alliance, sanctified by common sorrows, endeared by stolen victories shared in fearful secrecy.

"She says it's my fault, just as you do. But you know her way."

I became conscious that what I had said would

be, in fact, singularly hard to bear when it fell from Princess Heinrich's judicial lips.

" She told me that I had lost him, and that I had only myself to thank for it; and—she said it was perhaps partly because my complexion had lost its freshness." Victoria paused, and then ended, " That's a lie, you know."

I seemed to be young again; we were again laying our heads together, with intent to struggle against our mother. I cared not a groat for William Adolphus, but it would be pleasant to me to help my sister to bring him back to his bearings; and the more pleasant in view of Princess Heinrich's belief that the things could not be done.

" As far as being pleasant to him goes," Victoria resumed, " I don't believe that the creature's pleasant to him either. At least he came home in a horribly bad temper last night."

" And what did you say to him? "

" Oh, I—I told him what I thought."

" How we all waste opportunities! " I reflected. " You ought to have soothed him down. He was annoyed last night."

Of course she asked how I knew it, and in the fresh-born candour of revived alliance I told her the story of our evening. I have observed before on the curious fact that women who think nothing of their husbands are nevertheless annoyed when other people agree in their estimate. Victoria was very indignant with Coralie for slighting William Adolphus and showing a ready disposition to transfer her attentions to me.

" It's only because you're king," she said. But she did not allow her vexation to obscure her perception. Her frown gave place to a smile as she looked up, saying: "It would be rather fun if you flirted with her."

I raised my eyebrows. Whence came this new complaisance toward my flirtations?

"Just enough, I mean, to disgust William Adolphus," she added. "Then, as soon as he'd given up, you could stop, you know. Everything would be right then."

"Except mother, you mean."

"Why, yes, except mother. And she'd be splendidly wrong," laughed Victoria.

Nobody who studies himself honestly or observes his neighbours with attention will deny value to an excuse because it may be merely plausible. After all, to wear even a transparent garment is not quite the same thing as to go naked. I do not maintain that Victoria's suggestion contributed decisively to the prosecution of my acquaintance with Coralie Mansoni, but it filled a gap in the array of reasons and impulses which were leading me on, and gave to the matter an air of sport and adventure most potent in attraction for such a mood as mine. I was in rebellion against the limits of my position and the repression of my manner of life. To play a prank like this suited my humour exactly. When Victoria left me, I sent word of my intention to be present at Coralie's theatre that evening, and invited William Adolphus to join me in my box. I received the answer that he would come.

When we arrived at the theatre Coralie was already on the stage. She was singing a song; she had a very fine voice; her delivery and air, empty of real feeling, were full nevertheless of a sensuous attraction. My brother-in-law laid his elbows on the front of the box and stared down at her; I sat a little back, and, after watching the scene for a few moments, began to look at the house. Immediately opposite me I saw Varvilliers with a party of ladies and men; he bowed and smiled as I caught his eye. In another box I saw Wetter, gazing at the singer as intently as William Adolphus himself. There must certainly be something in a girl who exercised power over two men so different. And Wetter was a person of importance and prominence, accepted as a political leader, and consequently a fine target for gossip; his feelings must be strongly engaged before he exposed himself to comment. I fell to studying his face; he was pale; when I took my glass I could see the nervous frown on his brow and the restless gleam of his eyes. By my side William Adolphus was chuckling with bovine satisfaction at an allusion in Coralie's song; his last night's pique seemed forgotten. I leaned forward and looked again at Coralie. She saw me and sang the next verse straight at me. (She did the same thing once more in later days.) I saw people's heads turn toward my box, and drew back behind the shelter of the hangings.

At the end of the act my brother-in-law turned to me, blew his nose, and ejaculated, "Superb!" I nodded my head. "Splendid!" said he. I nodded again. He launched on a catalogue of Coralie's attractions, but seemed to check himself rather suddenly.

"I don't suppose she's your sort, though," he remarked.

"Why not?" I asked with a smile.

"Oh, I don't know. You like clever women who can talk and so on. She'd bore you to death in an hour, Augustin."

" Would she?" said I innocently. I was amused
at William Adolphus' simple cunning. " I daresay I
should bore her too."

" Perhaps you would," he chuckled. " Only she
wouldn't tell you so, of course."

" But Wetter doesn't seem to bore her," I observed.

" Good God, doesn't he?" cried my brother-
in-law.

There were limits to the amusement to be got
out of him. I yawned and looked across the house
again. Wetter's place was empty. I drew William
Adolphus' attention to the fact.

" I wonder if the fellow's gone behind?" he said
uneasily.

" We'll go after the next act."

" You'll go?"

" Of course I shall send and ask permission."
William Adolphus looked puzzled and gloomy.

" I didn't know you cared for that sort of thing;
I mean the theatre and all that."

" We haven't a Coralie Mansoni here every day,"
I reminded him. " I don't care for the ordinary run,
but she's something remarkable, isn't she?"

He muttered a few words and turned away. A
moment later Varvilliers knocked at the door of my
box and entered. Here was a good messenger for
me. I sent him to ask whether Coralie would receive me after the next act. He went off on his
errand laughing.

I need not record the various stages and the gradual progress of my acquaintance with Coralie Mansoni. It would be for the most part a narrative of
foolish actions and a repetition of trivial conversa-
tions. I have shown how I came to enter on it, led

by a spirit of rebellion and the love of a joke, weary
of the repression that was partly inevitable, partly
self-imposed, glad to find an outlet for my youthful
impulses in a direction where my action would in-
volve no political danger. On one good result I can
pride myself; I was undoubtedly the instrument of
sending my brother-in-law back to his wife a hum-
bled and repentant man. Coralie had no scruple
about allowing him to perceive that her attentions
had been paid to his rank, not to himself; and his
rank was now eclipsed. A few days of sulking was
followed by a violent outburst; but my position was
too strong. He could not quarrel seriously with his
wife's brother on such a ground. He returned to
Victoria, and, I had no doubt, received the castiga-
tion which he certainly deserved. My interest in him
vanished as he vanished from the society that centred round Mlle. Mansoni. At the same time my
share in his defeat and humiliation left a soreness
between us which lasted for a long while.

I myself had by this time fallen into a severe conflict of feeling. My temperament was not like Varvilliers'. For an hour or two, when I was exhilarated
with society and cheered by wine, I could seem to
myself such as he naturally and permanently was.
But I was not a native of the clime. I raised myself
to those heights of unmoral serenity by an effort and
an artifice. He forgot himself easily. I was always
examining myself. That same motive, or instinct, or
tradition of feeling (I do not know how best to describe it) on whose altar I had sacrificed my first
passion was still strong in me. I did not fear that
Coralie would or could exercise a political influence
over me, but I was loth that she should possess a
control of any sort. I clung obstinately to the con-

13

ception of myself as standing alone, as being independent and under the power of nobody in any respect. This was to me a stronger check than the restraint of accepted morality. Looking back on the matter, and judging myself as I should judge any young man, I am confident that my passion would easily have swept away the ordinary scruples. It was my other conscience, my King's conscience, that raised the barrier and protracted the resistance. Here is another case of that reaction of my position on myself which has been such a feature of my life. Varvilliers' unreasoned philosophy did not cover this point. Here I had to fight out the question for myself. It was again a struggle between the man and the king, between a natural impulse and the strength of an intellectual conception. I perceived with mingled amusement and bitterness how entirely Varvilliers failed to appreciate the condition of my mind or .to conceal his surprise at my alternate hot and cold fits, urgency followed by a drawing-back, eagerness to be moving at moments when nothing could be done, succeeded by refusals to stir when the road was clear. I believe that he came to have a very poor opinion of me as a man of the world; but his kindness toward me never varied.

But there was one to whom my mind was an open book, who read easily and plainly every thought of it, because it was written in the same characters as was his own. The politician who risked his future, the debtor who every day incurred new expenses, the devotee of principles who sacrificed them for his passion, the deviser of schemes who ruined them at the demand of his desires, here was the man who could understand the heart of his King. Wetter was my sympathizer, and Wetter was my rival. The relations between us in those days were strange. We did not quarrel, we felt a friendliness for one another. Each knew the price the other paid or must pay as well as he knew his own price. But we were rivals. Varvilliers was wrong when he said that Coralie cared nothing about Wetter. She cared, although it was in a peculiar fashion that she cared. Truly he could give her little, but he was to her a sign and a testimony of her power, even as I myself in another way. Mine was the high rank, the great position. In conquering me lay the open and notorious triumph, but she was not insensible to the more private joy and secret exultation that came to her from dominating a ruling mind, and filling with her own image a head capacious enough to hold imperial policies and shape the destinies of kingdoms. Wetter and I, each in our way, broke through the crust of seemingly consistent frivolity that was on her, and down to a deep-seated tendency toward romance and the love of power. She could not rule directly, but she could rule rulers. I am certain that some such idea was in her head, alloying, or at least refining, a grosser self-interest. Therefore Wetter, no less than I, was of value to her. She would not willingly have let him go, even although he could give her nothing and she did not care for him in the only sense of which my friend the Vicomte took account. I came to realize how it was between her and him before very long, and to see how the same ultimate instinct of her nature made her long to gather both him and me into her net. Thus she would have bowing before her the highest and the strongest heads in Forstadt. That she so analyzed and reasoned out her wishes it would be absurd to suppose, but we— he and I—performed the task for her. Each knew that the other was at work on it; each chafed that she would consent to be but half his; each desired to rule alone, not to be one of two that were ruled. All this had been dimly foreshadowed to me when I sat in the theatre, looking now at Coralie as she sang her song, now at Wetter's frowning brows and tight-set lips. I must add that my position was rendered peculiarly difficult by the fact that Wetter not only owed me deference, but was still in my debt for the money I had lent him. He had refused to consider it a gift, but was, and became every day more, incapable of repaying it.

We were at luncheon at her villa one day, we three, and with us, of course, Madame Briande, an exceedingly well-informed and tactful little woman. Coralie had been very silent and (as usual) attentive to her meal. The rest had chattered on many subjects. Suddenly she spoke.

"It has been very amusing," she said, with a little yawn that ended in a rather weary smile. "For my part I can conceive only one thing that could increase the entertainment."

"What's that, Coralie?" asked Madame Briande.

Coralie waved her right hand toward me and her left toward Wetter.

"Why, that we should have for audience and as spectators of our little feast your subjects, sire, and, monsieur, your followers."

Clearly Coralie had been maturing this rather startling speech for some time; she launched it with an evident enjoyment of its malice. A moment of astonished silence followed; madame's tact was strained beyond its uttermost resources; she smiled nervously and said nothing; Wetter turned red. I looked full in Coralie's eyes, drained my glass of cognac, and laughed.

"But why should that be amusing?" I asked. "And, at least, shall we not add to our imaginary audience the crowd of your admirers?"

"As you will," said she with a shrug. "Whomever we add they would see nothing but two gentlemen getting under the table, oh, so quickly!"

Madame Briande became visibly distressed.

"Is it not so?" drawled Coralie in lazy enjoyment of her excursion.

"Why," said I, "I should most certainly invoke the shelter of your tablecloth, mademoiselle. A king must avoid being misunderstood."

"I thought so," said she with a long look at me. "And you, monsieur?" she added, turning to Wetter.

"I should not get under the table," said he. He strove to render his tone light, but his voice quivered with suppressed passion.

"You wouldn't?" she asked. "You'd sit here before them all?"

"Yes," said he.

Madame Briande rose. Her evident intention was to break up the party. Coralie took no notice; we men sat on, opposite one another, with her between us on the third side of the small square table.

"Must not a politician avoid—being misunderstood?" she asked Wetter.

"Unless there is something else that he values more," was the reply.

She turned to me, smiling still.

"Would not that be so with a king also?"

"Certainly, if there could be such a thing."

"But you think there could not?"

"I can't call such a thing to mind, mademoiselle."

"Ah, you can't call it to mind! No, you can't call it to mind. It seems to me that there is a difference, then, between politicians and kings."

Madame Briande was moving about the room in evident discomfort. Wetter was sitting with his hand clenched on the table and his eyes downcast.

Coralie looked long and intently at him. Then she turned her eyes on me. I took out a cigarette, lit it, and smiled at her.

"You—you would get under the table?" she asked me.

"You catch my meaning perfectly."

"Then aren't you ashamed to sit at it?"

"Yes," said I, and laughed.

"Ah!" she cried, shaking her fist at me, and herself laughing. Then she leaned over toward me and whispered, "You shall retract that."

Wetter looked up and saw her whispering to me, and laughing as she whispered. He frowned, and I saw his hand tremble on the table. Though I laughed and fenced with her and defied her, I was myself in some excitement. I seemed to be playing a match; and I had confidence in my game.

Wetter spoke abruptly in a harsh but carefully restrained voice.

"It is not for me to question the King's account of himself," he said, "but so far as I am concerned your question did me a wrong. Openly I come here, openly I leave here. All know why I come, and what I desire in coming. I ask nothing better than to declare it before all the city."

She rose and made him a curtsey, then she gave a slight yawn and observed:

"So now we know just where we are."

"The King has defined his position with great accuracy," said Wetter with an open sneer.

"Yes? What is it?" she asked.

"His own words are enough; mine could add no clearness—and——"

"Might give offence?" she asked.

"It is possible," said he.

"Then we come to this: which is better, a king under the table or a politician at it?" She burst out laughing.

Madame Briande had fled to a remote corner. Wetter was in the throes of excitement. A strange coolness and recklessness now possessed me. I was insensible of everything at this moment except the impulse of rivalry and the desire for victory. Nothing in the scene had power to repel me, my eyes were blind to everything of ugly aspect in it.

"To define the question, mademoiselle, should be but a preliminary to answering it," said I, with a bow.

"I would answer it this minute, sire, but——"

"You hesitate, perhaps?"

"Oh, no; but my hair-dresser is waiting for me."

"Let no such trifle detain you then," I cried. "For I, even I the coward, had sooner——"

"Be misunderstood?"

"Why, precisely. I had sooner be misunderstood than that your hair should not be perfectly dressed at the theatre."

Wetter rose to his feet. He said "Good-bye" to Coralie, not a word more. To me he bowed very low and very formally. I returned his salutation with a cool nod. As he turned to the door Coralie cried:

"I shall see you at supper, *mon cher?*"

He turned his head and looked at her.

"I don't know," he said.

"Very well. I like uncertainty. We will hope."

He went out. I stood facing her for a moment.

"Well?" said she, looking in my eyes, and seeming to challenge an expression of opinion.

"You are pleased with yourself?"

"Yes."

"You have done some mischief."

"How much?"

"I don't know. But you love uncertainty."

"True, true. And you seem to think that I love candour."

"Don't you?"

"I think that I love everything and everybody in the world except you."

I laughed again. I knew that I had triumphed.

"Behold your decision," I cried, "and the hair-dresser still waits!"

She did not answer me. She stood there smiling. I took her hand and kissed it with much and even affected gallantry. Then I went and paid a like attention to Madame Briande. As the little woman made her curtsey she turned alarmed and troubled eyes up to me.

"Oh, *mon Dieu!*" she murmured.

"Till to-night," smiled Coralie.

CHAPTER XVI.

I was reading the other day the memoirs of an eminent English man of letters, now dead. He had paid a long visit to Forstadt, and had much to say (sometimes, I think, in a vein of veiled irony) about Victoria, her literary tastes and her literary circle. Finding amusement enough to induce me to turn over a few more pages, I came on the following passage:

"With the King himself I conversed once only; but I saw him often and heard much about him. He was then twenty-four—a tall and very thin young man, with dark brown hair and a small mustache of a lighter tint. His nose was aquiline, his eyes rather deep set, his face long and inclining to the hatchet-shape. He had beautiful hands, of which he was said to be proud. He stooped a little when walking, but displayed considerable dignity of carriage. He was accused of haughtiness, except toward a few intimates. Unquestionably his late adviser, Hammerfeldt, had imbued him with some notions as to his position which it is hardly unjust to call mediæval. A wit, or would-be wit, said of him that he postulated God in order to legitimize the powers of Augustin, his deputy. Certain persons very closely acquainted with him (I withhold names) gave a curi-

ous account of his character. Usually he was re-
served and even secretive, cautious, cold, and free
from enthusiasms and follies alike. But at times he
appeared to be taken with moods of strong feeling.
Then he would speak freely to the first person who
might be by, was eager for merriment and dissipa-
tion, not fastidious as to how he came by what he
wanted, seeming forgetful of the sterner rule by
which his daily life was governed. A reaction would
generally follow, and the King would appear to take
a revenge on himself by acid and savagely humorous
comments on his own acts and on the companions of
his hours of relaxation. So far as I studied him for
myself, I was led to conclude that he possessed a very
impressionable and passionate temperament, but contrived, in general, to keep it in repression. There
were one or two scandals related about him; but
when we consider his position and temptations, we
must give credit either to his virtues or to his discretion that such stories were not more numerous.
I liked him and thought well of him, but I do think
that he enjoyed a disposition likely to result in a
happy life for himself. He was said to have great
attractions for women; but I am not aware that he
admitted persons of either sex to his confidence or
friendship. He was, I imagine, jealous of even ap-
pearing to be under any influence."

This impression of me was written just about the
time of my acquaintance with Coralie Mansoni and
of the events which led to a sudden break in it. The
judgment of me seems very fair and marked by considerable acumen. I have quoted it because it may
serve in some degree to explain my conduct at the
time. It also appears to have an interest of its own
as an independent appreciation formed by a fair-

minded and competent observer. I wish that the
same hand had painted an adequate portrait of Wetter, for his character better deserved study than my
own; but with the curious prejudice against politicians that so often affects the minds of students
and men of letters (those hermits of brain-cells) the
writer dismisses Wetter, briefly and almost contemp-
tuously, as an able but unscrupulous politician, ad-
dicted to extravagances and irregularity in private
life. He gives more space to William Adolphus
than to Wetter! So difficult it is even for superior
minds to remain altogether unaffected by the lus-
tre of rank; the old truism could not be better
exhibited.

I kept my appointment and went again to Coralie's in the evening. I took with me Vohrenlorf,
my aide-de-camp (brother to the General, my former
governor); there had been a dinner at the palace, and
we were both in uniform. I had hardly expected
Wetter to come that evening, but he was already
there when I arrived. He seemed in an excited state;
I found afterward that he was fresh from the delivery
of a singularly brilliant and violent speech in the
Chamber. I saluted him with intentional and marked
politeness. He made no more response than purest
formality demanded. I was aggrieved at this, for
I desired to be friendly with him in spite of our
rather absurd rivalry. Turning away from him, I
sat down by Coralie and asked her if supper were
ready.

"We're waiting for Varvilliers," she answered.

"But where is Madame Briande?"

"She went upstairs. I wanted a word with Wetter. She'll be down directly."

"A word with Wetter?"

"Why not, sire?" she asked with aggressive innocence.

"There can be no reason why not, mademoiselle," I replied, smiling.

We were interrupted by Varvilliers' arrival. He also had dined at the palace, and was in full dress.

"How gay my little house is to-night," drawled Coralie, as she rang the bell and ordered, in exactly the same manner, the descent of Madame Briande and the ascent of supper. Both orders were promptly obeyed, and we were left alone. Servants were never allowed to remain in waiting on these occasions.

Varvilliers was in fine vein that night, and Wetter seconded him. The one glittered with sharp-cut gems of speech, the other struck chords of deep and touching music. I played a more modest part, madame and Vohrenlorf were audience, Coralie seemed the judge whose hand was to award the prize. Yet she was indolent, and appeared to listen to no more than half of what was said. We finished eating and began to smoke ; the wine still went round. Suddenly a pause fell on us. A *mot* from Varvilliers had set *finis* to our subject, and another delayed presenting itself. To my surprise Wetter turned to me.

"In the Chamber to-night, sire," he said, "there was a question about your marriage."

I perceived at once the malice which inspired his remark, but I answered him gaily, and in a tone that was in harmony with the scene.

"I wish to heaven," said I, "there were a question about it anywhere else. Alas, it is a certainty."

"Why, so is death, sire," cried Varvilliers, "but we do not discuss it at supper."

"Does M. de Varvilliers quarrel with my choice

of a subject?" asked Wetters. He spoke calmly now, but it was not hard to discern his great excitement.

"I quarrel, sir, with nobody except quarrellers," answered the Frenchman impatiently.

"Well, then——" began Wetter.

"I think you forget my presence," I said coldly, "and this lady's also." I waved my hand toward Coralie. She lay back in her chair, smiling and holding an unlighted cigarette between her fingers.

"I forget, sire, neither your presence nor your due," said Wetter. With that he took a pocket-book from his pocket and flung it on the table before me. "There is my debt," he said.

I sat back in my chair and did not move.

"You choose a strange time for business," I observed. "Vohrenlorf, see what is in this pocket-book."

Vohrenlorf examined it, then he came and whispered in my ear, "Notes for 90,000 marks." It was the amount Wetter owed me with accrued interest. I was amazed. He could not have raised the money except at a most extravagant rate. I made no remark, but I knew that he had risked ruin by this repayment, and I knew well why he had made it. He would not have me for creditor as well as for king and rival.

Varvilliers burst out laughing.

"Upon my word," said he, "these gentlemen of the Chamber can think of nothing but money. Don't you wonder at them, mademoiselle?"

"Money is good to think of," said Coralie reflectively.

"An admirable candour, isn't it, sire?" he said, turning to me and pointing to Coralie.

I was disturbed and out of humour. Again I was in conflict. I thought of what she was, and wondered that such men, and men so placed, as Wetter and I should quarrel about her; I looked in her face and felt a momentary conviction that all the world might fall to fighting on her account; at least things more absurd have surely happened. But I answered smoothly and composedly. (That trick at least I had learned.)

"Sincerity is our hostess's greatest charm," said I.

Wetter laughed loudly and sneeringly. Coralie turned a gaze of indifferent curiosity on him. He puzzled her, tiresomely sometimes. I knew that he meant an insult. My blood runs hot at such moments. I was about to speak when Varvilliers forestalled me. He leaned across the table and said in a very low voice to Wetter:

"Sir, his Majesty is the only gentleman in Forstadt who can not resent an insult."

I recollect well little Madame Briande's pale face, as she half rose from her seat with clasped hands. Coralie still smiled. Vohrenlorf was red and fierce, with his hand on the hilt of his sword. Varvilliers was calm, cool, polished in demeanour.

For a moment or two Wetter sat silent, his eyes intently fixed on the Vicomte's face. Then he said in a tone as low as Varvilliers' had been:

"I think his Majesty remembers his disabilities too late—or has them remembered for him."

Vohrenlorf rose to his feet, carried away by anger and excitement.

"Sir——" he cried loudly.

"Vohrenlorf, be quiet. Sit down," said I. "M. Wetter is right."

None spoke. Even Coralie seemed affected to

gravity; or was it that we had touched the spring of her dramatic instinct? After a few minutes I turned to Madame Briande and introduced some indifferent topic. I spoke alone and found no answer. Coralie was now regarding me with obvious curiosity.

"The air of this room is hot," said I. "Shouldn't we be better in the other? If the ladies will lead the way, we'll follow immediately."

"I'm very well here," said Coralie.

"Oblige me," said I, rising and myself opening the door that led to the inner room.

After a moment's hesitation Coralie passed out, and madame followed her. I closed the door behind them and, turning, faced the three men. Wetter stood alone by the mantelpiece; the others were still near the table.

"In everything but the moment of his remark M. Wetter was right," said I. "I didn't remember in time that I am not placed as other men; I will not remember it now. Varvilliers, you mustn't be concerned in this. Vohrenlorf, I put myself in your hands."

"Good God, you won't fight?" cried Varvilliers.

"Vohrenlorf will do for me what he would for any gentleman who put himself in his hands," said I.

The position was too hard for young Vohrenlorf. He sank into a chair and covered his face with his hands. "No, no, I can't," he muttered. Wetter stood still as a rock, looking not at any of us, but down toward the floor. Varvilliers drank a glass of wine and then wiped his mustache carefully with a napkin.

"Your Majesty," said he, "will not do me the

injustice to suppose that I am not in everything and most readily at your command. But I would beg the honour of representing your Majesty in this affair."

"Impossible!" said I briefly.

"Consider, sire. To fight you is ruin to M. Wetter."

"As regards that, would not M. Wetter in his turn reflect too late?" I asked stiffly.

Vohrenlorf looked up with a hopeless dazed expression. Varvilliers was at a loss. Wetter's figure and face were still unmoved. A sudden idea came into my head.

"There is no need for M. Wetter to be ruined," said I. "Whatever the result may be it shall seem an accident."

Wetter looked up with a quick jerk of his head. I glanced at the clock.

"In four hours it will be light," I said. "Let us meet at six in the Garden Pavilion at the Palace. Varvilliers, since you desire to assist us, I have no doubt M. Wetter will accept your services. It will be well to have no more present than necessary. The Pavilion, gentlemen, I need hardly remind you, is fitted up for revolver practice. Well, there are targets at each end. It will be unfortunate, but not strange, if one of us steps carelessly into the line of fire."

They understood my idea. But Varvilliers had an objection.

"What if both of you?" he asked, lifting his brows.

"That's so unlikely," said I. "Come, shall it be so?"

Wetter looked me full in the face, and bowed low.

"I am at his Majesty's orders," said he. He spoke now quite calmly.

Varvilliers and Vohrenlorf seemed to regard him with a sort of wonder. At the risk of ridicule I must confess to something of the same feeling. A bullet is no respecter of persons, and has no sympathy with ideas which (as the Englishman observes) it is hardly unjust to call mediæval. Yes, even I myself was a little surprised that Wetter should meet me in a duel. But, while I was surprised, I was glad.

"I am greatly indebted to M. Wetter," I said, returning his bow, "in that he does not insist on my disabilities."

For the briefest moment he smiled at me; I think my speech touched his humour. Then he grew grave again, and thanked Varvilliers formally for the offer of his services.

"There remains but one thing," said I. "We must assure the ladies that any difference of opinion there was between us is entirely past. Let us join them."

Vohrenlorf opened the door of the inner room and I entered, the rest following. Madame Briande sat in a straight-backed chair at the table; she had a book before her, but her restless anxious air made me doubt whether she had read much of it. I looked round for Coralie. There on the sofa she lay, her head resting luxuriously on the cushions and her bosom rising and falling in gentle regular breathing. The affair had not been interesting enough to keep Coralie awake. But now Vohrenlorf shut the door rather noisily; she opened her eyes, stretched her arms and yawned.

"Ah! You've done quarrelling?" she asked.

14

"Absolutely. We're all friends again, and have come to say farewell."

"Well, I'm very sleepy," said she, with much resignation. "Go and sleep well, my friends."

"We're forgiven for our bad manners?"

"Oh, but you were very amusing. You're all going home now?"

"So we propose, mademoiselle."

Her eyes chanced to fall on Wetter. She pointed her finger at him and began to laugh.

"What makes you as pale as a ghost, my friend?" she asked.

"It's late; I'm tired," he answered lamely and awkwardly.

She turned a shrewd glance on me. I smiled composedly.

"Ah, well, it's no affair of mine," she said.

In turn we took farewell of her and of madame. But, as I was going out, she called me.

"In a minute, Vohrenlorf," I cried, waving my hand toward the door. The rest passed out. Madame had wandered restlessly to the fireplace at the other end of the room. I returned to Coralie's sofa.

"You're going too?" she asked.

"Certainly," said I. "I must rest. I have to rise early, and it's close on two o'clock."

"You don't look sleepy."

"I depart from duty, not from inclination."

"You'll come to see me to-morrow?"

"If I possibly can. Could you doubt it?"

"And why might you possibly not be able?"

"I am a man of many occupations."

"Yes. Quarrelling with Wetter is one."

"Indeed that's all over."

" I'm not sure I believe you."

" You reduce me to despair. How can I convince you? "

Madame Briande walked suddenly to the door and went out. I heard her invite Vohrenlorf to take a glass of cognac, and his ready acceptance. Coralie was sitting on the sofa now, looking at me curiously.

" I have liked you very much," she said slowly. " You are a good fellow, a good friend. I don't know how it is—I feel uncomfortable to-night. Will you draw back a curtain and open a window? It's hot."

I obeyed her; the cool night air rushed in on us, fresh and delicious. She drew her legs up sideways on the sofa, clasping her ankles with her hand.

" Don't you know," she cried impatiently, " how sometimes one is uncomfortable and doesn't know why? It seems as though something was going to happen, one's money to be lost, or one's friends to die or go away; that somehow they had misfortunes preparing for one."

" I know the feeling well enough, but I'm sure you needn't have it to-night."

" Oh, I don't know. It doesn't come without a reason. You've no superstitions, I suppose? I have many; as a child I learned them all. They're never wrong. Yes, something is to happen."

I shrugged my shoulders and laughed.

" You'll come to-morrow? " she asked, with increased and most unusual urgency.

" If possible," I answered again.

" But why won't you promise? Why do you always say ' if possible '? You're tiresome with your

' if possible.' " She shrugged her shoulders petulantly.

" I might be ill."

" Yes, and you might be dead, but——" She had begun petulantly and impatiently, as though she were angry at my excuse and meant to exhibit its absurdity. But now she stopped suddenly. In the pause the wind moaned.

" I hate that sound," she cried resentfully. " It comes from the souls of the dead as they fly through the air. They fly round and round the houses, crying to those who must join them soon."

" Ah, well, these people were, doubtless, often wrong when they were alive. Why must they be always right when they're dead?"

" No, death is near to-night. I wish you would stay with me—here, talking and forgetting it's night. I would make you coffee and sing to you. We would shut the window and light all the lights, and pretend it was day."

" I can't stay," I said. " I must get back. I have business early."

It is difficult to be in contact with such a mood as hers was that night and not catch something of its infection. Reason protests, but imagination falls a ready prey. I had no fear, but a sombre apprehension of evil settled on me. I seemed to know that our season of thoughtless, reckless merriment was done, and I mourned for it. There came over me a sorrow for her, but I made no attempt to express what she certainly would not have understood. To feel for others what they do not feel for themselves is a distortion of sympathy which often afflicts me. Her discomfort was purely childish, a sudden fear of the dark night, the dark world, the

ways of fortune so dark and unknowable. No self-
questioning and no sting of conscience had any part
in it. She had been happy, and she wanted to go
on being happy; but now she was afraid she was
going to be unhappy, and she shrank from unhappiness as from a toothache. I took her hand and kissed
and caressed it.

"Go to bed, my dear," said I. "You'll be laughing at this in the morning. And poor Vohrenlorf is
waiting all this while for me."

"Go, then. You may kiss me though."

I bent down and kissed her.

"Your lips are very hot," she said. "Yet you
look cool enough."

"I am even rather cold. I must walk home briskly. Good-night."

"You'll make it up with poor Wetter?"

"Indeed our difference is over, or all but over."

"Good. I hate my friends to quarrel seriously.
As for a little, it's amusing enough."

With that she let me go. The last I saw of her
was as she ran hastily across the room, slammed
down the window, and drew the curtain across it.
She was afraid of hearing more of those voices of
the night that frightened her. I thought with a smile
that candles would burn about her bed till she woke
to rejoice in the sun's new birth. Ah, well, I myself
do not love a blank darkness.

Vohrenlorf and I walked home together. We entered by the gardens, the sentry saluting us and opening the gate. There was the Pavilion rising behind
my apartments, a long, high, glass-roofed building.
The sight of it recalled my thought from Coralie to
the work of the morning. I nodded my head toward
the building and said to Vohrenlorf:

"There's our rendezvous."

He did not answer, but turned to me with his lips quivering.

"What's the matter, man?" I asked.

"For God's sake, sire, don't do it. Send him a message. You mustn't do it."

"My good Vohrenlorf, you are mad," said I.

Yet not Vohrenlorf was mad, but I, mad with the vision of my two phantoms—freedom and pleasure.

CHAPTER XVII.

DECIDEDLY MEDIÆVAL.

I was in the Garden Pavilion only the other morning with one of my sons, teaching him how to use his weapons. Suddenly he pointed at a bullet-mark not in any of the targets, but in the wainscoting above and a little to the right of them.

" There's a bad shot, father! " he cried.

" But you don't know what he aimed at," I objected.

" At a target, of course! "

" But perhaps his target was differently placed. That shot is many years old."

" Anyhow he missed what he shot at, or he wouldn't have struck the wainscoting," the boy persisted.

" Why, yes, he missed, but he may have missed only by a hair's breadth."

" Do you know who fired the shot? "

" Yes. It's a strange story; perhaps you shall hear it some day."

This little scene recalled with vividness my memories of the morning when Wetter and I met in the Pavilion. I had hit on a good plan. I was known to practise often, and Wetter was given to the same pursuit. Indeed we had shot against one another in club matches before now, and come off very equal.

207

It was not likely that suspicion would be aroused; the very early hour was our vulnerable point, but this could not be helped. Had we come later, we should have been pestered by attendants and markers. In other respects the ordinary arrangements for matches suited our purpose well. There was a target at either end of the Pavilion; each man chose an end to fire from. When he had discharged his bullet he retreated to a little shelter, of which there were two at each end, one for the shooter, one for the marker. His opponent then did the like. To account for what was meant to occur this morning we had only to make it believed that one of us, Wetter or I, as chance willed, had incautiously stepped out of his shelter at the wrong time. To render this plausible we agreed to pretend a misunderstanding; the man hit was to have thought that his opponent would fire only one shot, the man who escaped would express deepest regret, but maintain that the arrangement had been for two successive shots. I had very little doubt that these arrangements for baffling inconvenient inquiry would prove thoroughly adequate. For the rest, I made up a packet for Varvilliers containing a present for Coralie. To make any other preparations would not have been fair to Wetter; for my death, if it happened, must seem absolutely accidental. After all I did not feel such confidence in my value to the country, or in my wisdom, as to desire to leave my last will and testament. Victoria would do very well, no doubt. It was odd to think of her sleeping peacefully in the opposite wing, without an idea that anything touching her fortunes was being done in the Garden Pavilion.

The external scene is clearer to me than the picture of my own mind; yet there also I can trace the main outlines. The heat of passion was past; I was no longer in the stir of rivalry. I knew that it was through and because of Coralie that I had come into this position, and that Wetter had done what he had. But the thought of her, and the desire to conquer him in her favour or punish him for seeking it, were no more my foremost impulses. I can claim no feeling so natural, so instinctive, so pardonable because so natural. I was angry with him. I had waived my rank and set aside my state; that still I was eager and glad to do; but I waived them and forgot them, because only thus could I avenge them. By his challenge, his insult, his defiance, he had violated what I held sacred in me, and almost the only thing that I held sacred. I hear now the Englishman's mocking epithet in my ears—" Mediæval!" I did not hear it then. Wetter had insulted the King; the King would cease to be the King to punish him. I had this cool anger in my heart when I went with Vohrenlorf to the Pavilion at six in the morning. But half the bitterness of it was due to my own inmost knowledge that my acts had led him on; that, if he had committed the sacrilege, my hand had flung open the doors of the shrine. He had defaced the image; it was I who had taught him no more to reverence it. Because he reminded me of this, I thought that I hated him, as we took our way to the Pavilion.

Men who have been through many of these affairs have told me that on the first occasion they felt some fear, or, at least, an excitement so great as to seem like fear. I recollect no such feeling. This was not because I was especially courageous or more indifferent to death than other men; it did not occur to me that I should be killed or even hit. Coralie had a strong presentiment of evil for some one; I had none for myself. If she were right, it seemed to me that Wetter's fate must prove her so.

The other pair came punctually. They had encountered some slight obstacle in entering. The sentry had been seized with scruples, and the officer of the guard had been summoned. Varvilliers pleaded an express appointment with me, and the officer, surprised but conquered, had let them pass. All this Varvilliers told us in his usual airy manner, Wetter sitting apart the while. The clock struck a quarter past six.

"We waste time, Vicomte," said I, and I sat down in a chair, leaving him to make the arrangements with Vohrenlorf, or, rather, to announce them to Vohrenlorf; for my second was unmanned by the business, and had quite lost his composure.

Varvilliers had just measured the distance and settled the places where we were to stand, when there was a step outside and a knock at the door. The seconds looked round. Wetter sprang to his feet.

"Open it, Vohrenlorf. We're doing nothing secret," I said, with a smile.

Varvilliers nodded approvingly.

"But our visitor mustn't stay long," he observed.

"It's one of my privileges to send people away," said I reassuringly.

The door opened, and in walked William Adolphus! He was in riding boots and carried a whip. It was his custom to rise early for a gallop in the park; he must have heard our voices as he passed by.

"You're early," he cried in boisterous merriment. "What's afoot?"

"Why, a wager between Wetter and myself," I answered. "A match."

"What for?"

"Upon my word, we haven't fixed the stakes; it's pure rivalry." Then I began to laugh. "How odd you should come!" I said. Indeed it seemed strange, for, if the whole affair were traced back to the egg, William Adolphus' flirtation was the origin of it. His appearance had the appropriateness of an ironically witty comment on some hot-headed folly.

"I've half a mind to stay and see you shoot."

"By no means; you'd make me nervous."

"I'll bet a hundred marks on Wetter."

"I take you there," said I. "But I hear your horse being walked up and down outside."

"Yes, he's there."

"It's a chilly morning. Don't keep him waiting. Vohrenlorf, see the Prince mounted."

Varvilliers laughed; even Wetter smiled.

"All right, you needn't be in such a hurry. I'm going," said William Adolphus.

"But I'm glad you came," said I, laughing again, and, as the door closed behind him, I added, "Most lucky! His evidence will be invaluable. Fortune is with us, Varvilliers."

"A man of ready wit is with us, sire," he answered in his pleasant courtliness; then, as we heard William Adolphus trotting off and Vohrenlorf came back, he went on, "All is ready."

Wetter seemed absolutely composed. I marvelled at his composure. No doubt his ideas were not mediæval, as mine were; yet it seemed strange to me that he should fire at me as he would at any other man. I did not then understand the despair which underlay his iron quietness. I was set thinking, though, the next moment, when Varvilliers stepped forward holding a pair of single-barrelled pistols. Wetter opened his lips for the first time:

" Why not revolvers? "

" If we allow a second shot, Vohrenlorf and I will reload. Pardon, sire, have you any other weapon about you? "

I answered " No," and Wetter made the same reply to a like question. But I had seen a sudden change pass over his face when he was told that revolvers were not to be used. An idea entered my head and would not be dislodged; a man might fire more calmly at the King if he were resolved in no case to outlive the King. I said nothing; what could I say or do now? But strangely and suddenly, under the influence of this thought, my anger died away. I saw with his eyes and felt with his heart; I saw how he stood, and I knew that I had brought him to that pass. Was it strange that he fired at me without faltering, although I might be ten times a king? It seemed to me almost just that he should kill me. Varvilliers would not give him a revolver. Did Varvilliers also suspect? I think his fear was rather of our extreme rage against one another. It occurred to me that I would not aim at my opponent. But then I thought I had no right to act thus; it would make matters worse for him if I fell. Besides my own life did not seem to me a thing to be thrown away lightly.

Varvilliers produced another pair of pistols, similar to those which Wetter and I now held. He loaded both, fired them into the targets, and placed one on a shelf at either end of the room.

" Those are the first shots. You understand? The gentleman who is hit made the mistake of not expecting a second shot. Now, sire—if you are ready?"

We took up our positions, each six feet in front of the targets; a bullet which hit me would, but for the interruption, have struck on, or directly above or below, the outermost target on the right-hand side.

Vohrenlorf and Varvilliers stood on either side of the room; the latter was to give the signal. Indeed Vohrenlorf could not have been trusted with such a duty.

"I shall say fire, one—two—three," said Varvilliers. "You will both fire before the last word is ended. Are you ready?"

We signified our assent. Wetter was pale, but apparently quite collected. I was very much alive to every impression. For example, I noticed a man's tread outside and the tune that he was whistling. I lifted my pistol and took aim. At that moment I meant to kill Wetter if I could, and I thought that I could. It did not even occur to me that I was in any serious danger myself.

"Are you ready? Now!" said Varvilliers, in his smooth distinct tones.

I looked straight into Wetter's eyes, and I did not doubt that I could send my bullet as straight as my glance. I felt that I saw before me a dead man.

I am unable to give even to myself any satisfactory explanation of my next act. It was done under an impulse so instantaneous, so single, so simply powerful as to defy analysis. I have the consciousness of one thought or feeling only; but even to myself it seems absurd and inadequate to account for what I did. Yet I can give no other reason. I had no relenting toward Wetter as a man, as companion, or as former friend. I was not remorseful about my own part in the affair, and did not now accuse myself of being responsible for the quarrel. Suddenly—and I record the feeling for what it is worth—it came upon me that I must not kill him. Why? That Englishman would laugh. I am inclined to laugh myself. Well, I was only twenty-four, and, moreover, in a state of high tension, fresh from great emotional excitement and a sleepless night. Because he was one of my people, and great among them; because he might do great things for them; because he was one of those given to me, for whom I was answerable. I can get no nearer to it—it was something of that kind. Some conception of it may be gained if I say that I have never signed a death-warrant without a struggle against a somewhat similar feeling. Whatever it was, it resulted in an inability to try to kill him. As Varvilliers' voice pronounced in clear quiet tones "Fire!" I shifted my aim gently and imperceptibly. If it were true now, the ball would pass his ear and bury itself in the wainscoting behind.

"One—two—three!"

I fired on the last word; I saw the smoke of Wetter's pistol; he stood motionless. In an instant I felt myself hit. I was amazed. I was hit, shot through the body. I staggered, and should have fallen; Vohrenlorf ran to me, and I sank back in his arms. My head was clear, and I saw the order of events that followed. Varvilliers also had started toward me. Suddenly he stopped. Wetter had rushed across the room toward where the cartridges lay. Varvilliers sprang upon him and caught him resolutely by the shoulders. I myself cried, "Stop

"On my honour, a pure accident," said Varvilliers.

him!" even as I sank on the ground, my shoulders propped up against the wall. Before more could happen there was a loud rapping at the door, and the handle was twisted furiously. Somebody cried, " Go for a doctor!" Then came Varvilliers' voice, " You go, Wetter. We trust you to go. Who the devil's at the door?" He sprang across and opened it. Vohrenlorf was asking me in trembling whispers where I was hit. I paid no heed to him. The door opened, and to my amazement William Adolphus ran in, closely followed by Coralie Mansoni. I was past speaking, soon I became past consciousness. The last I remember is that Coralie was kneeling by me, Vohrenlorf still supporting me, the rest standing round. Yet, though I did not know it, I spoke. Varvilliers told me afterward that I muttered, " An accident—my fault." I heard what they said, though I was unconscious of speaking myself.

"It wasn't!" Coralie cried.

"On my honour, a pure accident," said Varvilliers.

Then the whole scene faded away from me.

There can be no doubt that it was Wetter's intention to take his own life in case he hit me. I had discovered this resolution; Varvilliers was not behind me. Had revolvers been employed no power could have hindered Wetter from carrying out his purpose. But Varvilliers had prevented this, and by despatching my antagonist to seek medical aid had put him on his *parole*. He returned with one of my surgeons in a very short space of time; perhaps the desperate fit had passed then, perhaps he had come to feel that he must face the consequences of his act. I know that Varvilliers spoke to him again and very urgently, obtaining at last a pledge from him that

he would at least await the verdict on my case. But
when he had fired at me he had considered himself as a man in any event doomed to death. We
are strangely at fault in our forecasts of fate. He
was uninjured; I, who had been confident of escaping unhurt, lay on the edge between life and death.
My presentiment was signally falsified.

But we must be just even to superstitions. I had
my presentiment, and it was wrong. Coralie Mansoni also had hers, and most unfortunately, for from
hers came the sole danger that threatened the success of our scheme and impaired the perfection of
our pretences. Had William Adolphus been a man
of strong will no harm would have been done; but
he was as wax in her hands. When he left us, he
went on his ride, and in the park he met her, driving herself in her little pony-chaise. She had been
quite unable to sleep, she said, and had been tempted
by the fine morning; had he seen the King? William Adolphus, without a thought of indiscretion,
described how he had found us in the Pavilion. In
an instant her mind, inflamed by her fancies and
readily suspicious, was on fire with fear; fear turned
to an instinctive certainty. My brother-in-law was
amazed at her agitation; she swept away his opposition; he must take her to the Pavilion, or she would
go alone; nothing else would serve. But he should
have held her where she was by main force rather
than bring her; the one fatal thing was to allow
her to appear in the affair at all. He could not with-
stand her; he did not know the extent of his error,
but he knew that to bring her within the precincts
of the palace was a sore indiscretion. She overbore
him; they burst together into the room, as I have
described. And, being there, she would not go, and

was seen by two doctors, by Baptiste, and by the shooting-master, who came to carry me to my apartments. Then at last Varvilliers prevailed on her to allow herself to be smuggled out through the back gate of the gardens, and himself took her to her house in a condition of great distress and collapse. She, at least, was not deceived by the pretence of an accident.

Were other people? I feel myself on doubtful ground. What was said at the moment I know only by hearsay, for I was incapable of attending to anything for three months. There was an enormous amount of gossip and of talk; there were, I think, many hints and smiles; there were hundreds of people who knew the truth, but were careful not to submit their versions to the test of publicity. But what could be done? Varvilliers and Vohrenlorf, men of unblemished honour, were firm in their assertions and unshaken in their evidence; Wetter's obvious consternation at the event was invoked as confirmatory evidence. As soon as I was able to give my account, my voice and authority were cast decisively into the same scale. Men might suspect and women might gossip.· Nothing could be done; and as soon as the first stir was over, Wetter left for a tour abroad without any opposition, and carrying with him a good deal of sympathy. The King's own carelessness was of course responsible, but it was very terrible for Wetter, so they said.

But a point remains; how did we account for Coralie and the presence of Coralie? In fact we never did account very satisfactorily for Coralie. We sacrificed—or rather Varvilliers and Vohrenlorf sacrificed—William Adolphus without hesitation, saying truly enough that he had brought her. Victoria was extremely angry and my brother-in-law much aggrieved. But I must admit that the story met with very hesitating acceptance. Some denied it altogether, the more clear-sighted perceived that, even were its truth allowed, it presupposed more than it told. There was something in the background; that was what everybody thought. What? That was what nobody knew. However I am afraid that there were quite enough suspicion and enough talk to justify my English friend in his remark about the one or two scandals which attached themselves to my name. I beg leave to hope that his charitable expression of surprise that there were not more may be considered equally well justified.

While I lay ill, Princess Heinrich was the dominant influence in the administration of affairs. When I recovered, I found that Coralie Mansoni was no longer playing in Forstadt, and had left the town some weeks before. I put no questions to my mother. I also found that Varvilliers had resigned his official position in the French service, and remained in Forstadt as a private person. Here again, at Varvilliers' own request, I put no questions to my mother. Finally I was informed that the Bartensteins had offered themselves for a visit. Again I put no questions to my mother. I determined, however, not to be laid on the shelf again for three months, if I could help it.

Such is the history of my secret duel with Wetter and of my acquaintance with Coralie Mansoni up to the date of that occurrence. Such also is the story of that apparently very bad shot which my little son found in the wainscoting of the Garden Pavilion. But it was not such a very bad shot; not everybody would have gone so near and yet made sure of not hitting.

CHAPTER XVIII.

At Artenberg, whither we went when I was con-
valescent, the family atmosphere recalled old days.
We were all in disgrace—Victoria because she had
not managed her husband better, William Adolphus
for behaviour confessedly scandalous, I by reason of
those rumours at which I have hinted. My sister
and brother-in-law were told of their faults and
warned, the one against professors, the other against
actresses. My delinquencies were treated with absolute silence. Princess Heinrich reminded me how
I had degraded my office by a studious, though cold,
deference toward it on her own part. The king
was the king, be he never so unruly. His mother
could only disapprove and grieve in silence. But
in the hands of Princess Heinrich silence was a
trenchant weapon. William Adolphus also was very
sulky with me. I found some excuse for him. Toward his wife he wore a hang-dog air; from Princess Heinrich he fairly ran away whenever he could.
In these relations toward one another we settled
down to pass a couple of summer months at Artenberg. Now was early July. In August would come
the visit of the Bartensteins.

Beside this great fact all else troubled me little.
I fell victim to an engrossing selfishness. The quar-

rels and woes of my kindred went unnoticed, except when they served for a moment's amusement. To the fortunes of those with whom I had lately been so much concerned, of Wetter and of Coralie, I was almost indifferent. Varvilliers wrote to me, and I answered in friendly fashion, but I did not at that time desire his presence. So far as my thoughts dwelt on the past, they overleaped what was immediately behind, and took me back to my first rebellion, my first struggle against the fate of my life, my first refusal to run into the mould. I remembered my Governor's comforting assurance that I had still six years; I remembered the dedication of my early love to the Countess. Then I had cherished delusions, thinking that the fate might be avoided. Herein lay the sincerity and honesty of that first attachment, and an enduring quality which made good for it its footing in memory. In it I was not passing the time or merely yielding to a desire for enjoyment. I was struggling with necessity. The high issue had seemed to lend some dignity even to a boy's raw love-making, a dignity that shone dimly through thick folds of encircling absurdity. I had not been particularly absurd in regard to Coralie Mansoni, but neither had there been in that affair any redeeming worthiness or dignity of conception or of struggle. Now all seemed over, struggle and waywardness, the dignified and undignified, the absurdly pathetic and the recklessly impulsive. The six years were nearly gone. Princess Heinrich's steady pressure contracted their extent by some months. The coming of the Bartensteins was imminent. The era of Elsa began.

Old Prince Hammerfeldt had left a successor behind him in the person of his nephew, Baron von

Bederhof, and this gentleman was now my Chancellor and my chief official adviser.   He was a portly man of about fifty, with red cheeks and black hair. He was high in favour with my mother, the husband of a buxom wife, and the father of nine children. As is not unusual in cases of hereditary succession, he was adequate to his office, although he would certainly not have been selected for it unless he had been his uncle's nephew; but, being the depositary of Hammerfeldt's traditions (although not of his brains), he contrived to pass muster.   He came at this time to Artenberg, and urged on me the necessity of a speedy marriage.

"The recent danger, so providentially averted," he said, "is a stronger argument than any I could use."

"It certainly is," said I politely.   As a fact, it might be stronger than any he would be likely to use, and yet not be impregnable.

"For the sake of your people, sire, do not delay."

"My dear Baron," said I, "send for the young lady to-morrow.   I haven't seen her since she was a child, so let her bring a letter of identification."

"You joke!" said he.   "There can be no doubt. Her parents will accompany her."

"True, true!" I exclaimed, in a tone of relief. "There will be really no substantial risk of having an impostor planted on us."

"I am confident," observed Bederhof, "that the marriage will be most happy."

"You are?"

"Undoubtedly, sire."

"Then we won't lose a moment," I cried.

Bederhof looked slightly puzzled, but also rather complimented.   He cleared his throat (if only he could have cleared his head as often and as thoroughly as he did his throat!) and asked, " Er—there are no complications? "

" I beg your pardon, Baron."

" I am ashamed to suggest it, but people do talk. I mean—no other attachment? "

" I have yet to learn, Baron," said I with dignity, " that such a thing, even if it existed, would be of any importance compared to the welfare of the kingdom and the dynasty."

" Not of the least! " he cried hastily.

" I never suspected you of such a paradox really," I assured him with a smile. " And if the lady should harbour such a thing that would be of equal insignificance."

" My uncle, the Prince——" he began.

" Knew all this just as well as we do, my dear Baron," I interrupted. " Come, send for Princess Elsa. I am all impatience."

Even the stupidest of men may puzzle a careful observer on one point—as to the extent of his stupidity. I did not always know whether Bederhof was so superlatively dull as to believe a thing, or merely so permissibly dull as to consider that he ought to pretend to believe it. Perhaps he had come himself not to know the difference between the two attitudes; certain ecclesiastics would furnish an illustration of what I mean. Princess Heinrich's was quite another complexion of mind. She assumed a belief with as much conscious art as a bonnet or a mantle; just as you knew that the natural woman beneath was different·from the garment which covered her, so you were aware that my mother's real opinion was absolutely diverse from the view she professed. In both cases propriety forbade any reference to the natural naked substratum. The Princess, with an art that scorned concealment, congratulated me upon my approaching happiness, declared that the marriage was one of inclination, and, having paid it this seemly tribute, at once fell to discussing how the public would receive it. I believe, however, that she detected in me a certain depression of spirits, for she rallied me (again with a superb ignoring of what we were both aware of) on being moped at the moment when I should have been exultant.

"I am looking at it from Elsa's point of view," I explained.

"Elsa's? Really I don't see that Elsa has anything to complain of. The position's beyond what she had any right to expect."

All was well with Elsa; that seemed evident enough; it was a better position than Elsa had any right to expect. Poor dear child, I seemed to see her rolling down the bank again, expecting and desiring no other position than to be on her back, with her little legs twinkling about in the air.

"I think," said I meditatively, "that it would be a good thing if, in providing wives, they reverted to the original plan and took out a rib. One wouldn't feel that one's rib had any particular right to complain at having its fortunes mixed up with one's own."

My mother remained silent. I looked across the terrace and saw Victoria's three-year-old girl playing about.

"The child's so like William Adolphus," said I, sighing.

My mother rose with deliberate carelessness and walked away.

It may be wondered why I did not rebel. I must

answer, first, from the binding force of familiarity;
I hated the thing, but it had made good its place
in the map of my life; secondly, from the impossibility of inflicting a slight; thirdly, because I rather
chose to bear the ills I had than fly to others that
I knew not of. Who revolts save in the glowing
hope of bettering his lot? I must marry; who was
there to be preferred before Elsa? It did not occur
to me that I might remain single; I should have
shared the general opinion that such an act was little removed from treason. It would not only be to
end my own line, it would be to install the children
of William Adolphus. I did not grant even a moment's hospitality to such an idea. Bederhof was
right, the marriage was urgent; I must marry—just
as occasionally I was compelled to review the troops.
I had as little aptitude for one duty as for the other,
but both were among my obligations. I was so
rooted in this attitude that I turned to Victoria with
a start of surprise when she said to me one day:

"She's very pretty; I daresay you'll fall in love
with her."

She was pretty, if her last portrait spoke truth;
she was a slim girl, of very graceful figure, with
small features and large blue eyes, which were merry
in the picture, but looked as if they could be sad
also. I had studied this attractive shape attentively;
yet Victoria's suggestion seemed preposterous, incongruous—I had nearly said improper. A moment
later it set me laughing.

" Perhaps I shall," I said with a chuckle.

" I don't see anything amusing in the idea," observed Victoria. " I think you're being given a much
better chance than I ever had."

The old grudge was working in her mind; by

covert allusion she was recalling the part I had taken in the arrangement of her future. Yet she had contrived to be jealous of her husband; that old puzzle recurs.

"I suppose," I mused, "that I'm having a very good chance." I looked inquiringly at my sister.

"If you use it properly. You can be very pleasant to women when you like. She's sure to come ready to fall in love with you. She's such a child."

"You mean that she'll have no standard of comparison?"

"She can't have had any experience at all."

"Not even a baron over at Waldenweiter?"

"What a fool I was!" reflected Victoria. "Mother was horrid, though," she added a moment later. She never allowed the perception of her own folly to plead on behalf of Princess Heinrich. "I expect you'll go mad about her," she resumed. "You see, any woman can manage you, Augustin. Think of——"

"Thanks, dear, I remember them all," I interposed.

"The question is, how will mother treat her," pronounced Victoria.

It was not the question at all; that Victoria thought it was merely illustrated the Princess's persistent dominance over her daughter's imagination. I allow, however, that it was an interesting, although subordinate speculation.

The Bartensteins' present visit was to be as private as possible. The arrangement was that Elsa and I should be left to roam about the woods together, to become well known to one another, and after about three weeks to fall in love. The Duke was not to be of the party on this occasion (wise

Duke!) and, when I had made my proposal, mother and daughter would return home to receive the father's blessing and to wait while the business was settled. When all was finished, I should receive my bride in state at Forstadt, and the wedding would be solemnized. In reply to my questions Bederhof admitted that he could not at present fix the final event within a fortnight or so; he did not, however, consider this trifling uncertainty material.

"No more do I, my dear Baron," said I.

"Here," said he, "is the picture of your Majesty which Princess Heinrich has just sent to Bartenstein."

I looked at the lanky figure, the long face, and the pained smile which I had presented to the camera.

"Good gracious!" I murmured softly.

"I beg your pardon, sire?"

"It is very like me."

"An admirable picture."

What in the world was Elsa feeling about it? Thanks to this picture, I was roused from the mood of pure self-regard and allowed my mind to ask how the world was looking to Elsa. I did not find encouragement in the only answer that I could honestly give to my question.

Just at this time I received a letter from Varvilliers containing intelligence which was not only interesting in itself, but seemed to possess a peculiar appositeness. He had heard from Coralie Mansoni, and she announced to him her marriage with a prominent operatic impresario. "You have perhaps seen the fellow," Varvilliers wrote. "He has small black eyes and large black whiskers; his stomach is very big, but, for shame or for what reason I know not, he hides it behind a bigger gold locket. Coralie detests him, but it has been her ambition to sing in grand opera. 'It is my career, *mon cher*,' she writes. Behold, sentiment is sacrificed, and we shall hear her in Wagner! She thinks that she performs a duty, and she is almost sure that it need not be very onerous. She is a sensible woman, our dear Coralie. For the rest I have no news save that Wetter is said to have broken the bank at baccarat, and may be expected shortly to return home and resume his task of improving the condition and morals of the people. I hear reports of your Majesty that occasion me concern. But courage! Coralie has led the way!"

"Come," said I to myself aloud, "if Coralie, although she detests him, yet for her career's sake marries him, it little becomes me to make wry faces. Haven't I also, in my small way, a career?"

But Coralie hoped that her duty would not be very onerous. I had nothing to do with that. The difference there was in temperament, not circumstances.

I have kept the Duchess and Elsa an intolerably long while on their journey to Artenberg. In fact they came quickly and directly; we were advised of their start, and two days of uncomfortable excitement brought us to the hour of their arrival. For once in her life Princess Heinrich betrayed signs of disturbance; to my wonder I detected an undisguised look of appeal in her eyes as she watched me at my luncheon which I took with her on the fateful day. I understood that she was imploring me to treat the occasion properly, and that its importance had driven her from her wonted reserve. I endeavoured to reassure her by a light and cheerful demeanour, but my effort was not successful enough to prevent her from saying a few words to me after the meal. I assured her that Elsa should receive from me the most delicate respect.

"I'm not afraid of your being too precipitate," she said. "It's not that."

"No, I shall not be too precipitate," I agreed.

"But remember that—that she's quite a girl, and "—my mother broke off, looked at me for a moment, and then looked away—"she'll like you if you make her think you like her," she went on in a moment.

I seemed suddenly to see the true woman and to hear the true opinion. The crisis then was great; my mother had dropped the veil and thrown aside her finished art.

"I hope to like her very much," said I.

Princess Heinrich was a resolute woman; the path on which she set her foot she trod to the end.

"I know what you've persuaded yourself you feel about it," she said bluntly and rather scornfully. "Well, don't let her see that."

"She would refuse me?"

"No. She'd marry you and hate you for it. Above all, don't laugh at her."

I sat silently looking at Princess Heinrich.

"You're so strange," she said. "I don't know what's made you so. Have you no feelings?"

"Do you think that?" I asked, smiling.

"Yes, I do," she answered defiantly. "You were the same even as a boy. It was no use appealing to your affections."

I had outgrown my taste for wrangles. But I certainly did not recollect that either Krak or my mother had been in the habit of appealing to my affections; Krak's appeals, at least, had been addressed elsewhere.   Yet my mother spoke in absolute sincerity.

"It's only just at first that it matters," she went on in a calmer tone.   "Afterward she won't mind. You'll learn not to expect too much from one another."

"I assure you that lesson is already laid to my heart," said I, rising.

My mother ended the interview and resumed her mask.   She called Victoria to her and sent her to make a personal inspection of the quarters prepared for our guests.   I sat waiting on the terrace, while William Adolphus wandered about in a state of conscious and wretched superfluousness.   I believe that Victoria had forbidden him to smoke.

They came; there ensued some moments of embracing.   Good Cousin Elizabeth was squarer and stouter than six years ago.   Her cheeks had not lost their ruddy hue.   She was a favourite of mine, and I was glad to find that her manner had not lost its heartiness as she kissed me affectionately on both cheeks.   At the same time there was a difference. Cousin Elizabeth was a little flurried and a little apologetic.   When she turned to Elsa I saw her eye run in a rapid anxious glance over her daughter's raiment.   Then she led her forward.

"She's changed since you saw her last, isn't she?" she asked in a mixture of pride and uneasiness.   "But you've seen photographs, of course," she added immediately.

I bent low and kissed my cousin's hand.   She was very visibly embarrassed, and her cheeks turned red.   She glanced at her mother as though asking what she ought to do.   In the end she shook hands and glanced again, apparently in a sudden convic-

tion that she had done the wrong thing. There can
be very little doubt that we ought to have kissed
one another on the cheek. Victoria came up, and
I turned away to give my arm to Cousin Elizabeth.

"She's so young," whispered Cousin Elizabeth,
hugging my arm.

"She's a very pretty girl," said I, responsively
pressing Cousin Elizabeth's fingers.

Cousin Elizabeth smiled, and I felt her pat my
arm ever so gently. I could not help smiling, in
spite of my mother's warning. I heard Victoria
chattering merrily to Elsa. A gift of inconsequent
chatter is by no means without its place in the world,
although we may prefer that others should supply
the commodity. I heard Elsa's bright sweet laugh
in answer. She was much more comfortable with
Victoria. A minute later the arrival of Victoria's
little girl made her absolutely happy.

I had been instructed to treat the Duchess with
the most distinguished courtesy and the highest
tributes of respect. My mother and I put her between us and escorted her to her rooms. Elsa, it
was considered, would be more at her ease without
such pomp. My mother was magnificent. On such
occasions she shone. Nevertheless she rather alarmed
honest Cousin Elizabeth. A perfect manner alarms
many people; it seems so often to exhibit an un-
holy remoteness from the natural. Cousin Elizabeth was, I believe, rather afraid of being left alone
with my mother. For her sake I rejoiced to meet
her servants hurrying up to her assistance. I returned to the garden.

Elsa had not gone in; she sat on a seat with
Victoria's baby in her arms. Victoria was standing

by, telling her how she ought and ought not to hold the little creature. William Adolphus also had edged near and stood hands in pockets, with a broad smile on his excellent countenance. I paused and watched. He drew quite near to Victoria; she turned her head, spoke to him, smiled and laughed merrily. Elsa tossed and tickled the baby; both Victoria and William Adolphus looked pleased and proud. It is easy to be too hard on life; one should make a habit of reflecting occasionally out of what very unpromising materials happiness can be manufactured. These four beings were at this moment, each and all of them, incontestably happy. Ah, well, I must go and disturb them!

I walked up to the group. On the sight of me Victoria suppressed her kindliness toward her husband; she did not wish me to make the mistake of supposing that she was content. William Adolphus looked supremely ashamed and uncomfortable. The child, being suddenly snatched by her mother, puckered lips and brows and threatened tears. Elsa sprang up with heightened colour and stood in an attitude of uneasiness. Why, yes, I had disturbed their happiness very effectually.

"I didn't mean to interrupt you," I pleaded.

"Nonsense; we weren't doing anything," said Victoria. "I'll show you your rooms, Elsa, shall I?"

Elsa, I believe, would have elected to be shown something much more alarming than a bedroom in order to escape from my presence. She accepted Victoria's offer with obvious thankfulness. The two went off with the baby. William Adolphus, still rather embarrassed, took out a cigar. We sat down side by side and both began to smoke.—There was a silence for several moments.

"She's a pretty girl," observed my brother-in-law at last.

"Very," I agreed.

"Seems a bit shy, though," he suggested, with a sidelong glance at me.

"She seemed to be getting on very well with you and the baby."

"Oh, yes, she was all right then," said William Adolphus.

"I suppose," said I, "that I frighten her rather."

William Adolphus took a long pull at his cigar, looked at the ash carefully, and then gazed for some moments across the river toward Waldenweiter. It was a beautiful evening, and my eyes followed in the same direction. Thus we sat for quite a long time. Then William Adolphus gave a laugh.

"She's got to get used to you," he said.

"Precisely," said I.

For that was pretty Elsa's task in life.

CHAPTER XIX.

GREAT PROMOTION.

I SHOULD be doing injustice to my manners and
(a more serious offence) distorting truth, if I represented myself as a shy gaby, afraid or ashamed to
make love because people knew the business on
which I was engaged. Holding a position like mine
has at least the virtue of curing a man of such folly;
I had been accustomed to be looked at from the day
I put on breeches, and, thanks to unfamiliarity with
privacy, had come not to expect and hardly to miss
it. The trouble was unhappily of a deeper and more
obstinate sort, rooted in my own mind and not due
to the covert stares or open good-natured interest
of those who surrounded me. There is a quality
which is the sign and soul of high and genuine pleasure, whether of mind or body, of sight, feeling, or
imagination; I mean spontaneity. This characteristic, with its included incidents of unexpectedness,
of suddenness, often of unwisdom and too entire
absorption in the moment, comes, I take it, from
a natural agreement of what you are with what you
do, not planned or made, but revealed all at once
and full-grown; when the heart finds it, it knows
that it is satisfied. The action fits the agent—the
exercise matches the faculty. Thenceforward what
you are about does itself without your aid, but pours

into your hand the treasure that rewards success, the very blossom of life. There may be bitterness, reproaches, stings of conscience, or remorse. These things are due to other claims and obligations, artificial, perhaps, in origin, although now of binding force. Beneath and beyond them is the self-inspired harmony of your nature with your act, sometimes proud enough to claim for itself a justification from the mere fact of existence, oftener content to give that question the go-by, whispering softly, "What matters that? I am."

By some such explanation as this, possibly not altogether wide of the mark, I sought to account for my disposition in the days that followed Elsa's arrival. I was conscious of an extreme reluctance to set about my task. I have used the right word there; a task it seemed to me. The trail of business and arrangement was over it; it was defaced by an intolerable propriety, ungraced by a scrap of uncertainty; its stages had been marked, numbered, and catalogued beforehand. Bederhof knew the wedding-day to within a fortnight, the settlement to within a shilling, the addresses of congratulation to a syllable. To this knowledge we were all privy. God save us, how we played the hypocrite!

I am fully aware that there are men to whom these feelings would not have occurred. There are probably women in regard to whom nobody would have experienced them in a very keen form. Insensibility is infectious. We have few scruples in regard to the unscrupulous. We feel that the exact shade of colour is immaterial when we present a new coat to a blind man. Had Hammerfeldt left as his legacy the union with some rude healthy creature, to follow his desire might have been an easy thing—

one which, on a broad view of my life, would have been relatively insignificant. I should have disliked my duty and done it, as I did a thousand things I disliked. But I should not have been afflicted with the sense that where I endured ten lashes another endured a thousand; that, being a fellow-sufferer, I seemed the executioner; that, myself yearning to be free, I was busied in forging chains. It was in this light that Elsa made me regard myself, so that every word to her from my lips seemed a threat, every approach an impertinence, every hour of company I asked a forecast of the lifelong bondage that I prepared for her. This was my unhappy mood, while Victoria laughed, jested, and spurred me on; while William Adolphus opined that Elsa must get used to me; while Cousin Elizabeth smiled open motherly encouragement ; while Princess Heinrich moved through the appropriate figures as though she graced a stately minuet. I had come to look for little love in the world; I was afflicted with the new terror that I must be hated.

Yet she did not hate me; or, at least, our natures were not such as to hate one another or to be repugnant naturally. Nay, I believe that we were born to be good and appreciative friends. Sometimes in those early days we found a sympathy of thought that made us for the moment intimate and easy, forgetful of our obligation, and frankly pleased with the society which we afforded one another. Soon I came to enjoy these intervals, to look and to plan for them. In them I seemed to get glimpses of what my young cousin ought to be always; but they were brief and fleeting. An intrusion ended them; or, more often, they were doomed to perish at my hands or at hers. A troubled shyness would suddenly eclipse her mirth ;

or I would be seized with a sense that my cheating
of fate was useless, and served only to make the fate
more bitter. She seemed to dread any growth of
friendship, and to pull herself up abruptly when she
felt in danger of being carried away into a genuine
comradeship. I was swiftly responsive to such an
attitude; again we drew apart. Here is an extract
from a letter which I wrote to Varvilliers:

"MY DEAR VARVILLIERS: The state of things
here is absurd enough. My cousin and I can't like,
because we are ordered to love; can't be friends, because we must be mates; can't talk, because we must
flirt; can't be comfortable alone together, because
everybody prepares our *tête-à-tête* for us. She is in
apprehension of an amourousness which I despair
of displaying; I am ashamed of a backwardness
which is her only comfort. And the audience grows
impatient; had the gods given them humour they
would laugh consumedly. Surely even they must
smile soon, and so soon as they smile I must take
the leap; for, my dear friend, we may be privately
unhappy, but we must not be publicly ludicrous.
To-day, as we walked a yard apart along the terrace,
I seemed to see a smile on a gardener's face. If it
were of benevolence, matters may not advance just
yet; if I conclude that amusement inspired it, even
before you receive this I may have performed my
duty and she her sacrifice. Pray laugh at and for
me from your safe distance; in that there can be no
harm. I laugh myself sometimes, but dare not risk
sharing my laugh with Elsa. She has humour, but
to ask her to turn its rays on this situation would
be too venturous a stroke. An absolute absorption
in the tragic aspect is probably the only specific which

will enable her to endure. Unhappily the support of pure tragedy, with its dignity of unbroken gloom, is not mine. I forget sometimes to be unhappy in reflecting that I am damnably ridiculous. What, I wonder, were the feelings of Coralie at the first attentions of her big-bellied impresario? Did stern devotion nerve her? Was her face pale and her lips set in tragic mode? Or did she smile and yawn and drawl and shrug in her old delightful fashion? I would give much to be furnished with details of this parallel. Meanwhile Bederhof tears his hair, for I threaten to be behind time, and the good Duchess tells me thrice daily that Elsa is timid. Princess Heinrich has made no sign yet; when she frowns I must kiss. So stands the matter. I must go hence to pray her to walk in the woods with me. She will flush and flutter, but, poor child, she will come. What I ask she will not and must not refuse. But, deuce take it, I ask so little! There's the rub! I hear your upbraiding voice, 'Pooh, man, catch her up and kiss her!' Ah, my dear Varvilliers, you suffer under a confusion. She is a duty; and who is impelled by duty to these sudden cuttings of a knot? And she does a duty, and would therefore not kiss me in return. And I also, doing duty, am duty. Thus we are both of us strangled in the black coils of that belauded serpent."

I did not tell Varvilliers everything. Had I allowed myself complete unreserve I must have added that she charmed me, and that the very charm I found in her made my work harder. There was a dainty delicacy about her, the freshness of a flower whose velvet bloom no finger-touch has rubbed. This I was to destroy.

But at last from fear, not of the gardener's smiles, but of my own ridicule, I made my start, and, as I foreshadowed to Varvilliers, it was as we walked in the woods that I began.

"What of that grenadier?" I asked her—she was sitting on a seat, while I leaned against a tree-trunk—"the grenadier you were in love with when I was at Bartenstein. You remember? You described him to me."

She blushed and laughed a little.

"He married a maid of my mother's, and became one of the hall-porters. He's grown so fat."

"The dream is ended then?"

"Yes, if it ever began," she answered. "How amused at me you must have been!"

Suddenly she perceived my gaze on her, and her eyes fell.

"He was Romance, Elsa," said I. "He has married and grown fat. His business now is to shut doors; he has shut the door on himself."

"Yes," she answered, half-puzzled, half-embarrassed.

"He had an unsuccessful rival," said I. "Do you recollect him? A lanky boy whom nobody cared much about. Elsa, the grenadier is out of the question."

Now she was agitated; but she sat still and silent. I moved and stood before her. My whole desire was to mitigate her fear and shrinking. She looked up at me gravely and steadily. It went to my heart that the grenadier was out of the question. Her lips quivered, but she maintained a tolerable composure.

"You should not say that about—about the lanky boy, Augustin," said she. "We all liked him. I liked him."

"Well, he deserved it a little better then than now. Yet perhaps, since the 'grenadier——"

"I don't understand what you mean about the grenadier."

"Yes, don't you?" I asked with a smile. "No dreams, Elsa, that you told to nobody?"

She flushed for a moment, then she smiled. Her smiling heartened me, and I went on in lighter vein.

"One can never be sure of being miserable," I said.

"No," she murmured softly, raising her eyes a moment to mine. The glance was brief, but hinted a coquetry whose natural play would have delighted —well, the grenadier.

She seemed very pretty, sitting there in the half-shade, with the sun catching her fair hair. I stood looking down on her; presently her eyes rose to mine.

"Not of being absolutely miserable," said I.

"You wouldn't make anybody miserable. You're kind. Aren't you kind?"

She grew grave as she put her question. I made her no answer in words; I bent down, took her hand, and kissed it. I held it, and she did not draw it away. I looked in her eyes; there I saw the alarm and the shrinking that I had expected. But to my wonder I seemed to see something else. There was excitement, a sparkle witnessed to it; I should scarcely be wrong if I called it triumph. I was suddenly struck with the idea that I had read my feelings into her too completely. It might be an exaggeration to say that she wished to marry me, but was there not something in her that found satisfaction in the thought of marrying me? I remembered with a new clearness how the little girl who rolled down the hill

had thought that she would like to be a queen. At
that moment this new idea of her brought me pure
relief. I suppose there were obvious moralizings to
be done; it was also possible to take the matter to
heart, as a tribute to my position at the cost of myself. I felt no soreness, and I did no moralizing.
I was honestly and fully glad that for any reason
under heaven she wished to marry me.

Moreover this touch of a not repulsive worldli-
ness in her sapped some of my scruples. What I
was doing no longer seemed sacrilege. She had one
foot on earth already then, this pretty Elsa, lightly
poised perhaps, and quite ethereal, yet in the end
resting on this common earth of ours. She would
get used to me, as William Adolphus put it, all the
sooner. I took courage. The spirit of the scene
gained some hold on me. I grew less repressed in
manner, more ardent in looks. I lost my old desire
not to magnify what I felt. The coquetry in her
waged now an equal battle with her timidity.

"You're sure you like me?" she asked.

"Is it incredible? Have they never told you how
pretty you are?"

She laughed nervously, but with evident pleasure.
Her eyes were bright with excitement. I held out
my hands, and she put hers into them. I drew her
to me and kissed her lightly on the cheek. She
shrank suddenly away from me.

"Don't be frightened," I said, smiling.

"I am frightened," she answered, with a look
that seemed almost like defiance.

"Shall we say nothing about it for a little while?"

This proposal did not seem to attract her, or to
touch the root of the trouble, if trouble there were.

"I must tell mother," she said.

"Then we'll tell everybody." I saw her looking at me with earnest anxiety. "My dear," said I, " I'll do what I can to make you happy."

We began to walk back through the wood side by side. Less on my guard than I ought to have been, I allowed myself to fall into a reverie. My thoughts fled back to previous love-makings, and, having travelled through these, fixed themselves on Varvilliers. It was but two days since I sent him a letter almost asserting that the task was impossible to achieve. He would laugh when he heard of its so speedy accomplishment. I began in my own mind to tell him about it, for I had come to like telling him my states of feeling, and no doubt often bored him with them; but he seemed to understand them, and in his constant minimizing of their importance I found a comfort. I had indeed almost followed the advice he would have given me—almost taken her up and kissed her, and there ended the matter. A low laugh escaped from me.

"Why are you laughing?" Elsa asked, turning to me with a puzzled look.

"I've been so very much afraid of you," I answered.

"You afraid of me!" she cried. "Oh, if you only knew how terrified I've been!" She seemed to be seized with an impulse to confidence. "It was terrible coming here to see whether I should do, you know."

"You knew you'd do!"

"Oh, no. Mother always told me I mightn't. She said you were—were rather peculiar."

"I don't know enough about other people to be able to say whether I'm peculiar."

She laughed, but not as though she saw any point

in my observation (I daresay there was none), and walked on a few yards, smiling still. Then she said:

"Father will be pleased."

"I hope everybody will be pleased. When you go to Forstadt the whole town will run mad over you."

"What will they do?"

"Oh, what won't they do? Crowds, cheers, flowers, fireworks, all the rest of it. And your picture everywhere!"

She drew in her breath in a long sigh. I looked at her and she blushed.

"You'll like that?" I asked with a laugh.

She did not speak, but nodded her head twice. Her eyes laughed in triumph. She seemed happy now. My pestilent perversity gave me a shock of pain for her.

When we came near the house she asked me to let her go alone and tell her mother. I had no objection to offer. Indeed I was glad to escape a hand-in-hand appearance, rather recalling the footlights. She started off, and I fell into a slower walk. She almost ran with a rare buoyancy of movement. Once she turned her head and waved her hand to me merrily. I waited a little while at the end of the terrace, and then effected an entry into my room unperceived. The women would lose no time in telling one another; then there would be a bustle. I had now a quiet half-hour. By a movement that seemed inevitable I sat down at my writing-table and took up a pen. For several minutes I sat twirling the quill between my fingers. Then I began to write:

"My dear Varvilliers: The impossible has happened, and was all through full of its own impossibility. I have done it. That now seems a little thing. The marvel remains. 'An absolute absorption in the tragic aspect'—you remember, I daresay, my phrase; that was to have been her mood—seen through my coloured glasses. My glasses! Am I not too blind for any glasses? She has just left me and run to her mother. She went as though she would dance. She is merry and triumphant. I am employed in marvelling. She wants to be a queen; processions and ovations fill her eyes. She is happy. I would be happy for her sake, but I am oppressed by an anticipation. You will guess it. It is unavoidable that some day she will remember myself. We may postpone, but we can not prevent, this catastrophe. What I am in myself, and what I mean to her, are things which she will some day awake to. I have to wait for the time. Yet that she is happy now is something, and I do not think that she will awake thoroughly before the marriage. There is therefore, as you will perceive, no danger of anything interfering with the auspicious event. My dear friend, let us ring the church bells and sing a *Te Deum;* and the Chancellor shall write a speech concerning the constant and peculiar favour of God toward my family, and the polite piety with which we have always requited His attentions. For just now all is well. She sleeps.

" Your faithful friend,

" AUGUSTIN."

I had just finished this letter when Baptiste rushed in, exclaiming that the Duchess had come, and that he could by no means prevent her entry. The truth of what he said was evident; Cousin Elizabeth herself was hard on his heels. She almost ran

in, and made at me with wide-opened arms. Her
honest face beamed with delight as she folded me in
an enthusiastic embrace. Looking over her shoulder, I observed Baptiste standing in a respectful attitude, but struggling with a smile.

"You can go, Baptiste," said I, and he withdrew, smiling still.

"My dearest Augustin," panted Cousin Elizabeth, "you have made us all very, very happy. It
has been the dream of my life."

I forget altogether what my answer was, but her
words struck sharp and clear on my mind. That
phrase pursued me. It had been the dream of Max
von Sempach's life to be Ambassador. There had
been a dream in his wife's life. It was the dream of
Coralie's life to be a great singer; hence came the
impresario with his large locket and the rest. And
now, quaintly enough, I was fulfilling somebody
else's dream of life—Cousin Elizabeth's! Perhaps I
was fulfilling my own; but my dream of life was
a queer vision.

"So happy! So happy!" murmured Cousin
Elizabeth, seeking for her pocket-handkerchief. At
the moment came another flurried entry of Baptiste.
He was followed by my mother. Cousin Elizabeth
disengaged herself from me. Princess Heinrich came
to me with great dignity. I kissed her hand; she
kissed my forehead.

"Augustin," she said, "you have made us all very
happy."

The same note was struck in my mother's stately
acknowledgment and in Cousin Elizabeth's gushing
joy. I chimed in, declaring that the happiness I gave
was as nothing to what I received. My mother appeared to consider this speech proper and adequate,

Cousin Elizabeth was almost overcome by it. The letter which lay on the table, addressed to Varvilliers, was fortunately not endowed with speech. It would have jarred our harmony.

Later in the day Victoria came to see me. I was sitting in the window, looking down on the river and across to the woods of Waldenweiter. She sat down near me and smiled at me. Victoria carried with her an atmosphere of reality; she neither harboured the sincere delusions of Cousin Elizabeth nor (save in public) sacrificed with my mother on the shrine of propriety. She sat there and smiled at me.

" My dear Victoria," said I, " I know all that as well as you do. Didn't we go through it all before, when you married William Adolphus? "

" I've just left Elsa," my sister announced. " The child's really half off her head; she can't grasp it yet."

" She is excited, I suppose."

" It seems that Cousin Elizabeth never let her count upon it."

" I saw that she was pleased. It surprised me rather."

" Don't be a goose, Augustin," said Victoria very crossly. " Of course she's pleased."

" But I don't think she cares for me in the very least," said I gravely.

For a moment Victoria stared. Then she observed with a perfunctory politeness:

" Oh, you mustn't say that. I'm sure she does." She paused and added: " Of course it's great promotion for her."

Great promotion! I liked Victoria's phrase very much. Of course it was great promotion for Elsa. No wonder she was pleased and danced in her walk;

no wonder her eyes sparkled. Nay, it was small wonder that she felt a kindliness for the hand whence came this great promotion.

"Yes, I suppose it is—what did you say? Oh, yes—great promotion," said I to Victoria.

"Immense! She was really a nobody before."

A hint of jealousy lurked in Victoria's tones. Perhaps she did not like the prospect of being no longer at the head of Forstadt society.

"There's nobody in Europe who would have refused you, I suppose," she pursued. "Yes, she's lucky with a vengeance."

I began to laugh. Victoria frowned a little, as though my laughter annoyed her. However I had my laugh out; the picture of my position, sketched by Victoria, deserved that. Then I lit a cigarette and stood looking out of the window.

"Poor child!" said I. "How long will it last?"

Victoria made no answer. She sat where she was for a few moments; then she got up, flung an arm round my neck, and gave me a brief business-like kiss.

"I never knew anybody quite so good as you at being miserable," she said.

But I was not miserable. I was, on the whole, very considerably relieved. It would have been much worse had Elsa really manifested an absolute absorption in the tragic aspect. It was much better that her thoughts should be filled by her great promotion.

I heard suddenly the sound of feet on the terrace. A moment later loud cheers rang out. I looked down from the window. There was a throng of the household, stable, and garden servants gathered in front of the window of my mother's room.

On the steps before the window stood Elsa's slim graceful figure. The throng cheered; Elsa bowed, waved, and kissed her hand to them. They cried out good wishes and called blessings on her. Again she kissed her hand to them with pretty dignity. A pace behind her on either side stood Princess Heinrich and Cousin Elizabeth. Elsa held the central place, and her little head was erect and proud.

Poor dear child! The great promotion had begun.

CHAPTER XX.

AN INTERESTING PARALLEL.

I HAD a whimsical desire that somebody, no matter who, should speak the truth about the affair. That I myself should was out of the question, nor would candour be admissible from any of my family; even Victoria could do no more than kiss me. Elsa did not know the truth; her realization of it lay in the future—the future to me ever so present. Varvilliers would not tell it; his sincerity owned always the limit of politeness. I could not look to have my whim indulged; perhaps had there seemed a chance of fulfilment I should have turned coward. Yet I do not know; the love of truth has been a constant and strong passion in my mind. Hence come my laborious trackings of it through mazes of moods and feelings; painful trifling, I daresay. But my whim was accomplished; why and under what motive's spur it is hard to guess.

I sent a message to the Chamber announcing my betrothal; a debate on the answer to be returned followed. Here was a proper and solemn formality, rich in coloured phrases and time-honoured pretence. No lie was allowed place that could not prove its pedigree for five hundred years. Then when Bederhof and the rest had prated, there rose (*O si audissem*) a man with a pale-lined face, in which passion had almost destroyed mirth, or at least compelled it to put on the servile dress of bitterness, but with eyes bright still and a voice that rang through the Chamber. Wetter was back, back from wounding me, back from his madness of Coralie, back from his obscure wanderings and his reported bank-breakings. Somewhere and somehow he had got money enough to keep him awhile; and with money in his pocket he was again and at once a power in Forstadt. There must have been strange doings in that man's soul, worthy of record; but who would be so bold as to take up the pen? His reappearance was remarkable enough. I asked whether he did what he did in malice, in a rivalry that our quarrel and our common defeat at the hands of the paunchy impresario could not wipe out, or whether he discerned that I should join in his acid laugh, and, as I read his speech, cry to myself, " Lo, here is truth and a man who tells it ! "

For he rose, there in the Chamber, when Bederhof's sticky syrup had ceased to flow. He spoke of my betrothal, sketching in a poet's mood, with the art of an orator, that perfect love whereof men dream; painting with exquisite skill the man's hot exultation and the girl's tremulous triumph, the spontaneous leap of heart to heart, the world without eclipsed and invisible; the brightness, the glory, and the unquestioning confidence in their eternity. His voice rose victorious out of falterings; his eyes gleamed with the vision that he made. Then, while still they wondered as men shown new things in their own hearts, his lips curved in a smile and his tones fell to a moderate volume. " Such," said he, " are the joys which our country shares with its King. Because they are his they are ours; because they

17

are his they are hers. Hers and his are they till their lives' end; ours while our hearts are worthy to conceive of them."

They were silent when he sat down. He had outraged etiquette; nobody had ever said that sort of thing before on such an occasion. Bederhof searched in vain through an exhaustive memorandum prepared in the Chancellery. He consulted the clerks. Nobody had ever said anything in the least like it. They were puzzled. It was all most excellent, most loyal, calculated to impress the people in the most favourable way. But, deuce take it, why did the man smile while he talked, and why did his voice change from a ring of a trumpet to the rasp of a file? The Chamber at large was rather upset by Wetter's oration.

Ah, Wetter, but you had an audience fit though small! I read it—I read it all. I, in my study at Artenberg; I, alone. My mind leaped with yours; my lips bent to the curve of yours. Surely you spoke to please me, Wetter? To show that one man knew? To display plainest truth by the medium of a giant's lies? I could interpret. The language was known to me; the irony was after my own heart.

" It's dashed queer stuff," said William Adolphus, scratching his head. " All right in a story book, you know; but in the Chamber! Do you think he's off his head?"

" I don't think so, William Adolphus," said I.

" Victoria says it's hardly—hardly decent, you know."

" I shouldn't call it exactly indecent."

" No, not exactly indecent," he admitted. " But what the devil did he want to say it there for?"

" Ah, that I can't answer."

My brother-in-law looked discontented. Yet as a rule he resigned himself readily enough to not understanding things.

"Victoria says that Princess Heinrich requested the Duchess to manage that Elsa——"

"My dear William Adolphus, the transaction sounds complicated."

"Complicated? What do you mean? Princess Heinrich requested the Duchess not to let Elsa read it."

"Ah, my mother has always good reasons."

"But Elsa had read it already."

"How unfortunate wisdom always is! Did Elsa like it?"

"She told Victoria that it seemed great nonsense."

"Yes, she would think so."

"Well, it is, you know," said William Adolphus.

"Of course it is, my dear fellow," said I.

Yet I wanted to know more about it, and observing that Varvilliers was stated to have been present in the Diplomatic Gallery, I sent for him to come to Artenberg and describe the speech as it actually passed. When I had sent my message I went forth in search of my *fiancée*. She had read the report already; my mother's measures had been taken too late. What did pretty Elsa think? She thought it was all great nonsense. Poor pretty Elsa!

My heart was hungry. Wetter had broken—as surely he had meant to break—the sleep of memory and the sense of contrast. I went to her not with love, but with some vague expectation, a sort of idea that, contrary to all likelihood, I might again have in some measure what had come to me before, springing now indeed not whence I would, but whence it could, yet being still itself though grown in an alien soil. The full richness of native bloom it could not win, yet it might attain some pale grace and a fragrance of its own. For these I would compound and thank the malicious wit that gave them me. But she thought it all great nonsense; nay, that was only what she had told Victoria. My mother was wise, and my mother had requested that she should not read it.

When I came to her she was uncertain and doubtful in mood. She did not refer to the speech, but a consciousness of it showed in her embarrassment and in the distrustful mirth of her eyes. She did not know how I looked upon it, nor how I would have her take it; was she to laugh or to be solemn, to ridicule or to pretend with handsome ampleness? There were duties attached to her greatness; was it among them to swallow this? But she knew I liked to joke at some things which others found serious; might she laugh with me at this extravagance?

"Well, you've read the debate?" I asked. "They all said exactly the proper things."

"Did they? I didn't know what the proper things were."

"Oh, yes; except that mad fellow Wetter. It's a sad thing, Elsa; if only he weren't a genius he'd have a great career."

She threw a timid questioning glance at me.

"Victoria says that he talked nonsense," she remarked.

"Victoria declares that it was you who said it."

"Well, I don't know which of us said it first," she laughed. "Princess Heinrich said so too; she said he must have been reading romances and gone mad, like Don Quixote."

"You've read some?"

"Oh, yes, some. Of course, it's different in a story."

So had observed William Adolphus. I marked Victoria as the common origin.

"You see," said I tolerantly, "he's a man of very emotional nature. He's carried away by his feelings, and he thinks other people are like himself." And I laughed a little.

Elsa also laughed, but still doubtfully. She seemed ill at ease. I found her venturing a swift stealthy glance at me; there was something like fear in her eyes. I was curiously reminded of Victoria's expression when she came to Krak with only a half of her exercise written, and mistrusted the validity of her excuse. (Indeed it was always a bad one.) What, then, had Wetter done for her? Had he not set up a hopeless standard of grim duty, frowning and severe? My good sister had meant to be consolatory with her "great nonsense," remembering, perhaps, the Baron over there at Waldenweiter. Elsa was looking straight before her now, her brows puckered. I glanced down at the hand in her lap and saw that it trembled a little. Suddenly she turned and found me looking; she blushed vividly and painfully.

"My dearest little cousin," said I, taking her hand, "don't trouble your very pretty head about such matters. Men are not all Wetters; the fellow's a poet if only he knew it. Come, Elsa, you and I understand one another."

"You're very kind to me," she said. "And—and I'm very fond of you, Augustin."

"It's very charming of you, for there's little enough reason."

"Victoria says several people have been." She hazarded this remark with an obvious effort. I laughed at that. There was also a covert hint of surprise in her glance. Either she did not believe Victoria fully, or she was wondering how the thing had come about. Alas, she was so transparent! I found myself caught by a momentary wish that I had chosen (as if I could choose, though!) a woman of the world, whose accomplished skill should baffle all my scrutiny and leave me still the consolations of uncertainty; it is probable that such a one would have extorted from me a belief in her love for five minutes every day. Not for an instant could that delusion live with Elsa's openness. Yet perhaps she would learn the trick, and I watch her mastery of it in the growth. But at least she should not learn it on my requisition.

Elsa sat silent, but presently a slight meditative smile came on her lips and made a little dimple in her chin. Her thoughts were pleasant then; no more of that grim impossible duty. Had Wetter's wand conjured any other idea into her mind? Had his picture another side for her imagination? It seemed possible enough; it may well have seemed possible to Princess Heinrich when she requested that Elsa should not read the speech. Princess Heinrich may have preferred that such notions should not be suggested at all under the circumstances of the case. There was always a meaning in what Princess Heinrich did.

"What are you thinking of, Elsa?"

"Nothing," she answered with a little start. "Is he a young man?"

"You mean Wetter?"

"Yes."

"Oh, a few years over thirty. But he's made the most of his time in the world. The most, not the best, I mean, you know."

Her thoughts had been on Wetter and Wetter's words. Since she had smiled I concluded that my guess was not far off. Elsa turned to me with a blush and the coquettish air that now and then sat so prettily on her innocence.

"I should think he might have made love rather well," she said.

"I shouldn't wonder in the least," said I. "But he might be a little tempestuous."

"Yes," Elsa acquiesced. "And that wouldn't be nice, would it?"

"Not at all nice," said I, and laughed. Elsa joined in my laugh, but doubtfully and reluctantly, as though she had but a dim glimmer of the reason for it. Then she turned to me with a sudden radiant smile.

"Fancy!" said she. "Mother says I must have forty frocks."

"My dear," said I, "have four hundred."

"But isn't it a lot?"

"I suppose it is," I remarked. "But have anything you ought to have. You like the frocks, Elsa?"

She gave that little emphatic double nod of hers.

We talked no more of the frocks then, but during the few days which followed Elsa's perusal of Wetter's speech there was infinite talk of frocks and all the rest of the furnishings and appurtenances of Elsa's new rank. The impulse which moved women so different as my mother, the Duchess, and Victoria, to a common course of conduct was doubtless based on an universal woman's instinct. All the three seemed to set themselves to dazzle the girl with the glories and pomp that awaited her; at the same time William Adolphus became pressing in his claims on my company. Now Victoria never really supposed that I desired to spend my leisure with William Adolphus; she set him in motion when she had reason to believe that I had better not spend it with some other person. So it had been in the days of the Countess and in Coralie's epoch; so it was now. The idea was obvious; just at present it was better for Elsa to think of her glories than to be too much with me; she was to be led to the place of sacrifice with a bandage over her eyes, a bandage that obscured the contrasted visions of Wetter's imagination and of my actual self. I saw their plan and appreciated it, but seeing did not forbid yielding. I was not hoodwinked, but neither was I stirred to resistance. It seemed to me then that kindness lay in not obtruding myself upon her, in being as little with her as courtesy and appearances allowed, in asking the smallest possible amount of her thoughts and making the least possible claim on her life. They asked me to efface myself, to court oblivion, to hide behind the wardrobe. It was all done with a soothing air, as though it were a temporary necessity, as though with a little patience the mood would pass, almost as though Elsa had some little ailment which would disappear in a few days; while it lasted, men were best out of the way, and would show delicacy by asking no questions. The way in which women act, look, and speak, when they desire to create that impression, is clear and unmistakable; a wise man goes about his business or retires to his smoking-room, his papers, and his books.

The treatment seemed to answer well, and its severity was gradually relaxed. William Adolphus,

sighing relief I doubt not (for I was well-nigh as
tedious to him as he to me), went off to his horses. .
I was again encouraged to be more with Elsa, under
a caution to say nothing that could excite her. She
met me with a quiet gay contentment, seemed pleased
to be with me, and was profuse and sincere in thanks
for my kindness. Sometimes now she talked of our
life after we were married, when Princess Heinrich
would be gone and we alone together. She was occupied with innocent wonderings how we should get
on, and professed an anxiety lest she should fail
in keeping me amused. Then she would take refuge
in reminding herself of her many and responsible
duties. She would have nearly as much to do as
I had, she said, and was not her work really almost
as important as mine?

"Princess Heinrich says that the social influence
I shall wield is just as important to the welfare of
the country," she would say, with that grave inquiring look in her pretty blue eyes.

"All the fashionable folk in Forstadt will think
it much more important," said I, laughing. "Especially the young men, Elsa."

"As if I should care about that!" she cried scornfully.

Now and then, at intervals, while I talked to her,
the idea of doing what my mother had meant by
exciting her came into my head, the idea of satisfying her unconscious longings and of fulfilling for her
the dream which had taken shape under the wand
of that magician Wetter. I believed then that I
could have succeeded in the task; there may be vanity in that opinion, but neither lapse of time nor later
experience has brought me to renounce it. Why,
then, did I yield to the women's prescription, and

renounce the idea of gaining and chaining her love and her fancy for myself? Nothing in her gives the answer to that question; it must be sought in my mind and my temper. I believed and I believe that if I could have stirred myself I could have stirred her. The claim is not great; Wetter had done half the work for me, and nature was doing the better part of the rest. I should have started with such an advantage that the battle must have been mine. This is not merely perceived in retrospect; it was tolerably clear to me even at the time. But the impulse in me was wanting. I could have won, but I did not truly desire to win. I could have given what she asked, but my own heart was a niggard. It was from me more than from her that the restraint came; it was with me to move, and I could not stir. She was lovable, but I did not love her; she had love to give, but I could not ask for it. To marry her was my duty, to seem to desire the marriage my *rôle*. There obligation stopped; inclination refused to carry on the work. I had driven a bargain with fate; I would pay the debt to the last farthing, but I could not open my purse again for a gratuity or a bounty. I acquiesced with fair contentment in it, and in the relations which it produced between Elsa and myself. There was a tacit agreement among all of us that a calm and cousinly affection was the best thing, and fully adequate to the needs of the situation. The advice of the women chimed in with my own mood. Making love to her would have seemed to them a dangerous indiscretion, to me a rather odious taking advantage of one who was not a free agent, and a rather humiliating bit of pretence besides. We had all made up our minds that matters had better be left considerably below boiling-point.

While things stood thus I received a letter from Varvilliers (who was at Forstadt) accepting my invitation to Artenberg. His acceptance signified, he went on:

"Of course all the town is full of you and your *fiancée*—her portrait is everywhere, your name and hers in every mouth. There is another coupled with them, surely in a strange conjunction! When they speak of you and the Princess they speak of Wetter also. It is recalled that you and he were friends and associates, companions in amusement and sport (especially, of course, in pistol practice!). Hence springs a theory that the fellow's odd rhapsody (mad and splendid!) was directly inspired by yourself, that you chose him as your medium, desiring to add to the formal expressions usual on such occasions an unofficial declaration of your private feelings. So you are hailed as a model and most romantic lover, and every tea-table resounds with your praises. Early indiscretions (forgive a pen itself indiscreet) are forgotten, and you are booked for the part of the model husband, an example of the beauty (and the duty) of marriages of inclination in high places. Believe me, your popularity is doubled. And the strange fellow himself, having money in his pocket and that voice of his in magnificent order, is to be seen everywhere, smiling mysteriously and observing a most significant reticence when he is pressed to say that he spoke at your request and to your pattern. But for your Majesty's own letters I should not have ventured to be a dissenter from the received opinion; if you bid me, at any moment I will gladly renounce my heresy and embrace the orthodox faith. Meanwhile I am wondering what imp holds sway in Wetter's brain;

and I am laughing a little at this new example of the
eternal antagonism between what is the truth and
what is thought to be the truth. If mankind ever
stumbled on absolute naked verity, what the devil
would they make of it? By the way, I hear that
Coralie is to make her *début* in Paris in a week or
two. She being now reputably impresarioed, the
Sempachs have shown her some civility. I told
Wetter this when I last ran against him at the club.
He raised his brows, twisted his lips, scratched his
chin, looked full in my face and said with a smile,
' My dear Vicomte, Madame Mansoni is passionately
attached to her husband. They are ideal lovers.'
Your Majesty shall interpret, if it be your pleasure.
I leave the matter alone."

This fellow Wetter was very impertinent with his
speeches and his parallels. But, good heavens, he
had eyes to see! Madame Mansoni and her impresario were ideal lovers! Surely the world was grown
young again! Elsa also made her *début* in a few
weeks; I was her impresario. And she was passionately attached to her impresario! I lay back in my
chair, laughing and wishing with all my heart that I
could have a talk with Wetter.

CHAPTER XXI.

ON THE ART OF FALLING SOFT.

THE economy of belief which wisdom practices forbids us to embrace fanciful theories where commonly observed facts will serve our turn. They talk now about strange communications of mind to mind, my thought speaking to yours a thousand miles away. Perhaps; or perhaps there is a new fashion in ghost stories. In any case there was no need of these speculations to account for Wetter being near me at the very time when I was longing for his presence. From the moment I read his speech I knew that he was thinking of me; that my doings were stuff for his meditations; that his mind entered into mine, read its secrets, and was audience to all its scenes. Is not the desire to meet, at least to see, the natural sequence of such an interest and such a preoccupation? Given the wish, what was simpler than its gratification? He need ask no leave from me, and need run no risk of my rebuff or of Princess Heinrich's stiffness. He knew all the world of Forstadt. From favour or fear every door opened when he knocked at it. He knew, among the rest, Victoria's Baron over at Waldenweiter. From no place could he better observe the King. Nowhere else was it so easy for a man to meet the King. He came to Waldenweiter; I jumped to the conclusion that to be near me was his only object. By a stableman's chance remark, overheard as I was looking at my horses, I learned of his presence on the morning of the day when Varvilliers was to arrive at Artenberg. We were coming together again, we three who had met last for pistol practice in the Garden Pavilion.

About two o'clock I went out alone and got into my canoe. It was a beautiful day; no excuse was needed for a lounge on the water. I paddled up and down leisurely, wondering how soon the decoy would bring my bird. A quarter of an hour proved enough. I saw him saunter down to the water's edge. He perceived me, lifted his soft hat, and bowed. I shot across the space between, and brought the canoe up to the edge of the level lawn that bordered on the river.

"Why, what brings you here?" I cried.

His lips curved in a smile, as he replaced his hat in obedience to a sign from me.

"A passion for the Baroness, sire," said he.

"Ah, that's only a virtuous pretence," I laughed. "You've a less creditable motive?"

"Why, possibly; but who tells his less creditable motives?"

I looked at him curiously and attentively. He had grown older, the hair by his ears was gray, and life had ploughed furrows on his face.

"Well," said I, "a man might do even that who talks romance to the Chamber."

He gave a short laugh as he lit his cigarette.

"Your Majesty has done me the honour of reading what I said?"

"I am told that I suggested it. So runs the gossip in town, doesn't it?"

"And your opinion on it?"

"Why, what brings you here?" I cried.

"I think I won't expose myself to your fire again," said I. "It was careless last time; it would be downright folly now."

" Then we are to say no more about it? " he asked gravely.

" Not a word. Tell me, how came you to know that Coralie loves her impresario? You told Varvilliers so."

His lips twitched for a moment, but he answered, smiling:

" Because she has married him."

" I heard something of ambition in the case, of her career demanding the sacrifice."

" A slander, sire, depend on it. It is said in envy of her good fortune."

" Come, come, you love the Baroness so much, that you must have all the world in love."

" Indeed I can think of nobody more in love than I am."

" Think of me, Wetter."

" As though your Majesty could ever be absent from my thoughts," said he with a bow, a wave of his cigarette, and a smile.

I laughed outright in sheer enjoyment of his sword-play.

" And since we parted where have you been? " I asked.

" I have walked through hell, in such company as the place afforded," he answered, with a shrug that spoke ill for hell's resources.

" And you've come out the other side? "

" Is there another side? "

" Then you're still there? "

" Upon my word I don't know. It's so like other places—except that I picked up money there."

" I heard that."

" My resurrection made it obvious."

A silence fell on both of us; then our eyes met, and he smiled kindly.

" I knew you meant the speech for me," I said.

" I was not entitled to congratulate you officially."

" You have raised a mountain of misconception about me in Forstadt," I complained.

" A mountain-top is a suitable regal seat, and perhaps the only safe one."

" Won't you speak plainly to me? "

" Yes, if it's your pleasure."

" I have least of it of any pleasure in the world."

" Well, then, the Countess von Sempach grows no younger."

" No? "

" And Coralie Mansoni has married her impresario."

" I know it."

" And my hair is gray, and your eyes are open."

. We both laughed and fell again to smoking in silence. At last I spoke.

" Her hair is golden and her eyes are shut," said I. " Why did you try to open them? "

" Wasn't it to look on a fine sight? "

" But you knew that the sight wasn't there."

" She looked? "

" For an instant. Then they turned her head the other way."

" It was pure devilry in me. You should have seen the Chamber! Good God! Bederhof, now! "

His eyes twinkled merrily, and my laugh answered their mirth.

" One can always laugh," said I with a shrug.

" It was invented for the world before the Fall, and they forgot to take it away afterward," he said. " But you? You take things seriously? "

" What I have to do, yes."

" But what you have to feel? "

" In truth I am not even there a consistent laugher."

" Nor I, or we shouldn't talk so much about it. Look at Varvilliers. Does he laugh on a theory? "

" He's coming to Artenberg to-day. There at least he'll laugh without any effort. Are you staying here long? "

" No, sire. One scene of despair, and I depart."

" I should like to see you oftener."

" Why not? You are finally, and I for the time, respectable. Why not, while my money lasts? "

" I have money of yours."

" You have more than money of mine."

He looked me in the face and held out his hand. I grasped it firmly.

" Are you making a fool of this Baroness? " I asked.

" Don't be afraid. She's making one of me. She is very happy and content. I am born to make women happy."

I laughed again. He was whimsically resigned to his temperament, but the mischief had not touched his brain. Then the Baroness' hold on him was not like Coralie Mansoni's; he would fight no duel for her. He would only make a fool of the greatest man in Forstadt. That feat was always so easy to him.

" Well," he said, " I must return to my misery."

" And I to my happiness," said I. " But you'll come to Artenberg? "

18

"It's Princess Heinrich's house," he objected with a smile.

"For the time, yes. Then come to me at Forstadt."

"Yes; unless I have disappeared again."

He put his hand on the bows of my canoe and thrust me out into the stream. Then he stood baring his head and crumpling up the soft hat in his fist. I noticed now that his hair was gray all over his head. He resumed his hat, put his hands in his pockets, and waited without moving, till I turned my back to him. Having reached the opposite bank, I looked round. He was there still. I waved my hand to him; he returned the signal. Then we both began to climb the hill, I to Artenberg, he to Waldenweiter; he to his misery, I to my happiness. And—which is better, who knows? At any rate the Baroness was pleased.

I mounted through the woods slowly, although I had been detained longer than I expected, and was already too late to greet Varvilliers on his arrival. As I came near the terrace I heard the ring of merry voices. The ladies and gentlemen of the household were all there, making a brave and gay group. In the centre I saw my family and Elsa. Varvilliers himself was standing by Princess Heinrich's side, talking fast and with great animation. Bursts of glad laughter marked his points. There was not a hint of care nor a touch of bitterness. Here was no laughing on a theory, as Wetter called it, but a simple enjoyment, a whole-hearted acceptance of the world's good hours. Were they not nearer truth? Were they not, at least, nearer wisdom? A reaction came on me. In a sudden moment a new resolve entered my head; again Varvilliers roused the impulse that he had power to rouse in me. I would make trial of this mode of living and test this colour of mind. I had been thinking about life when I might have been exulting in it. I ran forward to the group, and, as they parted to let me through, I came quickly to Varvilliers with outstretched hands. He seemed to me a good genius. Even my mother looked smiling and happy. The faces of the rest were alight with gaiety. Victoria was in the full tide of a happy laugh, and did not interrupt it on account of my arrival. Elsa's lips were parted in a smile that was eager and wondering. Her eyes sparkled; she clasped her hands and nodded to me in a delicious surprised merriment. I caught Varvilliers by the arm and made him sit by me. A cry arose that he should repeat the last story for the King's benefit. He complied at once, and launched on some charming absurdity. Renewed applause greeted the story's point. A rivalry arose who should cap it with a better. The contact of brains struck sparks. Every man was wittier than his wont; every woman more radiant. What the plague had I and Wetter been grumbling and snarling at down there on the river?

The impulse lasted the evening out. After dinner we fell to dancing in the long room that faced the gardens. My mother and the Duchess retired early, but the rest of us set the hours at defiance and revelled far on into the night. It was as though a new spirit had come to Artenberg; the very servants wore broad grins as they bustled about, seeming to declare that here at last was something like what a youthful king's court should be. William Adolphus was boisterous, Victoria forgot that she was learned and a patroness of the arts, Elsa threw herself into the fun with the zest and abandonment of a child.

I vied with Varvilliers himself, seeking to wrest from him the title of master of the revels. He could not stand against me. A madman may be stronger than the finest athlete. No native temper could vie with my foreign mood.

Suddenly I knew that I could do to-night what I had vainly tried to do; that to-night, for to-night at least, I felt something of what I desired to feel. The blood ran free in my veins; if I did not love her, yet I loved love, and for love's sake would love Elsa. If to-night the barrier between us could be broken down, it need never rise again; the vision, so impossible a few hours before, seemed now a faint reflection of what must soon be reality. I looked round for her, but I could not see her. I started to walk across the room, threading my way through the merry company, who danced no longer, but stood about in groups, bandying chaff and compliments. Engrossed with one another, they hardly remembered to give me passage. Presently I came on William Adolphus, making himself very agreeable to one of his wife's ladies.

"Have you seen Elsa?" I asked him.

"What, you've remembered your duty at last, have you?" he cried, with a burst of laughter.

"No; I believe I've forgotten it at last," I answered. "Where is she?"

"I saw her with Varvilliers on the steps outside the window."

I turned in the direction which he indicated, and stepped out through the open window. Day was dawning; I could make out the gray shape of Waldenweiter. Was the scene of despair played there yet? I gave but a passing thought to old Wetter, his mad doings and wry reflections. I was hot on

another matter, and, raising my voice, I called, " Varvilliers! Where are you, Varvilliers?"

"I am not Varvilliers, but here I am," came in
answer from across the terrace.

"Wetter!" I whispered, running down the steps
and over to where he stood. "What brings you
here?"

"I couldn't sleep. I saw your lights and I rowed
across. I've been here for an hour."

"You should have come in."

"No. I have been very well here, in the fringe
of the trees."

"You have had your scene?"

"No; he would not sleep after dinner. Early to-
morrow! And then I go. Enough of that. I have
seen your Princess."

"You have? Wetter, I am in love with her. Tell
me where she went. She has suddenly become all
that I want. I have suddenly become all that I ought
to be. Tell me where she is, Wetter!"

"It is not your Princess; it is the dance, the wine,
the night."

"By God, I don't care what it is."

"Well, then, she's with Varvilliers, at the end of
the terrace, I imagine; for they passed by here as
I lay in my hole watching."

"But he would have heard my cry."

"It depends upon what other sounds were in his
ears. They seemed very happy together."

I saw that he rallied me. I smiled, answering:

"I'm not in the mood for another duel."

He shrugged his shoulders, and then caught me
by the hand.

"Come, let's slink along," he said. "We may get
a sight of them."

"I can't do that."

"No? Perhaps you can't. Walk up to them, send him away, and make your love to her. I'll wait for you here. You'll like to see me before the night's out."

I looked at him for a moment.

"Shall I like to see you?" I asked.

"Yes," he answered. "The olive after the sweets." He laughed, not bitterly, I thought, but ruefully.

"So be it," I said. "Stay here."

I started off, but he had laid a cold hand on my heart. I was to want him; then I should be no lover, for a lover wants but one. Yet I nerved myself and cried again loudly, "Varvilliers!" This time I was answered. I saw him and Elsa coming toward me; his voice sounded merry and careless as he shouted, "Here I am, sire"; a moment later they stood before me. No, there was no ground for Wetter's hint, and could be none. Both were merely happy and gay, both utterly unembarrassed.

"Somebody wants you inside, Varvilliers," said I, with a nod.

He laughed, bowed gracefully to Elsa, and ran off. He took his dismissal without a sign of grudge. I turned to her.

"Oh, dear," she said with a little yawn, "I'm tired. It must be very late."

I caught her by both hands.

"Late!" I cried. "Not too late, Elsa!" I bent down and kissed both her hands. "Why did you run away?" I asked.

"I didn't know you wanted me," she said in a sort of wonder.

I looked full in her eyes, and I knew that there

was in mine the look that declares love and asks for
it. If her eyes answered, the vision might be reality.
I pressed her hands hard. She gave a little cry,
the sparkle vanished from her eyes, and their lids
drooped. Yet a little colour came in her cheeks and
the gray dawn showed it me. I hailed it with eagerness and with misgiving. I thought of Wetter waiting there among the trees, waiting till the moment
when I wanted him.

"Do you love me, Elsa?" I asked.

The colour deepened on her cheeks. I waited
to see whether her eyes would rise again to mine;
they remained immovable.

"You know I'm very fond of you," she murmured.

"But do you love me?"

"Yes, of course I love you. Please let my hands
go, Augustin."

If Wetter were listening, he must have smiled at
the peal of laughter that rang out from me over the
terrace. I could not help it. Elsa started violently
as I loosed her hands; now she looked up at me
with frightened eyes that swam in tears. Her lips
moved; she tried to speak to me. I was full of brutal
things and had a horrible longing to say them to
her. There was a specious justice in them veneering
their cruelty; I am glad to say that I gave utterance to none of them. We were both in the affair,
and he is a poor sort of villain who comforts himself
by abusing his accomplice.

"You're tired?" I asked gently.

"Very. But it has been delightful. M. de Varvilliers has been so kind."

"He's a delightful fellow, Varvilliers. Come, let
me take you in, and we'll send these madcaps to bed."

She put her hand on my arm in a friendly trustful fashion, and I found her eyes fixed on mine with a puzzled regretful look. We walked most of the way along the terrace before she spoke.

"You're not angry with me, Augustin?"

"Good heavens, no, my dear," said I.

"I'm very fond of you," she said again as we reached the window.

At last they were ready for bed—all save myself. I watched them as they trooped away, Elsa on Victoria's arm. Varvilliers came up to me, smiling in the intervals that he snatched from a series of yawns.

"A splendid evening!" he said. "You surpassed yourself, sire."

"I believe I did," said I. "Go to bed, my friend."

"And you?"

"Presently. I'm not sleepy yet."

"Marvellous!" said he, with a last laugh and a last yawn.

For a few moments I stood alone in the room. There were no servants about; they had given up waiting for us, and the lights were to burn at Artenberg till the hour of rising. I lit a cigarette and went out on the terrace again. I had no doubt that Wetter would keep his tryst. I was right; he was there.

"Well, how did you speed?" he asked with a smile.

"Marvellously well," said I.

He took hold of the lapels of my coat and looked at me curiously.

"Your love scene was short," he said.

"Perhaps. It was long enough."

"To do what?"

"To define the situation."

"Did it need definition?"

"I thought so half an hour ago."

"Ah, well, the evening has been a strange one, hasn't it?"

"Let's walk down to the river through the woods," said I. "I'll put you across to Walden-weiter."

He acquiesced, and I put my arm through his. Presently he said in a low voice:

"The dance, the wine, the night."

"Yes, yes, I know," I cried. "My God, I knew even when I spoke to her. She saw that a brute asked her, not a man."

"Perhaps, perhaps not; they don't see everything. She shrank from you?"

"The tears were very ready."

"Ah, those tears! Heavens, why have we no such appeals? What matter, though? You don't love her."

"Do you want me to call myself a brute again? Wetter, any other girl would have been free to tell me that I was a brute."

"Why, no. No man is free even to tell you that you're a fool, sire. The divinity hedges you."

I laughed shortly and bitterly. What he said was true enough.

"There is, however, nothing to prevent you from seeing these things for yourself, just as though you were one of the rest of us," he pursued. "Ah, here's the river. You'll row me across?"

"Yes. Get into the boat there."

We got in, and I pulled out into mid-stream. It was almost daylight now, but there was still a grayness in the atmosphere that exactly matched the tint of Wetter's face. Noticing this suddenly I pointed it out to him, laughing violently.

"You are Lucifer, Son of the Morning," I cried. "How art thou fallen from heaven, O Lucifer, Son of Morning!"

"I wouldn't care for that if I had the trick of falling soft," said he. "Learn it, O King, learn it! On what padded bed falls William Adolphus!"

My laugh broke again through the morning loud and harsh. Then I laid myself to the oars, and we shot across to the bank of Waldenweiter. He shook my hand and sprang out lightly.

"I must change my clothes and have my scene, and then to Forstadt," said he. "Good-day to you, sire. Yet remember the lesson of the moralist. Learn to fall soft, learn to fall soft." With a smile he turned away, and again I watched him mount the slope of Waldenweiter.

In such manner, on that night at Artenberg, did I, having no wings to soar to heaven and no key wherewith to open the door of it, make to myself, out of dance, wine, night, and what not, a ladder, mount thereby, and twist the door-handle. But the door was locked, the ladder broke, and I fell headlong. Nor do I doubt that many men are my masters in that art of falling soft.

CHAPTER XXII.

THE next morning all Artenberg had the air of
being rather ashamed of itself. Styrian traditions
had been set at naught. Princess Heinrich considered that the limits of becoming mirth had been over-
stepped; the lines of her mouth had their most downward set. Nothing was said because the King had
led the dance, but disgrace was in the atmosphere.
We had all fallen from heaven—one may mean many
things by heaven—and landed with more or less severity, according to the resources of padding with
which Nature furnished us. To Varvilliers' case,
indeed, the metaphor is inadequate; he had a para-
chute, sailed to earth gaily with never a bruise, and
was ready to mount again had any of us offered to
bear him company. His invitation, given with a
heartiness that mocked his bidden companions, found
no acceptance. We were all for our own planet in
the morning. It was abundantly clear that revels
must be the exception at Artenberg. Victoria was
earnestly of this opinion. In the first place, the physical condition of William Adolphus was deplorable;
he leered rueful roguishness out of bilious eyes, and
Victoria could not endure the sight of him; secondly, she was sure that I had said something—what she
did not know, but something—to Elsa; for Elsa had

been found crying over her coffee in bed in the morning.

"And every word you say to her now is of such supreme importance," Victoria observed, standing over my writing-table.

I took my cigarette out of my mouth and answered perversely enough, but with an eye to truth all the same.

"Nothing that I say to her now is of the very least importance, Victoria."

"What do you mean?" she cried.

"Much what you do," I rejoined, and fell to smoking again.

Victoria began to walk about the room. I endured patiently. My eyes were fixed on Waldenweiter. I wondered idly whether the scene of despair had been enacted yet.

"It's not the smallest good making ourselves unhappy about it," Victoria announced, just as she was on the turn at the other end of the room.

"Not the smallest," I agreed.

"It's much too late."

"A great deal too late."

Victoria darted down and kissed my cheek.

"After all, she ought to think herself very lucky," she decided. "I'm sure everybody else considers her so."

"Under such circumstances," said I, "it's sheer perversity in her to have her own feelings on the matter."

"But you said something that upset her last night," remarked my sister, with a return to the point which I hoped she had lost sight of. This time I lowered my guard in surrender.

"Certainly. I tried to make love to her," said I.

"There, you see!" she cried reproachfully. Her censure of the irrelevant intrusion of such a subject was eloquent and severe.

"It was all Wetter's fault," I remarked, sighing.

"Good gracious! what's it got to do with Wetter? I hate the man!" As she spoke her eyes fell on a box which stood on my writing-table. "What's that?" she asked.

"Diamonds," I answered. "The necklace for Elsa."

"You bought the big one you spoke of? Oh, Augustin, how fortunate!"

I looked up at Victoria and smiled.

"My dear Victoria," said I, "it is the finger of Providence. I'll present them to her after luncheon."

"Yes, do; and mind you don't upset her again."

Alas! I had no desire to "upset" her again. The fit had passed; my only relations toward it were those of an astonished spectator or a baffled analyst. It was part of the same mood that had converted Artenberg into a hall of revelry, of most unwonted revelry. But to-day, with Princess Heinrich frowning, heaven at a discount, and everybody rather ashamed of themselves, was it likely that I should desire to upset her again? The absence of any such wish, combined with the providential diamonds, would (it might reasonably be hoped) restore tranquillity to Elsa. Victoria was quite of this optimistic opinion.

Our interview was interrupted by the arrival of Bederhof, who came to take my final commands with regard to the marriage arrangements. The whole programme was drawn out neatly on a sort of chart (minus the rocks and shoals, of course). The Duchess and her daughter were to stay at Artenberg for another week; it would then be the end of August. On the 1st of September they would reach home, remain there till the 1st of October, when they and the Duke would set out for Forstadt; they were to make their formal entry on the 4th, and on the 12th (a week being allowed for repose, festivities, and preparations) the marriage would be solemnized; in the evening of that day Elsa and I were to come back to Artenberg to pass the first days of our married life.

"I hope your Majesty approves?" said Bederhof.

"Perfectly," said I. "Let us go and find the Princess. Hers must be the decisive word;" and with my programme in one hand and my diamonds in the other I repaired to the Duchess's room, Bederhof following in high contentment.

I imagine that there must have been a depression in my looks, involuntary but reassuring. It is certain that Elsa received me with more composure than I had ventured to hope. She studied Bederhof's chart with grave attention; she and her mother put many questions as to the ceremonial; there was no doubt that Elsa was very much interested in the matter. Presently my mother came in; the privy council round Bederhof grew more engrossed. The Chancellor was delighted; one could almost see the flags and hear the cannon as his descriptive periods rolled out. Princess Heinrich sat listening with a rather bitter smile, but she did not cut him short. I leaned over the back of her chair. Once or twice Elsa glanced at me, timidly but by no means uncheerfully. Behind the cover of the chair-back I unfastened my box and got out my necklace. Then I waited for Elsa's next look. It seemed entirely in keeping with the occasion that I, as well as Bederhof, should have my present for her, my ornament, my toy.

" Their Majesties' carriage will be drawn by four gray horses," said Bederhof. The good Duchess laughed, laid her hand on Elsa's, and whispered, " Their Majesties ! " Elsa blushed, laughed, and again glanced at me. My moment had come. I held up my toy.

" Their Majesties will be dressed in their very best clothes," said I, " with their hair nicely brushed, and perhaps one of them will be so charming as to wear a necklace," and I tossed the thing lightly over the chair-back into Elsa's lap.

She caught it with a little cry, looked at it for a moment, whispered in her mother's ear, jumped up, and, blushing still, ran round and kissed me.

" Oh, thank you ! " she cried.

I kissed her hand and her cheek. My mother smiled, patiently it seemed to me; the Duchess was tremulously radiant; Bederhof obviously benign. It was a pretty group, with the pretty child and her pretty toy for the centre of it. Suddenly I looked at my mother; she nodded ever so slightly. I was applauded and commanded to persevere.

Bederhof pursued his description. He went through it all; he rose to eloquence in describing our departure from Forstadt. This scene ended, he seemed conscious of a bathos. It was in a dull, rather apologetic tone that he concluded by remarking :

" Their Majesties will arrive at Artenberg at seven o'clock, and will partake of dinner."

There appeared to be no desire to dwell on this somewhat inglorious conclusion to so eventful a day. A touch of haste betrayed itself in my mother's manner as she asked for the list of the guests. Elsa had dropped her necklace in her lap, and sat looking before her with an absent expression. The names of distinguished visitors, however, offered a welcome diversion. We were all in very good spirits again in a few minutes. Presently the names bored Elsa; she jumped up, ran to a mirror, and tried on her necklace. The names bored me also, but I stood where I was. Soon a glance from her summoned me, and I joined her. The diamonds were round her neck, squeezed in above the high collar of her morning gown.

"They'll look lovely in the evening," she said.

"You'll have lots more given you," I assured her.

"Do you think so?" she asked, in gleefulness dashed with incredulity.

"Scores," said I solemnly.

"I am very grateful to you for—for everything," she said almost in a whisper, with a sort of penitence that I understood well enough, and an obvious desire to show every proper feeling toward me.

"I delight to please you above all things now," I answered; but even to myself the words sounded cold and formal. Yet they were true; it was above all things my wish to persuade her that she was happy. To this end I used eagerly the aid of the four (or was it six?) gray horses, the necklace, and "Their Majesties."

In the next few days I was much with Elsa, but not much alone with her. There was, of course, no want of ready company, but most of those who offered themselves merely intensified the constraint which their presence was expected to remove. Even Victoria overdid her part rather, betraying an exaggerated fear of leaving us to ourselves. Varvilliers' admirable tact, his supreme apparent unconsciousness, and his never-failing flow of gaiety made him our ideal companion. I missed in him that sympathy with my sombre moods which bound me to Wetter, spirit to spirit; but for lighter hours, for hours that must be made light, he was incomparable. With him Elsa bloomed into merriment, and being, as it were, midway between us, he seemed to me to bridge the gulf of mind and temperament that separated her from me. Hour by hour she grew happier, less timid, more her true self. I took great comfort from this excellent state of things. No doubt I must be careful not to upset her (as Victoria said), but she was certainly getting used to me (as William Adolphus said). Moreover, I was getting used to her, to the obligations she expressed, and to the renunciations she involved. But I had no more wish to try to upset her.

It must be a familiar fact to many that we are very prone to mistake or confuse the sources of our pleasure and the causes of such contentment as we achieve. We attribute to our surroundings in general what is due to one especial part of them; for the sake of one feature the landscape's whole aspect seems pleasant; we rob Peter with intent to pay Paul, and then in the end give the money to somebody else. It is not difficult to see how Elsa and I came to think that we got on better with one another because we both got on so well with Varvilliers, that we were more comfortable together because he made us both comfortable, that we came nearer to understanding each other because he understood us so admirably. We did not perceive even that he was the occasion of our improved relations, far less did we realize that he was their cause and their essence; that it was to him I looked, to him she

looked; and that while he was between there could
be no rude direct contact of her eyes with mine, nor
of mine with hers. Onlookers see most of the game,
they say, but here the onlookers were as blind as the
players; there was an air of congratulation at Artenberg; the King and his bride were drawing closer
together. The blindness was complete; Varvilliers
himself shared it. Of his absolute good faith and
utter unconsciousness I, who doubt most things,
can not doubt. Had he been Wetter, I should have
been alert for the wry smile and the lift of the brows;
but he was his simple self, a perfect gentleman un-
spoiled by thought. Such are entirely delightful;
that they work infinite havoc with established relations between other people seems a small price to pay
for the privilege which their existence confers upon
the world. My dear friend Varvilliers, for whom
my heart is always warm, played the mischief with
the relations between Elsa and myself, which we
all (very whimsically) supposed him to be improving.

It was a comparatively small, although an inter-
estingly unusual, thing that I came to enjoy Elsa's
society coupled with Varvilliers', and not to care
much about it taken alone; it was a more serious,
though far more ordinary, turn of affairs that Elsa
should come to be happy enough with me provided
that Varvilliers were there to—shall I say to take the
edge off me?—but cared not a jot to meet me in his
absence. The latter circumstance is simply and con-
ventionally explained (and, after all, these conventional expressions are no more arbitrary than the
alphabet, which is admitted to be a useful means of
communicating our ideas) by saying that Elsa was
falling in love with Varvilliers; my own state of mind

would deserve analysis, but for a haunting notion that
no states of mind are worth such trouble. Let us
leave it; there it was. It was impossible to say which
of us would miss Varvilliers more. He had become
necessary to both of us. The conclusion drawn by
the way of this world is, of course, at once obvious;
it followed pat from the premise. We must both of
us be deprived of him as soon as possible. I am not
concerned to argue that the world is wrong; and
the very best way to advance a paradox is to look
as though you were uttering a platitude. In this art
the wittiest writer cuts a poor figure beside the laws
of society.

The end of the week approached. Elsa was to
go; Varvilliers was to go. So the arrangement stood;
Elsa was to return, about Varvilliers' return nothing
had been said. The bandage was still over the eyes
of all of us; we had not perceived the need of
settling anything about him. He was still as insignificant to us as he was to Princess Heinrich
herself.

This being the state of the case, there enters to
me one morning my good Cousin Elizabeth, tear-
fully radiant and abundantly maternal. The reason
was soon declared. Elsa had been found crying
again, and wondering vaguely what she was crying about. It was suggested to her that her grief
was due to approaching departure; Elsa embraced
the idea at once. It was pointed out that a month's
absence from me was involved; Elsa sighed deeply
and dabbed her eyes. Cousin Elizabeth dabbed hers
as she told the story; then she caught me in her
arms, kissed me, and said that her happiness was
complete. What was I to do? I was profoundly
surprised, but any display of that emotion would

have been inappropriate and ungracious. I could appear only compassionate and gratified.

"Things do happen right sometimes, you see," pursued Cousin Elizabeth, triumphing in this refutation of some little sneer of mine which she had contested the day before. "I knew you had come to care for her, and now she cares for you. I never was indifferent to that side of it. I always hoped. And now it really is so! Kiss me, Augustin dear."

I kissed Cousin Elizabeth. I was miles away in thought, lost in perplexed musings.

"I comforted her, and told her that the time would soon pass, and that then she would have you all to herself, with no tiresome people to interrupt. But the poor darling still cried a little. But one can't really grieve, can one? A little sorrow means so much happiness later on, doesn't it? And though I couldn't comfort her, you'll be able to, I daresay. What's a month?"

"Nothing," said I. I was conscious of realizing that it was at all events very little.

"I shall expect to see her quite smiling after she's had a little talk with you," was Cousin Elizabeth's parting speech. It won from me a very reassuring nod, and left me in mazes of bewilderment. There was nothing in particular which I believed, but I disbelieved one thing very definitely. It was that Elsa wept because she must be absent from me for a month—a month delightfully busied with the making of four hundred frocks.

Impelled partly by duty but more by curiosity, I went in search of her. Having failed to find her in the house or on the terrace, I descended into the hanging woods, and made for an arbour which she and I and Varvilliers had fallen into the habit of frequenting. A broad grass path ran up to the front of it, but, coming as I did, I approached it by a side track. Elsa sat on the seat and Varvilliers stood before her. He was talking; she leaned forward listening, with her hands clasped in her lap and her eyes fixed on his face. Neither perceived me. I walked briskly toward them, without loitering or spying, but I did not call out. Varvilliers' talk was light, if it might be judged by his occasional laughs. When I was ten yards off I called, " Hallo, here you are! " He turned with a little start, but an easy smile. Elsa flushed red. I had not yet apprehended the truth, although now the idea was dimly in my mind. I sat down by Elsa, and we talked. Of what I have forgotten. I think, in part, of William Adolphus, I laughing at my brother-in-law, Varvilliers feigning to defend him with good-humoured irony. It did not matter of what we talked. For me there was significance in nothing save in Elsa's eyes. They were all for Varvilliers, for him sparkled, for him clouded, for him wondered, laughed, applauded, lived. Presently I dropped out of the conversation and sat silent, facing this new thing. It was not bitter to me; my mood of desire had gone too utterly. There was no pang of defeated rivalry. But I knew why Elsa had cried, who had power to bring, and who also had power to dry, her tears.

Suddenly I saw, or seemed to see, a strange and unusual restraint in Varvilliers' manner. He missed the thread of a story, stumbled, grew dull, and lost his animation. He seemed to talk now for duty, not for pleasure, as a man who covers an awkward moment rather than employs to the full a happy opportunity. Then his glance rested for an instant on my face. I do not know what or how much my face told him, but I did not look at him unkindly.

"I must go, if I may," he said addressing me. "I promised to ride with Vohrenlorf, and the time is past."

He bowed to Elsa and to me.

"We shall see you this afternoon?" she asked.

He bowed again in acquiescence, but with an air of discomfort. Elsa looked at him, and from him to me. She flushed again, opened her lips, but did not speak; then she bent her head down, and the blush spread from neck to forehead.

"Go, my dear friend, go," said I.

He looked at me as though he would have spoken, almost as though he would have protested or excused himself, inadmissible as such a thing plainly was. I smiled at him, but waved my hand to dismiss him. He turned and walked quickly away along the broad grass path. I watched him till he was out of sight; all the while I was conscious of an utter motionlessness in Elsa's figure beside me.

We must have sat there a long while in that unbroken eloquent silence, hardly moving, never looking at one another. For her I was full of grief; a wayward thing it was, indeed, of fate to fashion out of Varvilliers' pleasant friendship this new weapon of attack. She had been on the way to contentment—at least to resignation—but was now thrust back. And she was ashamed. Poor child! why, in Heaven's name, should she be ashamed? Should she not better have been ashamed of a fancy so ill directed as to light on me when Varvilliers was by? For myself I seemed to see rising before me the need for a new deception, a hoodwinking of all the world, a secret that none must know or suspect, that she and I must

have between us for our own. The thing might pass;
she was young. Very likely, but it would not pass
in time. There were the frocks. Ah, but the wardrobe that half hid me would not suffice to obscure
Varvilliers. Or would it? I smiled for an instant.
Instead of hiding behind the wardrobe, I saw myself
becoming part of it, blending with it. Should I take
rank as the four-hundred-and-first frock? " Willingly give thyself up to Clotho, allowing her to spin thy
thread into whatever things she pleases." Even into
a frock, O Emperor? Goes the philosophy as far as
that?

At last I turned to her and laid my hand gently
on her clasped hands.

" Come, my dear," said I, " we must be going
back. They'll all be looking for us. We're too important people to be allowed to hide ourselves."

As I spoke I jumped to my feet, holding out my
hand to help her to rise. She looked up at me in an
oddly pathetic way. I was afraid that she was going
to speak of the matter, and there was nothing to be
gained by speaking of it. " Give me your hand," I
said with a smile, and she obeyed. The pleading in
her eyes persisted. As she stood up, I kissed her
lightly on the forehead. Then we walked away together.

That afternoon I was summoned to Princess
Heinrich's room to drink tea with her and the Duchess. Cousin Elizabeth was still exuberant; it seemed
to me that a cold watchfulness governed my mother's
mood. Relations between my mother and myself
have not always been cordial ; but I have never failed
to perceive and respect in her a fine inner sincerity, an aptitude for truth and a resolute facing of
facts. While Cousin Elizabeth talked, the Princess

sat smiling with her usual faint smile; it never showed the least inclination to become a laugh. She acquiesced politely in the rose-coloured description of Elsa's feelings and affections. She had perception enough to know that the picture could not be true. Presently I took the liberty of informing her by a glance that I was not a partner in the delusion. She showed no surprise; but the fruit of my act was that she detained me by a gesture, after Cousin Elizabeth had taken her leave. For a few moments she sat silent; then she remarked:

"The Duchess is a very kind woman, very anxious to make everybody happy."

"Yes," said I carelessly.

"But it must be in her own way. She is romantic. She thinks everybody else must be the same. You and I know, Augustin, that things of that kind occupy a very small part of a man's life. My sex deludes itself. And when a man occupies the position you do, it's absurd to suppose that he pays much attention to them."

"No doubt Cousin Elizabeth exaggerates," said I, standing in a respectful attitude before my mother.

"Well, I daresay you remember the time when Victoria was a girl. You recollect her folly? But you and I were firm—you behaved very well then, Augustin—and the result is that she is most suitably and most happily married."

I bowed. I did not think that any agreement of mine could be worthy of the magnificent boldness of Princess Heinrich's statement.

"Girls are silly; they pass through a silly time," she pursued, smiling.

A sudden remembrance shot across me.

" It doesn't do to take any notice of such things," said I gravely.

Happily, perhaps, Princess Heinrich was not awake to the fact that she herself was being quoted to herself.

" I'm glad to hear you say so," she said. " You have your work to do. Don't waste your time in thinking of girls' megrims—or of their mothers' nonsense."

I left her presence with a strong sense that Providence had erred in not making her a saint, a king, or anything else that demands a resolute repression of human infirmities. Some people are content to triumph over their own weaknesses; my mother had an eye also for the frailty of others.

She made no reference at all to Varvilliers. There was always something to be learned from Princess Heinrich. From early youth I was inured to a certain degree of painfulness in the lesson.

" Willingly give thyself up to Clotho." My mother was more than willing. She was proud; and, if I may be allowed to vary the metaphor, she embarked on the ship of destiny with a family ticket.

CHAPTER XXIII.

To many the picture presented by my life might seem that of a man who detects the trap and yet walks into it, sinks under burdens that he might cast aside, groans at chains that he could break, and will not leave the prison although the door-key is in his pocket. Such an impression my record may well give, unless it be understood that what came upon me was not an impossibility of movement, but a paralysis of the will to move. In this there is nothing peculiar to one placed as I was. Most men could escape from what irks, confines, or burdens them at the cost of effacing their past lives, breaking the continuity of existence, cutting the cord that binds together, in a sequence of circumstances and incidents, youth, and maturity, and age. But who can do the thing? One man in a thousand, and he generally a scoundrel.

Our guests returned to Bartenstein, the Duchess still radiant and maternal, Elsa infinitely kind, infinitely apologetic, a little tearful, never for an instant wavering in her acceptance of the future. Varvilliers took leave of me with great friendliness; there was in his air now just a hint of amusement, most decorously suppressed; he was charmingly unconscious of any possible seriousness in the position.

My mother went to visit Styrian relatives. Victoria and William Adolphus had taken a villa by the seaside. I was quite alone at Artenberg, save for my faithful Vohrenlorf, and Vohrenlorf was bored to death. That will not appear strange; to me it seemed enviable. A prisoner under sentence probably discerns much that is attractive even in the restricted life of his jailer.

In a day or two there came upon me a persistent restlessness, and with it constant thoughts of Wetter. I wondered where he was and what he did; I longed to share the tempestuousness of his life and thoughts. He brought with him other remembrances, of the passions and the events that we two had, in friendship or hostility, witnessed together. They had seemed, all of them, far behind in the past, belonging to the days when, as old Vohrenlorf had told me, I had still six years. Now I had only a month; but the images were with me, importunate and pleading. I was asking whether I could not, even now, save something out of life.

Three days later found me established in a hotel in the Place Vendôme at Paris, Vohrenlorf my only companion. I was in strictest *incognito;* Baron de Neberhausen was my name. But in Paris in August my *incognito* was almost a superfluity for me, although a convenience to others. It was very hot; I did not care. The town was absolutely empty. Not for me! Here is my secret. Wetter was in Paris. I had seen it stated in the newspaper. What brought the man of moods to Paris in August? I could answer the question in one way only: the woman of his mood. I did not care about her; I wanted to see him and hear again from his own lips what he thought of the universe, of my part and his in it, and of the ways of the Power that ruled it. In a month I should be on my honeymoon with Cousin Elsa. I fought desperately against the finality implied in that.

On the second evening I gave Vohrenlorf the slip, and went out on the Boulevards alone. In great cities nobody is known; I enjoyed the luxury of being ignored. I might pass for a student, a chemist, at a pinch, perhaps, for a poet of a reflective type. My natural manner would seem no more than a touch of youth's pardonable arrogance. I sat down and had some coffee. It was half-past ten, and the pavements were full. I bought a paper and read a paragraph about Elsa and myself. Elsa and myself both seemed rather a long way off. It was delicious to make believe that this here and this now were reality; the kingship, Elsa, the wedding and the rest, some story or poem that I, the student, had been making laboriously before working hours ended, and I was free to seek the Boulevards. I was pleased when a pretty girl, passing by, stared hard at me and seemed to like my looks; this tribute was my own; she was not staring at the king.

Satisfaction, not surprise, filled me when, in about twenty minutes, I saw Wetter coming toward the *café*. I had taken a table far back from the street, and he did not see me. The glaring gaslight gave him a deeper paleness and cut the lines of his face to a sharper edge. He was talking with great animation, his hands moving constantly in eager gesture. I was within an ace of springing forward to greet him—so my heart went out to him—but the sight of his companion restrained me, and I sat chuckling and wondering in my corner. There they were, large as life, true to Varvilliers' description; the big stomach and the locket that a hyperbole, so

"My dear friend, have you forgotten me?"

inevitable as to outstrip mere truth in fidelity, had called bigger. Besides there were the whiskers, the heavy jowl, the infinite fatness of the man, a fatness not of mere flesh only, but of manner, of air, of thought, of soul. There was no room for doubt or question. This was Coralie's impresario, Coralie's career, her duty, her destiny; in a word, everything to Coralie that poor little Cousin Elsa was to me. Nay, your pardon; that I was to Cousin Elsa. I put my cigar back in my mouth and smoked gravely; it seemed improper to laugh.

The two men sat down at an outer table. Wetter was silent now, and Struboff (I remembered suddenly that I had seen Coralie described as Madame Mansoni-Struboff) was talking. I could almost see the words treacling from his thick lips. What in Heaven's name made him Wetter's companion? What in Heaven's name made me such a fool as to ask the question? Men like Struboff can have but one merit, and, to be fair, but one serious crime. It is the same; they are the husbands of their wives.

I could contain myself no longer. I rose and walked forward. I laid my hand on Wetter's shoulder, saying:

"My dear friend, have you forgotten me—Baron de Neberhausen?"

He looked up with a start, but when he saw me his eyes softened. He clasped my hand.

"Neberhausen?" he said.

"Yes; we met in Forstadt."

"To be sure," he laughed. "May I present my friend to you? M. le Baron de Neberhausen, M. Struboff. You will know Struboff's name. He gives us the best operas in the world, and the best singing."

" M. Struboff's fame has reached me," said I, sitting down.

Evidently Struboff did not know me; he received the introduction without any show of deference. I was delighted. I should have seen little of the true man had he been aware from the first who I was. Things being as they were, I could flatter him, and he had no motive for flattering me. A mere baron had no effect on him. He resumed the interrupted conversation; he was telling Wetter how he could make money out of music, and then more music out of the money, then more money out of the music, and so on, in an endless chain of music and money, money and music, money, music, money. Wetter sat looking at him with a smile of malicious mockery.

" Happy man! " he cried suddenly. " You love only two things in the world, and you've married both."

Struboff pulled his whisker meditatively.

" Yes, I have done well," he said, and drained his glass. " But hasn't Coralie done well too? Where would she have been but for me? "

" Indeed, my dear Struboff, there's no telling, but I suppose in the arms of somebody else."

" Your own, for example? " growled the husband.

" Observe the usual reticences," said Wetter, with a laugh. " My dear Baron, Struboff mocks my misery by a pretended jealousy. You can reassure him. Did Madame Mansoni ever favour me? "

" I can speak only of what I know," I answered, smiling. " She never favoured you before me."

He caught the ambiguity of my words, and laughed again. Struboff turned toward me with a stare.

" You also knew my wife? " he asked.

"I had the honour," said I. "In Forstadt."

"In Forstadt! Do you know the king?"

"Not so well as I could wish," I answered. "About as well as I know Wetter here."

"That's admirably well!" cried Wetter. "Well enough not to trust me."

The fat man looked from one to the other of us in an obtuse suspicion of our hilarity.

"The king admired my wife's talents," said he. "We intend to visit Forstadt next year."

"Do you?" said I, and Wetter's peal broke out again.

"The king will find my wife's talent much increased by training," pursued Struboff.

"Damn your wife's talent!" said Wetter, quite suddenly. "You talk as much about it as she does of your beauty."

"I hope madame is well?" I interposed quickly and suavely, for Struboff had grown very red and gave signs of temper. Wetter did not allow him to answer. He sprang to his feet and dragged Struboff up by the arm.

"Take his other arm!" he cried to me. "Bring him along. Come, come, we'll all go and see how madame is."

"It's nearly eleven," remonstrated Struboff sourly. "I want to go to bed."

"You? You go to bed? You, with your crimes, go to bed? Why, you couldn't sleep! You would cower all night! Go to bed! Oh, my dear Struboff, think better of it. No, no, we'll none of us go to bed. Bed's a hell for men like us. For you above all! Think again, Struboff, think again!"

Struboff shrugged his fat shoulders in helpless bad temper. I was laughing so much (at what, at what?) that I could hardly do my part in hustling him along. Wetter set a hot pace, and Struboff soon began to pant.

"I can't walk. Call a cab!" he gasped.

"Cab? No, no. We can't sit still. Conscience, my dear Struboff! *Post equitem*—you know. There's nothing like walking for sinners like us. Bring him along, Baron, bring him along!"

"Perhaps M. Struboff doesn't desire our company," I suggested.

"Perhaps!" shouted Wetter, with a laugh that turned a dozen heads toward him. "Oh, my dear Struboff, do you hear this suggestion of our friend the baron's? What a pity you have no breath to repudiate it!"

But now we were escaping from the crowd. Crossing in front of the Opera House, we made for the Rue de la Paix. The pace became smarter still; not only was Struboff breathless with being dragged along, but I was breathless with dragging him. I insisted on a cab. Wetter yielded, planted Struboff and me side by side, and took the little seat facing us himself. Here he sat, smiling maliciously, as the poor impresario mopped his forehead and fetched up deep gasps of breath. Where lay the inspiration of this horseplay of Wetter's?

"Quicker, quicker!" he cried to the driver. "I am impatient, my friends are impatient. Quick, quick! Only God is patient."

"He's mad," grunted Struboff. "He's quite mad. The devil, I'm hot!"

Wetter suddenly assumed an air of great dignity and blandness.

"In offering to present us to madame at an hour possibly somewhat late," he said, "our dear M. Struboff shows his wonted amiability. We should be failing in gratitude if we did not thank him most sincerely."

"I didn't ask you to come," growled Struboff.

Wetter looked at him with an air of grieved surprise, but said nothing at all. He turned to me with a ridiculous look of protest, as though asking for my support. I laughed; the mad nonsense was so welcome to me.

We stopped before a tall house in the Rue Washington; Wetter bundled us out with immense haste. There were lights in the second-floor windows. "Madame expects us!" he cried with a rapturous clasping of his hands. "Come, come, dear Struboff! —Baron, Baron, pray take Struboff's arm; the steps to heaven are so steep."

Struboff seemed resigned to his fate; he allowed himself to be pushed upstairs without expostulation. He opened the door for us, and ushered us into the passage. As he preceded us, I had time for one whisper to Wetter.

"You're still mad about her, are you?" I said, pinching his arm.

"Still? Good Heavens, no! Again!" he answered.

The door that faced us was thrown open, and Coralie stood before me in a loose gown of a dark-red colour. Before she could speak, Wetter darted forward, pulling me after him.

"I have the distinguished honour to present my friend, M. de Neberhausen," he said. "You may remember meeting him at Forstadt."

Coralie looked for a moment at each of us in turn. She smiled and nodded her head.

"Perfectly," she said; "but it is a surprise to see

20

him here, a very pleasant surprise." She gave me her hand, which I kissed with a fine flourish of gallantry.

"This gentleman knows the King very well," said Struboff, nodding at her with a solemn significance. "There's money in that!" he seemed to say.

"Does he?" she asked indifferently; and added to me, "Pray come in. I was not expecting visitors; you must make excuses for me."

She did not seem changed in the least degree. There was the same indolence, the same languid, slow enunciation. It struck me in a moment that she ignored her husband's presence. He had gone to a sideboard and was fingering a decanter. Wetter flung himself on a sofa.

"It is really you?" she asked in a whisper, with a lift of her eyelids.

"Oh, without the least doubt!" I answered. "And it is you also?"

Struboff came forward, tumbler in hand.

"Pray, is your King fond of music?" he asked.

"He will adore it from the lips of Madame Struboff," I answered, bowing.

"He adored it from the lips of Mlle. Mansoni," observed Wetter, with a malicious smile. Struboff glared at him; Coralie smiled slightly. An inkling of Wetter's chosen part came into my mind. He had elected to make Struboff uncomfortable; he did not choose that the fat man should enjoy his victory in peace. My emotions chimed in with his resolve, but reason suggested that the ethical merits were more on Struboff's side. He was Coralie's career; the analogy of my own relation toward Elsa urged that he who is a career is entitled to civility. Was not I Elsa's Struboff? I broke into a sudden laugh; it passed as a tribute to Wetter's acid correction.

"You are studying here in Paris, madame?" I asked.

"Yes," said Coralie. "Why else should we be here now?"

"Why else should I be here now?" asked Wetter. "For the matter of that, Baron, why else should you be here now? Why else should anybody be here now? It is even an excuse for Struboff's presence."

"I need no excuse for being in my own home," said Struboff, and he gulped down his liquor.

Wetter sprang up and seized him by the arm.

"You are becoming fatter and fatter and fatter. Presently you will be round, quite round; they'll make a drum of you, and I'll beat you in the orchestra while madame sings divinely on the boards. Come and see if we can possibly avoid this thing," and he led him off to the sofa. There they began to talk, Wetter suddenly dropping his burlesque and allowing a quiet, earnest manner to succeed his last outburst. I caught some mention of thousands of francs; surely there must be a bond of interest, or Wetter would have been turned out before now.

Coralie moved toward the other end of the room, which was long, although narrow. I followed her. As she sat down she remarked:

"He has lent Struboff twenty thousand francs; but for that I must have sung before I was ready."

The situation seemed a little clearer.

"But he is curious," she pursued, fixing a patiently speculative eye on Wetter. "You would say that he was fond of me?"

"It is a possible reason for his presence."

"He doesn't show it," said she, with a shrug.

I understood that little point in Wetter's code; besides, his humour seemed just now too bitter for love-making. If Coralie felt any resentment, it did not go very deep. She turned her eyes from Wetter to my face.

"You're going to be married very soon?" she said.

"In a month," said I. "I'm having my last fling. You perceived our high spirits?"

"I've seen her picture. She's pretty. And I've seen the Countess von Sempach."

"You know about her?"

"Have you forgotten that you used to speak of her? Ah, yes, you've forgotten all that you used to say! The Countess is still handsome."

"What of that? So are you."

"True, it doesn't matter much," Coralie admitted. "Does your Princess love you?"

"Don't you love your husband?"

A faint slow smile bent her lips as she glanced at Struboff—himself and his locket.

"Nobody acts without a motive," said I. "Not even in marrying."

The bitterness that found expression in this little sneer elicited no sympathetic response from Coralie. I was obliged to conclude that she considered her marriage a success; at least that it was doing what she had expected from it. At this moment she yawned in her old, pretty, lazy way. Certainly there were no signs of romantic misery or tragic disillusionment about her. Again I asked myself whether my sympathy were not more justly due to Struboff—Struboff, who sat now smoking a big cigar and wobbling his head solemnly in answer to the emphatic taps of Wetter's forefinger on his waistcoat. The question was whether human tenderness lay anywhere under those wrappings; if so, M. Struboff might be a proper object of compassion, his might be the misery, his (O monstrous thought!) the disillusionment. But the prejudice of beauty fought hard on Coralie's side. I always find it difficult to be just to a person of markedly unpleasant appearance. I was piqued to much curiosity by these wandering ideas; I determined to probe Struboff through the layers.

Soon after I took my leave. Coralie pressed me to return the next day, and before I could speak Wetter accepted the invitation for me. There was no very strong repugnance in Struboff's face; I should not have heeded it had it appeared. Wetter prepared to come with me. I watched his farewell to Coralie; his smile seemed to mock both her and himself. She was weary and dreary, but probably only because she wanted her bed. It was a mistake, as a rule, to attribute to her other than the simplest desires. The moment we were outside, Wetter turned on me with a savagely mirthful expression of my own thoughts.

"A wretched thing to leave her with him? Not the least in the world!" he cried. "She will sleep ten hours, eat one, sing three, sleep three, eat two, sleep—— Have I run through the twenty-four?"

"Well, then, why are we to disturb ourselves?" I asked.

"Why are we to disturb ourselves? Good God, isn't it enough that she should be like that?"

I laughed, as I blew out my cigarette smoke.

"This is an old story," said I. "She is not in love with you, I suppose? That's it, isn't it?"

"It's not the absence of the fact," said he, with

a smile; "it's the want of the potentiality that is so deplorable."

"Why torment Struboff, though?"

"Struboff?" he repeated, knitting his brows. "Ah, now Struboff is worth tormenting! You won't believe me; but he can feel."

"I was right, then; I thought he could."

"You saw it?"

"My prospects, perhaps, quicken my wits."

My arm was through his, and he pressed it between his elbow and his side.

"You see," said he, "perversity runs through it all. She should feel; he should not. It seems she doesn't, but he does. Heavens, would you accept such a conclusion without the fullest experiment? For me, I am determined to test it."

"Still you're in love with her."

"Agreed, agreed, agreed. A man must have a spur to knowledge."

We parted at the Place de la Concorde, and I strolled on alone to my hotel. Vohrenlorf was waiting for me, a little anxious, infinitely sleepy. I dismissed him at once, and sat down to read my letters. I had the feeling that I would think about all these matters to-morrow, but I was also pervaded by a satisfaction. My mind was being fed. The air here nourished, the air of Artenberg starved. I complimented Paris on a virtue not her own; the house in the Rue Washington was the source of my satisfaction.

There was a letter from Varvilliers; he wrote from Hungary, where he was on a visit. Here is something of what he said:

"There is a charming lady here, and we fall in

love, all according to mode and fashion. (The buttons are on the foils, pray understand.) It is the simplest thing in the world; the whole process might, as I believe, be digested into twelve elementary motions or thereabouts. The information is given and received by code; it is like playing whist. 'How much have you?' her eyes ask. 'A passion,' I answer by the code. 'I have a *penchant*,' comes from her side of the table. 'I am leading up to it,' say I. 'I am returning the lead.' Good! But then comes hers (or mine), 'I have no more.' Alas! Well then, I lead, or she leads, another suit. It's a good game; and our stakes are not high. You, sire, would like signals harder to read, I know your taste. You're right there. And don't you make the stakes higher? I have plunged into indiscretion; if I did not, you would think that Bederhof had forged my handwriting. Unless I am stopped on the frontier I shall be in Forstadt in three weeks."

I dropped the letter with a laugh, wondering whether the charming lady played the game as he did and a stake as light. Or did she suffer? Well, anybody can suffer. The talent is almost universal. There was, it seemed, reason to suppose that Struboff suffered. I acquiesced, but with a sense of discontent. Pain should not be vulgarized. Varvilliers' immunity gave him a new distinction in my eyes.

CHAPTER XXIV.

STRUBOFF'S inevitable discovery of my real name
was a disaster; it delayed my operations for three
days, since it filled his whole being with a sense of
abasement and a hope of gain, thereby suspending
for the time those emotions in him which had excited my curiosity. Clearly he had unstinted visions
of lucrative patronage, dreams, probably, of a piece
of coloured ribbon for his button-hole, and a right
to try to induce people to call him " Chevalier."
He made Coralie a present, handsome enough. I
respected the conscientiousness of this act; my
friendship was an unlooked-for profit, a bonus on the
marriage, and he gave his wife her commission. But
he seemed cased in steel against any confidence; he
trembled as he poured me out a glass of wine. He
had pictured me only as a desirable appendage to a
gala performance; it is, of course, difficult to realize that the points at which people are important to
us are not those at which they are important to themselves. However I made progress at last. The
poor man's was a sad case; the sadder because only
with constant effort could the onlooker keep its sad-
ness disengaged from its absurdity, and remember
that unattractiveness does not exclude misery. The
wife in a marriage of interest is the spoiled child of

304

romancers; scarcely any is rude enough to say, " Well, who put you there?" The husband in such a partnership gains less attention; at the most, he is allowed a subordinate share of the common stock of woe. The clean case for observation—he miserable, she miles away from any such poignancy of emotion—was presented by Coralie's consistency. It was not in her to make a bargain and pull grimaces when she was asked to fulfil it. True, she interpreted it in her own way. " I promised to marry you. Well, I have. How are you wronged, *mon cher?* But did I promise to speak to you, to like you? *Mon Dieu!* who promised, or would ever promise, to love you?" The mingled impatience and amusement of such questions expressed themselves in her neglect of him and in her yawns. Under his locket, and his paunch, and his layers, he burned with pain; Wetter was laying the blisters open to the air, that their sting might be sharper. At last, sorely beset, he divined a sympathy in me. He thought it disinterested, not perceiving that he had for me the fascination of a travesty of myself, and that in his marriage I enjoyed a burlesque presentiment of what mine would be. That point of view was my secret until Wetter's quick wit penetrated it; he worked days before he found out why I was drawn to the impresario; his discovery was hailed with a sudden laugh and a glance, but he put nothing into words. Both to him and to me the thing was richer for reticence; in the old phrase, the drapery enhanced the charms which it did not hide.

A day came when I asked the husband to luncheon with me. I sent Vohrenlorf away; we sat down together, Struboff swelling with pride, seeing himself telling the story in the wings, meditating the appearance and multiplication of paragraphs. I said not a word to discourage the visions; we talked of how Coralie should make fame and he money; he grew enthusiastic, guttural, and severe on the Steinberg. I ordered more Steinberg, and fished for more enthusiasm. I put my purse at his disposal; he dipped his fingers deep, with an anxious furtive eagerness. The loan was made, or at least pledged, before it flashed across my brain that the money was destined for Wetter—he wanted to pay off Wetter. We were nearing the desired ground.

"My dear M. Struboff," said I, "you must not allow yourself to be embarrassed. Great properties are slow to develop; but I have patience with my investments. Clear yourself of all claims. Money troubles fritter away a man's brains, and you want yours."

He muttered something about temporary scarcity.

"It would be intolerable that madame should be bothered with such matters," I said.

He gulped down his Steinberg and gave a snort. The sound was eloquent, although not sweet. I filled his glass and handed him a cigar. He drank the wine, but laid the cigar on the table and rested his head on his hand.

"And women like to have money about," I pursued, looking at the veins on his forehead.

"I've squandered money on her," he said. "Good money."

"Yes, yes. One's love seeks every mode of expression. I'm sure she's grateful."

He raised his eyes and looked at me. I was smoking composedly.

"Were you once in love with my wife?" he asked

bluntly. His deference wore away under the corrosion of Steinberg and distress.

"Let us choose our words, my dear M. Struboff. Once I professed attachment to Mlle. Mansoni."

"She loved you?"

"It is discourteous not to accept any impression that a lady wishes to convey to you," I answered, smiling.

"Ah, you know her!" he cried, bringing his fist down on the table.

"Not the least in the world," I assured him. "Her beauty, her charm, her genius—yes, we all know those. But her soul! That's her husband's prerogative."

There was silence for a moment, during which he still looked at me, his thick eyelids half hiding the pathetic gaze of his little eyes.

"My life's a hell!" he said, and laid his head between his hands on the table. I saw a shudder in his fat shoulders.

"My dear M. Struboff," I murmured, as I rose and walked round to him. I did not like touching him, but I forced myself to pat his shoulder kindly. "Women take whims and fancies," said I, as I walked back to my seat.

He raised his head and set his chin between his fists.

"She took me for what she could get out of me," said he.

"Shall we be just? Didn't you look to get something out of her?"

"Yes. I married her for that," he answered. "But I'm a damned fool! I saw that she loathed me; it isn't hard to see. You see it; everybody sees it."

"And you fell in love with her? That was breaking the bargain, wasn't it?" It crossed my mind that I might possibly break my bargain with Elsa. But the peril was remote.

"My God, it's maddening to be treated like a beast. Am I repulsive, am I loathsome?"

"What a question, my dear M. Struboff!"

"And I live with her. It is for all day and every day."

"Come, come, be reasonable. We're not love-sick boys."

"If I touch a piece of bread in giving it to her, she cuts herself another slice."

How I understood you in that, O dainty cruel Coralie!

"And that devil comes and laughs at me."

"He needn't come, if you don't wish it."

"Perhaps it's better than being alone with her," he groaned. "And she doesn't deceive me. Ah, I should like sometimes to say to her, ' Do what you like; amuse yourself, I shall not see. It wouldn't matter.' If she did that, she mightn't be so hard to me. You wonder that I say this, that I feel it like this? Well, I'm a man; I'm not a dog. I don't dirty people when I touch them."

I got up and walked to the hearthrug. I stood there with my back to him. He blew his nose loudly, then took the bottle; I heard the wine trickle in the glass and the sound of his noisy swallowing. There was a long silence. He struck a match and lit his cigar. Then he folded up the notes I had given him, and the clasp of his pocket-book clicked.

"I have to go with her to rehearsal," he said.

I turned round and walked toward him. His uneasy deference returned, he jumped up with a bow and an air of awkward embarrassment.

" Your Majesty is very good. Your Majesty pardons me? I have abused your Majesty's kindness. You understand, I have nobody to speak to."

" I understand very well, M. Struboff. I am very sorry. Be kind to her and she will change toward you."

He shook his head ponderously.

" She won't change," he said, and stood shuffling his feet as he waited to be dismissed. I gave him my hand. (O Coralie, you and your bread! I understood.)

" She'll get accustomed to you," I murmured, with a reminiscence of William Adolphus.

" I think she hates me more every day." He bowed over my hand, and backed out with clumsy ceremony.

I flung myself on the sofa. Was not the burlesque well conceived and deftly fashioned? True, I did not seem to myself much like Struboff. There was no comfort in that; Struboff did not seem to himself much like what he was. "Am I repulsive, am I loathsome?" he cried indignantly, and my diplomacy could answer only, " What a question, my dear M. Struboff!" If I cried out, asking whether I were so unattractive that my bride must shrink from me, a thousand shocked voices would answer in like manner, " Oh, sire, what a question!"

Later in the day I called on Coralie and found her alone. Speaking as though from my own observation, I taxed her roundly with her coldness to Struboff and with allowing him to perceive her distaste for him. I instanced the matter of the bread, declaring that I had noticed it when I breakfasted with them. Coralie began to laugh.

" Do I do that? Well, perhaps I do. You've

felt his hand? It is not very pleasant. Yes, I think I do take another piece."

"He observes it."

"Oh, I think not. He doesn't care. Besides he must know. Have I pretended to care for him? Heavens, I'm no hypocrite. We knew very well what we wanted, he and I. We have each got it. But kisses weren't in the bargain."

"And you kiss nobody now?"

"No," she answered simply and without offence. "No. Wetter doesn't ask me, and you know I never felt love for him; if he did ask me, I wouldn't. These things are very troublesome. And you don't ask me."

"No, I don't, Coralie," said I, smiling.

"I might kiss you, perhaps."

"I have something to give too, have I?"

"No, that would be no use. I should make nothing out of you. And the rest is nonsense. No, I wouldn't kiss you, if you did ask."

"Perhaps Wetter will ask you now. I have lent your husband money, and he will pay Wetter off."

"Ah, perhaps he will then; he is curious, Wetter. But I shan't kiss him. I am very well as I am."

"Happy?"

"Yes; at least I should be, if it were not for Struboff. He annoys me very much. You know, it's like an ugly picture in the room, or a dog one hates. He doesn't say or do much, but he's there always. It frets me."

"Madame, my sympathy is extreme."

"Oh, your sympathy! You're laughing at me. I don't care. You're going to be married yourself."

"What you imply is not very reassuring."

"It's all a question of what one expects," she said with a shrug.

"My wife won't mind me touching her bread?" I asked anxiously.

"Oh, no, she won't mind that. You're not like that. Oh, no, it won't be in that way."

"I declare I'm much comforted."

"Indeed you needn't fear that. In some things all women are alike. You needn't fear anything of that sort. No woman could feel that about you."

"I grow happier every moment. I shouldn't have liked Elsa to cut herself another slice."

Coralie laughed, sniffed the roses I had brought, and laughed again, as she said:

"In fact I do. I remember it now. I didn't mean to be rude; it came natural to do it; as if the piece had fallen on the floor, you know."

Evidently Struboff had analyzed his wife's feelings very correctly. I doubted both the use and the possibility of enlightening her as to his. Kisses were not in the bargain, she would say. After all, the desire for affection was something of an incongruity in Struboff, an alien weed trespassing on the ground meant for music and for money. I could hardly blame her for refusing to foster the intruder. I felt that I should be highly unjust if, later on, I laid any blame on Elsa for not satisfying a desire for affection should I chance to feel such a thing. And as to the bread Coralie had quite reassured me. I looked at her. She was smiling in quiet amusement. Evidently her fancy was tickled by the matter of the bread.

"You notice a thing like that," she said. "But he doesn't. Imagine his noticing it!"

"I can imagine it very well."

"Oh no, impossible. He has no sensibility. You laugh? Well, yes, perhaps it's lucky."

During the next two or three days I was engaged almost unintermittently with business which followed me from home, and had no opportunity of seeing more of my friends. I regretted this the less, because I seemed now to be possessed of the state of affairs. I resigned myself to the necessity of a speedy return to Forstadt. Already Bederhof was in despair at my absence, and excuses failed me. I could not tell him that to return to Forstadt was to begin the preparations for execution; a point at which hesitation must be forgiven in the condemned. But before I went I had a talk with Wetter.

He stormed Vohrenlorf's defences and burst into my room late one night.

"So we're going back, sire?" he cried. "Back to our work, back to harness?"

"You're going too?" I asked quietly.

He threw back his hair from his forehead.

"Yes, I too," he said. "Struboff has paid me off; I have played, I have won, I am rich, I desire to serve my country. You don't appear pleased, sire?"

"When you serve your country, I have to set about saving mine," said I dryly.

"Oh, you'll be glad of the distraction of public affairs," he sneered.

"Madame Mansoni-Struboff has not fulfilled my hopes of her. I thought you'd have no leisure for politics for a long while to come."

"The pupil of Hammerfeldt speaks to me," he said with a smile. "You would be right, very likely, but for the fact that madame has dismissed me."

"You use a conventional phrase?"

" Well then, she has—well, yes, I do use a conventional phrase."

" I shall congratulate M. Struboff on an increased tranquillity."

The evening was chilly, and I had a bit of fire. Wetter sat looking into it, hugging his knees and swaying his body to and fro. I stood on the hearthrug by him.

" I have still time," he said suddenly. " I'm a young man. I can do something still."

" You can turn me out, you think? "

" I don't want to turn you out."

" Use me, perhaps? "

" Tame you, perhaps."

I looked down at him and I laughed.

" Why do you laugh? " he asked. " I thought I should have roused that sleeping dignity of yours."

" Oh, my friend," said I, " you will not tame me, and you will not do great things."

" Why not? " he asked, briefly and brusquely.

" You'll play again, you'll do some mad prank, some other woman will—let us stick to our phrase—will not dismiss you. When an irresistible force encounters an immovable object—— You know the old puzzle? "

" Interpret your parable, O King! "

" When a great brain is joined to an impossible temper—result? "

" The result is nothing," said he, taking a fresh grip of his knees.

" Even so, even so," I nodded.

" But I have done things," he persisted.

" Yes, and then undone them. My friend, you're a tragedy." And I lit a cigarette.

He sat where he was for a moment longer; then he sprang up with a loud laugh.

"A tragedy! A tragedy! If I make one, by Heaven the world is rich in them! Take Struboff for another. But your Majesty is wrong. I'm a farce."

"Yes, you're a bit of a farce," said I.

He laid his hand on my arm and looked full and long in my face.

"So you've made your study of us?" he asked. "Oh, I know why you came to Paris! Coralie, Struboff, myself—you have us all now?"

"Pretty well," said I. "To understand people is both useful and interesting; and to a man in my position it has the further attraction of being difficult."

"And you think Bederhof is too strong for me?"

"He is stupid and respectable. My dear Wetter, what chance have you?"

"There's a river in this town. Shall I jump in?"

"Heavens, no! You'd set it all a-hissing and a-boiling."

"To-night, sire, I thought of killing Struboff."

"Ah, yes, the pleasures of imagination! I often indulge in them."

"Then a bullet for myself."

"Of course! And another impresario for Coralie! You must look ahead in such matters."

"It would have made a great sensation."

"Everywhere, except in the bosom of Coralie."

"Your cleverness robbed the world of that other sensation long ago. If I had killed you!"

"It would have been another—another impresario for my Princess."

"We shall meet at Forstadt? You'll ask me to the wedding?"

" Unless you have incurred Princess Heinrich's anger."

" I tell you I'm going to settle down."

" Never," said I.

" Be careful, sire. The revolver I bought for Struboff is in my pocket."

" Make me a present of it," I suggested.

He looked hard in my eyes, laughed a little, drew out a small revolver, and handed it to me.

" Struboff was never in great danger," he said.

" I was never much afraid for Struboff," said I. " Thanks for the revolver. You're not quibbling with me? "

" I don't understand."

" There's no river in this town; no institution called the Morgue? "

· " Not a trace of such things. Do you know why not? "

" Because it's the king's pleasure," said I, smiling and holding out my hand to him.

" Because I'm a friend to a friend," he said, as he took my hand. Then without another word he turned and walked out quickly. I heard him speak to Vohrenlorf in the outer room, and laugh loudly as he ran down the stairs.

He had reminded me that I was a pupil of Hammerfeldt's. The reminder came home to me as a reproach. I had been forgetful of the Prince's lessons; I had allowed myself to fall into a habit of thought which led me to assume that my happiness or unhappiness was a relevant consideration in judging of the merits of the universe. The assumption is so common as to make us forget that so far from being proved it is not even plausible. I saw the absurdity of it at once, in the light of my recent discoveries. Was God shamed because Struboff was miserable, because Coralie was serenely selfish, because Wetter was tempestuous beyond rescue? I smiled at all these questions, and proceeded to the inference that the exquisite satisfaction of my own cravings was probably not an inherent part of the divine purpose. That is, if there were such a thing; and if there were not, the whole matter was so purely accidental as not to admit of any one consideration being in the least degree more or less relevant than another. "Willingly give thyself up to Clotho, allowing her to spin thy thread into whatever things she pleases." That was an extremely good maxim; but it would have been of no service to cast the pearl before Coralie's impresario. I would use it myself, though. I summoned Vohrenlorf.

"We have stayed here too long, Vohrenlorf," said I. "My presence is necessary in Forstadt. I must not appear wanting in interest in these preparations."

"Undoubtedly," said he, "they are very anxious for your Majesty's return."

"And I am very anxious to return. We'll go by the evening train to-morrow. Send word to Bederhof."

He seemed rather surprised and not very pleased, but promised to see that my orders were executed. I sat down in the chair in which Wetter had sat, and began again to console myself with my Stoic maxim. But there was a point at which I stuck. I recalled Coralie and her bread, and regarded Struboff not in the aspect of his own misery (which I had decided to be irrelevant), but in the light of Coralie's feelings. It seemed to me that the philosopher should have spared more consideration to this side of the matter.

Had he reached such heights as to be indifferent not only to his own sufferings, but to being a cause of suffering to others? Perhaps Marcus Aurelius had attained to this; Coralie Mansoni, by the way, seemed most blessedly to have been born into it. To me it was a stone of stumbling. Pride came to me with insidious aid and admired while I talked of Clotho; but where was my ally when I pictured Elsa also making her surrender to the Fates? My ally then became my enemy. With a violent wrench I brought myself to the thought that neither was Elsa's happiness a relevant consideration. It would not do, I could not maintain the position. For Elsa was young, fresh, aspiring to happiness as a plant rears its head to the air. And our wedding was but a fortnight off.

"Am I repulsive, am I loathsome?"

"What a question, my dear M. Struboff!"

I had that snatch of talk in my head when I fell asleep.

The next day but one found me back at Forstadt. They had begun to decorate the streets.

CHAPTER XXV.

A SMACK OF REPETITION.

THE contrast of outer and inner, of the world's myself and my own myself, of others as they seem to me and to themselves (of the reality they may be, through inattention or dulness, as ignorant as I), which is the most permanent and the dominant impression that life has stamped on my mind, was never more powerfully brought home to me than in the days which preceded my marriage to my cousin Elsa. As I have said, they had begun to decorate the streets; let me summarize all the rest by repeating that they decorated the streets, and went on decorating them. The decorative atmosphere enveloped all external objects, and wrapped even the members of my own family in its spangled cloud. Victoria blossomed in diamonds, William Adolphus sprouted in plumes; my mother embodied the stately, Cousin Elizabeth a gorgeous heartiness; the Duke's eyes wore a bored look, but the remainder of his person was fittingly resplendent. Bederhof was Bumble in Olympus; beyond these came a sea of smiles, bows, silks, and uniforms. Really I believe that the whole thing was done as handsomely as possible, and the proceedings are duly recorded in a book of red leather, clasped in gold and embellished with many pictures, which the Municipality of. Forstadt presented to Elsa in remembrance of the auspicious event. It lies now under a class case, and, I understand, excites much interest among ladies who come to see my house.

Elsa was a puzzle no longer; I should have welcomed more complexity of feeling. The month which had passed since we parted had brought to her many reflections, no doubt, and as a presumable result of them a fixed attitude of mind. William Adolphus would have said (and very likely did say to Victoria) that she had got used to me; but this mode of putting the matter suffers from my brother-in-law's bluntness. She had not defied Clotho, but neither had she altogether given herself up to Clotho. She had compromised with the Formidable Lady, and, although by no means enraptured, seemed to be conscious that she might have come off worse. What was distasteful in Clotho's terms Elsa attempted to reduce to insignificance by a disciplined arrangement of her thoughts and emotions. Much can be done if one will be firm with would-be vagrants of the mind. The pleasant may be given prominence; the disagreeable relegated to obscurity; the attractive installed in the living apartments; the repellant locked in a distant cellar, whence their ill-conditioned cries are audible occasionally only and in the distance. What might have been is sternly transformed from a beautiful vision into a revolting peril, and in this new shape is invoked to applaud the actual and vilify what is impossible. This attitude of mind is thought so commendable as to have won for itself in popular speech the name of philosophy—so even with words Clotho works her will. Elsa, then, in this peculiar sense of the term was philosophical about the business. She was balanced in her attitude, and, left to herself, would maintain equilibrium.

"She's growing fonder and fonder of you every day," Cousin Elizabeth whispered in my ear.

"I hope," said I, with a reminiscence, "that I am not absolutely repulsive to her." And in order not to puzzle Cousin Elizabeth with any glimmer of truth I smiled.

"My dearest Augustin" (that she seemed to say "Struboff" was a childish trick of my imagination), "what an idea!" ("What a question, my dear M. Struboff!")

I played too much, perhaps, with my parallel, but I was not its slave. I knew myself to be unlike Struboff (in my case Coralie scouted the idea of a fresh slice of bread). I knew Elsa to be of very different temperament from Coralie's. These variances did not invalidate the family likeness; a son may be very like his father, though the nose of one turns up and the other's nose turns down. We were, after making all allowances for superficial differences—we were both careers, Struboff and I. I need none to point out to me my blunder; none to say that I was really fortunate and cried for the moon. It is admitted. I was offered a charming friendship; it was not enough. I could give a tender friendship; I knew that it was not enough.

And there was that other thing which went to my heart, that possibility which must ever be denied realization, that beginning doomed to be thwarted. As we were talking once of all who were to come on the great day, I saw suddenly a little flush on Elsa's cheek. She did not look away or stammer, or make any other obvious concession to her embarrassment, but the blush could not be denied access to her face and came eloquent with its hint.

"And M. de Varvilliers—he will be there, I suppose?" she asked.

"I hope so; I have given directions that he shall be invited. You like him, Elsa?"

"Yes," she said, not looking at me now, but straight in front of her, as though he stood there in his easy heart-stealing grace. And for an instant longer the flush flew his flag on her cheek.

But Struboff had been so mad as to fall in love with Coralie, and to desire her love out of no compassion for her but sheerly for itself. Was I not spared this pang? I do not know whether my state were worse or better. For with him, even in direst misery, there would be love's own mad hope, that denial of impossibility, that dream of marvellous change which shoots across the darkest gloom of passion. Or at least he could imagine her loving as he loved, and thereby cheat the wretched thing that was. I could not. In dreary truth, I was toward her as she toward me, and before us both there stretched a lifetime. If an added sting were needed, I found it in a perfectly clear consciousness that a great many people would have been absolutely content, and, as onlookers of our case, would have wondered what all the trouble was about. There are those who from a fortunate want of perception are called sensible; just as Elsa by her resolute evasion of truth would be accorded the title of philosophical.

Victoria was the prophet of the actual, picking out with optimistic eye its singular abundance of blessedness. I do not think that she reminded me that Elsa might have had but one eye, one leg, or a crooked back, but her felicitations ran on this strain. Their obvious artificiality gave them the effect of sympathy, and Victoria would always sanction this interpretation by a kiss on departure. But she had her theory; it was that Elsa only needed to be wooed. The "only" amused me, but even with that point waived I questioned her position. It left out imagination, and it left out Varvilliers, who had become imagination's pet. Nevertheless, Victoria spoke out of experience; she did not blush at declaring herself "after all very comfortable" with William Adolphus. Granted the argument's sincerity, its force could not be denied with honesty.

"We're not romantic, and never have been, of course," she conceded.

"My dear Victoria, of course not," said I, laughing openly.

"We have had our quarrels."

"The quarrels wouldn't trouble me in the least."

"We don't expect too much of one another."

"I seem to be listening to the address on the wedding day."

"You're an exasperating creature!" and with that came the kiss.

Victoria's affection was always grateful to me, but in the absence of Wetter and Varvilliers, neither of whom had made any sign as yet, I was bereft of all intellectual sympathy. I had looked to find some in the Duke, and some, as I believe, there was; but its flow was checked and turned by what I must call a repressed resentment. His wife's blind heartiness was impossible to him, and he read with a clear eye the mind of a loved daughter. With him also I ranked as a necessity; so far as the necessity was distasteful to Elsa, it was unpalatable to him. Beneath his friendliness, and side by side with an unhesitating acceptance of the position, there lay this grudge, not acknowledged, bound to incur instant absurdity as the price of any open assertion of itself, but set in his mind and affecting his disposition toward me. He was not so foolish as to blame me; but I was to him the occasion of certain fears and shrinkings, possibly of some qualms as to his own part in the matter, and thus I became a less desired companion. There was something between us, a subject always present, never to be mentioned. As a result, there came constraint. My pride took alarm, and my polite distance answered in suitable terms to his reticent courtesy. I believe, however, that we found one common point in a ludicrous horror of Cousin Elizabeth's behaviour. Had she assumed the air she wore, she must have ranked as a diplomatist; having succeeded in the great task of convincing herself, she stands above those who can boast only of deceiving others. To Cousin Elizabeth the alliance was a love match; had she possessed the other qualities, her self-persuasion would have been enough to enable her to found a religious sect and believe that she was sent from heaven for its prophet.

Amid this group of faces, all turned toward the same object but with expressions subtly various, I spent my days, studying them all, and finding (here has been nature's consolation to me) relief from my own thoughts in an investigation of the mind of others. The portentous pretence on which we were engaged needed perhaps a god to laugh at it, but the smaller points were within the sphere of human ridicule; with them there was no danger of amusement suffering a sudden death, and a swift resurrection in the changed shape of indignation.

There was already much to laugh at, but now a new occasion came, taking its rise in a thing which seemed very distinct, and appertaining to moods and feelings long gone by, a plaything of memory destined (as it had appeared) to play no more part in actual life. The matter was simply this: Count Max von Sempach was on leave, and proposed with my permission to be in Forstadt for the wedding festivities.

Bederhof had heard legendary tales; his manner was dubious and solemn as he submitted the Count's proposal to me; Princess Heinrich's carelessness of reference would have stirred suspicion in the most guileless heart; William Adolphus broke into winks and threatened nudges; I invoked my dignity just in time. Victoria was rather excited, rather pleased, looking forward to an amusing spectacle. Evidently something had reached Cousin Elizabeth's ears, for she overflowed with unspoken assurances that the news was of absolutely no importance, that she took no notice of boyish follies, and did not for a moment doubt my whole-hearted devotion to Elsa. Elsa herself betrayed consciousness only by not catching my eye when the Sempachs' coming cropped up in conversation. For my own part I said that I should be very glad to see the Count and the Countess, and that they had a clear claim to their invitation. My mother's manner had shown that she felt herself in no position to raise objections; Bederhof took my commands with resigned deference. I was aware that his wife had ceased to call on the Countess some time before Count Max went Ambassador to Paris.

Max had done his work very well—his appointment has been quoted as an instance of my precocious

insight into character—and his work did not appear
to have done him any harm. When he called on me
I found him the same sincere simple fellow that
he had been always. By consent we talked of private affairs, rather than of business. He told me
that Toté was growing into a tall girl, that his other
children also shot up, but (he added proudly) his
wife did not look a day older, and her appearance
had, if anything, improved. She had been happy at
Paris, he said, " but, to be sure, she'd be happy anywhere with the children and her home." The mod-
esty of the last words did not conceal his joyous confidence. I felt very kindly toward him.

" Really you're an encouragement to me at this
moment," I said. " You must take me to see the
Countess."

" She will be most honoured, sire."

" I'd much rather she'd be a little pleased."

He laughed in evident gratification, assuring me
that she would be very pleased. He answered for
her emotions in the true style of the blessed partner;
that is an incident of matrimony which I am content
to have escaped. I doubted very much whether she
were so eager for the renewal of my acquaintance
as he declared. I recollected the doubts and fears
that had beset her vision of that event long ago.
But my part was plain—to go, and to go speedily.

" To the Countess'? " exclaimed Victoria, to
whom I mentioned casually my plans for the afternoon. " You're in a great hurry, Augustin."

" It's no sign of hurry to go to a place at the
right time," said I, with a smile.

" I don't call it quite proper."

" I go because it is proper."

" If you flirt with her again——"

"My dear Victoria, what things you suggest!"

Victoria returned to her point.

"I see no reason why you should rush off there all in a minute," she persisted.

Nevertheless I went, paying the tribute of a laugh to the picture of Victoria flying with the news to Princess Heinrich. But the Princess' eye could tell a real danger from an imaginary one; she would not mind my seeing the Countess now.

I went quite privately, without notice, and was not expected. Thus it happened that I was ushered into the drawing-room when the Countess was not there to receive me. There I found Toté undeniably long-legged and regrettably shy. The world had begun to set its mark on her, and she had discovered that she did not know how to behave to me. I was sorry not to be pleasant company for Toté; but, perceiving the fact too plainly to resist it I sent her off to hasten her mother. She had not been gone a moment before the Countess came in hurriedly with apologies on her lips.

Not a day older! O my dear Max! Shall we pray for this blindness, or shall we not? She was older than she had been, older than by now she should be. Yet her charm hung round her like a fine stuff that defies time, and a gentle kindness graced her manner. We began to talk about anything and nothing. She showed fretful dread of a pause; when she spoke she did not look me in the face. I could not avoid the idea that she did not want me, and would gladly see me take my leave. But such a feeling was, as it seemed to me, inhuman —a falseness to our true selves, born of some convention, or of a scruple overstrained, or of a fear not warranted.

" Have you seen Elsa? " I asked presently, and
perhaps rather abruptly.

" Yes," she said, " I was presented to her. She
was very sweet and kind to me."

" She's that to me too," I said, rising and standing by her chair.

She hesitated a moment, then looked up at me;
I saw emotion in her eyes.

" You'll be happy with her?" she asked.

" If she isn't very unhappy, I daresay I
shan't be."

" Ah!" she said with a sort of despairing sigh.

" But I don't suppose I should make anybody
particularly happy."

" Yes, yes," she cried in low-voiced impetuosity.
" Yes, if——" She stopped. Fear was in her eyes
now, and she scanned my face with a close jealous
intensity. I knew what her fear was, her own expression of it echoed back across the years. She
feared that she had given me occasion to laugh at
her. I bent down, took her hand, and kissed it
lightly.

" Perhaps, had all the world been different," said
I, with a smile.

" I'm terribly changed?"

" No; not terribly, and not much. How has it
been with you?"

Her nervousness seemed to be passing off; she
answered me in a sincere simplicity that would neither exaggerate nor hide.

" All that is good, short of the best," she said.
" And with you?"

" Shall I say all that is bad, short of the worst?"

" We shouldn't mean very different things."

" No; not very. I've done many foolish things."

"Have you? They all say that you fill your place well."

"I have paid high to do it."

"What you thought high when you paid," she said, smiling sadly.

I would not do her the wrong of any pretence; she was entitled to my honesty.

"I still think it high," I said, " but not too high."

"Nothing is too high?"

"But others must help to pay my score. You know that."

"Yes, I know it."

"And this girl will know it."

"She wouldn't have it otherwise."

"I know, I know, I know. She would not. It's strange to have you here now."

"Max would come. I didn't wish it. Yet—" She smiled for a moment and added: " Yet in a way I did wish it. I was drawn here. It seemed to concern me. Don't laugh. It seemed to be part of my story, too; I felt that I must be there to hear it. Are you laughing?"

"I've never laughed."

"You're good and kind and generous. No, I think you haven't. I'm glad of it, because——"

"Yes? Why?"

"Because even now I can't," she whispered. "No, don't think I mean—I mean a thing which would oblige you to laugh now. It's all over, all over. But that it should have been, Augustin?" My name slipped from unconscious lips. " That it should have been isn't bad to me; it's good. That's wicked? I can't help it. It's the thing—the thing of my life. I've no place like yours. I've nothing to make it come second. Ah, I'm forgetting again

how old I am. How you always make me forget it!
I mustn't talk like this."

"We shall never, I suppose, talk like this again.
You go back to Paris?"

"Yes, soon. I'm glad."

"But it's not hard to you now?"

She seemed to reflect, as though she were anxious to give me an answer accurately true.

"Not very hard now," she said at last, looking
full at me. "Not very hard, but very constant, always with me. I love them all, all my folk. But it's
always there."

"You mean—What do you mean? The thought
of me?"

"Yes, or the thought that somehow I have just
missed. I'm not miserable. And I like to dream—
to be gorgeous, splendid, wicked in dreams." She
gave a laugh and pressed my hand for a moment.
"Toté grows pretty," she said. "Don't you think
so?"

"Toté was unhappy with me, and I let her go.
Yes, she's pretty; she won't be like you, though."

"I'll appeal to you again in five, in ten years,"
said she, smiling, pleased with my covert praise.
"Oh, it's pleasant to see you again," she went on
a moment later. "I'm a bad penitent. I wish I
could be with you always. No, I am not dreaming
now. I mean, just in Forstadt and seeing you."

"A moment ago you were glad to go back to
Paris."

"Ah, you assume more ignorance of us than you
have. Mayn't I be glad of one thing and wish another?"

"True; and men can do that too."

I felt the old charm of the quick word coming
22

from the beautiful lips, the twofold appeal. Though passion was gone, pleasure in her remained; my love was dead. As I sat there I wished it alive again; I longed to be back in the storm of it, even though I must battle the storm again.

"After all," she said, with a glance at me, " I have my share in you. You can't think of your life without thinking of me. I'm something to you. I'm one among the many foolish things—You don't hate the foolish things?"

"On my soul, I believe not one of them; and if you're one, I love one of them."

"I like you to say that."

A long silence fell on us. The thing had not come in either of the fashions in which I had pictured it, neither in weariness nor in excitement. It came full with emotions, but emotions that were subdued shadows of themselves, of a mournful sweetness, bewailing their lost strength, yet shrinking from remembrance of it. Would we have gone back if we could? Now I could not answer the question. Yet we could weep, because to go back was impossible. But it was with a slight laugh that at last I rose to my feet to say good-bye.

"It's like you always to laugh at the end," she said, a little in reproach, but more, I think, in the pleasure of recognising what was part of her idea of me. "You used often to do it, even when you were—even before. You remember the first time of all—when we smiled at one another behind your mother's back? That oldest memory comforts me. Do you know why? I was never so many centuries older than you again. I'm not so many even now. You look old, I think, and seem old; if we're nearer together, it's your fault, not my merit. Well, you must go. Ah, how you fill time! How you could have filled a woman's life!"

" Could have? Your mood is right."

" Surely she'll be happy with you? If you could love her?"

" Not even then. I'm not to her measure."

" Are you unhappy?"

" It's better than the worst, a great deal better. Good-bye."

I pressed her hand and kissed it. With a sudden seeming formality she curtseyed and kissed mine.

" I don't forget what you are," she said, " because I have fancied you as something besides. Good-bye, sire. Good-bye, Augustin."

" There's a name wanting."

" Ah, to Cæsar I said good-bye five years ago." The tears were in her eyes as I turned away and left her.

I had a fancy to walk back alone, as I had walked alone from her house on the day when I cut the bond between us that same five years ago. Having dismissed my carriage, I set out in the cool of the autumn evening as dusk had just fallen, and took my way through the decorated streets. Only three days more lay between the decorations and the occasion they were meant to grace. There was a hum of gaiety through all the town; they had begun their holiday-making, and the shops did splendid trade. They in Forstadt would have liked to marry me every year. Why not? I was to them a sign, a symbol, something they saw and spoke of, but not a man. I reviewed the troops every year. Why should I not be married every year? It would be but the smallest extension of my functions, and all on the lines of logic. I could imagine Princess Heinrich according amplest approval to the scheme.

Suddenly, as I passed in meditation through a quiet street, a hand was laid on my shoulder. I knew only one man who would stop me in that way. Was he here again, risen again, in Forstadt again, for work, or mirth, or mischief? He came in fitting with the visit I had paid. I turned and found his odd, wry smile on me, the knit brows and twinkling eyes. He lifted his hat and tossed back the iron-gray hair.

"I am come to the wedding, sire," said he, bowing.

"It would be incomplete without you, Wetter."

"And for another thing—for a treat, for a spectacle. They've written an epithalamium, haven't they?"

"Yes, some fool, according to his folly."

"It is to be sung at the opera the night before? At the gala performance!"

"You're as well up in the arrangements as Bederhof himself."

"I have cause. Whence come you, sire?"

"From paying a visit to the Countess von Sempach."

He burst into a laugh, but the look in his eyes forbade me to be offended.

"That's very whimsical too," he observed. "There's a smack of repetition about this. Is fate hard-up for new effects?"

"There's variety enough here for me. There were no decorations in the streets when I left her before."

"True, true; and—for I must return to my tidings—I bring you something new." He paused and enjoyed his smile at me. "Who sings the marriage song?" he asked.

"Heavens, man, I don't know! I'm not the manager. What is it to me who sings the song?"

"You would like it sung in tune?"

"Oh, unquestionably."

"Ah, well, she sings in tune," he said, nodding his head with an air of satisfaction. "She is not emotional, but she sings in tune."

"Does she, Wetter? Who is she?"

He stood looking at me for a moment, then broke into another laugh. I caught him by the arm; now I laughed myself.

"No, no?" I cried. "Fate doesn't joke, Wetter?"

"Fate jokes," said he. "It is Coralie who will sing your song. To-morrow they reach here, she and Struboff. Yes, sire, Coralie is to sing your song."

We stood looking at one another; we both were laughing. "It's a great chance in her career," he said.

"It's rather a curious chance in mine," said I.

"She sings it, she sings it," he cried, and with a last laugh turned and fairly ran away down the street, like a mischievous boy who has thrown his squib and flies from the scene in mirthful fear.

When Fortune jested she found in him quick-witted loving audience.

CHAPTER XXVI.

PRINCESS HEINRICH held a reception of all sorts
and conditions of those in Forstadt who were re-
ceivable. So comprehensive was the party that to
be included conveyed no compliment, to be left out
meant a slap in the face. But the scene was gorgeous, and the Princess presided over it with fitting
dignity. Elsa and I stood by her for a while, all in
our buckram, living monuments of bliss and exalted-
ness. It was like a prolonged interview with the
photographer. Then I slipped away and paid marked
and honorific courtesy to Bederhof's wife and Bederhof's daughters, tall girls, not over-quick to be married, somehow quite inevitable if one considered
Bederhof himself. Rising from my plunge, I looked
round for Elsa. She had left my mother and taken
a seat in a recess by the window. There she sat, looking, poor soul, rather weary, speaking now and then
to those who, in passing by, paused to make their
respects and compliments to her. She wore my diamonds; all eyes were for her; the streets were splendidly decorated. Was she content? With all my
heart I hoped that she was.

People came and buzzed about me, and I buzzed
back to them. I had learned to buzz, I believe, with
some grace and facility, certainly with an almost en-

334

tire detachment of my inner mind; it would be intolerable for the real man to be engrossed in such performances. Looking over the head of the President of the Court of Appeal (he was much shorter than his speeches), I saw Elsa suddenly lean forward and sign with her fan to a lady who passed by. The lady stopped; she sat down by Elsa; they entered into conversation. For a while I went on buzzing and being buzzed to, but presently curiosity conquered me.

"In the pleasure of your conversation I mustn't forget what is my first duty just now, gentlemen," I said with a smile.

They dissolved from in front of me with discreet smiles. I sauntered toward the recess where Elsa sat. Glancing at Princess Heinrich, I saw her watching all that went forward, but she was hemmed in by eminent persons. And why should she interpose, if Elsa desired to talk to the Countess von Sempach?

I leaned over the arm of my betrothed's chair. They were talking of common affairs. From where I was I could not see Elsa's face, so I moved and stood leaning on a third chair between them. The Countess was gay and brilliant; kind also, with a tenderness that seemed to throw out feelers for friendship. To me she spoke only when I addressed her directly; her attention was all for Elsa. In Elsa's eyes, not skilled to conceal her heart, there was, overpowering all other expression, a curiosity, a study of something that interested and puzzled her, a desire to understand the woman who talked to her. For Elsa had heard something; not all, but something. She was not hostile or disturbed; she was gracious and eager to please; but she was inquiring and searching. At her heart's bidding her wits were

on the move. I knew the maze that they explored.
She was asking for the Countess' secret. But which
secret? For to her it might well seem that there
were two. Rumour said that I had loved the Countess. It would be in the way of the natural woman
for Elsa to desire to find out why, the trick of the
charm that a predecessor (let the word pass) had
wielded. But rumour said also that the Countess
had loved me. Was this the deeper harder secret
that Elsa sought to probe, this the puzzle to which
she asked an answer? Perhaps, could she find an
answer that satisfied, there would be new heaven and
new earth for her. Here seemed to me the truth, the
reason of the longing question in her eyes. Jealousy
could not inspire that; certainly not a jealousy of
what was long gone by, of a woman who to Elsa's
fresh girlhood must be faded and almost sunk to
middle age. " How did you contrive to love him? "
That was Elsa's question, asked beneath my understanding gaze.

There was a little stir by the door, and a man
came through the group that loitered round it, hastily
shaking hands here, nodding there, as he steered his
course toward Princess Heinrich. I knew that Varvilliers would come to the wedding, but had not been
aware that he was already in Forstadt. My companions did not notice him, but I watched his interview
with my mother. Even she unbent to him, disarmed
by a courtesy that overcame the protest of her judgment; she detained him in conversation nearly ten
minutes, and then pointed to where we were, direct-
ing him to join us.

" Ah, here comes Varvilliers," said I. " I'm delighted to have him back. You've met him, Countess? "

" Oh, yes, sire, in Paris," she answered.

For a few moments I kept my eyes from Elsa's face and looked toward Varvilliers, smiling and beckoning. When I turned toward her she was bright and composed. He joined us, and she welcomed him with cordiality. He launched on an account of his doings; then came to our affairs, commiserating us on the trial of our ceremonies. For a while we talked all to all; then I began to tell the Countess a little story. Varvilliers and Elsa fell into a conversation apart. She had made him sit by her. I bent down over my chair back, to converse more easily with my Countess. All this was right enough, unless the talk were to continue general.

I do not know how long we went on thus; some time I know it was. At last it chanced that the Countess made no answer to what I said, and leaned back in her chair with a thoughtful smile. I sighed, raised my head, and looked across the room. I heard the other two in animated talk and their gay laughter; for the moment my mind was not on them. Suddenly Wetter passed in front of me; he had once been President of the Chamber, and Princess Heinrich knew her duty. He was with William Adolphus, who seemed in extremely good spirits. Wetter paused opposite to me and bowed. I returned his salutation, but did not invite him to join us; I hoped to speak to him later. Thus it was for a bare instant that he halted. But what matters time? Its only true measure lies in what a man does in it. Wetter's momentary halt was long enough for one of those glances of his to play over the group we made. From face to face it ran, a change of expression marking every stage. It rested at last on me. I turned my head sharply toward Elsa; her

cheek was flushed; her eyes glistened; her body was
bent forward in an eagerness of attention, as though
she would not lose a word. Varvilliers was given
over to the spirit of his talk, but he watched the
sparks that he struck from her eyes. I glanced again
at Wetter; William Adolphus had seized his arm
and urged him forward. For a second still he stood;
he tossed his hair back, laughed, and turned away.
Why should he stay? He had said all that the situation suggested to him, and said it with his own merciless lucidity.

I echoed his laugh. Mine was an interruption to
their talk. Elsa started and looked up; Varvilliers'
face turned to me. He looked at me for a moment,
then a strange and most unusual air of embarrassment spread over him. The Countess did not speak,
and her eyes were downcast. Varvilliers was himself
again directly; he began to speak of indifferent matters; he was not so awkward as to let this incident
be the occasion of his leave-taking. A minute or
two passed. I looked at him and held out my hand.
At the same instant the Countess asked a signal
from Elsa, and it was given. We all stood together
for a moment, then they left us, she accepting his arm
to cross the room. Elsa sat down again and did not
speak. I found no words either, but leaned again
over my chair, regarding the scene in absent moodi-
ness. I was thinking how odd a thing it was, and
how perfect, that absolute contentment of the one
with the other, that mutual sufficiency, that fitting
in of each to each, that ultimate oneness of soul which
is the block from which is hewn love's image. And
the block is there, though by fate's caprice it lie un-
shaped. The thing had been between the Countess
and myself; its virtue had availed to abolish differ-

ence of years, to rout absurdity, to threaten the strongest resolution of my mind. It was between Elsa and Varvilliers. In none other had I found it for myself; in none other would Elsa find it. It was not for her in me. Then in vain had been the questioning of her eyes, in vain the eager longing of her parted lips. She had not ears to hear the secret of the Countess. At this moment I forgot again that my, or even her, happiness was not a relevant consideration in forming a judgment of the universe. It is, in fact, a difficult thing to remember. My pride was ablaze with hatred of being taken because I could not be refused. I was carried away by a sudden impulse. I threw myself into the chair by Elsa, saying:

" How it would surprise and scatter all these good people if you suddenly announced that you'd changed your mind, Elsâ! What a rout! what a scurry! What a putting out of lights, and a pulling down of poles, and a furling up of flags, and a countermanding of orders to the butcher and the baker! Good heavens! Think of my mother's face, or, indeed, of your mother's face! Think of Bederhof's face, of everybody's face!" And I fell to laughing.

Elsa also laughed, but with a nervous discomfort. Her glance at me was short; her eyes dropped again.

" What made you think of such a thing?" she asked in a hesitating tone.

" I don't know," said I. Then I turned and asked, " Have you never thought of it?"

" Never," she said. " Indeed, never. How could I?"

It was impossible to doubt the sincerity of her disclaimer. She seemed really shocked and amazed at the notion.

"And now! To do it now! When everything is ready!" She gave a pretty little gasp. "And go back with mother to Bartenstein!" she went on, shaking her head in horror. "How could you imagine it? Fancy Bartenstein again!"

Evidently I was preferable to Bartenstein again, to the narrow humdrum life there. No poles, no flags, no illuminations, no cheers, no dignity! Diamonds even scarce and rare! I tried to take heart. It was something to be better than Bartenstein again.

"And what would they think of me? Oh, it's too absurd! But of course you were joking?"

"Oh, not more than usual, Elsa. You might have found me even more tiresome than Bartenstein."

"Nonsense! It would always be better here than at Bartenstein."

Clearly there was no question in her mind on this point. Forstadt and I—let me share, since I may not engross the credit—were much better than going back to Bartenstein.

She was looking at me with an uneasy, almost suspicious air.

"What made you ask that question?" she said abruptly.

I looked round the room. Among the many groups in talk there were faces turned toward us, regarding us with a discreet good-humoured amusement. The King forgot his duties and talked with his lady-love. Every moment buttressed the reputation of our love match. Let it be so; it was best. Yet the sham was curiously unpleasant to me.

"Why did you ask me that question, Augustin? You had a reason?"

"No, none; except that in forty-eight hours it will be too late to ask it."

She leaned toward me in agitated pleading.

"I do love you, Augustin. I love nobody so much as you—you and father."

I and father! Poor girl, how she admitted while she thought to deny! But I was full of a pity and a tenderness for her, and forgot my own pride.

"You're so good to me; and there's no reason why you should like me."

"Like?" said I. "A gentleman must pretend sometimes, or so it's thought."

"Yes. What do you mean?" Pleased coquetry gleamed for a moment in her eyes. "Do you mean— love me?"

"It is impossible, is it?" I asked, and I looked into her eyes as though I desired her love. Well, I did, that she might have peace.

She blushed, and suddenly, as it were by an uncontrollable immediate impulse, glanced round. Whose face did she seek? Was it not his who last had looked at her in that fashion? He was not in sight. Her gaze fell downward. Ah, that you had been a better diplomatist, Elsa. For though a man may know the truth, he loves sometimes one who will deny it to him pleasantly. He gains thereby a respite and an intermission, the convict's repose between his turns on the treadmill or the hour's flouting of hard life that good wine brings. But it was impossible to rear on stable foundations a Pleasure House of Pretence. With every honest revelation of her heart Elsa shattered it. I can not blame her. I myself was at my analytic undermining.

"You'll go on then?" I asked, with a laugh.

She laughed for answer. The question seemed to

her to need no answer. What, would she go back
to Bartenstein—to insignificance, to dulness, and to
tutelage? Surely not!

"But I'm not very like the grenadier," I said.

She understood me and flushed, relapsing into
uneasiness. I saw that I had touched some chord
in her, and I would willingly have had my words
unsaid. Presently she turned to me, and forgetting
the gazers round held out her hands to mine. Her
eyes seemed dim.

"I'll try—I'll try to make you happy," she said.

And she said well. Letting all think what they
would, I rose to my feet and bowed low over the
hand that I kissed. Then I gave her my arm, and
walked with her through the lane that they made
for us. Surely we pretended well, for somehow,
from somewhere, a cheer arose, and they cheered us
as we walked through. Elsa's face was in an instant
bright again. She pressed my arm in a spasm of
pleasure. We proceeded in triumph to where Princess Heinrich sat; away behind her in the foremost row of a group of men stood Wetter—Wetter
leading the cheers, waving his handkerchief, grinning
in charmingly diabolical fashion. The suitability of
Princess Heinrich's reception of us I must leave to
be imagined; it was among her triumphs.

I fell at once into the clutches of Cousin Elizabeth, my regard for whom was tempered by a prefer-
ence for more restraint in the display of emotion.

"My dearest boy," she said, pulling me into a
seat by her, "I saw you. It makes me so happy."

A thing, without being exactly good in itself, may
of course have incidental advantages.

"It was sure to happen. You were made for one
another. Dear Elsa is young and shy, and—and she

"I'll try—I'll try to make you happy."

didn't quite understand." Cousin Elizabeth looked almost sly. "But now the weight is quite off my mind. Because Elsa doesn't change."

"Doesn't she?" I asked.

"No, she's constancy itself. Once she takes up a point of view, you know, or an impression of a person, nothing alters it. Dear me, we used to think her obstinate. Only everybody gave way to her. That was her father's fault. He never would have her thwarted. But she's turned out very well, hasn't she? So I can't blame him. I know your mother thought us rather lax."

"Ah, my mother was not lax."

"It only shows there's room for both ways, doesn't it? What was I saying?"

I knew what she had been saying, but not which part of it she desired to repeat. However she found it for herself in a moment.

"Oh, yes! No, she never changes. Just what she is to you now she'll be all her life. I never knew her to change. She just loves you or she doesn't, and there it rests. You may feel quite safe."

"How very satisfactory all this is, Cousin Elizabeth!"

"Satisfactory?" she exclaimed, with a momentary surprise at my epithet. But her theory came to the rescue. "Oh, I know you always talk like that. Well, I don't expect you to talk like a lover to me. It's quite enough if you do it to Elsa. Yes, it is— satisfactory, isn't it?" The good creature laughed heartily and squeezed my hand. "She'll never change," she repeated once again in an ample, comfortable contentment. "And you don't mind showing what you feel, do you?"

Cousin Elizabeth was chaffing me.

"On my word, I forgot how public we were," said I. "My feelings ran away with me."

"Oh, why should you be ashamed? They might laugh, but I'm sure they envied you."

It was strange enough, but it is very likely that they did. For my own part, I have learned not to envy people without knowing a good deal about them and their affairs.

"Because," pursued Cousin Elizabeth, "I have always in my heart hated merely arranged marriages. They're not right, you know, Augustin. They may be necessary, but they're not right."

"Very necessary, but quite wrong," I agreed.

"And at one time I was the least bit afraid— However I was a silly old woman. Do look at her talking to your mother. Oh, of course, you were looking at her already. You weren't listening to my chatter."

But I had listened to Cousin Elizabeth's chatter. She had told me something of interest. Elsa would never change; she took a view and a relation toward a person and maintained them. What she was to me now she would be always.

"My dear cousin, I have listened with keen interest to every word that you've said," I protested truthfully.

"That's your politeness. I know what lovers are," said Cousin Elizabeth.

I looked across to the Duke's passive tired face. The thought crossed my mind that Cousin Elizabeth must have depended on observation rather than on experience for the impressions to which she referred. However she afforded me an opportunity for escape, which I embraced with alacrity.

As I passed my mother, she beckoned to me. Elsa had left her, and she was alone for the moment. It seemed that she had a word to say to me, and on the subject concerning which I thought it likely enough that she would have something to say—the engagement of Coralie to sing at the gala performance.

"Was there not some unpleasant talk about this Madame Mansoni?" she asked.

"Well, there was talk," said I, smiling and allowing my eyes to rest on the figure of William Adolphus, visible in the distance. "It would have been better not to have her, perhaps. It can be altered, I suppose."

"Bederhof sanctioned it without referring to you or to me. It has become public now."

"Oh, I didn't know that."

"Yes; it's in the evening papers."

"Any—any remarks?"

"No, except that the Vorwärts calls it an extraordinarily suitable selection."

"The Vorwärts? Yes," said I thoughtfully. Wetter wrote for the Vorwärts. "Perhaps then to cancel it would make more talk than to let it stand. The whole story is very old."

Princess Heinrich permitted a smile to appear on her face as with a wave of her fan she relegated Coralie to a proper insignificance. She was smiling still as she added:

"There's another old acquaintance coming to assist at the wedding, Augustin. I telegraphed to ask her, and she has answered accepting the invitation in the warmest terms."

"Indeed! Who is that, pray?"

"The Baroness," said my mother.

23

I stared at her; then I cried with a laugh, "Krak? Not Krak?"

"Yes, Krak, as you naughty children used to call her."

"Good Heavens, does the world still hold Krak?"

"Of course. She's rather an old woman, though. You'll be kind to her, Augustin? She was always very fond of you."

"I will treat Krak," said I, "with all affection."

Surely I would, for Krak's coming put the crown of completeness on the occasion. But I was amazed; Krak was utterly stuff of the past.

My mother did not appear to desire my presence longer; I had to take up my own position and receive farewells.

A dreary half hour passed in this occupation; at last the throng grew thin. I broke away and sauntered off to a buffet for a sandwich and a glass of champagne. There I saw Wetter and Varvilliers standing together and refreshing their jaded bodies. I joined them at once, full of the news about Krak. It fell rather flat, I regret to say; Krak had not significance for them, and Wetter was full of wild brilliant talk. Varvilliers' manner, on the other hand, although displaying now no awkwardness or restraint, showed unusual gentleness and gravity with an added friendliness very welcome to me. I stood between my friends, sipping my wine and detaining them, although the room was nearly empty. I felt a reluctance to part and an invincible repugnance to my bed.

"Come to my quarters," I said, "and we'll have cigars."

Varvilliers bowed ready assent. Wetter's face twisted into a smile.

" I must plead excuse to the command," he said.

" Then you're a rascal, Wetter; I want you, man, and you ought not to be expected anywhere this time of night."

" Not at home, sire? "

" Home least of all," said Varvilliers, smiling.

" But I have guests at home," cried Wetter. " I've left them too long. But Her Royal Highness didn't invite them; besides it was necessary to practise the song."

" What? Are they with you? "

" Should I send them to a hotel, sire? My friends the Struboffs! No, no! "

Sipping my wine, I looked doubtfully from one to the other.

" The King," observed Wetter to Varvilliers, " would be interested in hearing a rehearsal of the song."

" But," said I, " Krak comes to-night, and I daren't look as if I'd sat up beyond my hour."

Wetter laid his finger on my arm.

" One more night," he said. Varvilliers laughed. " I have the same old servant. He's very discreet! "

" But you'll put it in the Vorwärts! "

" No, no, not if the meeting-place is my own house."

" I'll do it! " I cried. " Come, let's have a carriage."

" Mine waits," said Varvilliers, " at your disposal. I'll see about it," and off he ran. Wetter turned to me.

" An interesting quartette there in the recess," said he.

" And an insolent fellow looking on at it," said I.

" I'll write an article on your impulsive love-making before all the world."

" Do; I can conceive nothing more politic."

" It shall teem with sincerity."

" Never a jest anywhere in it? Not one for me? "

" No. Jests are in place only when one tells the truth. A lie must be solemn, sire."

" True. Write it to your mood."

And to his mood he wrote it, eloquently, beautifully, charged with the passion of that joy which he realized in imagination, but could not find in his stormy life. I read it two or three days later at Artenberg.

" Hey for the wedding-song and one night more! " he cried.

We rolled off, we three, in Varvilliers' carriage.

CHAPTER XXVII.

OF GRAZES ON THE KNEE.

THERE was no doubt that they practised the marriage-song. Coralie's voice echoed through the
house as we entered. For a moment we paused in
the hall to listen. Then Wetter dashed up the stairs,
crying, " Good God! Wooden, wooden, wooden!"
We followed him at a run; he flung the door open
and rushed in. Coralie broke off her singing and
came to greet me with a little cry of pleased surprise. Struboff sat at the piano, looking rather bewildered. Supper was spread on a table at the other
end of the room. When Struboff tried to rise, Wetter thrust him back into his seat. " No, no, the King
doesn't want to talk to you," he said. " He wants
to hear madame sing, to hear you play. Coralie,
come and sing again, and, for God's sake sing it as if
it meant something, dear Coralie."

" It's such nonsense," said Coralie, with a pout-
ing smile.

" Nonsense? Then it needs all your efforts. As
if—as if, I say—it meant something."

Varvilliers, laughing, flung himself on a sofa, I
stood at the end of the piano, Wetter was ges-
ticulating and muttering on the hearthrug. Struboff put his fingers on the keys again and began to
play; after a sigh of weariness Coralie uplifted her

voice. It came fresh and full; the weariness was of the spirit only. The piece was good, nay, very good; there were feeling and passion in the music. I looked at Struboff. His fingers moved tenderly, tears stood in his little eyes. Coralie shouted perfect notes in perfect heartlessness.

"My God!" muttered Wetter from the hearth-rug, and bounded across to her. He caught her by the arm.

"Feel, feel, feel!" he cried angrily.

"Don't be so stupid," said Coralie.

"She can't feel it," said Struboff, taking his handkerchief and wiping brow and eyes.

"She's a fortunate woman," remarked Varvilliers from his sofa.

"You'd think she could," said Wetter, taking both her hands and surveying her from top to toe. "You'd think she could understand. Look at her eyes, her brows, her lips. You'd think she could understand. Look at her hands, her waist, her neck. It's a little strange, isn't it? See, she smiles at me. She has an adorably good temper. She doesn't mind me in the least. It's just that she happens not to be able to feel."

During all this outburst Struboff played softly and tenderly; a large tear formed now in each of his eyes, and presently trickled over the swelling hillocks underneath his cheek bones. Coralie was smiling placidly at Wetter, thinking him mad enough, but in no way put out by his criticism.

"I can feel it," said Wetter, in a whimsically puzzled tone. "Why should I feel it? I'm not young or beautiful, and my voice is the worse for wear, because I've had to denounce the King so much. Nevertheless I can feel it."

"You can make a big fool of yourself," observed Coralie, breaking into a laugh and snatching her hands away from him.

"Yes, yes, yes, I should hope so," he cried. "She catches the point! Is there hope? No, she won't make a fool of herself. There's no hope." He sank into a chair with every appearance of dejection.

"I think it's supper-time," she said, moving toward the table. "What are you still playing for?" she called to Struboff.

"Let him play," said I. "Perhaps he would rather play than sup."

"It's very likely," Coralie admitted with a shrug. Struboff looked at me for a moment, and nodded solemnly. He was playing low now, giving a plaintive turn to the music that had been joyful. ·

"No, you shall try it once again," cried Wetter, leaping up. "Once again! A verse of it! I'll stand opposite to you. See, like this; and I'll look at you. Now try!"

She was very good-natured with him, and did as he bade her. He took his stand just by her, behind Struboff, and gazed into her face. I could see him; his lips twitched, and his eyes were set on her in an ardour of passion.

"Look in my eyes and sing!" he commanded.

"Ah, you're silly," she murmured in her pleasant lazy drawl. She threw out her chest, and filled the room with healthy tuneful sound.

"Stop!" he cried. "Stop! I can endure no more of it. Can you eat? Yes, you can eat. In God's name, come and eat, dear Coralie."

Coralie appealed to me.

"Don't you think I sing it very well?" she

asked. "I can fill the Grand Opera House quite easily."

"You sing it to perfection," said I. "There's nothing wrong, nothing at all. Wetter here is mad."

"Wetter is certainly mad," echoed Varvilliers, rising from the sofa.

"Wetter is damned mad," said Wetter.

"Wetter is right—ah, so right," came in a despairing grumble from poor Struboff, who still played away.

"To supper, to supper!" cried Wetter. "You're right, all of you. And I'm right. And I'm mad. To supper! No, let Struboff play. Struboff, you want to play. Play on."

Struboff nodded again and played on. His notes, now plaintive, now triumphant, were the accompaniment to our meal, filling the pauses, enriching, as it seemed, the talk. But Coralie was deep in *foie gras*, and paid no heed to them. Wetter engaged in some vehement discussion with Varvilliers, who met him with good-humoured pertinacity. I had dropped out of the talk, and sat listening dreamily to Struboff's music. Suddenly Coralie laid down her knife and turned to me.

"Wouldn't it be nice if I were going to be married to you?" she asked.

"Charming," said I. "But what of our dear M. Struboff? And what of my Cousin Elsa?"

"We wouldn't trouble about them." She was looking at me with a shrewd gaze. "No," she said, "you wouldn't like it. Shall we try another arrangement?" She leaned toward me and laid her pretty hand on my arm. "Wetter and I—I am not very well placed, but let it pass—Wetter and I, Varvilliers and the Princess, you and the Countess."

I made no sign of appreciating this rather penetrating suggestion.

"You're more capricious than fortune, more arbitrary than fate, madame," said I. "Moreover, you have again forgotten to provide for M. Struboff."

She shrugged her shoulders and smiled.

"No," she said meditatively. "I don't like that after all. It might do for M. de Varvilliers, but the Countess is too old, and Wetter there would cut my throat. We can't sacrifice everything to give Varvilliers a Princess." She appeared to reflect for a few seconds. "I don't know how to arrange it."

"Positively I should be at a loss myself if I were called upon to govern the world at short notice."

"I think I must let it alone. I don't see how to make it better."

"Thank you. For my own part I have the good luck to be in love with my cousin."

Coralie lifted her eyes to mine. "Oh, no!" she drawled quietly. Then she added with a laugh, "Do you remember when you fought Wetter?"

"Heavens! yes; fools that we were! Not a word of it! Nobody knows."

"Well, at that time you were in love with me."

"Madame, I will have the honour of mentioning a much more remarkable thing to you."

"If you please, sire," she said, taking a bunch of grapes and beginning to eat them.

"You were all but in love with me."

"That's not remarkable. You're too humble. I was; ah, yes, I was. I was very afraid for you. *Mon ami*, don't you wish that, instead of being King here, you were the Sultan?"

I laughed at this abrupt and somewhat unceremonious question.

"In fact, Coralie," said I, "there are only two really satisfactory things to be in this life; all else is miserable compromise."

"Tell them to me."

"A Sultan or a monk. And—pardon me—give me the latter."

"Well, I once knew a monk very well, and——" began Coralie in a tone of meditative reminiscence. But, rather to my vexation, Wetter spoiled the story by asking what we were talking about with our heads so close together.

"We were correcting Fate and re-arranging Destiny," I explained.

"Pooh, pooh!" he cried. "You'd not get rid of the tragedy, and only spoil the comedy. Let it alone, my children."

We let it alone, and began to chatter honest nonsense. This had been going on for a few minutes, when I became aware suddenly that Struboff had ceased playing my wedding-song. I looked round; he sat on the piano-stool, his broad back like a tree-trunk bent to a bow, and his head settled on his shoulders till a red bulge over his collar was all that survived of his neck. I rose softly, signing to the others not to interrupt their conversation, and stole up to him. He did not move; his hands were clasped on his stomach. I peered round into his face; its lines were set in a grotesque heavy melancholy. At first I felt very sorry for him; but as I went on looking at him something of Coralie's feeling came over me, and I grew angry. That he was doubtless very miserable ceased to plead for him, nay, it aggravated his offence. What the deuce right had this fellow to make misery repulsive? And it was over my wedding song that he had tortured himself into this ludicrous condition! Yet again it was a pleasant paradox of Nature's to dower this carcass with the sensibility which might have given a crowning charm to the beauty of Coralie. In him it could attract no love, to him it could bring no happiness. Probably it caused him to play the piano better; if this justifies Nature, she is welcome to the plea. For my part, I felt that it was monstrously bad taste in him to come and be miserable here and now in Forstadt. But he overshot his mark.

"Good God, my dear Struboff!" I cried in extreme annoyance, "think how little it matters, how little any of us care, even, if you like, how little you ought to care yourself! You've tumbled down on the gravel; very well! Stop crying, and don't, for Heaven's sake, keep showing me the graze on your knee. We all, I suppose, have grazes on our knees. Get your mother to put you into stockings, and nobody will see it. I've been in stockings for years." I burst into a laugh.

He did not understand what I would be at; that, perhaps, was hardly wonderful.

"The music has affected me," he mumbled.

"Then come and let some champagne affect you," I advised him irritably. "What, are you to spoil a pleasant evening?"

He looked at me with ponderous sorrowful reproach.

"A pleasant evening!" he groaned, as he blew his nose.

"Yes," I cried loudly. "A damnably pleasant evening, M. Struboff," and I caught him by the arm, dragged him from his stool, and carried him off to the table with me. Here I set him down between Varvilliers and myself; Wetter and Coralie, deep in low-voiced conversation, paid no heed to him. He began to eat and drink eagerly and with appetite.

"You perceive, Struboff," said I persuasively, "that while we have stomachs—and none, my friend, can deny that you have one—the world is not empty of delight. You and I may have our grazes—Varvilliers, have you a graze on the knee by chance?—but consider, I pray you, the case of the man who has no dinner."

"It would be very bad to have no dinner," said Struboff, in full-mouthed meditation.

"Besides that," said I lightly—I grew better tempered every moment—"what are these fine-spun miseries with which we afflict ourselves? To be empty, to be thirsty, to be cold—these are evils. Was ever any man, well-fed, well-drunk, and well-warmed, really miserable? Reflect before you answer, Struboff."

He drained a glass of champagne, and, I suppose, reflected.

"If he had his piano also——" he began.

"Great Heavens!" I interrupted with a laugh.

Coralie turned from Wetter and fixed her eyes on her husband. He perceived her glance directly; his appetite appeared to become enfeebled, and he drank his wine with apologetic slowness. She went on looking at him with a merciless amusement; his whole manner became expressive of a wish to be elsewhere. I saw Varvilliers smothering a smile; he sacrificed much to good manners. I myself laughed gently. Suddenly, to my surprise, Wetter caught Coralie by the wrist.

"You see that man?" he asked, smiling and fixing his eyes on her.

"Oh, yes, I see my husband," said she.

"Your husband, yes. Shall I tell you something? You remember what I've been saying to you?"

"Very well; you've repeated it often. Are you going to repeat it now out loud?"

"Where's the use? Everybody here knows. I'll tell you another thing." He leaned forward, still holding her wrist tightly. "Look at Struboff," he said. "Look well at him."

"I am giving myself the pleasure of looking at M. Struboff," said Coralie.

"Very well. When you die—because you'll grow old, and you'll grow ugly, and at last, after you have become very ugly, you'll die."

Coralie looked rather vexed, a little perturbed and protesting. Wetter had touched the one point on which she had troubled herself to criticise the order of the universe.

"When, I say, you die," pursued Wetter, "when, after growing extremely ugly, you die, you will be sent to hell because you have not appreciated the virtues or repaid the devotion of my good friend M. Struboff. And, sire " (he turned to me), " when one considers that, it appears unreasonable to imagine that eternity will be in any degree less peculiar than this present life of ours."

"That's all very well," said Coralie, "but after having grown ugly I don't think I should mind anything else."

I clapped my hands.

"I think," said I, "if M. Struboff will pardon the supposition, that madame will be allowed to escape perdition. For, see, she will stand up and she will say quite calmly, with that adorable smile of hers——"

"They don't mind smiles there, sire," put in Varvilliers.

"She'll smile not to please them, but because she's
amused," said I. "She'll say with her adorable
smile, 'This and that I have done, this and that I
have not done. Perhaps I did wrong, I have not
studied your rules. But you can't send me to hell.'"

They all appeared to be listening with attentive
ears.

"Here's a good advocate," said Wetter. "Let us
hear the plea."

"'You can't send me to hell because I have not
pretended. I have been myself, and I didn't make
myself. I can't go to hell with the pretenders.'"

"But to heaven with the kings?" asked Varvilliers.

"With the kings who have not also been pretenders," said I.

"*Nom de Dieu*," said she, "I believe that I shall
escape, after all. So you and I will be separated,
Wetter."

"No, no," he protested. "Unless you're there
the place won't be itself to me."

We all laughed—Struboff not in appreciation, but
with a nervous desire to make himself agreeable—
and I rose from my seat. It was three o'clock in
the morning. Struboff yawned mightily as he drank
a final glass and patted his stomach. I think that we
were all happier than when we sat down.

"And after the occasion, whither?" I asked
them.

"I back to France," answered Varvilliers.

"We to Munich," said Coralie, with a shrug.

"I the deuce knows where," laughed Wetter.

"I also the deuce knows where. Come, then, to

our next merry supper!" I poured out a glass
of wine. They all followed my example, and we
drank.

"But we shall have no more," said Wetter.

A moment's silence fell on us all. Then Wetter
spoke again. He turned to them and indicated me
with a gesture.

"He's a good fellow, our Augustin."

"Yes, a good fellow," said Varvilliers.

"A very good fellow," muttered Struboff, who
was more than a little gone in liquor.

"A good fellow," said Coralie. Then she stepped
up to me, put her hands on my shoulders, and kissed
me on both cheeks. "A good fellow, our little Augustin," said she.

There was nothing much in this; casual phrases
of goodwill, spoken at a moment of conviviality, the
outcome of genuine but perhaps not very deep feeling,
except for that trifle of the kisses almost an ordinary
accompaniment or conclusion of an evening's entertainment. I was a good fellow; the light praise had
been lightly won. Yet even now as I write, looking
back over the years, I can not, when I accuse myself
of mawkishness, be altogether convinced by the self-
denunciation. For what it was worth, the thing came
home to me; for a moment it overleaped the barriers
that were round me, the differences that made a
hedge between me and them; for a moment they had
forgotten that I was not merely their good comrade.
I would not have people forget often what I am; but
now and then it is pleasant to be no more than what
I myself am. And the two there, Wetter and Varvilliers, were the nearest to friends that I have known.
One went back to his country, the other the deuce
knew where. I should be alone.

Alone I made my way back from Wetter's house, alone and on foot. I had a fancy to walk thus through the decorated streets; alone to pause an instant before the Countess' door, recollecting many things; alone to tell myself that the stocking must be kept over the graze, and that the asking of sympathy was the betrayal of my soul's confidence to me; alone to be weak, alone to be strong; alone to determine to do my work with my own life, alone to hope that I must not render too wretched the life of another. I had good from that walk of mine. For you see, when a man is alone, above all, I think, when he is alone in the truce of night, one day's fight done and the new morning's battle not yet joined, he can pause and stand and think. He can be still; then his worst and his best steal out, like mice from their holes (the cat of convention is asleep), and play their gambols and antics before his eyes: he knows them and himself, and reaches forth to know the world and his work in it, his life and the end of it, the difference, if any, that he has made by spending so much pains on living.

It was four o'clock when a sleepy night-porter let me in. My servants had orders never to wait beyond two, and in my rooms all was dark and quiet. But when I lit a candle from the little lamp by the door, I saw somebody lying on the sofa in my dressing-room, a woman's figure stretched in the luxury of quiet sleep. Victoria this must be and none else. I was glad to see her there and to catch her drowsy smile as her eyes opened under the glare of my candle.

"What in the world are you doing here, my dear?" said I, setting down the candle and putting my hands in my pockets.

She sat up, whisking her skirts round with one hand and rubbing her eyes with the other.

"I came to tell you about Krak—Krak's come. But you weren't here. So I lay down, and I suppose I went to sleep."

"I suppose you did. And how's Krak?"

"Just the same as ever!"

"Brought a birch with her, in case I should rebel at the last?"

Victoria laughed.

"Oh, well, you'll see her to-morrow," she remarked. "She's just the same. I'm rather glad, you know, that Krak hasn't been softened by age. It would have been commonplace."

"Besides, one doesn't want to exaggerate the power of advancing years. You didn't come for anything except to tell me about Krak?"

Victoria got up, came to me, and kissed me.

"No, nothing else," she said. She stopped a moment, and then remarked abruptly, "You're not a bit like William Adolphus."

"No?" said I, divining in a flash her thought and her purpose. "Still—have you been with Elsa to-night?"

"Yes; after Cousin Elizabeth and mother left her. You—you'll be kind to her? I told her that she was very silly, and that I wished I was going to marry you."

"Oh, you did? But she wishes to marry me?"

"She means to, of course."

"Exactly. My dear, you've waited a long while to tell me something I knew very well."

"I thought perhaps you'd be glad to see me," she said, with a little laugh. "Where have you been? Not to the Countess'?"

24

" Indeed, no. To Wetter's."

" Ah! The singer? "

" The singer of my marriage-song, Victoria."

Victoria looked at me in a rather despairing fashion.

" Her singing of it," I added, " will be the most perfect and appropriate thing in the world. You'll be delighted when you hear it. For the rest, my dear sister, Hammerfeldt looks down from heaven and is well pleased."

Victoria sat on the sofa again. I went to the window, unfastened the shutters, and pulled up the blinds. A single star shone yet in the gray sky. I stood looking at it for a few minutes, then lit a cigarette, and turned round. Victoria was on the sofa still; she was crying in a quiet matter-of-fact way, not passionately, but with a rather methodical air. She glanced at me for a moment, but said nothing. Neither did I speak. I leaned against the wall and smoked my cigarette. For five minutes, I should suppose, this state of things went on. Then I flung away the cigarette, Victoria stopped crying, wiped her eyes, and got up.

" I rather wish we'd been born in the gutter," said she. " Good-night, dear."

She kissed me, and I bade her good-night.

" I must get some sleep, or I shall look frightful. I hope William Adolphus won't be snoring very loud, I hear him so plainly through the wall," she said as she started for the door.

CHAPTER XXVIII.

AS BEDERHOF ARRANGED.

OF the next day I have three visions.

I see myself with Krak and Princess Heinrich. Pride illuminated their faces with a cold radiance, and their utterances were conceived in the spirit of a *Nunc Dimittis.* They congratulated the world on its Ruler, the kingdom on its King, themselves on my account, me on theirs. To Krak I was her achievement; to my mother the vindication of the support she had given to Krak, and the refutation of my own grumblings and rebellion. How could I not be reminded of my coronation day? How not smile when the Princess, after observing regretfully that the Baroness would not be able to educate my children, bade me inculcate her principles in the mind of their tutor or governess. She was afraid, she said, that dear Elsa might be a little lacking in firmness, a little prone to that indulgence which is no true kindness in the end. " The very reverse of it, madame," added Krak.

" It's quite time enough for them to begin to do as they like when they grow up," said the Princess Heinrich.

" By then, though," said Krak, " they will have learned, I hope, to do what they ought."

" I hope so with all my heart, Baroness," said I.

" Victoria is absurdly weak with her child," Princess Heinrich complained.

Krak smiled significantly. She had never expected much of Victoria; the repression of exuberant wickedness had been the bounds of her hope.

Krak left us. There must have been some noticeable expression on my face as I watched her go, for my mother said with a smile:

" I know you think she was severe. I used to think so too, now and then. But see how well you've turned out, Augustin ! "

" Madame," said I, " my present excellence and my impending happiness reconcile me to everything."

" You had a very happy childhood," my mother observed. I bowed. " And now you are going to marry the girl I should choose for you above all others." Again I bowed. " And public affairs are quiet and satisfactory." A third time I bowed. " Kiss me, Augustin," said my mother.

This summary of my highly successful life and reign was delivered in Princess Heinrich's most conclusive manner. I had no thought of disputing it; I was almost surprised that the facts themselves did not suffer an immediate transformation to match the views she expressed. What matter that things were not so? They were to be deemed so and called so, so held and so proclaimed. My mother's courage touched my heart, and I kissed her with much affection. It is no inconsiderable achievement to be consistently superior to reality. I who fought desperate doubtful battles, crippled by a secret traitorous love of the enemy, could not but pay homage to Princess Heinrich's victorious front.

Next I see myself with Elsa, alone for a little while with Elsa exultant in her pomp, observed of

all, the envy of all, the centre of the spectacle, frocked
and jewelled beyond heart's desire, narcotized by fuss
and finery, laughing and trembling. I had found
her alone with difficulty, for she kept some woman
by her almost all the day. She did not desire to be
alone with me. That was to come to-morrow at
Artenberg. Now was her moment, and she strove ·
to think it eternal. It was not in her to face and
conquer the great enemy after Princess Heinrich's
heroic fashion; she could only turn and fly, hiding
from herself how soon she must be overtaken. She
chattered to me with nervous fluency, making haste
always to choose the topic, leaving no gap for the
entrance of what she feared. I saw in her eyes the
apprehension that filled her. Once it had bred in me
the most odious humiliation, an intense longing to
go from her, a passionate loathing for the necessity
of forcing myself on her. I was chastened now; I
should not be in so bad a case as Struboff; there
would be no question of a fresh slice of bread. But
I tried to harden myself against her, declaring that,
desiring the prize, she must pay the price, and deserved no pity on the score of a bargain that she herself had ratified. Alas, poor dear, she knew neither
how small the prize was nor how great the price,
and her eyes prayed me not to turn her fears to certainty. She would know soon enough.

Last comes the vision of the theatre, of the gala
performance, where Elsa and I sat side by side,
ringed about with great folk, enveloped in splendour,
making a spectacle for all the city, a sight that men
now remember and recall. There through the piece
we sat, and my mind was at work. It seemed to me
that all my life was pictured there; I had but to look
this way or that, and dead things rose from the grave

and were for me alive again. There was Krak's hard face, there my mother's unconquerable smile; a glance at them brought back childhood with its rigours, its pleasures snatched in fearfulness, its strange ignorance and stranger passing gleams of insight. Victoria's hand, ringed, and gloved, and braceleted, held her fan; I remembered the little girl's bare, red, rapped knuckles. Away in a box to the right, close by the stage, was the Countess with her husband; my eyes turned often toward her and always found hers on mine. Again as a child I ran to her, asking to be loved; again as a boy I loved her and wrung from her reluctant love; again in the first vigour and unsparing pride of my manhood I sacrificed her heart and my delight. Below her, standing near the orchestra, was Wetter; through my glass I could see the smile that never left his face as he scanned the bedizened row in which I sat. There with him, looking on, jesting, scoffing at the parade, there was Nature's place for me, not here playing chief part in the comedy. What talks and what nights had we had together; how together had we fallen from heaven and ruefully prayed for that trick of falling soft! See, he smiles more broadly! What is it? Struboff has stolen in and dropped heavily into a seat. Wetter waved a hand to him and laughed. Laugh, laugh, Wetter! It is your only gospel and therefore must be pardoned its inevitable defects. Laugh even at poor Struboff whose stomach is so gross, whose feelings so fine, who may not give his wife a piece of bread, and would ask no greater joy than to kiss her feet. And laugh at Varvilliers too, who, although he sits where he has a good view of us, never turns his eyes toward the lady by my side, but is most courteously unobservant of her alone among all the throng. Did she look at him? Yes, for he will not look toward her. Why, we are all here, all except Hammerfeldt, who looks down from heaven, and Coralie who is coming presently to sing us the wedding-song. Even Victoria's Baron is here, and Victoria's sobs of terror are in my ears again. Bederhof and his fellows are behind me. The real and the unreal, the dummies and the men, they are all here, each in his place in the tableau. When Coralie comes, we shall be complete.

The opera ended and the curtain fell. There was a buzz of talk.

"Our anthem comes now, Elsa," said I.

"Yes," she whispered, crushing the bizarre satin rag of a programme that they had given her. "I have never heard Madame Mansoni," she added. I glanced at her; there was a blush on her cheek. She had heard of Madame Mansoni, although she had not heard her sing.

I put up my glass again and looked at Wetter. He nodded slightly but unmistakably, then flung his head back and laughed again. Now we waited only for Coralie. With her coming we should be complete.

The music began. By arrangement or impulse, I knew not which, everybody rose to their feet. Only Elsa and I sat still. The curtain rose and Coralie was revealed in her rare beauty and her matchless calm. A moment later the great full feelingless voice filled the theatre; she had had no doubt that she could fill the theatre. I saw Struboff leaning back in his chair, his shoulders eloquent of despair; I saw Wetter with straining eyes and curling lips, Varvilliers smiling in mischievous remembrance of our rehearsal. By my side Elsa was breathing quick and fast. I turned to her; her eyes were sparkling in triumph and excitement. It was a grand moment. She felt my glance; her cheek reddened, her eyes dropped, her lip quivered; the swiftest covert glance flew toward where Varvilliers was. I turned away with a sort of sickness on me.

Coralie's voice rose and fell, chanting out her words. The deadness of her singing seemed subtle mockery, as though she would not degrade true passion to the service of this sham, as though the words were enough for such a marriage, and the spirit scorned to sanction it. Elsa's eyes were on her now, and the Countess leaned forward, gazing at her. The last verse came, and Coralie, with a low bow and a smile, sang it direct to me—to me across all the theatre, so plainly that now all heads were turned from her, the people facing round and looking all at me and at Elsa by my side. Every eye was on us. The song ended. A storm of cheers burst out. A short gasp or sob came from Elsa. The cheers swelled and swelled, handkerchiefs waved in the air. I rose to my feet, gave Elsa my hand, and helped her to rise. Then together we took a step forward and bowed to all. Silence fell. Coralie's voice rose again, repeating the last verse. Now all the chorus joined in. We stood till the song ended again, and through the tempest of cheers. There had been no such enthusiasm in Forstadt within the memory of man. The heart of the people went forth to us; it was a triumph, a triumph, a triumph!

The next day we were married, and in the evening my wife and I set out together for Artenberg. This was what Bederhof had arranged.

THE END.

MISS DOUGALL'S BOOKS.

*T*HE MORMON PROPHET. 12mo. Cloth, $1.50.

"A striking story. . . . Immensely interesting and diverting, and as a romance it certainly has a unique power."—*Boston Herald.*

"In 'The Mormon Prophet' Miss Lily Dougall has told, in strongly dramatic form, the story of Joseph Smith and of the growth of the Church of the Latter-Day Saints, which has again come prominently before the public through the election of a polygamist to Congress. . . . Miss Dougall has handled her subject with consummate skill. . . . She has rightly seen that this man's life contained splendid material for a historical novel. She has taken no unwarranted liberties with the truth, and has succeeded in furnishing a story whose scope broadens with each succeeding chapter until the end."—*New York Mail and Express.*

"Mormonism is not ordinarily regarded as capable of romantic treatment, but in the hands of Miss Dougall it has yielded results which are calculated to attract the general public as well as the student of psychology. . . . Miss Dougall has handled a difficult theme with conspicuous delicacy; the most sordid details of the narrative are redeemed by the glamour of her style, her analysis of the strangely mixed character of the prophet is remarkable for its detachment and impartiality, while in Susannah Halsey she has given us a really beautiful study of nobly compassionate womanhood. We certainly know of no more illuminative commentary on the rise of this extraordinary sect than is furnished by Miss Dougall's novel "—*London Spectator.*

"Miss Dougall may be congratulated both on her choice of a subject for her new book and on her remarkably able and interesting treatment of it. . . . A fascinating story, which is even more remarkable and more fascinating as a psychological study."—*The Scotsman.*

*T*HE MADONNA OF A DAY. 12mo. Cloth, $1.00 ; paper, 50 cents.

"An entirely unique story. Alive with incident and related in a fresh and captivating style."—*Philadelphia Press.*

"A novel that stands quite by itself, and that in theme as well as in artistic merit should make a very strong appeal to the mind of a sympathetic reader."—*Boston Beacon.*

*T*HE MERMAID. 12mo. Cloth, $1.00 ; paper, 50 cents.

"The author of this novel has the gift of contrivance and the skill to sustain the interest of a plot through all its development. 'The Mermaid' is an odd and interesting story."—*New York Times.*

*T*HE ZEIT-GEIST. 16mo. Cloth, 75 cents.

"One of the most remarkable novels."—*New York Commercial Advertiser.*

D. APPLETON AND COMPANY, NEW YORK.

TWO SUCCESSFUL AMERICAN NOVELS.

LATITUDE 19°. A Romance of the West Indies in the Year of our Lord 1820. Being a faithful account and true, of the painful adventures of the Skipper, the Bo's'n, the Smith, the Mate, and Cynthia. By Mrs. SCHUYLER CROWNINSHIELD. Illustrated. 12mo. Cloth, $1.50.

"'Latitude 19°' is a novel of incident, of the open air, of the sea, the shore, the mountain eyrie, and of breathing, living entities, who deal with Nature at first hand. . . . The adventures described are peculiarly novel and interesting. . . . Packed with incidents, infused with humor and wit, and faithful to the types introduced, this book will surely appeal to the large audience already won, and beget new friends among those who believe in fiction that is healthy without being maudlin, and is strong without losing the truth."—*New York Herald.*

"A story filled with rapid and exciting action from the first page to the last. A fecundity of invention that never lags, and a judiciously used vein of humor."—*The Critic.*

"A volume of deep, undeniable charm. A unique book from a fresh, sure, vigorous pen."—*Boston Journal.*

"Adventurous and romantic enough to satisfy the most exacting reader. . . . Abounds in situations which make the blood run cold, and yet, full of surprises as it is, one is continually amazed by the plausibility of the main incidents of the narrative. . . . A very successful effort to portray the sort of adventures that might have taken place in the West Indies seventy five or eighty years ago. . . . Very entertaining with its dry humor."—*Boston Herald.*

A HERALD OF THE WEST. An American Story of 1811–1815. By J. A. ALTSHELER, author of "A Soldier of Manhattan" and "The Sun of Saratoga." 12mo. Cloth, $1.50.

"'A Herald of the West' is a romance of our history which has not been surpassed in dramatic force, vivid coloring, and historical interest. . . . In these days when the flush of war has only just passed, the book ought to find thousands of readers, for it teaches patriotism without intolerance, and it shows, what the war with Spain has demonstrated anew, the power of the American people when they are deeply roused by some great wrong."—*San Francisco Chronicle.*

"The book throughout is extremely well written. It is condensed, vivid, picturesque. . . . A rattling good story, and unrivaled in fiction for its presentation of the American feeling toward England during our second conflict."—*Boston Herald.*

"Holds the attention continuously. . . . The book abounds in thrilling attractions. . . . It is a solid and dignified acquisition to the romantic literature of our own country, built around facts and real persons."—*Chicago Times-Herald*

"In a style that is strong and broad, the author of this timely novel takes up a nascent period of our national history and founds upon it a story of absorbing interest."—*Philadelphia Item.*

"Mr. Altsheler has given us an accurate as well as picturesque portrayal of the social and political conditions which prevailed in the republic in the era made famous by the second war with Great Britain."—*Brooklyn Eagle.*